Straight Up

Also by Catriona McCloud

Growing Up Again

Straight Up

Catriona McCloud

First Published in Great Britain in 2008 by
Orion Books, an imprint of The Orion Publishing Group Ltd
Orion House, 5 Upper Saint Martin's Lane
London WC2H 9EA
An Hachette Livre UK Company

1 3 5 7 9 10 8 6 4 2

A CIP catalogue record for this book is
available from the British Library.

ISBN (Hardback) 978 0 7528 7490 6
ISBN (Trade Paperback) 978 0 7528 7491 3

Typeset by Deltatype Ltd,
Birkenhead, Merseyside

Printed and bound in Great Britain at
Mackays of Chatham plc, Chatham, Kent

www.orionbooks.co.uk

For Lisa Moylett
(on whom not a word is based)
with love and thanks

Thanks to:

Natalie Braine, Susan Heady, Bradley Honey, Olivier Lepreux, Neil McRoberts, Larry Madden, Lisa Milton, Lisa Moylett, Diane Nelson, Sara O'Keeffe, Cesar Revoredo Giha, Nathalie Sfakianos, Emma Wallace and Melissa Weatherill.

Chapter 1
How I Became a Widow

To start at the beginning is not an option, so let's start in the taxi from LAX, heading into Beverly Hills.

There were two of them up front, husband and wife, her driving and him wrestling with the map and shouting at her, 'Right side, right side, right side of road. No, no, other right, this one. Look my hand.' Then: 'Look *road* when you driving.' Then: 'Open eyes when you driving. All times!'

Perhaps it was finding out that I was being driven along an eight-lane highway by someone who had to be told to keep her eyes open that let death slip into the background and hang about, waiting for a job to do.

'Out of interest,' I asked him, 'why are you speaking English? Is it part of the service? Because I'd be just as happy . . .'

The man shook his head.

'No Spanish, this one,' he said, jerking his thumb at his wife, who was changing lanes and murmuring continually under her breath, possibly praying. 'And I got no Portuguese.' He sighed, making a hissing noise through his teeth. 'Marriage,' he said.

Nothing strange about sitting in the back of a taxi listening to someone in the front grumble about his marriage, of course, but it was the first time for me that the wife had been right there beside him, her eyes flashing at me in the rear-view mirror and her foot going down on the gas in retort.

'I wouldn't know,' I said coldly, knowing which side my bread was buttered. The worst *he* could do was get us lost; I was sticking with the driver. I smiled at her and she snapped her eyes back to the road.

'You no married?' said the man, stroking his stubbled chin. 'Nice girl like you? Wass wrong with you men in ...?'

'England,' I said. 'Good question and I'm not in the market for another one so I'm never going to know the answer.'

'Aha!' he cried, smacking the map against the dashboard. 'You divorce! English just same like America, hey? Everybody divorce.' He nudged his wife. 'Everybody divorce, divorce. Here's another one same like all the other one.' They laughed together for a minute or two until, noticing that the car was drifting across the lanes, he started shouting again and she went back to her mumbled prayer.

But I wasn't divorced like everyone else was divorced. I wasn't another one just like all the other ones. It was different with me. It wasn't a dissolved contract, an agreement to disagree. Under the circumstances, my circumstances, the ones I never even thought about, my divorce was the kind of betrayal, abandonment, tragedy, that was more like ...

'I'm a widow, actually,' I said, getting just the right plucky little tremor in my voice. Briefly, the woman's eyes caught mine in the mirror again. Yes, I thought, I'm a widow – tragic and blameless – and you're still lumbered. I win.

The man rattled off a long string of what I assumed were prayers of respect to the soul of my dead husband and crossed himself several times.

'How he die?' he asked at last, when he was done. 'When?'

'He died a year ago today,' I said. 'In a car crash.'

This time the '*Pai nosso*'s and the '*Santo Dios del Cielo*'s lasted even longer and kept breaking out from both of them off and on all the way to the hotel.

OK, so obviously at this point my widowhood could have faded like rising smoke as the taxicab drew away and ended our threesome for ever. It was never what you would call a plan. But it just so happened that almost immediately afterwards I found myself in need of some leverage and there it was, the nearest thing to hand.

The Beverly Hills Hotel was Germolene pink and looked as though it had only been finished that afternoon, the foliage in the gardens dripping from the last burst of the sprinkler, lilies as sturdy as ornamental lamp posts with rivulets running into their crowns, yuccas big enough to hang hammocks from with droplets wavering on their leaf tips, everything glistening in the sinking sun. I could hear what I assumed was a tape of cicadas and songbirds trilling away softly somewhere.

Eventually, a team of bellhops bore down on me where I had been dumped out four taxis back from the door, slapped my luggage into a neat block on a trolley and took off for the foyer at a trot with me stumbling after. Inside, it goes without saying, was sumptuous; that pearly, almond-scented, wall-to-wall, perfect *American* sumptuousness which I had never seen before and which, seventeen hours after pulling my front door shut behind me at home, was enough to make my throat ache with sobs of relief. (Since then I have learned that it is not American sumptuousness at all. It's California sumptuousness, and it only really kicks in above $500 a night.)

The bellhops, whisking my trolley up to check-in, were chasing tips and they wouldn't have raised an eyebrow even if I'd had string holding my trousers up and all my stuff in carrier bags. The girls behind the desk, on the other hand, stared woodenly at me and my luggage as I advanced. One turned and whispered something to the other, who slipped off her stool and went through a door to the back. To be fair, they had a point: I was hot, I was dishevelled, I had got my matching set of suitcases for £39.99 in Morrison's and I looked – even to myself as I passed the enormous lobby mirrors – like a just-released hostage, at about the overnight stop in Syria stage, after a meal but before the debriefing by the CIA and long before a reunion with my family.

One time, after a party, I crashed with a friend and woke up, smoky, sweating pure vodka, with Alice Cooper make-up, barbecue sauce on my face and sick in my hair, to see my friend's four-year-old sister – pink and perfect, breathing rosebuds and blinking little duckling feathers – staring at me in bewilderment.

'Go away,' I managed to croak and she scampered off, howling.

That is how I felt crossing the lobby of the Beverly Hills Hotel – like a lone elastoplast in an empty swimming pool – and I didn't blame them for blanking me.

'Verity Drummond,' I said when I got to the desk at last. 'I'd like to check in.'

She just managed not to say 'I'm sure you would' and began clicking her mouse.

'I don't see a reservation, Ms Drummond,' she said presently. 'And I'm afraid the hotel is full—'

'Clara Callan, possibly?' I said. She frowned, no more than a twitch, but it never looks good to start offering aliases and so I tried to explain. 'It's my professional name and since this is a business trip I thought my agent would probably have ...' I let it trail off waiting for the magic word to take effect, but if anything her face grew even frostier, as though I had hit the pause button and put her on 'still'. Just too late, I got it. In Edinburgh, where I come from, even in London, having an agent gives one a bit of an air. But in Los Angeles having an agent is like having a mobile phone, or actually not even as neutral as that. Having an agent, in Los Angeles, is like having a satellite dish stuck to the front of your house, a tattoo on your shoulder blade and an interesting font on your number plate. I tried to think.

The first thought was that Clovis – my agent – would never make a mistake like this. Clovis is efficiency made flesh, never throws a stone unless she has at least two birds lined up in its path and always keeps one finger free in case of a new pie. And besides the efficiency, there's the fact that Clovis would never do this to *me*. Which sounds smug, I know, but it's no more than the truth because an agent is like a mother, only better; she is absolutely one hundred per cent for you and behind you all the way. Clovis told me so when I signed up with her and every day since, she's shown me that she meant it.

However, efficiency and devotion aside, it was possible that, for tax purposes or even just to make life interesting, she might have made a reservation I had to sniff out with a bit of flair. Take my upgrade on the flight over. Clovis always buys the cheapest ticket, but on flights booked through the agency I've never once sat in economy class. And it's true that it's forgery, but it's forgery so harmless and so inventive that she deserves to get away with it for the sheer spark it took to come up with it in the first place. I don't know how she manages her male clients, but for me she issues a statement of second trimester health. That is, a note from a medical doctor saying that, even though I am somewhere between the third and sixth month of pregnancy, I am in excellent shape and quite safe to fly. It works like a charm at the check-in desk – bumped up every time – and they tell the cabin crew so I get extra pillows too. Only I have to remember and *not* do what I did on the flight over from JFK today, which was to ask for a large gin and tonic as soon as we'd taken off. British Airways wouldn't have blinked, but United has a wholesome streak a mile wide and the first-class stewardess clearly wanted to have me arrested for foetus abuse on touchdown.

It also means I need to wear baggy clothes, and now the desk clerk at the Beverly Hills was shooting them little glances, unimpressed.

'Is there a chance that the room was booked under the name of Clovis Parr?' I said.

'Your stage name?' asked the clerk witheringly. And I think you will be forced to agree that this was out-and-out cheek. She now deserved whatever she got.

'She's my . . . She's the member of my staff who took care of it for me,' I said. 'It was booked a month ago. Did you have any new staff start about a month ago?'

'Do you have your confirmation with you?' said the clerk, with a patient-sounding although actually fairly irritated sigh.

Of course I did and I wished I'd thought of it first so that it could have been me who issued the patiently irritated sigh. I flicked it across the desk at her.

'Ah,' she said reading it and looking, all of a sudden, tremendously pleased. 'Yes,' she said. 'This isn't the first time it's happened. I should really have guessed.' She looked me up and down again, still smiling. 'You're not booked in at the Beverly Hills Hotel, Ms Drummond. Your booking is for the Beverly Hills *Plaza* Hotel. I'm so sorry.' And of course it was at this moment that her colleague returned, bringing with her a barrel-chested security man in a braided jacket.

'It's OK, Merle,' she said. 'She's leaving. Beverly Hills *Plaza* again. We should have guessed right away.'

Sweeping out with my remaining shreds of dignity clutched about me was one option, but I'd had a very long day – more than a day long now – and I wanted to stay in this cool, vanilla-scented, pearly perfect womb. I wanted them to want me to stay. I wanted to nod to Merle in the mornings on the way to breakfast and chat to the receptionists while they looked up opening times of attractions and ordered taxis for me. I belonged here.

And surely they wouldn't be so cruel as to stop me, not a woman on the anniversary of her bereavement, five months preg— no, that wouldn't work. So it was either the widow *or* the second trimester and a pregnant woman might throw up in their perfect bathrooms or look overweight in their perfect gym, so I let my head droop for a moment and when I raised my eyes again they were brimming with grief.

Fat lot of good it did me. No, I could not use their phone to cancel the other booking even though I had no charge left on mine, and no, they could not do me a walk-in rate and no, I certainly could not call London to see if Clovis could fix it up from that end. I got to phone for a cab but, after that, those two bitches (and Merle) turfed me out on the anniversary of my beloved husband's death by shooting while making a documentary in east LA, when I had come all this way to lay flowers at the site and had, quite understandably, not noticed my assistant's error in my pain. Actually, they would have let me wait in the lobby, but I was too hurt to be near them and so I slogged back to the street. Still, the street was Sunset Boulevard; it could have been worse.

Maybe I should have told them I was an orphan instead – or as well, I thought to myself, sitting down on my bags on the grass verge, but if they were the kind of people who had no sympathy for a widow ... The memory was stirring inside me of the only other time I had ever met with such indifference. I smiled in spite of myself. Even with the treachery and abandonment that came along in the end I would always smile when I remembered how we first met.

It was at a wedding. Our place cards threw us together, but Kim didn't say hello, didn't even notice me at first, just got drunk and heckled the speeches with someone else at the table who seemed to be an old pal.

'I give it six months,' drawled the pal, whose name was Phil.

'Cynic,' Kim said. 'I think Joe and Carol are going to make it. They go together like widows and orphans, Philly boy.'

I gasped. They turned.

'I find that very offensive,' I said. I was trying to sound haughty but my voice was trembling.

'Oh?' said Kim. He looked at my wedding finger. 'No ring,' he said, 'so if you're a widow you're over him.'

'I'm not a widow,' I said, my eyes filling.

'Oh dear,' said Kim. 'What a great start. You are Little Orphan ...?'

'Verity,' I said, stunned into giving a straight answer.

'I'm Little Orphan Kim,' said Kim. 'Mine drove off the road, coming back drunk from a party when I was ten. What about you?'

'My father was killed before I was born,' I said, using exactly the words my granny always used to me. 'He was a soldier. And my mother died having me.' I waited for his apologies.

'You win,' said Kim, cheerfully. 'Who brought you up?'

'My granny.'

'Ah, then we're drawing even again,' said Kim. 'I was brought up by three guardians and a Swiss trust fund. I'd have given my right arm for a granny. It's a dead heat, wouldn't you say?'

I couldn't say anything. I just stared at him. And then he moved the arm he had draped around the back of my chair and hugged me.

'It sucks though, doesn't it?' he said. 'Especially at weddings.'

'I'm dreading my own,' I said quietly. 'All the holes where the people should be.'

'So forget widows and orphans,' said Kim, 'and I'm sorry I upset you. Joe and Carol go together like ...'

'Sex and violence?' offered Phil.

Probably, I concluded, standing up as a taxi drew into the kerb beside me, the documentary was a step too far and it was just as well I was leaving. If I had talked myself into a room, they might have blabbed my history around the staff and in these days of on-line news archives it wouldn't have been long before someone was googling for the report and when they didn't find it I would have had to say he was undercover and then I would have had to explain why and it could have got complicated. Better this way. I humped my bags into the back of the taxi while the driver revved the engine and watched me.

'Beverly Hills Plaza Hotel, please,' I said, once I was in.

'Heh, heh, heh,' said the driver. 'First time in LA?'

The Beverly Hills Plaza was a perfectly nice hotel. It looked like a liner and had hair nets of fairy lights wrapped around the trunks of the palm trees, switched on already and just beginning to glow as the daylight faded. It didn't smell of vanilla and walking across the carpet in the lobby didn't make me think of the blush on a peach-blossom petal, but it was fine.

Soon, my blood pounding from a savagely hot shower and my teeth throbbing from a mini-bar coke so cold it must have had some extra chemicals in to keep it liquid – America can be very extreme – I crawled into bed, so tired that, for once, I did it without thinking. I lay and listened to the sounds coming through my open windows, the back one letting in the clink of glasses and the laughter from the poolside, the front one seeming to suck the noise and heat of the road right into my room. I should get up and shut them, I thought, watching the net curtains billow and stream. Or turn off the air-conditioning. One or the other. I would, in just a minute, but those curtains were mesmerising the way they floated up and whispered down again. So clean. The traffic was pulsing along out there, going wow, wow, wow as it passed, and yet these curtains were soft and white enough to wrap a baby in.

One of the very few good things about the whole divorce calamity had been leaving our house on the Wandsworth Bridge Road where no matter what I did, no matter how many hours I spent with a damp cloth or the latest attachment, the curtains were always gritty with that special greasy London grit, the books on the shelves trapping it in their pages and between their covers so that they made a scraping noise when you moved one of them. So I didn't. I left them behind. I left them all, thinking I could replace them with clean ones off Amazon second-hand. (But you don't.

You'd never actually throw out your Maya Angelous, unless you're a pseud, but you're hardly going to get a new set when the old lot's gone. George Eliot; all those Viragos; and those other ones, black and white, like Viragos but even more so. What were they called again . . . ?)

The bedside phone was ringing and the air-conditioning unit was howling like a juicer full of prunes. I flailed, dizzy in the sweeping arcs of light that folded in on each other across the ceiling, and grabbed the receiver.

'Good morning, California Sunrise,' said Clovis's voice.

'It's pitch black outside,' I said.

'I woke you in time to see it,' she chirped at me. 'Listen, I'm going out for lunch but I wanted to say—'

'Hang on,' I said. I stumbled over to the control panel and switched the air off then pulled the heavy curtains shut to stop the headlight show and got back into bed. Clovis was still talking.

'. . . might take more than one, but just do what she says and don't go ape about the coverage, OK?'

'Clov—'

'Have a nice day now!' she sang and rang off.

Which was not exactly adequate preparation for the most important meeting of my life. Unless – as could be the case – this wasn't an important meeting at all. You would think, what with crossing an ocean, that it had to be but nothing about this business was ever what it seemed.

I wrote a novel. I'm not a writer, I'm a florist, but while I was off on the sick leave that became the unemployment during the divorce apocalypse, sitting around in my dressing gown trying to fill the hours, I started typing and once I had started I couldn't stop. It was nothing so obvious as writing it all down to get it out of my system; *Straight Up* wasn't based on my life at all. I was very firm with myself about that. I lived in London, so I set it in Switzerland. It was summer so I set it in winter. I was a female so it was about a male. Nevertheless, for some reason, while my husband was scraping me off himself and skipping into the distance with *her* I got through it writing a story about a man who falls into a chasm in the Alps, goes through a Homeric struggle to get out again and dies alone, inches from safety, wretched, starving and with his broken bones poking through his skin.

My granny never read it, but three of her friends stuck with it right through to the end so, instead of putting it in a box in the attic with my school report cards, I made a dozen copies and sent it out to some agents. Back it came. I sent it out. Back it came. I sent it out one last time – fresh copies and a much more confident covering letter that I wrote after a jug of Pimm's – and back it came. Then, when I had just about given up, Clovis rang me. She was, she said, a friend of a friend, who had heard about the book, or read it in someone else's office or something – I was never quite sure *how* she got hold of the manuscript, truth be told – but she wanted to take me on. She loved it, she said. Loved the title, loved the ending, loved the writing. *That* was welcome news; after three months trying to think up new words for 'white' every day it was about time someone appreciated the effort. She didn't ask for a single sentence of rewrites either – she just started selling.

But now came the strange part. I didn't know much about the book business, but I thought I knew that some publisher somewhere would buy the book and publish it. Everyone knows that. Hardback, paperback, USA, translation. Talking book, large print, film rights, the end. Right? Wrong. Clovis started by selling the television rights in Italy. Why, I asked her, would they want to buy the right to adapt something that didn't even exist yet? Because it's a great story, she told me, and Italian television isn't like the BBC. I had been there by this time and met them and I could only agree.

Next, I was sure, would be a London hardback launch. Clovis convinced me otherwise. We need, she told me, to create a buzz. A reverse buzz. A zzub. A radio station in Prague can't give you more than they can give you even if the paperback is hurling itself into every supermarket trolley that passes, but the big publishing houses have budgets you wouldn't believe and with a bit of zzub – with Internet reviews and illicit tapes of the Czech adaptation on eBay – the sky's the limit. It was faintly embarrassing to have to tell people about the Radio Prague angle if ever they asked me when the book was coming out, especially since neither the radio show nor the TV play had actually been made yet, but now I was beginning to see how right Clovis was about this, as well as everything else. Here I was after all, in Beverly Hills, about to meet someone who wanted to make the film of the Czech monologue of the Italian docudrama of the book to be. And once there's a Hollywood film in the frame, as Clovis said, need she say more?

The only worry was that I couldn't be sure who I was meeting. All I knew was that her name was Jasmine, and Clovis just knew I would love her.

'But who is she?' I had said. 'Is she a producer? Does she work for a studio?'

'No, no, no,' Clovis had told me. 'That's not how it ... don't worry.'

'Is she an agent then?'

'She's a contact.'

'Yeah, I know that, but what *is* she? What does it say on her card?'

'She's an associate.'

'An associate what, though?'

'This isn't like you,' said Clovis. 'You're usually a very trusting person. What's wrong?'

I didn't really know what was wrong. Why was I quibbling? I hadn't had a clue who any of the Czechs were, and the Italians could have come from central casting with their wrist kisses and their '*bellissima*'s, but that was different. Nobody knows anything about any of that, but Hollywood? You're brought up on Hollywood. Tallulah Bankhead thinking she could be Scarlett O'Hara; Burt Reynolds nearly getting to be Rocky; the money men asking what was wrong with *Being John Travolta*? In Hollywood, it's just that much more humiliating not to have a clue.

'Jasmine,' said Clovis at last, 'is a scout. A sniffer. A tracker. She doesn't work for anyone. She sniffs out hot property and tracks it down.'

'But I thought you said you phoned her?'

Clovis sighed and after a minute's tussle she smiled at me.

'I did phone her, Verity, love, I phoned her *back*. Because she phoned me. Because she heard that your book was hot property. Because it is.'

'Has she read it?'

'She loves the sound of you.'

'What? Why? What did you say?' I blurted, panicking for no reason. Clovis couldn't have said anything – she didn't *know* anything. I hadn't wanted her pity and so I hadn't *told* her anything.

'Nothing,' said Clovis, of course. 'I just mentioned a bit about your background.'

'What do you mean?' I said.

'You know, a simple flower seller from the streets of London town.'

'Buy a bunch of violets from a pore gel, guvnor?'

'That's the idea,' Clovis said.

I was still sitting up in bed when the phone rang for the second time.

'Verity?' said a new voice.

'Hello?'

'It's Jasmine,' the voice said. It was smoky, almost rasping, the vowel a long creak that made me think of a cat stretching, but warm and nasal too, like Barbra Streisand cuddling up to the microphone and making fifty thousand fans feel like it was just the two of them in the stadium together. 'I'm on my way into town,' Jasmine said. 'But I'm about to hit some traffic. So, have breakfast, I'll pick you up, we'll go see some sights and talk over lunch. OK?'

'I—'

'It's just you, right?' she went on. 'You're alone? No one else along for the ride?'

'It's just me,' I said.

'Fabulous,' said Jasmine. 'If you had some guy on your tail, seeing the sights would mean museums, but if it's just you and me we know what we mean, right? Right? Verity?'

'Absolutely,' I said, trying to sound hearty. 'Shopping.'

'You OK?'

'I'm fine.'

'Oh God,' said Jasmine. 'Was it recent?'

'I'm sorry?'

'You're divorced, right? Me too.'

'Actually,' I said, and I swear I wasn't even conscious of planning to speak, never mind of choosing what to say, 'I'm a widow.'

So, by such a string of odd little occurrences and coincidences, it came to pass. There was nothing deliberate about it. It wasn't a decision; nothing to do with me at all really. It was partly down to bad driving, partly down to two snooty receptionists' poor customer care, and partly just down to the depressing American divorce rate in general. And anyway, it made sense to tell Jasmine too. After all, as far as California was concerned, I *was* a widow. One hundred per cent of the people in this place who knew anything about me at all knew I was a widow. It would be silly to start muddying the waters now.

Chapter 2

The Perfect Italian

Breakfast at the Beverly Hills Plaza was opulent enough to make me wonder what Germolene Towers could have pulled to outdo it. There were white raspberries in the halved papayas – they looked a bit like maggots, but they're much rarer so you've got to be impressed – and the egg chef was a polyglot and a master of his art, tipping out perfect spheres from his poaching pan with a flick of the wrist and a kind word in German for the tourists ahead of me in the queue. After breakfast I waited in my room, hopping up and down between the sofa, the windows and the air unit, which was now in an irresolvable loop of overheating and overcooling and sucking every drop of moisture from the atmosphere as it strained away. When I could feel my bottom eyelids moving downwards if I opened my mouth too far, I went to put more face cream on, put on too much, scraped back my hair to scrub it off, forgot about my mascara and had just taken that off too when the buzzer sounded.

Jasmine. My first sight of Jasmine. I'll never forget it. Not only was she groomed beyond my wildest aspirations – sleek, pressed, glossed and polished from her precision parting to the top coat on her little toenail – she was also, underneath all that, spellbindingly beautiful, with a beauty that instantly made you think she must be a genius. That's how beautiful she was: so, so beautiful she didn't even look dumb. And although meeting another woman for the first time while wearing a shower cap and with splats of cleanser all down the front of your dress would usually seem like a problem, it didn't matter with Jasmine because, even if you spent the next month in a spa drinking melted snow and having surgery, when you came to stand beside her you would still look like a sat-on pie.

Her hair was black and hung down, not chemically or mechanically straightened, but just heavy under its own silky weight. Her face poked out from it, high beaky nose, wicked-stepmother eyebrows, a long red mouth that dipped downwards in the middle and up into points in the corners when she smiled. And cheekbones. God, what cheekbones. If everyone looked like Jasmine then little children learning to draw faces would draw eyes, nose, mouth and cheekbones; cheekbone shape would be on your passport description; somewhere in the world some tribe would have thought of something to do to the cheekbones of marriageable girls and London punks would have taken it up too.

Eventually I stopped gazing and put out my hand, but Jasmine's mouth split into the v-shaped grin showing glittering little ice-white teeth and she stepped forward to hug me.

'Welcome to California,' she said. 'You only shake hands when you really hate someone. Musta been tough in the eighties, huh? Full foundation all day long and everyone in *Miami Vice* sports coats. No wonder there's a dry cleaners on every block.' She followed me to the bathroom doorway and watched me prink. 'So we'll talk over lunch – hey, you need to tell me what you're in the mood for so I can get a table – but before that I thought we could have some fun.'

'Talk about the script over lunch, you mean?' I said.

'Clovis said you love flowers, so we could go out to the valley and look at some.' Jasmine waved a languid hand towards the window as if to indicate that the world out there was full of flowers, if anyone cared. I screwed up my nose to show that I could take them or leave them too. 'But there's this great place up in Burbank,' she went on, much more animated. 'Sells wardrobe from the studios – the real thing. We can loop back along Santa Monica for Cahuenga, take in Rodeo, Sunset ... you want to see the Walk of Fame? We'll stop at the corner of Hollywood and Vine, show you the sign, huh?'

Who wouldn't be sidetracked by all of that?

*

Jasmine drove with one arm slung along the seatback behind me and held the steering wheel by hooking a finger over it at the bottom.

'Where is everyone?' I said. Rodeo Drive was deserted apart from a slow snake of enormous cars, and the shops looked closed. 'When do the stores open?'

'They're open,' said Jasmine. 'It's subtle lighting, so the rest of us can't see in.'

I still didn't understand it. If the shops were full of millionaires' wives buying gold shoes why was there no one on the sidewalk? Why was there no one moving from store to store? The car in front of us glided over to the kerb and stopped. A blade of a figure in a pink trouser suit got out, scurried across the sidewalk and disappeared, then the car glided out again and carried on up the street.

'Got it,' I said. 'Drivers.'

'You got it,' said Jasmine. 'They call the car when they're good to go. It's an art form, look.'

Four cars ahead, something that looked like an army truck, except in lavender, swooped in to arrive kerbside just as an ancient woman in a leather coat made the ten-foot journey from the door to the road. One shop doorman ushered her into the back of the truck while another lifted the bags up and put them into the boot as it popped open, then they both waited respectfully until she had pulled away. The whole operation took ten seconds, beginning to end.

'Pretty slick,' said Jasmine. 'I like it better when they balls it up. Rodeo Drive fender benders are the *best.*' I was aware of her stiffening slightly. 'Not that I'm into car wrecks or anything, as a rule. Sorry.'

'For what?' I asked.

'If he, ah … I hope you don't mind me asking … how *did* he …?'

I stalled, momentarily. I had forgotten about that. But the car crash had been a cheap shot and my husband's death was too important to be cheapened like that again. Sacred, really, in a way. I needed something more respectful now. There was the documentary, true, but that had failed once already. Jasmine was looking at me, and I realised that from her end there was no good reason for the hesitation, so now I had that to explain too and my mind went, unusually, unhelpfully, completely blank. Then when it rebooted, none of the things I could think of – leukaemia, sailing accident, MRSA – could explain the pause. So the pause lengthened.

'It's OK,' said Jasmine at last. 'You don't have to tell me.'

Bugger it, I thought. Now she would assume it was something disgusting that I was ashamed of and didn't want to say out loud. She would think it was suicide, or AIDS. (But would a Californian think there was anything disgusting about suicide or AIDS? No, of course she wouldn't, but now she'd think that *I* did). I was making a real mess of this. Clovis had told me that Jasmine was an important person to get on my side – at least she hadn't told me, but I bet she should have – and yet here I was, after ten minutes, showing her that I was so shallow it was no wonder my husband had killed himself or been driven into the arms of another to catch things from.

I sneaked a look across at her, keeping my head to the front and swivelling my eyes as far left as they would go so that it almost hurt them. What did she mean by saying I didn't have to tell her? How could she be so uninquisitive? She looked perfectly serene, tapping a little tune out on the steering wheel with her sharp red nails and checking over her shoulder with a graceful arc of her perfect olive neck. She smiled at me as she turned to face front again and said:

'Really. Don't worry about it. I shouldn't have asked.'

And all of a sudden, I knew exactly why she wasn't seething with curiosity. She was going to get the story from Clovis instead.

'Can I ask you a favour?' I blurted.

'Sure.'

'Can you not mention it – my husband, I mean – to Clovis?'

'Sure,' she said again, very smoothly, as though this had been the last thing on her mind. And then she blew it. She didn't ask why not. What person in a million wouldn't ask why not? I might just conceivably have bought the calm 'sure's if she'd acted naturally and asked me why not.

'She doesn't know,' I said.

'Clovis doesn't know that your husband died?' She sounded surprised. Time to concentrate.

'It's hard to explain. I knew this trip was coming up and I knew that Clovis would cancel it and I knew that it would be better if I did come – take my mind off things, you know – but that sounds so callous, I didn't want to admit it. You understand? If I was any kind of person at all, I wouldn't even want to take my mind off it. So I didn't tell her. Pretty shitty, when she's been so good to me.'

Of course Jasmine believed me. People always do when you admit something bad about yourself; when those who tell *real* lies tell lies they try to make themselves sound good. That's why they so rarely get away with it. And that's why I never do it.

'Don't be silly,' said Jasmine, reaching over and giving my leg a squeeze.

Rather forward, I found myself thinking, prissily, and only really because my legs were relaxed and her olive claw fingers disappeared into my flesh and if I'd known it was coming I would have lifted my thigh off the seat and tensed it. Anyway, ten minutes later I was clutching her round the waist like a fetish corset, practically standing in her shoes with her, so I could hardly talk.

'You gotta do it,' Jasmine had said as she was parking, squeezing into a space about six inches longer than the car. 'Look at the view.'

'Exactly,' I answered. 'I can see it from here. It's lovely.'

'Come on!' said Jasmine. 'You gotta get a picture of you with the sign behind you.'

I knew the rules for being shown around someone's hometown and so I let myself be led to what she told me was the best spot – the intersection of Hollywood and Vine. Right on the intersection, in the middle of the road, with tourist buses whisking past on all sides.

'Let go and lemme get my camera,' Jasmine said, picking at my arms with her sharp fingernails and laughing.

'Yeek!' I screamed as a rubbish lorry went past close enough for me to feel the heat coming off its sides. The driver leaned out and howled at us.

'Get in back with da rest a da garbage, ya tree,' screeched Jasmine, then turned back to me. 'One picture.'

Sensing that resistance was useless, I peeled myself off her and stood with my shoulders round my ears and my best attempt at a smile while she framed the shot.

'Gotcha!' she said, looking down into her camera and nodding. 'Shame about the yellow ribbons, but it's beautiful of you.' She grabbed my arm and hustled me back to the sidewalk, holding up her hand like a cop to slow the traffic and ignoring the horns honking.

'What's with those ribbons?' I asked her. 'Iraq?'

'They're for Roman Polanski,' said Jasmine, and then snorted at the look on my face. 'Nah, it's Eye-raq.' She slid back into the car and waited for me to join her, gazing up at the hillside in the distance. 'You know the most impressive thing about the Hollywood sign, Verity? Only one person has ever jumped off it to kill herself. Isn't that amazing? Only one.'

'You'll never make a tour guide,' I said, buckling my seat belt again before I turned to look at her. Her face was reddening, her eyes so wide that the tips of her lashes touched her cheeks and eyebrows and bent over. I had never seen lashes long enough to do that before.

'I'm so sorry,' she said. Aha, I thought. I was right.

'It's OK,' I told her. 'That wasn't what happened. What letter did she jump off?'

'The H. I woulda jumped off the Y if it was me.'

'Oh yeah,' I said. 'No question. The Y. Symmetrical. Jumping off the H—'

'Makes you look like a quitter.'

'Hardly worth slogging all the way up there and then jumping off the H.'

In agreement then, we veered back out into the traffic and headed north.

At noon, Jasmine laden with the General Hospital scrubs that she said all her friends wore as pyjamas and me clutching the overshirt of a lesser Desperate Housewife, we left the cool air of It's a Wrap and stepped back out into a sauna.

'God,' Jasmine said. 'It's October, for Chrissake. What is going *on* with this weather? Let's eat somewhere with air, huh? You don't want to go back to your hotel, do you? Nah, me either. Whaddaya in the mood for? Italian?'

'No,' I said. 'Anything but Italian.'

'Mexican? French? Japanese?'

'American?' I suggested.

Jasmine, thinking hard, opened her mouth wide like a choirboy and drummed her fingers on her stretched cheek.

'You don't mean fried chicken and mashed potato, right?' she said. I shrugged. 'Oh, you do?' Another little drumbeat. 'OK, I'll get my office to grab us a table.' She pushed some buttons on her mobile while steering out of the cark park. 'Hey,' she said into the phone. 'Get me The Farm. Outside. Nah, they got air outside. And only call me for Chicago. Anyone else say I'll call back.' She dinked off her phone and threw it over her shoulder.

'We're going to The Farm,' she said to me.

'With the outside air,' I said.

'Funny,' said Jasmine. 'Hey!' She swivelled round on the seat and looked intently at me. 'I just got what you said back there. Anything but Italian. You don't like Italian food?'

'It's not that.'

'I'm Italian,' said Jasmine. 'What do you eat when you're home if you don't eat pasta? Is it tomatoes? If it's tomatoes I can show you a pasta sauce, takes seven minutes, no tomatoes. Grated zucchini, lemon, parmigiano.'

'It sounds lovely,' I told her. 'My husband . . .' I caught my breath and hoped that would be enough.

The truth of the matter was that I had eaten Italian food under very dismal circumstances every night for months, while the divorce train was derailing, and although I adored it – for, as Jasmine said, what would you eat when you're home if you didn't eat pasta? – it was beginning to pall.

'What?' said Jasmine, cutting into my thoughts. 'Was he Italian?'

'No,' I said. 'My husband and I . . .'

The whole story was that there was an Italian – a very indifferent Italian – down beyond our house on the Wandsworth Bridge Road and I ate dinner there, all alone, every night. I got off the tube at

Fulham Broadway and walked down, past our house, ate a plate of noodles and walked back. In the summertime there wasn't much to see through the gritty, grey curtains of the kitchen, although sometimes I could tell from beads of condensation on the small window below the area steps that someone was having a shower. Kim always showered in the mornings and so when I saw the steam I knew it was *her*, standing on the rough bit in the bath, reaching out towards the wire rack for the soap that would be making my bathroom smell like someone else's house because it wasn't my soap. It was hers.

Now that winter was coming, of course, there were much richer pickings. On the way down lights would be on and shutters would still be open and the kitchen, sometimes even the basement bedroom, would be there as plain as day through the grey film. On the way back, although the shutters would be barred, I could tell from the light seeping around the edges whether they were still up or were in bed, reading or whatever. Also, three times in the last year I had seen him on the street: once putting the rubbish out and twice grimly thundering up and down the steps with bags of shopping while our car sat illegally in the road, hazard lights beseeching and boot open.

So the problem with Italian food, although I could hardly tell Jasmine this, was that every night on the way down my stomach would already be churning and on the way back the taste in my mouth, as I saw the slivers of light from the bedside lamps, if they were reading or something, was burned garlic and sour tomatoes – it really was a very indifferent Italian – and inside me, I would feel the Parmesan re-forming itself into a lump.

'What?' said Jasmine. 'You ran a restaurant? I thought you were in flowers.'

'No,' I said. Would a widow go out and eat in the same bad Italian every night for six months? What was I going to say?

'We just went to them a lot,' I began but, before I could go on, Jasmine laid her hand on my arm.

'You went to them a lot?' she said kindly. 'Verity, honey. I gotta say – you need to fight this. When I got divorced everything reminded me of my ex-husband. Jeez, *I* reminded me of my ex-husband. But you gotta resist; you gotta get back in the game. How you gonna get through the rest of your life without eating a little pasta?'

This was all wrong. She was divorced and I was a widow and there was no way she should get to tell me things – it was a simple matter of precedence. I only had myself to blame, though: I must look as if I was overreacting, as if I was exactly the kind of widow who could be told what to do by a mere divorcee. I had to reclaim some ground, quickly.

'It was more than that,' I told her. 'I met my husband in a terrible Italian restaurant, a real shocker, with hard-boiled eggs and pickled beetroot in the Insalata Mista – a British problem you wouldn't understand – and then for our first date we went to a slightly better one, great salads but Wall's vanilla. Then we had a bit of a setback, didn't see each other for months and when we bumped into ourselves again where should we be but ...'

'A better Italian?' said Jasmine. She was interested now.

'Slightly,' I said. 'The food was OK, but the waiters were English and the wine was Chilean. And so it turned into a quest. Our search for the perfect Italian. We combed London for it. Well, Europe generally. Even Italy a few times. And ever since he died ... I had a good plate of minestrone by accident once, served by the perfect waiter – broken English and flirty but not too flirty – and I cried in the toilets for an hour.'

'Oh God,' said Jasmine. 'If only you'd come here together, before. We have Gino Angelini, oh my God, we have Il Cielo ... People hold their weddings there and go back every year for anniversaries. Oh, *God*.'

'It sounds lovely,' I said. 'But you're right – I do need to get over it now.'

Jasmine put her head down on the steering wheel, parping the horn, which made her jerk up again. 'I could just die for saying that,' she groaned. Then: 'Oh my God, I can't believe I just said I could *die*.'

'Please,' I said. 'Don't worry.' I heaved a sigh. 'I know you're right. Thank you for telling me.'

'God,' croaked Jasmine. I reached over and patted her leg, smiling bravely.

She was still groaning now and then and I was still smiling through my grief when we drew up at the restaurant. She flicked the car into neutral, sprang out and tossed the keys to a parking attendant.

'There's not that much we need to discuss, really,' she said, once we were sitting at our table. She snapped her fingers. The water boy turned, frowning, but his face smoothed and then softened into near idiocy as he saw Jasmine and moved towards her.

'Ice water?' he said, gazing.

'And can you tilt the shade, hon?' said Jasmine. 'Just a tad, to get the sun out of Ms Drummond's eyes. You're a blessing in a cold, empty world.'

The water boy gulped, gave me a respectful look and cranked the sunshade around so that Jasmine and I were plunged into darkness, ignoring the loud tutting from the next table where two large tourists were now sitting out in the midday glare.

'Shouldn't we talk about the film?' I said. 'The movie?' I was stroking the tablecloth and menu stand, thinking they had to be filthy – we were only feet away from the traffic and the exhausts of the SUVs – but they felt smooth enough under my fingers.

Jasmine blew a kiss at the water boy, and then shook her head at me.

'Not us, not now,' she said. 'I've straightened it all out with Clovis already, I know what I can take to the table.'

'I thought we'd be talking about the cast and the location and everything,' I said, trying not to sound as disappointed as I felt.

'Money,' said Jasmine. 'That's all we talk. And I know what Clovis wants. The rest is up to *Jesus*.'

I glanced up from my menu. She was looking over my shoulder with her eyes and mouth wide open. I hesitated. Jasmine, on our short acquaintance, didn't seem the type to bring the Lord to the lunch table. Of course, she might just have been saved that minute but if so she didn't look very pleased about it.

'Jasmine?' I said, but before she could answer, a vision appeared and spoke unto us.

'Verity,' the vision said. 'I'm so pleased to meet you. You have to excuse me butting in. It's not professional and I can tell from

Jasmine's face that she's mad at me, but I couldn't help it. Let me introduce myself. I'm the producer. I'm Patrice. I want to talk to you about our movie.'

The besotted water boy had already rushed up with a third chair and Patrice sank into it, without ever taking her eyes off my face.

'So, Verity,' she said. '*Straight Up*.' She stared at me. I stared back. It wasn't a question. I didn't know what she wanted me to say, and it was no use trying to read her face for clues. I smiled at her. She closed her eyes slowly and opened them again like a cat. Maybe that was the nearest to a smile she could manage.

To be fair, she might have been responding to a terrible accident with a chip pan, but here we were in Beverly Hills and I was taking a guess that most of what had happened to Patrice's face had sprung from vanity. Vanity which must now be satisfied: it was certainly beautiful – it just wasn't really a face. I looked at it, item by item, trying to reach an overall view.

Her cheeks were sculpted into perfect apples, her brows arching proudly above the chiselled hollows and her forehead a skating rink on the first day of winter, untrammelled, untrammellable. So plump and so sharply defined were her lips that they seemed to float in front of her, but it was a job well done. There was none of the inner tube about them; the perfect line where lip ended and skin began was still the most prominent point, but one more ounce, one more gram, if the surgeon had blinked, they would be monstrous.

In the middle, though, something had gone ever so slightly wrong. Her nose had a Mary Poppins point, and while she had avoided the nostrils-first look that a Mary Poppins point can sometimes lead to, the tilt, the flare, the joining of the frenulum, powdered and shaded as it was ... something about it was not quite right. It was like looking at Escher's impossible triangle; when you focussed on one part that one part was fine, but at the corners of your eyes the other parts were making no sense and some bit of your brain, busily getting on with interpreting the world without waiting to be asked, was troubled.

The problem on either side of her nose was easier to account for; you can't keep scooping out eye bags and lifting crow's feet forever and Patrice was getting near the end of the road.

Her hair though, twenty shades of professional red, was like the bought-in pudding at the dinner party of a very bad cook, rioting triumphant atop the careful and uneasy home-made face in the way that hair and puddings can do. Sure there were the long side curls, hiding the scars, and sure there was a definite raising of the hairline along the top, electrolysis probably or plucking. This was momentarily puzzling. If she'd had a lot of lifts wouldn't her hairline be too high and need lowering? Well, maybe it had started just above her lashes, Onassis-style. Or maybe it had been lowered too far and was on its way back. Or maybe there comes a point when all bets are off and anything can happen. Luckily, with forty still a long way away and never having had the funds to dabble, I wouldn't know.

'*Straight Up*,' she said again.

'This is my meeting, Patrice,' said Jasmine slowly. Patrice swivelled her eyes towards Jasmine's face.

'Your office told me where you were,' she said. 'And I just couldn't resist coming down and adding my voice to yours. I want to tell Verity about my vision for her story.'

'You don't have to,' I said. 'I'm not playing hard to get.' I wasn't sure what it was about her that made me blurt a reassurance. She was a producer and who was I? And she had to be older than me. She had to be ... I peered at her face but there was no help to be had there. Her clothes gave a bit of a clue; they were floating panels of silk, hard to tell where one garment ended and the next began, more like an abstract painting of clothing than actual clothes, and a very young woman, especially one in such good shape as Patrice – and she was in very good shape – would hardly waft around Beverly Hills in abstract clothing panels. Besides there was a kind of deliberation that was almost stateliness about her, a carefulness in her movements, that didn't seem young. The only other time I ever saw someone move like that, hold herself like that, it had been a friend of a friend who had quickly lost a large volume of her weight; she had become willowy and could have flitted around, but still she walked as though making sure not to bump into things, still, after all the years of sizing up chairs and measuring the gaps between the bodies in crowds, she hesitated and considered the air in front of her, making sure there was a space before she moved.

Patrice reminded me of that, not exactly, but something like. I smiled at her again.

'I see white,' she said.

'This is not the time,' said Jasmine. 'We only need to talk money and I've got it under control.'

'Lots of white,' Patrice went on. 'Lots of dazzle. I'd like to shoot it in sunshine, but not have much of the sky. Even on the surface shots. Just lots and lots of white.'

'It's going to be expensive,' I said. I was aware of Jasmine turning slightly to look at me. Patrice grew very still. 'Isn't it? Getting a crew into the snow somewhere. Where do you think you'll make it? Canada? Colorado?'

Patrice said nothing although her face, somehow, registered a change of emotion. It wasn't a frown, obviously, but something happened. Maybe her pupils dilated. As I waited for her to speak, Jasmine jumped in.

'It's the opposite of animation,' she said. 'In animation, snow scenes are the easiest of all. Cheapest background there is – nobody has to draw anything.'

'Or darkness,' I said. 'A pair of eyes in the dark and a voiceover. I bet that speeds up *Wallace and Grommit* no end.'

'Jasmine told me you were a complete industry outsider,' said Patrice.

'I am,' I answered. 'Sorry, I shouldn't be telling you what you know and I'm only guessing. Sorry. I'm a florist.'

'Really?' said Patrice. 'That's fascinating. I love flowers.' For the first time she seemed to shake off the dreamy intensity which was beginning to unnerve me a little. 'Do you do contract work or do you have a store?'

'I work in a shop, a store,' I said. 'Doing everything really. Weddings, funerals, christenings.'

'Tell me ...' Patrice began, then she sat back. 'Sorry,' she said. 'I should concentrate on the movie.'

'No,' said Jasmine, 'you shouldn't. You shouldn't even be in this meeting.'

Again, before I could help it I found myself jumping to Patrice's aid.

'I'm surprised that you're interested at all, really,' I told her. '*Straight Up* seems like it would be such a boys' film.' Again, hard to tell, but this time I was sure I had offended her. I began to backtrack. 'Do you get to pick what you work on or does the studio just give you jobs to do?'

'Patrice is an independent producer,' said Jasmine. 'And anyway, *you* wrote it and you're a girl too.'

'True,' I said. 'But in the written story, there's a lot of feelings and interior stuff. How are you going to do that in a film? And what's going to be left except the climbing if you take all that out?'

'You don't think I'm up to making an action adventure?' said Patrice.

'Sorry,' I said.

'Don't be,' she answered and she smiled. That was a sight to behold. Her top lip curled away from her teeth, large, perfect and many in number, and her bottom lip spread out across her chin in a movement unrelated to what was going on above. Nothing else moved a millimetre, but her eyes shone, and some of the carefulness disappeared from her the way it does when you close the door after the guests have gone. Something had changed and it never changed back again. It wasn't a big change; Patrice never got normal. But from that moment on she got on with the rest of us – in normal's orbit.

'OK,' said Jasmine. 'Patrice, I guess it's nice for Verity to meet the producer, so long as you let me run the meeting and don't get carried away with your dazzling white.' She gave Patrice a hard stare and was rewarded with another feline eye squeeze. A blonde girl was bobbing aerobically towards us through the tables, ducking the perimeters of the umbrellas, her ponytail leaping up to one side and then the other with each step.

'So,' said Jasmine, 'let's eat.'

'You're having a burger for lunch?' said Patrice once the waitress had taken our orders and we were alone again. 'And a coke?'

'I'm Scottish,' I told her. 'Bread, beef and sugar are made from wheat, grass and sugarcane plants. It's practically a salad.'

'Didn't I read somewhere that Scotland holds the title for the what is it?' said Jasmine.

'Heart attack capital of Europe,' I said.

'Doesn't that worry you?' asked Patrice, her face attempting an unsuccessful look of concern; there were enough puckers to make a frown but they were not in the expected places.

'Nah,' I said. 'The way I see it is that you can either live on lard and whisky and crump to the ground like a shot stag when you're sixty-five or you can scrabble away at wheatgerm and carrot juice and spend an extra twenty years drooling and babbling with your family itching to pillow you. No contest.'

Patrice looked as though she might cry; I would have given a lot to see where the water came from – God knows where her tear ducts were. It was my first, although by no means my last, experience of the idea that Americans – or rather Californians – don't believe that death is inevitable. I felt I'd dropped a bit of a brick and despite what Jasmine had said there seemed only one way to fill the silence that followed.

'So, lots of white,' I said. 'And lots of voiceover.'

'No voiceover,' said Patrice. 'I don't know much about adapting scripts but I do know that.'

'You usually work with original scripts?' I asked her. She fell silent and once again Jasmine stepped in.

'What Patrice means is that she won't be writing it,' she said. 'We'll be hiring a scriptwriter, or rather a team of scriptwriters.'

'You will?'

'Of course.'

'I mean,' I said to Jasmine, '*you* will? You just said, *we'll* be hiring. Do you work for Patrice's company? Now, why on earth wouldn't Clovis tell me that? I practically had to tie her to a chair and drip water on her to get your name.'

'That's Clovis for you,' said Jasmine. 'She wouldn't be the Clovis we love if she wasn't the Clovis we love!'

'Do you know her?' I said. 'I thought you'd just heard about the book.'

'I wouldn't say I know her,' said Jasmine.

'I don't know her,' said Patrice, sounding very definite.

'But I know *of* her,' said Jasmine. 'I mean, everyone knows everyone in this business. If you ever meet anyone who doesn't know everyone, you know that's no one you want to know.'

'That's what I meant,' said Patrice, a bit less definite now. 'I know her, obviously.'

I said nothing. Patrice watched me, looking unavoidably serene. Jasmine tried for serenity but spoiled it by drumming her nails on the tabletop and I could feel the judder of one of her feet ticcing away underneath. So did they know Clovis or didn't they? And whether they did know her or didn't know her, shouldn't they know which? I excused myself and went to find the loo.

But when I was sitting on the closed lid of the loo, staring at Clovis's number on my phone, I couldn't think of a way to ask what I wanted to ask without making it sound as if I was questioning Clovis and not Jasmine at all. I had slid off my sandals and I propped my bare feet against the back of the door. I love America. People say it's sanitised and phony, and maybe California isn't the place to come if you're looking for grit, but the thing about sanitised? The thing about phony? They're just two different words for clean. How many restaurant toilet doors would you touch with your bare feet in London? How many toilet lids would you close with your bare hand and then touch your phone? That, surely, was all that was wrong: I was a long way from home, talking to new people with a different way of expressing themselves. I was being silly. I left the cubicle and washed my hands – but only to try the hand scrub and the spritz with extract of real silk, not because I touched the toilet lid – and went back outside.

'Hey, kid,' said a voice as I passed under the canopy. A man was beckoning to me. I hesitated. But he was wearing a cream linen suit and a brown linen shirt and he had on brown rope sandals showing off beautiful brown feet. Crooks and grifters don't have pedicures. I walked over to him.

'Are you talking to me?' I said.

'None of my business,' he said. 'But those two at your table? You're getting stiffed out there.'

'I'm sorry?'

'I'm at the next table,' he said. 'I heard it all. She said she was a tracker, but now it turns out she works for the studio?'

'What studio?' I asked. 'Patrice is an independent producer. Who are you?'

'*I'm* a tracker,' he said. 'And I don't work for anyone, except me and possibly you. Does this producer have an option on it?'

'Umm,' I said. Two things were troubling me. For one, I didn't know whether you would say that Patrice had an option on anything exactly, we had only just met and for all her intensity she had hardly choked me with ideas about what she was going to do. On the other hand, this character, despite his linen and matt-finish toe polish (I thought, after a closer look), didn't seem to know that Patrice was a producer and Jasmine had just told me that anyone who didn't know everyone ...

'She does,' I said. 'Do you know Patrice?'

He had overheard the entire conversation so he could hardly admit that he didn't. He could hardly say there was a producer in LA that he didn't know.

'Sure, I know Patrice,' he said. 'I didn't know she had gone independent is all. Brave move. Very risky way to place your script.'

'Really?'

'My card,' he said, twitching one out of nowhere like a conjuror. 'Kenny Daateng. Century City,' it said. 'Give me a call if things free up again. Or even if they don't. I could look at the option contract for you, get you out of it, get you a better deal.'

'Don't you want to know what it's about?' I asked him. 'How do you know you're interested?'

'*Straight Up*, right?' he said. 'White, snow, ice, climbing. A real guy movie but a ton of feeling, right?' I was nodding and he clicked a wink at me. 'Send me over a copy of the book when you send the contract,' he said. 'Can't hurt to get started.'

Patrice and Jasmine had their heads bent close together across the table as I returned and were talking earnestly, one of Jasmine's hands patting Patrice's arm and the other hovering near the back of her hair. They were so intent and they sprang apart so electrically when they saw me that a thought popped into my head that would explain it all. Were they a couple? Was that 'we' that Jasmine had let slip not the company 'we' at all, but the couple 'we'? The one I didn't get to use any more? I decided to flush them out, or at least make them squirm.

'I don't know a lot about this,' I began, 'so I'm sorry if it's inappropriate, but do we have to talk just about the book? Is it weird to want to get to know you?' Patrice's face registered a series of expressions one after the other as I spoke. She looked blank, then receptive, then smooth, then alert, then drained. Reading between the lack of lines I would have said that on a normal face it would have been: caution, intrigue, relief, pleasure, alarm. 'For instance,' I went on, 'are you married?' I smiled sweetly and Patrice relaxed and smiled back, beamed almost, her eyes shining.

'No,' she said. 'I'm not. I was once, in another life, but not right now.'

'Children?' I asked and Patrice's smile widened to its capacity, her top lip beginning to get that crease above it, like Julia Roberts's gets, the one that reminds you that your mouth is one of the places where your insides begin.

'No,' she said again, and her beaming smile and shining eyes took in Jasmine too. 'Not yet.'

'Not right now?' echoed Jasmine. 'Not yet? Jeez, Patrice, you get much more positive, you'll end up on Oprah.' Obviously, I was wrong. They weren't a couple: Patrice had been married and wanted children and – I remembered – Jasmine had told me that morning that she was divorced. So what was going on with the almost hair-stroking and arm-patting and the 'we'?

'Oh, Jas,' said Patrice, as the food arrived. She was still looking insanely and mystifyingly happy. She turned to me and compressed her face into dimples, as though attempting a smirk. 'Jasmine thinks she'll never find another one,' she said then she picked up her fork, selected a chunk of pepper and placed it carefully in her mouth without touching her lips.

Jasmine was spiking beansprouts on to her fork, jabbing away at them. When she had a full load she nibbled the untidy ends off the bundle before putting them all in her mouth and chewing thoughtfully. Finally she swallowed and spoke.

'I'll never get married again,' she said. 'I'm willing to bet my own money. I've been divorced for seven years. I've been on at least two dates a week since then and the best run I've had is nine dates in a row. I'll bet you my own money and throw in a kidney that I will never find anyone I want to marry. You on?'

'Verity?' said Patrice, but I shook my head.

'I'd never lay a bet that someone as beautiful as Jasmine can't get a guy,' I said. 'I wouldn't give you—'

'Doughnuts to dollars?' said Patrice. 'I agree. But I meant how about you, as in, are you married?'

'I, I . . .' I stammered. 'I'm not sure.' Obviously I couldn't change the story now, not with Jasmine sitting right there, but I wished I could. There was something about Patrice that made me feel I could tell her anything, even the five act tragedy with Greek chorus and real flames that was my divorcerama. And like they said, here in California, everyone was divorced; there was no shame in it. It wasn't like home where my granny always lowered her eyes before she told me that some marriage had 'failed' in an echo of that voice that said the king's life was drawing peacefully to a close.

'You're not sure?' Patrice said.

'I'm sorry, Vee,' said Jasmine, reaching across to squeeze my hand supportively.

'I'm a widow,' I said. For the first time I felt no frisson as I said it but luckily a tone of blank dolefulness suited the message quite well. Patrice put her hands up in front of her face with a gasp. From front on you would almost have said she clapped her hands *to* her face, but as she turned slightly sideways to gape at Jasmine I could see that they had come to a dead stop a good couple of inches away from her flesh, as though repelled like magnets. Patrice's make-up survived.

'Not . . .' she began. 'I mean, the book, the story?'

'No!' I said. 'God, no.' But she didn't believe me.

'How can you *stand* to listen to people talking about it?' she said. 'Picking it over? If I had known!'

'Let's talk about Jasmine instead,' I went on, brightly, bravely. 'How did you find the first one?'

'Fell over him at work one day,' said Jasmine. 'But I wouldn't marry him again either, now that I'm paying attention. It's like when you go shopping for a new dress? You can't find anything you like so you get ready to leave in your own clothes and you hate them too.'

'Well, God help the rest of us,' said Patrice.

'It's not that,' said Jasmine. 'I'm not saying I think I'm unattractive. I'm saying there are no men to marry. None. Not in LA, anyway.'

I stared around at the other tables. Kenny Daateng in his cream linen suit was gone but there were others like him six deep in all directions, tanned, buffed, flossed and coordinated, any one of them could walk into a packed football stadium in England and be the handsomest man there.

'Jasmine, don't ever go to Bradford,' I said.

'Huh?' said Jasmine. 'No really. LA is a company town. All the men are actors. And marrying an actor is not something normal healthy people do much these days. It's like smallpox.'

I snorted. 'There are schools and shops and offices aren't there?' I said. 'So there must be teachers and salesmen and photocopier engineers and IT support staff.'

'Correction: actors and losers,' said Jasmine. 'Actors and losers.'

'But there are thousands of men even in the industry who aren't actors,' said Patrice.

'Like who?' said Jasmine.

'Sound editors,' said Patrice. 'Cameramen, FX guys, lighting specialists, set builders ...'

'*Crew*?' said Jasmine. 'You want me to marry *crew*?'

At her horror, obviously sincere, Patrice and I caught each other's eyes and started laughing, just as if we were old friends. That was it, I decided. That 'we' had been unavoidable with someone like Patrice because as soon as you met her you felt as if you'd known her for ever, could tell her anything, and would certainly pitch in and help adapt a script if she asked you.

Kenny in the suit didn't know anything, I decided. For the first time in months, sitting there, I felt happy. And for the first time in a lot longer – I might even call it ever, if that didn't sound so pathetic – I felt something else too. It wasn't just that they liked my story, it was more that all the teasing and the kind looks and hand squeezes made it feel like ... like a ... like a family, maybe? Well, like a sitcom, anyway.

Chapter 3

My Trouble with Pyjamas

Jasmine said the paperwork would take the rest of the day, so she and Patrice arranged to meet me for breakfast the following morning and in the meantime would I be OK? I assured her that, in the meantime, I would happily float around Beverly Hills in a taxi. Who wouldn't after all?

'You want us to drop you at the Farmers' Market?' said Jasmine. 'That's a trip. Or wait, no – go to 2 Rodeo. It's this beautiful little old cobbled street. Brand new.'

In the end they left me at the door of my hotel and drove off, Jasmine shouting at me that I wasn't to walk along Sunset Strip unless I wanted to go home in the hold. I felt a little slump, watching them go. Maybe I just wanted that thing I was feeling, that I didn't have a name for, to stay. Or maybe after one meeting I had got the bug and didn't want to be a tourist in this company town where everyone else was putting deals together and talking big money into tiny phones. As a first step on the road to becoming a player, I took Kenny Daateng's card out of my pocket and headed for the desk to sweet-talk my way into a shot of their Xerox machine.

'I love your beautiful country,' said the desk clerk, out of the blue, as we stood in the cramped office behind reception watching my manuscript whipping through the copier. It was one of those things people say in California that there's no answer for if you don't have the accent to say 'thank you so muuuch' without sounding silly.

'Well,' I said, trying at least, 'I love yours.' I tried to read his name badge.

'Bradley Honey,' he said. Or possibly, 'Bradley, honey.' I couldn't tell.

'Bradley,' I said.

'Brad.'

'Brad.'

'Really?' said Brad. 'You love America?'

'Absolutely,' I said. 'I mean, I haven't seen much of it, but California ...' I looked out of the window of the office at the car park and the fire escape of the building beyond it. 'California is ...' They always say that you can get anyone to believe anything so long as it's a compliment. 'California is just heaven.'

'Really?' His eyes were bulbous with pleasure now. 'All of it?'

'All of it. The architecture, the food, the people, the weather, the traffic.'

'The traffic? You love the traffic? Somebody else needs to hear this.' He looked around him as if trying to gather a crowd.

'It's the automatic cars,' I said. 'Everyone's driving around half-comatose because there's nothing for them to do. It makes for a lot of serenity on the roads.' His smile spread beyond his ears and I waited to hear if there would be a clink of enamel as it met round the back of his head. 'My country is just rude people eating bad food in old buildings with the rain coming in and then driving over each other on the way home.'

'Oh please,' he said. 'I'm sure that's not true.'

'Are you calling me a liar?' I asked him, and his smile faded for a beat before coming back even wider than before.

'I get that,' he said. 'The British sense of humour? I totally get it. In high school I was already Monty Python's biggest fan.'

There was a final sshhpp as the last page was sucked into the copier and Brad bent to remove the stack.

He was still on the desk when I passed through again an hour later.

'Hi!' he said. 'Hello again! How you doing? How you been?'

'How've I been since I saw you last?' I said. 'I've been through some ups and downs but I'm holding it together, just about.'

'I get that!' said Brad. 'Nudge, nudge, wink, wink, say no more.'

'Has the courier come yet?' I asked him. He shook his head and reached under the desk for the parcel.

'But you go on out if you need to,' he said. 'I can take care of it. I'm on until seven.'

'Well then I will,' I said. 'Thank you, Brad.'

'Thank *you*, Ms Drummond,' he said.

'Verity.'

'What a beautiful name,' said Brad. He smiled at me again and then grew solemn, stroking the package on the desk before him, smoothing the gummed edge of the Jiffy bag.

'Can I tell you something?' he said. I nodded. 'I really appreciate you trusting me with your book, and I just wanted to say, I'm only working here to pay my way through acting classes?' I nodded again. Of course he was. 'But I'm serious. I'm no wannabe. My cousin, at this very moment … no wait. My uncle, his father,' he paused, 'is the only US citizen ever, to take part in both the trooping of the colours and the last night of the proms.'

'What …' I began. I was going to continue 'does that have to do with anything?' but managed to turn it into '… does he play?'

Brad shook his head with his eyes shut in an expression of patient condescension.

'He's not a musician,' he said.

'Well,' I answered. 'That's quite something.'

'Telling me,' said Brad and because I had such a shaky grip on myself, feeling the giggles bubbling up inside me, I didn't dare to say any more. So I never asked, and I never found out. 'I speak to his son, my cousin, every day,' Bradley went on. 'So can I give you some advice?'

'With those credentials,' I said, 'I'd be a fool not to listen to it.' Bradley tried to hold his smile down to a dimpled smirk of pride.

'If I were you,' he said. 'I would use a different pseudonym. I really would.'

'Not Clara Callan?'

'I really wouldn't,' he said. 'Clara Callan says "Oprah's Bookclub" to me. For this ice-entrapment thing you got going here, you need something … not exactly snappy, but something intriguing. Something with menace, a little more Hollywood dark side, you know? I'm thinking …' he spread his hands wide and pushed one shoulder forward as though just about to hit the high note in his aria, '… Nils Noir,' he said. 'You like that?'

'Nils Noir?' I pretended to think about it for a while. 'It doesn't really sound like someone's name.'

'That's OK.'

'Well, if *that's* OK, I might have the perfect thing. It's dark and menacing, anyway. How about: The Widow?'

Bradley swallowed awkwardly, his Adam's apple descending down into his collar and bobbing up again. 'No way,' he breathed. 'You are not.'

'Ah,' I said. 'You've read it.'

He nodded.

'I'll make up a new title page on the PC back there,' he told me. '*Straight Up*. By. The Widow. Oh, my God, I'm so glad you did this on my shift.'

It wasn't until long after my afternoon touring Universal Studios with the population of Idaho, when I was sitting alone in a darkened cinema with a bucket of popcorn the size of a wheelie bin, that the little tiny doubt that had been nudging me all afternoon, like a lemon pip in a Jacuzzi, finally wedged itself in somewhere I could pick it out. It had been on my wish list of things to do while I was here, to sit alone in a cinema with a bucket of popcorn and watch an ancient film, preferably black and white, that I had seen a dozen times on the television but never on a big screen. I don't know where I got the idea that old movies played in cinemas all the time in America. Certainly, I couldn't find any in the listings so I had to make do with a pseudo-Ephron romcom that must have had Joan Crawford turning in her grave. After it had finished I had the usual tussle with myself, trying to decide whether to watch the credits to the end while everyone else left, because that's what serious film buffs do, or whether to leave as soon as the credits got boring because only pseuds watch right to the Dolby logo. As I watched the endless reams of names flash past, sound editors and lighting technicians and FX men, I couldn't stop myself thinking about script adaptors too and I knew I had to stop telling myself what I wished was true and start facing the facts. I was still in my seat when the lights came up and the kids with the black bin bags started sweeping down between the rows of seats to pick up the litter. No independent scout would say that she and a producer together would be hiring a writer to adapt a script. That 'we' just would not go away.

In fact, I'd had my doubts about Jasmine ever since I first heard her name, ever since Clovis wouldn't tell me straight who she was. My heart lurched in my chest as I thought this. What was I saying? If Clovis trusted Jasmine then everything had to be square, didn't it? Once again, something under my ribcage bumped. This time, I knew what it was. It was the thought of calling Clovis and asking her something that made it sound as if I didn't trust her. Just the thought, of even asking, and making it *sound* that way. Clovis was my agent, like a primary care-worker, a guardian angel, a patron saint, and if I told her what I was thinking it would crush her. Then I remembered: I couldn't call Clovis because it was six in the morning in London. Finally, the bumping stopped, and it probably wasn't my heart anyway; it was probably just all the popcorn.

Back in the hotel lobby, Bradley was still there.

'Verity,' he called across to the door as soon as I entered. 'At last. I have to talk to you and promise you won't get mad? He looked over each shoulder in an exaggerated caricature of a spy. 'I copied your script,' he said.

'I know,' I said slowly. 'I was there. Thank you.'

'No, no, no, no,' said Brad. 'I mean I copied it again. After you'd gone. And I sent it over to my cousin.'

'The son of the uncle who ...?' I gave up before working out how to summarise it.

'I never finished that story, did I?' said Brad. 'My cousin, my uncle's son ...' he paused dramatically, 'works in the mailroom at IFA. And he's going to send your script upstairs in the morning.'

'Wow,' I said, guessing that this was impressive. From the expression on Brad's face, it seemed I had guessed right.

'Pret-ty exci-ting,' he sang in a tremulous falsetto. 'And your own contact has already biked something back to you.' He plucked an envelope from under the desk and laid it reverentially on the counter, holding it by its edges like a DVD. 'This came right back like a boomerang while you were out.' Kenny Daateng's name and logo were stamped on the envelope, embossed really. Pretty swish.

'You're being discovered, Verity,' Brad breathed. 'Just like Lana Turner in the malt shop. Right here in my hotel, on my shift.' His eyes were sparkling with unshed tears and I didn't want to ruin it by pointing out that I was being 'discovered' while discussing a contract with a sniffer and producer my agent had already set me up with, which wasn't really the stuff of Hollywood legend. Thinking that, though, only reminded me that I wasn't completely convinced about the sniffer and producer after all.

'Can I ask you a question?' I said, copying his looking over one shoulder and then the other routine, like Inspector Clouseau. 'What would it mean to you if someone who said she worked for herself didn't.'

'Worked at what?' said Brad.

'Sniffing scripts.'

He winced and shook his head slowly.

'That's what I thought,' I said. 'Not good.'

'Who are we talking about? I can get my cousin to scope him out for you.'

'Really? Your cousin in the mailroom would know anyone who was anyone?'

'Or who had ever been anyone, or who was ever going to be anyone, or who had ever had lunch with anyone who was anyone ...' I thought Brad was on a loop but abruptly he stopped and said, 'What's the name?'

'Jasmine,' I said. 'Jasmine ... I can't remember her second name. I don't actually know if I ever heard it but if I did I've forgotten. It's Italian, I know that. Jasmine ... If I don't remember I'll phone my agent in London in the morning and get her to remind me.'

'And I'll ask my cousin to check her out,' said Bradley. 'When I call him tomorrow to tell him about this,' he tapped his finger on the embossed envelope sitting on the desk. 'Things could get interesting.'

*

I hate getting ready for bed. It's always been the worst time of the day for me. Sometimes I feel, as I emerge from the lattice of waistbands and earrings and bra straps, as though I'll keep going and end up just a pile of flesh and organs in the corner for someone to shovel away. And I hate putting on pyjamas I've had on already, never knowing if I got hot in them the night before while I was asleep or got twisted up in them while I was dreaming so that the seams were tight under my arms or the gusset was dug right into my bottom, but then I hate putting on clean pyjamas over the grubby body after a long hard day too, but I hate the feeling of getting dressed while damp from a shower and I hate lying in bed with nothing on except the sheets. So whichever way I play it, it's always been a problem, and sometimes, crazy as it sounds, I sit in the corner of my bedroom in my clothes and cry because I just can't face it again.

Funnily enough, my granny always said I loved having my nappy changed when I was a baby and would gurgle and wave my arms and legs about until I was trussed back up again and finished off with a good tight shawl, but knowing my granny it was probably just that I couldn't get a deep enough breath of air to gurgle with when she had me swaddled to her satisfaction and so nappy changing and bathtime were my only chances at exercise before the next clamp-down.

Apart from telling my granny, I've always kept my pyjama problem quiet. (Not that it's anything to be ashamed of, because it could have been that a scorpion ran up my leg one night when I was getting changed. I've never been anywhere with scorpions, as it happens, but my point is that there are a hundred perfectly respectable explanations for everything, if only you can think them up.)

Before the divorce bomb went off, of course, I had options. I would either fall on to the bed with Kim and take my clothes off one piece at a time as things progressed, so that afterwards when it was time to get into bed officially and go to sleep I'd kind of already be there. Or I'd get changed into my pyjamas just after dinner, as though I was only trying them on, and then I'd have time to get used to them by bedtime so it was almost as if I was going to sleep in my clothes and there wasn't the same scary kind of peeling-ness about the transition. Now though, these days, living in the bombed-out wasteland, it was just too sad to put on pyjamas at seven o'clock at night. I had tried; I had poured glasses of wine for myself, saved up phone calls to make, even bought a plug-in foot massager, but it still made me feel as if in a year or two I would be the woman who came round getting stale bread for the pigeons.

Except that it wasn't so bad in hotels, where you could waft about quite legitimately in a robe trying out bits of equipment and letting the complimentary products soak in. Tonight, for instance, by the time I gave up watching the adverts and the snatches of programme in between them and got into the acres of bed, I was dry-eyed and not thinking about my pyjamas at all.

'Jasmine, Jasmine, Jasmine,' I repeated to myself, lying in the dark watching the headlights on the ceiling again. I tried to conjure up Clovis's voice telling me her name. Italian, I told myself, so it would probably end in O. Jasmine Blah-O. Jasmine Bla-blah-O.

I didn't see it coming. I should have, but I didn't see it coming until it was there in my ear, in my head. That hated name, the name I used to laugh and joke about, the name that more recently I had been careful never to say out loud or even in my thoughts, never to write in an email, never even to read if I could help it.

Helen Marlowe. It billowed out of me like a big sulphurous cloud and hung over my bed, seeping.

Helen Marlowe. She was as cool and smooth as she sounded. Perhaps it was no more than careful dressing that did it. Her clothes were made for her by a dressmaker, as she told anyone who would listen, and not the mouse-like émigrée of straitened means that the word dressmaker usually implies, but a competent mother of three who lived in Essex and did her fittings in her new conservatory, letting down the blinds with a ffrrmp! before asking Helen to strip. So Helen's waistband never cut in and her shirt cuffs never rode up and this, added to her taste for plain fabrics in muted shades and her habit of wearing her silky hair in a ponytail tied at the nape of her neck, gave her a look of calm as though nothing could ruffle her. My name for her – oh yes, I knew her – was Palmolive.

'Palmolive?' Kim asked, the first time.

'Bland, alkaline, no zip,' I explained. 'Like a bar of soap that's been left in the bath and lost its corners. Or a half-sucked sweet. And then there's her toes.'

'What's wrong with her toes?' said Kim.

'No one will ever know,' I said. 'No one will ever see them. Court shoes, slingbacks, espadrilles. Women like Palmolive never show their toes.'

And then afterwards every time we saw her, which was perhaps four or five times a year, I would stare at Kim and then look hard at Helen Marlowe's satin, leather, or cotton covered toes (depending on the season), pull the corners of my mouth down and nod.

Only now, Kim had seen Helen Marlowe's toes as well as everything else she had to show him. I turned my pillows over and thrashed my feet out from under the sheets. And every time he looked at them he would sigh with happiness that I was gone and Helen Marlowe would smile an easy smile as though she was an oval floating candle with a smile on top and she was melting.

'Tell me a Verity story,' said Helen. She was lying on the bed in her bra and underskirt, her work clothes shed and properly disposed of – shoes in trees, suit hanging up to air on the back of the bathroom door, everything else in the laundry hamper – and her going out clothes laid over a chair. She would put them on, do her face, brush her hair and be ready in time to go, she always was, but first she was lying down. Helen, Kim was beginning to notice, lay down the way that other people had cups of tea. After breakfast, after work, whenever she came home from a shopping trip, when weekend guests finally drove away, Helen would head downstairs to the basement bedroom, strip to her underwear and lie down.

He remembered the way Verity used to hurl herself on to him fully dressed at bedtime and snatch off her clothes and his in a frenzy.

'Are you meditating?' he had asked Helen once, but she had only smiled.

'There's just time,' she said now. 'A quick Verity story to boost my confidence.' They were headed to a party at work, with dozens of colleagues – partners and secretaries – who had never met Helen and who were almost bound, Kim knew, to call her Verity possibly by mistake and possibly not.

'OK,' he said. 'Let me think. Did I tell you the one about the boots in the sale? Or no, how about the time I caught her shaking vinegar into the cat's basket?' Helen wriggled her shoulders against the banked up pillows in anticipation. 'OK, this is a 24-carat Verity special.

'I came home a bit early from work one night, it was a bank-holiday Monday, one of the many that Verity got off and I didn't, and there she was, in her PJs, shaking cider vinegar into the basket.'

'Why was she in her PJs?' Helen asked.

'Oh, just that she usually was,' said Kim. He looked at Helen lying flat on the bed in her underwear and remembered Verity in her PJs at teatime, out washing the front windows or running across to the shops for milk with her raincoat buttoned over the top but the striped flannel legs unrolling underneath it for everyone to see. 'That's not the point,' he said. 'She was shaking vinegar in the cat's basket, so naturally I asked her why.'

'And?' said Helen, giggling already.

'And she gave it a good go, said it was a flea remedy, or wait no – it wasn't the flea remedy – but it was to mask the smell of the flea remedy which otherwise would put the cat off going in the basket and if the cat went to sleep somewhere else the fleas would spread to there. Because you see this was an amazing new product – it's all coming back to me now – where you shook the powder on the bedding instead of the cat, much kinder really since cats hate being dusted, only if the cat took against the smell, you had to dab the cat's nose with vinegar so that it couldn't smell the flea stuff.'

'So why was she putting it in the basket?' said Helen, eyes shining with glee.

'Exactly. One of the worst trip-ups of her long career. And just to make sure, while she was still wondering whether I'd spotted that one I asked her: "What's it called?"'

'The flea stuff?' said Helen.

'And she looked stunned for a second and then said. "Flea".'

Helen cackled and Kim started to laugh too.

'But she recovered, she recovered. F-L-E-E, she assured me. A pun. Like Hoppit the rabbit repellent. And then she went into the usual detail overdrive, like she always did when she'd nearly blown it, you know. She told me not to tell anyone about it because she had got it

from Phil Coates who'd brought it back from Kenya where his mother uses it on the dogs and it wasn't licensed in Britain and that was why she had thrown the packaging away already and couldn't show me.'

'Was she expecting a sneak raid?' said Helen.

'God knows,' said Kim. 'Although to be fair Phil has been arrested a few times coming back through customs. I wouldn't keep the wrapper off any powder he gave me.'

'I hope you wouldn't take any powder he offered,' said Helen, who didn't approve of Phil. 'So did you ever find out the truth?'

'I guessed,' said Kim. 'After dinner, I went to load the dishwasher and it was full of coffee cups and side plates, the good ones, which was when Verity "revealed" that her granny's friend Pearl had dropped in in the afternoon with a bunch of ladies, all playing hooky from some country dancing championship at Earl's Court. Now pay attention, won't you. One of them had brought a Sealyham terrier and between them they had eaten all the coffee-walnut cake she had made the day before.'

Kim waited, but Helen never tried to work it out for herself. When she asked to be told a story she meant it.

'I was supposed to notice that Twiglet wouldn't go near his basket and ask why. Then Verity would tell me that it had been commandeered by the Sealyham terrier brought by the lady who along with a few others was responsible for the disappearance of the walnut cake.'

'When in fact?'

'My guess would be Verity had eaten the whole thing herself watching Chitty-Chitty-Bang-Bang *in her dressing gown.'*

'So she ate a cake and to cover it up she invented several old ladies, a country dance championship, and a dog complete with unlikely breed, she pickled the cat, got caught red-handed and made up a flea remedy?'

'Yeah,' said Kim. 'You've got to hand it to her, really.'

'You poor darling,' said Helen.

'Yeah,' said Kim again and he watched as Helen sat up and began to get dressed.

I had ways to stop myself thinking about it, though, the best of which was to focus on work instead; not in the sense of reminding myself what I had to do and what I'd forgotten to do and what I hoped my boss wouldn't find out I'd done – that was never going to send anyone off to sleep – but more like work-based fantasy, like work would be if the world was the way you thought it was when you were five and everybody in your class wanted to be a train driver or a ballerina. Back then, I had wanted to be a florist and now I was one and in bed at night when I needed something to dream about to get that name out of my head and put me to sleep I'd dream about being what being a florist would be if five-year-olds were in charge.

So … the Turner/Brooke wedding last month. They'd had peach rosebuds and little white lilies with the stamens snipped out, wires up the stems, ferns round the outside, peach and white embroidered ribbon tied in an eight-loop bow. A big peach and white bouquet for the big white bride, a small peach and white posy for each of the little peach bridesmaids, a peach buttonhole for the men, a spray of peach and white at either side of the altar, a peach and white nosegay every six places on the table and one peach silk rosebud poked through the ribbon holding shut the net of sugared almonds, peach and white.

But if it was up to me, oh if it was up to me … I would have given her scarlet dahlias for her bouquet, their raggy yellow eyes echoing the shape of crimson chrysanthemums, and Lucifer, like a freeze-frame of a firework, and orange marigolds and flame-coloured asters like surprised babies' eyes when someone goes Boo! and yellow Icelandic poppies that wouldn't last anyway so there would be nothing to stop the bride from plucking them out and giving them to her guests instead of sugared almonds in net. And the whole thing would be tied up with plaited straps of crocosmia. And the bridesmaids would each carry one humungous dahlia like a spirograph come to life, with a stem four feet long, that they could hold up to make an arch like soldiers do. And the poppies at the table could be in little honey jars and by the time the sun went down they would mostly have been pinched to be tucked behind girls' ears so then the water could be tipped out and candles put in the jars and they would glow and the shadows of the few wilting poppies left over would dance, enormous, around the walls.

Except that last month Icelandic poppies would have had to be flown in, and unless the ends were burned off the sap might give the bride a rash, so not poppies then, maybe Echinacea … but that would make three spiky shapes and nothing rounded … so instead …

In the morning, as usual, all I could remember were waves of red and orange, bursts of scarlet, as if I had spent the night in a late-Beatles drug dream. It always worked, always had, even back when the most my imagination ran to was daisies and ribbons. It worked every time.

Chapter 4

The Cat's Mother

Jasmine and Patrice were early for breakfast, both looking as fabulous as though they had spent all night getting ready. Patrice had surely been professionally blow dried, the red curls as perfect at the back as at the front and exuding the scent of melons as she tossed them carelessly around above another assemblage of clothing-like artistry. Jasmine was wearing a white dress, red stilettos and sunglasses inside, and should have looked like a footballer's girlfriend after her first big shop, but on Jasmine it worked. I was wearing clean jeans and a T-shirt from Marks and Spencer and looked, therefore, like the funny little friend who either turns out to be a stunner after a long makeover sequence with no sync-sound and a retro musical overlay, or gets killed in the first action scene and missed off the posters. (After two days in Beverly Hills, the movies were taking me over body and soul.)

Patrice swooped as soon as she spied me and gave me an expert air kiss, clamping both my arms in her hands to stop me touching her, darting in and out once on each side, just brushing the very ends of my hair with the very ends of hers. Jasmine, of course, folded me into a hug and squeezed me until something under my collarbone popped.

'We're good to go,' she sang as she sat down. 'Short stack of blueberry and Canadian,' she said to the waitress as Patrice opened her eyes wide as if trying to raise her eyebrows. 'What? It's a special occasion,' Jasmine said. 'We're celebrating. Fizzing virgins all round?'

'Fizzing ...?' I said.

'It's like buck's fizz, but with cranberry. Kind of disgusting name, when you think about it. But since we're celebrating ...'

'Oh, why not,' said Patrice. 'And I'll have granola with orchard and two per cent live, please.'

The waitress was looking at me.

'Toast?' I ventured. Jasmine laughed, patted me on the arm and took over, asking the waitress for eggs anyways and home fries.

'Before we get down to business, Verity,' said Patrice after draining her water glass and signalling for a refill, 'I really wanted to say how sorry I was about yesterday. Blurting out like that. And then saying nothing. I'm very, very sorry.'

I ran over the conversation from the previous day and took a guess.

'Do you mean about my husband?'

'I lost a man very close to me some time ago,' said Patrice. 'I don't mean my divorce, I wouldn't ... that was ... But I feel I know what you're going through, and I'm just so very sorry if I made it harder.'

'Oh, please,' I said. There was something *about* Patrice. She could do sincere without being mawkish, she could do caring without it seeming phoney even though she hardly knew me from a cold-caller, and once again just for a moment I wished that my widowhood would wither away and I could heave the real corpse – the dead, stinking corpse of my divorce – on the table to see what she might make of that.

'So you can talk to us, you know,' Patrice said. 'We're here for you.'

'I'm fine,' I said.

'Really?' said Jasmine. 'You're fine? How come?' I remembered, too late, what I had told her about not telling Clovis about Kim because I was so far from fine that I needed this trip to help me limp through the empty days.

'Well, no, obviously,' I said, 'I'm not *fine* fine. It's just that ...' Just that what, though? Why would I suddenly have said I was fine? Again, it was time to say something that made me look bad so that they would believe that I wasn't trying to make myself look good and they would think that what I was saying was true. 'I feel like a bit of a fraud, that's all,' I said. 'Because some of what's wrong isn't the fact that my husband—'

'What was his name?' said Patrice.

'Kim,' I told her.

'Nice name,' said Jasmine.

'Not so much the fact that's he's – that he died as the fact that before he died we weren't – things weren't – we might have – The fact is that if he hadn't – then we might not have—' I was sure that if Jasmine hadn't been there I would have been able to say it to Patrice, but Jasmine's face, intent with interest, her black darts of eyebrows pulled down in the middle as she sawed off a section of pancake stack and devoured it, was making it hard to spit it out.

'If he hadn't croaked you'd have dumped him anyway?' she said.

'Jasmine!' said Patrice, her hands doing that magnet-repulsion approach to her face again. I laughed.

'Sorry,' said Jasmine, looking anything but. 'If he hadn't passed you'd have parted?'

'Sounds like a country music ballad,' I said and even Patrice smiled.

'How come?' said Jasmine, and Patrice tutted and rolled her eyes so extravagantly that, just like Jasmine the day before, the ends of her eyelashes touched down. Only, because hers were thickened, lengthened and curled stiff, they caught under the ridge of her brows and she had to poke her eyebrows up with the tips of her fingers to unstick them.

I braced myself. I was determined to say it, but somehow I just took breath after breath in silence.

'What was the problem?' Jasmine prompted. 'I'll tell you first if you like. I divorced my husband because he changed from being the man I married to being someone I would never have got married to and couldn't stay married to. How about you, Patrice?'

'We turned out to have very different values,' said Patrice, nodding. 'There were areas of life – professional, ethical – where we just couldn't see eye to eye and besides, I was being prevented from growing, prevented from changing, being myself.'

It was my turn.

'My husband,' I said, 'was a shit.'

Jasmine and Patrice laughed so loud and long that people at other tables turned to look and joined in with a few chuckles of their own.

'You just saved yourself years in therapy, Vee,' said Jasmine. 'But tell us more. What flavour of shit? A drunken shit? A lazy shit? A cheating shit?'

'No!' I was already reeling from having said this much. I don't think I could have told them about *her*. They might think I deserved it for some reason, that if my husband had gone off with *her* there must be something wrong with me. What could I tell them instead? Something that would make them see that it was his fault and not mine. 'He was a lying shit,' I said.

'Woah,' said Jasmine. 'They're the very worst kind.'

'But my God,' said Patrice. 'You had to go through a funeral and everything. Did everyone know?'

I shook my head. 'No one knew. We hadn't told a soul we were separating.'

'Jeez,' said Jasmine. 'You had to pay a preacher and order a tombstone? Or, wait no, you Brits cremate, don't you? You had to scatter his ashes and all the time you hated him for being a lying shit? That must have been hell on a cracker.'

I got a sudden picture of Kim going up in flames and shuddered.

'Actually I did bury him,' I said, which didn't seem so bad somehow.

Jasmine snorted.

'Well, if you buried him,' she said, 'he's certainly lying now.'

'Jasmine!' said Patrice. 'You can't just say things whenever you think them. Have some decorum, have some tact, have some—'

'Have some more granola,' said Jasmine. 'It might loosen things off for ya back there.'

When we had finished eating, Jasmine brought out a document folder and slapped it on to the table, wiggling her eyebrows at me. Patrice wound her napkin around one finger and poked it towards the corners of her lips without touching.

'Just sign on the line, hon,' said Jasmine. 'And God bless Clovis for doing all the grunt work for you.'

Patrice folded her napkin slowly and rose, saying she was going to the bathroom. I waited, saying nothing until she had gone.

'Problem?' said Jasmine.

'A bit,' I said, my heart flapping in my throat. 'I know Clovis has worked it all out already and I like Patrice, a lot. She's lovely. I can't remember the last time I took to someone so much so fast …'

'But?' said Jasmine.

'I'm just not ready to make a firm commitment. Not yet. Not today.'

'Ah!' said Jasmine. She sat back in her chair, polishing her teeth with her tongue and nodding. 'I get it. It's him.'

'Him?' I asked. 'Who?'

'Kim, was it?' said Jasmine. 'After I got divorced I wouldn't trust someone who said they'd deliver a pizza. I know how it gets you.'

'I'm not divorced,' I reminded her. 'And it's nothing to do with Kim.'

Jasmine just grinned, her long red mouth dipping devilishly. 'You take the cake,' she said. 'You take the last cannoli, Vee, you really do. You're hesitating about sixty-five thousand dollars, for five years, offset, for a book that nobody's even read and yet you think you *don't* have trust issues?' She shook her head at me, but more in bewilderment than anything harsher. I was trying to take in what she had just said but even with the hopeless exchange rate that was a lot of money for a florist, and I think it showed.

'And speaking of pizza and cannoli,' Jasmine went on, 'I need to ask you about the Italian food. I was thinking about it again last night when I was writing my journal and now after what you said this morning, what's with the veto if you hated the guy anyway because he was a shit? I don't get that now. What's it all about?'

I was dumbstruck. If Jasmine was one of those sneaky journal-writing types always checking up on people, I would need to watch out for her. And anyway, it was her and Patrice and their 'we' that I didn't trust. What a nerve even to talk about trust when, as Kenny Daateng had said, she was as good as stiffing me, pretending to be an independent getting me a great deal, and in Patrice's pocket all along.

'It's complicated,' I said.

'He was a shit. Now he's dead,' said Jasmine. 'How complicated is that?'

'Extremely,' said Patrice's voice suddenly, making us both jump. 'Jasmine, how can you be so insensitive? It's much harder to get over a difficult relationship than a perfect one. Look at Paul McCartney.' Jasmine and I caught each other's eyes. 'And don't smirk at each other and think I can't see you,' said Patrice. 'I know I'm right. When I lost the man *I* lost it was far from straightforward, and it was all for the best that he went and I wouldn't have done it differently for anything, but it was still a long hard road to the end of the grief.' She sat down and arranged the various panels of her outfit around her. 'But are you all done with the paperwork?' she asked. 'Can we celebrate now?'

'Not quite,' Jasmine said.

'Oh?' said Patrice and her mouth stayed in the O-shape after she had finished speaking.

'I just need to talk to Clovis,' I told her. I could screw up the courage from somewhere, surely. Clovis wouldn't mind.

'So go,' Jasmine said to me, smiling as much as ever, but very firm. She shut the folder and pushed the contract towards me. 'Call her, chew it over, take your time. We'll wait in the lobby. We'll have some more coffee and when you're ready you come down.'

She kept the smile on her face and Patrice kept the silent 'o' on hers. I glanced between the two of them a few times – What rule of Hollywood etiquette was I trampling over here? – and then left.

Bradley was on the desk and he winked at me and gave me two thumbs up as I passed him, so I wheeled back and went over.

'Any news?' I said. 'I don't know how fast these things go.'

'Fast,' said Brad. 'When they go at all, they go way fast.'

'Only, I don't know if you need to know this but I've had a firm offer. Sixt— a high five-figure offer, all ready to go.'

'Get out of here,' said Bradley. 'High fives? No way. For rights or to option?'

'Just to option,' I said. 'But still. I thought you'd want to know.'

'No, Verity,' said Brad. 'Option is good. Clear or offset?'

'Oh, offset,' I said, enthusiastically. Brad leaned closer and spoke more quietly.

'No, actually, offset is bad,' he told me.

'Oh,' I said. 'Well, anyway, I just wondered if your cousin's people were still interested.'

'No way,' said Bradley. 'They were *interested* when you had *interest*. If someone's *moving*, they're not going to stay *interested*. They're going to *move*. Further. Faster. If someone's *offering*, they're going to *offer*. More. Better.'

'So your cousin should hear about this?' I said.

'He surely should,' said Brad, already hitching himself up to the phone to unlock the outside line with the key on his belt chain. 'I'll get back to you just as soon as I can.'

Up in my room, I thought it through. Of course, I should call Clovis and tell her that the deal she had put together was possibly not all that it seemed. And she *would* mind. She would be embarrassed; she might even be angry with me for being the bearer of the bad news. But if I gave her some good news too ... I hesitated, telling myself that I knew nothing about this, but I couldn't help wondering, if one person moved further and offered more than another one, how much further and much more would a third person move and offer than two? I called Kenny Daateng and his secretary put me straight through.

'Just to let you know, Mr Daateng,' I said. 'I've had an offer and I'm waiting for a second one to come through. High fives for a five year option. Offset, of course, but still a healthy start, don't you think?'

'High fives?' he said. I held my breath, waiting for him to notice that I didn't have a clue what I was talking about. 'Well, if that's so then ... I can get you low six easy.'

'Blimey,' I said. 'You've had time to read the book already?'

He cleared his throat and I could hear him shuffling papers at the other end.

'Sure, sure, I loved it,' he said. '*Straight Up*, right? Written by The Widow. Nice touch. I can see the poster now. I can see the title sequence. I'm thinking a blend of *North by Northwest* and *Panic Room* except in the Grand Canyon, from the bottom, straight up. You see? Straight up?'

'Is there snow in the Grand Canyon?' I said, trying to remember where it was, if I ever knew. Wasn't it in the Wild West?

'Right, the snow,' he said. 'You see the thing about snow is ... It's not really the snow, is it? It's the cliff.'

'But could you fall down a hole in the Grand Canyon and stay there?' I said. 'Isn't it full of tourists in helicopters? And people on charity abseils?'

'Low to mid sixes,' he said. 'Don't sign anything until I get back to you.'

'I won't,' I told him. 'I'm waiting to hear from IFA, anyway.'

'IFA?' he said and the sounds of rummaging got louder. I could hear slapping noises as bundles of paper fell to the floor. 'Well, for God's sake don't sign up with those guys till you hear some numbers. I'll be right back to you.'

After that, I sat on the edge of the bed for a while staring at the phone, wondering how fast fast was, how long it took someone to get right back, then feeling like Gordon Gekko I flipped open the folder to read the contract through.

I wouldn't go as far as to say I didn't understand it; I'm sure I could have said which words were nouns and which were verbs but it wasn't my job to trawl through every footnote with a toothpick. I phoned Clovis.

'Well, hello!' she cooed down the phone to me. 'How does it feel to be a lot richer than you were an hour ago? Are you going shopping? Listen, don't go to the stores, get Jasmine to take you to the discount mall at ... actually there are no discount malls in Beverly Hills, but—'

'Clovis, I just want to ...' I started.

'Well, of course you do,' she said. 'But hang on, I've got another call.' And the line went dead. That had been quite a long stretch of continuous phone time for Clovis, really, and I knew she'd get back to me in the end so I settled in for a wait, glad I wasn't paying the bill, but the line popped again two seconds later and Clovis's voice came back. 'It's Jasmine!' she said. 'On the other line. One thing I can say for the Americans, Verity, and that's beautiful manners. Not every scout phones up to say thank you once the deal is done.'

'Clov—'

'Hang on,' she sang and she was off again. This time I waited for a full minute, trying to organise how to break the good news without making it sound like I'd stepped in on Clovis's patch and done her job for her. When the line popped again all I could hear was breathing.

'Jasmine tells me you won't sign,' she said at last.

'I don't think it would be a good idea,' I said.

'Oh?' Clovis spoke mildly enough.

'I'm not trying to tell you your business, Clovis, honest I'm not, but I think Jasmine has been stringing you along. I don't think she's trying to get the best deal. The producer—'

'The *producer*?' said Clovis.

'I met her yesterday,' I said, 'And she and Jasmine—'

'You met the producer,' said Clovis. She didn't go on to say 'and you think you know everything' but I could hear her thinking it.

'I know that hardly makes me an expert, but if you would just listen.'

'Verity, love,' said Clovis. 'I've worked with Jasmine for, you know what? I'm not even going to get into it. This is the only deal on the table and—'

'Actually,' I said, 'I've got another offer on the table. A better one. Six figures.'

'*What*?' said Clovis loudly.

'I didn't plan it,' I said. 'A tracker called Kenny Daateng overheard us talking and gave me his card.'

'*What*?' This was even louder. 'I've *heard* of him!'

'And someone else who happened to see it while I was photocopying it for *him*, has given it to a bunch of people at IFA and—'

'*IFA*?' said Clovis, loud enough to make me jerk the phone away from my ear. 'Verity, what are you *doing* to me? Do you know who IFA are?'

'Um,' I said, feeling a lot less like Gordon Gekko now. 'A studio?'

'IFA,' said Clovis, 'is an agency.'

'Clovis, I swear,' I said, 'I had no idea. I just heard the name from my contact.'

'Your contact?' said Clovis. 'Verity, love, you're a florist. You've been there for thirty-six hours. What contact? What is going on?'

I always hated that way she had of calling me Verity comma love. That 'love' sounded, to me, a lot like 'idiot' somehow. But why would she be calling me an idiot when I had done all this on my own?

'It *is* good news, isn't it?' I said. 'I mean it can't be bad to have lots of different people all interested in an option. Can it? Clovis?'

There was a very long pause, a silence really.

'Of course it's not bad,' said Clovis. 'It's just so unexpected. And we're going to have to move fast. Listen, fax me the details of your contact and I'll take over the negotiation for you. I'll speak to IFA and make sure they know you have representation and they'll need to cut me in. And I'll begin to liaise with Mr Daateng's office and see what we can do. You just leave it all to me, OK? If any of them contacts you again you just refer them straight to me.' She waited for me to say something.

'OK,' I offered, at last.

'Now, I've got to go. Jasmine's still holding. I'll say as little as I can to her and you say nothing, right? We don't want to scare anyone away until we've got the very best deal that's going in the bag.' I heard the click of her hanging up and then her voice came again. 'Jas?' she said. I held my breath. 'You'll never believe what she's just told me. She thinks ...'

I dropped the phone into my lap and stared at it, swallowing repeatedly, fighting nausea. At last, I raised it again and holding my breath so they wouldn't hear me, put it against my ear. Clovis was still talking. 'I know. Darling, I *know*. Listen, you need to get her out of town. Will you stop telling me, Jas? I really do know. Just take her away from LA and for God's sake frisk her for business cards before you go.' The line went dead and very slowly, very quietly, I hung up my phone.

If there's one thing I hate in this world – more than putting on my pyjamas, which is the sort of thing anyone might get to hate if once they had put on their pyjamas right before bed and got an electric shock from the static off their nylon sheets or something, more than touching dry cottonwool, which is just squeamishness, no story there; more even than wildlife documentaries, which could easily just be squeamishness too because some of them are disgusting – it's hearing people talking about me. (And there are a hundred innocent reasons for that. It could be that it brought back memories of a schizophrenic episode with lots of voices or it could have been left over from family therapy where you all sat in a circle and told a nosy parker your secrets, except that those aren't really top notch innocent reasons, are they? Those are almost worse than … or it could be that you went to a hippy boarding school with a council that discussed everything to death, or came from a gossipy little village with people whispering about you in the post office. All I'm saying is that there are lots of perfectly respectable reasons why you might hate knowing that people are talking about you, like I do. Or even thinking they are. Even imagining that they must be.

I could just picture *them*, coming home to my house after work, taking their food out of my fridge and putting it on my table, opening the mail and getting a letter from my solicitor. They would talk about me and they would call me 'she' and 'her' until it was time to sit down to eat and Kim would say they shouldn't talk about 'her' any more so 'she' didn't ruin their dinner. I couldn't imagine what the food would be because I always did the shopping and Kim just ate whatever appeared or, when it was his turn to cook, cooked whatever was there to cook with. It would be very different now, that was for sure. One of the first times we ever saw Helen Marlowe, after all she was on hummus patrol.

She was standing by the buffet table at Gerry Mott's Eurovision party.

'Look,' I said to Kim. 'It's that woman with the hair ribbon. What's her name?'

'Helen,' Kim had reminded me. (Why had I not seen it then?)

'What's she doing?' I said. 'Come on, let's drift over and watch.'

What she was doing was forcing people to take a splodge of it on their paper plates instead of just sticking in bits of celery and eating it from the dish.

'It's all very well the first time,' we heard her say, 'but then you bite off the celery and then what? You put it back in the dish. When it's been in your mouth. Do you see the problem?'

'No,' said Phil. 'I've shared body fluids with everyone here at least once, so no I don't, to tell you the truth.'

Helen laughed but pushed a paper plate firmly into his hands.

'You haven't shared them with me,' she said.

'I'll hotfoot it over if I feel a sneeze coming on,' said Phil, and poked his finger into a bowl of pâté.

'She's a nightmare,' I said to Kim.

'Phil's getting beyond a joke,' he replied.

I hadn't seen Phil since the divorce boil burst and drowned me and I doubted very much if he was still welcome at our place these days, now that it wasn't our place any more, but I wished I could believe he was there right now sticking his finger in Helen Marlowe's pudding and licking it.

But it didn't start with them. It started with ... I shook my head to make the thoughts go away before I had even thought them. And now it was Clovis too. Talking about me, calling me 'her' and 'she', which was much worse than calling me Verity comma love stroke idiot. I shook my head again, faster, then I sat on the edge of the bed and ground the heels of my hands into my eye sockets. The memories came trickling back in all the same.

'She's fine,' said my granny, from the hall where the phone was. 'Yes, she's fine. Yes, of course she does. Well, what do you expect? She's doing as well as we could hope. She's fine.'

'Who was that?' I would ask her when she rang off and came back.

'No one,' she would say, picking her knitting up again and looking back at her pattern to find her place.

'Who were you talking about?' I would ask, and my granny would put her finger on a line in the pattern and look up.

'No one. Now, sit at peace and let Granny concentrate, will you?'

*

I screwed my eyes shut and pressed my spread hands over my skull, trying to squeeze the memories back down, but I knew it wouldn't work; you always hurt your wrists more than your head and the thoughts are safe inside where you can't reach them. You can't shrink any of it down when it's in your head. That's why you have to keep it out of your head, down in the pit of your belly where it can clench up so small it's almost gone. When it gets into your head, all you can do is walk away from whatever put it there.

They were sitting opposite each other on the lobby sofas when I finally went back down. Jasmine watched me coolly as I crossed the floor but Patrice had her hands clasped between her knees and was staring down at the floor.

'Well?' said Jasmine.

Patrice looked up and her eyes widened.

'Verity?' she said. 'You look terrible. What is it?'

'I really hate ...' But I couldn't say it. I couldn't tell them. There was no way to explain it. What I *could* explain was: 'I really hate being lied to,' I finished. After what I said about Kim, they would believe that. 'Jasmine, I don't believe that if you're an independent tracker and Patrice is an independent producer, you would say 'we', meaning you and her. I mean, why were you so annoyed that Patrice came to lunch yesterday? Why shouldn't I meet her? What did you think she was going to let slip? Why were you scared she was going to screw up? I don't think anyone is being honest here, and I hate it. And I've got a new agency who want me and a new buyer for them to talk to and that's that.'

'Jasmine! Jasmine!' Patrice's voice was a high tremulous whinny and her chest was rising and falling even faster than mine.

'Vee, what the hell are you talking about?' Jasmine said.

'Jasmine! Jasmine!'

'It's not you, Patrice,' I said, turning to her. Her shoulders were up around her ears and she held her hands out towards me, wringing them. I don't think I had ever seen anyone wring their hands before. 'I'm sorry,' I said. 'I could tell from the moment I met you that you're a lovely person. You're like sitting in front of a fire with a mug of Horlicks, except cooler, with no fire tartan and no hot flush if you drink too quickly. And I hope you do meet someone nice and get married again and have children because you'd make a fantastic mum.' Patrice blinked three times very fast and I wondered if perhaps I'd gone too far, even for California, but I meant it. 'I would be very happy for you to buy my book and make a movie out of it, but I just hate being ... lied to.' I glared at Jasmine. She glared at Patrice.

'What did I tell you?' Jasmine said. 'You weren't even supposed to be in that meeting and now look what's happened.'

We all glared at one another for another minute or two and then Patrice touched both her hands to her throat, fingertips together, and then swept them up over her face – not touching – breathing in very deeply and ending with a smile on her face. It was hard to see what the gesture had achieved unless she had rubbed some kind of drug on to her palms before she started and had inhaled it like menthol, but when she spoke her voice was calm again.

'I think,' she said, 'that it's time to put our cards on the table.'

'No way,' said Jasmine. 'Patrice, butt out of what you don't understand and for God's sake leave it to me.'

I glanced quickly between both of them. Had I really stumbled on something here?

'Don't worry,' said Patrice talking to Jasmine but looking at me, 'it's going to be OK. I'm sorry, Verity – we haven't been one hundred per cent straight with you so far. The truth is—'

'Patrice,' said Jasmine in a voice that would have stopped me if it had been me she was using it to. Patrice went on regardless.

'The truth is that this is not just a movie deal.'

'Jeeezus!'

'I want this script more than I can say. I would pay anything in the world for it. I would fly to London and give Clovis my right arm for it.'

'OK,' I said slowly. 'But I still don't understand—'

'Jasmine and I are old friends,' said Patrice. 'You were right about that. But she's not doing me favours at your expense, I assure you. Let me explain.'

'Patrice, *please*,' said Jasmine. Again, she was ignored.

'Jasmine is a scout, as you know,' Patrice told me. 'She works for her family business. They have all the money and all the power, and poor Jasmine gets no say about anything. She's just a drone.'

I flicked a quick look at Jasmine to see if she was offended, but she was nodding along now and looked, if anything, relieved.

'That's right,' she said. 'I'm a drone. And it's killing me. And I needed a fantastic deal, a stellar, galactic deal, something to make them stop jerking me around and give me a corner office. I can't pound the streets with a script under my arm any more.'

'I'm still not sure ...' I began. Again, Patrice interrupted me.

'I am a producer, again as you know. But what you didn't know is that I have more money than I know what to do with. Family money.'

'She's richer than God,' said Jasmine.

'And I really want this script. But nobody's going to be impressed if Jasmine puts through a deal for an old friend with money no object, are they? She needs everyone else in the business to think that she hustled this to the ground like a real player. So ...'

'We strung everyone along,' said Jasmine. 'The family, I mean, and you.'

'Only we didn't know how much getting strung along was going to hurt you,' said Patrice. 'And if we had, we wouldn't have done it. We're sorry.'

'Yeah,' said Jasmine.

'And it's not so bad, is it?' said Patrice. 'Now you know.'

'Does Clovis know?' I said.

'Clovis!' said Jasmine. 'Clovis can't believe it's for real. All that money? Clovis thinks she's died and gone to heaven.'

'Because I just mentioned another deal to her and she went completely—'

'I know!' said Jasmine. 'She told me! She's freaking out because she thinks you're screwing things up over here. Get this: she's so antsy she wants you out of town, away from everyone else who could scare Patrice away. She wants me to take you on a road trip so you can't do any more harm!'

That was exactly what I had overheard. Jasmine hadn't so much as shaded a single word of it.

'OK,' I said at last. 'I see. I understand.'

'This means more than you'll ever know to both of us,' Patrice said.

'Yeah,' said Jasmine. 'We're really not jerking you around.'

'But ...' I began, then I held up my hand. 'No! Don't interrupt me. I need to think it through. Surely the offer Patrice made – no offence, Patrice, because it is generous – isn't stellar. Isn't galactic.'

'What we're doing today is just the option,' Jasmine reminded me. 'It had to look believable – no offence, Vee, because it *is* a great story – but the stellar bit was going to come later.'

'Only now,' said Patrice, clapping her hands, 'if there's going to be a *real* bidding war ...'

'Yeah,' said Jasmine, beaming. 'I could be rowing my own canoe by Christmas.'

I was grinning along with them now, warm waves of unhoped for relief washing over me. Clovis had just been trying and failing to play it cool over a huge deal, that was all. And Jasmine and Patrice had just been caught up with their own concerns, and as soon as I challenged them they opened right up to me. My smile faded a little when I thought that. What would they think if they knew how very far from open I had been with them?

'What is it, Verity?' said Patrice. 'You look troubled.'

'You hate lying to Clovis, don't you?' Jasmine said.

'We don't have to,' I said, suppressing a twinge of guilt at hearing myself being taken as the benchmark of total candour that way. 'Surely. We can tell her we've straightened it all out between the three of us and—'

'No!' said Jasmine. 'I don't think so. I don't want anyone to know that this deal wasn't a battle for me. Not even Clovis. And I think she'll do a better job of whipping up the competition if she thinks it's for real, don't you?' I nodded, but my doubts must have shown on my face.

'And if it helps you,' Patrice went on, 'at least Clovis is never going to *know* that you were lying to her – except, let's not call it that. You can be very blunt sometimes, Jasmine – just like she's never going to know that we were ...'

'Lying to her too,' said Jasmine. Patrice ignored her. 'That's right,' Jasmine went on. 'She's just gonna be a little crazy for a while, thinking a fabulous deal is looking dicey and then she's gonna be as happy as a clam because it all works out in the end. She's gonna love you more than ever, Vee.'

'I'm still not quite sure that I've got it,' I said.

'Clovis is going to do her stuff trying to sell the script to the highest bidder,' said Jasmine. 'Patrice is going to top the highest bid – whatever it is – right, Patrice?' Patrice nodded. 'I'm going to be the genius who brokered the deal and you're going to forget we ever had this conversation, OK?'

'Only, Verity,' said Patrice, leaning forward and fixing me with what would have been a flinty stare if she'd been able to narrow her eyes. 'You have to promise me. You will sell it to me in the end, won't you? No matter what? Promise me you're not going to take it away?'

'I promise,' I said. 'But – if you don't mind me asking – why does it matter? Why this script? When you must see a dozen a day?'

'It just ... spoke to me,' said Patrice. 'It's just my baby. What can I say?'

'And we really are sorry,' said Jasmine, 'about not telling you all of this right away.' I tried to smile at her. 'So how about that road trip?'

'You don't have to do that,' I said.

'No, we do, we do, we do,' said Patrice. 'Right, Jasmine? If Clovis thinks we should, then we should, we will, we must.'

'Calm down, Patrice,' said Jasmine. 'We are.'

'And anyway,' said Patrice, 'we need to do something to say sorry. To make it up to you for ...'

'Lying,' said Jasmine. Patrice rolled her eyes. 'So,' said Jasmine. 'San Diego? San Francisco?'

'Not San Francisco,' said Patrice quickly.

'No?' I said. 'It looks lovely in the films.' I was trying to join in, even though inside I was cringing with guilt.

'I spent a lot of years there,' said Patrice. 'I know too many people. I never go back there now. How about Vegas?'

'*I* know too many people there,' said Jasmine. 'And it'll be too hot there in this crazy weather.'

'You're from Vegas?' I said. 'I didn't think anyone actually came from there.'

'Well, they do, and I'm one of them,' said Jasmine.

'It's kind of a long way, anyway,' I said, sickened at the thought of them dragging me around, showing me a good time, trying to make up for flannelling me, trying to help me forget my dead liar of a husband.

'What about Seattle?' said Patrice. 'It's a real down-to-earth, honest-to-God kind of town, Verity. Or Oregon?' I managed to smile at her, somehow. She was trying to think up the most authentic places she could take me.

'I don't want to go on a trip,' I said. 'I don't want to put you to all that trouble. And I'm on a trip already, remember.'

'It's no trouble,' said Patrice. 'We would love to, wouldn't we, Jasmine?'

'It's about time someone took some trouble for you, Vee,' Jasmine said.

'I need some fresh air,' I blurted, standing up.

'Good luck,' Jasmine shouted after me, as I made my way to the door. 'It's heading for eighty out there.'

Chapter 5

A Fine English Vintage

I wasn't wearing sunscreen and didn't have my sunglasses on, but it was October, for God's sake, how hot could it get? The answer was that walking along a dusty road with six lanes of traffic belching out fumes could get hotter than I'd ever felt without a lilo under me and an umbrella stuck in my drink. I stalked along the excuse for a sidewalk trying to get a hold of myself again.

Something was happening to me here that I didn't want to happen. For a start, I was losing the ability to make convincing connections; more than once I had struggled to get the simplest little story to make sense. But even worse than that, things that I had got separate were joining up. Thinking about granny on the phone, imagining Kim and *her*, letting her name into my head again. And I was being reckless too, hooking up with strangers, agreeing with them to lie to Clovis, acting like an idiot saying all that stuff about how great Patrice was, right to her face.

I jumped suddenly as a car horn blared and someone shouted at me from the far lane of the highway. See? I told myself. This was hardly normal behaviour; probably only prostitutes and winos walked along this dusty non-pavement. Over on the other side the car had stopped, half-hitched up on to the verge, and someone had got out and was waving his arms at me. I turned and started hurrying back towards the hotel. Thank God he was on the other side. What would I have done if he'd been over here and had kerb-crawled me? I watched from the corner of my eye as he got back into his car and edged back into the traffic again, then I scurried on.

There was a lot of hooting and blaring going on behind me; I stole a glance. The car – I was sure it was the same car – a filthy green one, low slung and enormous, was crossing the lanes. Now it was ahead of me, sitting in the island, turning – more horns – crossing the lanes again and pulling up right in front of my face. The driver's door opened and a shambling, sweating scarecrow in a bushwhacker's hat sprang out and opened his arms wide.

'Stone me!' he bellowed. 'Verity? What are you doing here?'

I gaped, rooted to the spot with amazement. It was Phil.

He swiped off his mirror shades and grinned at me, long snaggled teeth gnashing as he tried and failed to stop the fag dropping out of his mouth.

'So what's all this turdage about getting divorced?' he asked me, beating the ash off his shirt front and stooping to retrieve the cigarette from the dust. 'What *do* you get up to when Uncle Phil's not there to look after you, eh?' He threw an arm around my shoulders and shook me. God, he stank. Phil didn't believe in deodorant and was a bit suspicious of too much soap. 'Come on, then,' he said. 'Has your car broken down? Where are you staying? Where will I take you?'

Where was I staying? I was staying in a hotel about a minute's drive away, in the lobby of which were two business associates who thought I was a widow who hated lies and here was my husband's best friend from school offering to take me back there and shouting about my divorce.

'Do you have time for coffee?' I asked.

'Coffee?' said Phil and he clapped a hand to his chest as if I had shot him. 'Have you forgotten?'

'Sorry!' I had. Coffee was a sore point with Phil.

'But we could go and have an early pipe-opener,' said Phil. 'There's a place just down the road here pretending to be the Pink Palace but they do the fizziest virgin in town.'

'I've already had a fizzing virgin this morning,' I said.

'Well, how much time have you got?' asked Phil, scrubbing his jaw and staring around as though at distant horizons.

'I'm all yours,' I told him.

'In that case,' he said, going back to his car and opening the door into the lane of traffic, making a station wagon swerve, 'believe it or not, I've found this place down in Venice that does a bloody excellent cup of tea and a marmite sandwich. And ...' He paused while I shovelled the burger boxes and coke cans off the passenger seat of his car and climbed in, 'Battenberg cake. I kid you not.' He clicked his indicator on and leaped out into the traffic again, ignoring the skids and screaming horns behind him.

'This is it?' I asked, politeness failing me as I looked around. 'This is what we drove all this way to get to?'

Sweet Caroline's was a prefab shack with a few parking spaces marked out in the concrete outside – hardly worth abandoning Patrice and Jasmine for. Inside, a sea of Formica tables and stackable chairs stretched to a counter where a row of large and only partially covered male bottoms spilled over the edges of their stools. A sign behind the counter proclaimed: NO SHIRT, NO SHOES, NO SUGAR! As the screen door banged shut on its spring behind us a tiny woman stretched up to peer over the heads of the men at the counter and yelled.

'Start boilin' that kettle, Pop, the redcoats are here!'

'Caroline,' said Phil.

'Prince Philip,' said the tiny woman coming around the end of the counter to bring us menus. One of the bottoms wobbled as its owner gave a laugh.

'I'll have the usual,' said Phil, and he leaned towards me. 'A pot of tea made with boiling water and tea leaves, Vert. It's like a miracle,' He leaned back again. 'And an egg and cress sandwich, please, Caroline.'

'I'll just have a glass of mineral water,' I said.

'Just soda, ice tea, or juice, hon,' said Caroline, flipping over a page of her order book and reaching for the pen that hung on a spiral plastic chain from a loop on her overall. 'We don't got no mineral water here.'

'Have the tea,' said Phil. 'Don't you understand what I'm telling you? You're English, for God's sake. She'll have tea, Caroline, and cake.'

'I'm Scottish,' I reminded him as Caroline disappeared.

'Oh please,' groaned Phil. 'Spare me. You sound like the bloody Welsh. Right. What happened? Tell Uncle Phil.'

'Hasn't Kim told you?' I said, feeling my way. How could I know what to tell him if I didn't know what he had heard?

'Haven't seen him,' said Phil. 'I've been stuck out here since Christmas, for my sins.'

'Yeah, what are you doing here?' I asked. Phil ignored me.

'He emailed me and told me you'd left.'

'Hah!' I said. 'He told you I left? Well, that's one way to describe it, I suppose. The other way is to say that it was Kim's house and I didn't have much choice.'

'So? What happened?'

Again I took my time. What should I say? I couldn't tell Phil that Kim was a lying shit; they'd known each other since schooldays. Maybe, though, since Phil had met *her* and already hated her, it would be safe to …

'I take it you haven't heard about …' I paused and took a deep breath, 'Kim's new paramour?'

'No!' said Phil loud enough to check the murmur of conversation from the faces belonging to the bottoms at the bar. 'He hasn't! He didn't!'

This was all very gratifying, and very, very Phil. He himself was not boyfriend material, being faithless, lazy and immune to falling in love, as well as having the deodorant problem, but he was very loyal to his friends. Of course, had Kim been sitting here instead of me it would have been: 'Quite right, mate, good for you. Off she goes and don't get caught again.' But since I was the one in the chair he was, for the moment, on my side.

'He has and he did,' I said, smiling ruefully.

'And when you say "new"?' went on Phil, rising to his feet and shuffling the ketchup bottle and napkin dispenser out of the way as Caroline returned with the tea tray. 'How new do you mean?'

'Well,' I said, sighing and trying to sound brave, 'not as new as she should be considering how recently he was still married to me.' Caroline shot me a glance but there was no scorn in it and I didn't mind. She was wearing three different sets of wedding and engagement rings on various fingers but none on the ring finger of her left hand and, with her four-inch dark roots and waitress uniform, she looked the very picture of disappointed love.

'Men,' she said, as if to confirm it. 'Never believe that all men are bastards,' she went on, 'but never believe that you're looking at one of the other ones.' She turned a sarcastic smile on Phil. 'I don't mean you, hon.' She turned back to me. 'Except I do.'

'Isn't she a smasher?' said Phil. 'Reminds me of Matron.' He took a gargantuan bite out of his egg sandwich and began chewing, with a piece of cress sticking out of his mouth like Ermentrude the cow. 'So who *is* the usurper? Anyone we know?'

I took another deep breath.

'Helen,' I said.

Phil narrowed his eyes and considered while swallowing and then ripping off another bite, then his eyebrows shot up in surprise.

'Helen Thingy? The one with the calculator? Nooo!'

'Calculator?' I said.

'To divide the bill,' he said. 'Who had a starter, and who wasn't drinking and cigars were out of the equation.'

I smiled. I didn't remember the night in question, but I knew Phil. He always had a starter and two puddings and a cigar with his liqueur and was always too drunk, after downing three times as much wine as anyone else, to see why we couldn't just divide the bill the easy way. It was more to do with a low boredom threshold than with meanness, though; he never had any money, but he would rather hand over his credit card and pay for everything than wait for Helen and her calculator to work out the gulf between his excesses and her little soup and salad and single glass of wine. And he didn't care how many times the waiter came back to say the machine had said no, he would just keep rummaging in pockets and producing more and more cards until he struck a winner.

'Well, no wonder he was cagey in his email,' said Phil. 'I never could stand the woman. Kim knows that.'

'Listen,' I said, an unpleasant thought suddenly occurring to me, 'don't tell him I told you. In fact, don't tell him you saw me if you'd rather. I mean, if it would make things awkward for you.' Phil was wrapping a wad of napkins around the handle of the teapot, but he stopped and frowned at me.

'Awkward?' he said. 'What do you mean? Look at this, Vert. The tea is so hot you can't touch the handle of the teapot to pour it out. It's like a little corner of Tunbridge in here.'

Of course it wouldn't be awkward for Phil. He had divided his childhood and adolescence between his father's place in Cornwall where his second stepmother was installed, his first stepmother's house in the grounds where his half-sisters lived, and the farm in Kenya his mother shared with his stepfather, to where his father's mother had retired because she said the dry heat was good for her rheumatic old bones. Phil, I realised, was the one person in the world who wouldn't take sides in a divorce.

'I won't say a word,' he assured me. 'If Kim doesn't want me to know he's shacked up with the dullest woman in Christendom, I don't blame him. Besides, I don't expect I'll see him any time soon.'

'Oh?' I said.

'My exile has hardly begun,' said Phil. 'It stretches to a dwindling point in the haze.'

'Yeah, you never answered me. What *are* you doing here?'

Phil groaned and put his head down on the table, hanks of hair flopping forward into the breadcrumbs and bobbles of hardboiled egg on his sandwich plate. I smoothed it back, unthinkingly, only remembering when I touched it that Phil didn't really believe in washing his hair. I wiped my hand surreptitiously on my napkin.

'I'm learning the wine trade,' he said, turning his head sideways to lie with one cheek on the tabletop. 'It's unspeakable.'

'Kim said something about that,' I remembered, dredging back through long-ago and half-forgotten chats.

'It's an abomination,' said Phil. '*English wine.*' I had to laugh; he said it the way that people say 'certain death' or 'fried in lard'. 'My own father, my own flesh and blood. And you know the worst of it, Vert? The worst irony? On a clear day you can *see* sodding France from the headland on our place.'

'Maybe that's what gave him the idea,' I said. 'What's wrong with it anyway?'

'What's …' Phil lapsed into silence as though words failed him and he poured himself another, restorative, cup of tea. 'What's wrong with it? The same thing that's wrong with English vodka and English salmon. Vodka comes from Russia; salmon comes from Scotland and sodding wine comes from bleeding, sodding France. And Spain, and Italy at a push, Germany if you're not fussy, and Portugal when you're a student, and Greece but only when you're in Greece and *that is all*.'

'I take it your father doesn't agree?'

'Oh, my father's cock-a-bloody-hoop. He's got grants and stewardship schemes and business start-up awards dropping out of his hairy arse and euro signs popping up in his greedy little eyes and he couldn't care less if he's making me and the rest of the family a laughing stock.'

'The girls will never find husbands now,' I said, winking at him. Phil winked back. He never minded being wound up on account of his poshness. 'And has he had a vintage yet? What does it taste like?'

'A vintage,' scoffed Phil. 'The expression is *un cru*. It's French. That's a clue. He squeezed out the first few barrelsful two years ago. It was utterly filthy, like Ribena with an aspirin in it. So of course it sold out and he won the newcomer of the year award from Southwest Wine. The English have no palates.'

'And now you're roped in?'

'Incarcerated at Fresno State on a graduate course,' said Phil. 'Fresno State. I ask you. The hottest, driest place on earth anyone has ever tried to grow grapes and make wine. And they're proud of it. Put it on their posters in big red letters. That and "Raisin Capital of the World". I *ask* you.'

'It doesn't seem the obvious place to learn about vineyards in England,' I agreed.

'Vineyards?' said Phil. 'Do you know what they call vineyards here? Wineries. Can you believe that? *Wineries*. There's even one with a tasting room called a wineteria. So thank God it's me who's here, in a way, and not the old man. He'd probably think it was a great idea to have a wineteria of his own.'

'Surely not,' I said.

'Oh, you wouldn't believe the half of it, Vert. It's not just the English wine, he's doing hay-wain rides around *les vignes* – where exactly the wainful of hay is supposed to have come from on a farm covered in grapevines I can't tell you – pick-and-press days, bottle-your-own sessions, with labels for the kiddies to colour in, Christmas wine clubs, cheese and wine-tasting nights with a band and dancing. It's like effing Disneyland, with my father right in the middle of it all like Mickey Sodding Mouse.'

'It sounds very energetic,' I said. 'I always pictured your father – from what Kim told me – as a typical . . .' I couldn't think how to put it. Kim had described Phil's father as a typical shambling toff, having good caviar flown in for parties but with his elbows coming through his jersey – an older version of Phil, in other words. Kim had described long summers down at Trepolgas, running wild, playing at archery with real arrows and sleeping beside a bonfire on the beach, with Phil's father drifting vaguely about somewhere in the background, crossing paths from time to time with the children, and wife number two coming down to the camp every day or so with a pan of stew.

'He was,' said Phil, reaching over and pinching the strip of marzipan that I had unwound from around my Battenberg cake. 'Absolutely typical. But, I suppose, with three wives and six children to support – God, he sounds like a sheikh, doesn't he? – and he's cracking on now. I remember my grandfather saving up to die, but he did it with decent, time-honoured stinginess, not by turning Trepolgas into the Alton Towers of grapes.' He put his head back and lowered the strip of marzipan slowly into his mouth. 'Gritty,' he said. 'Good sign, that. Home-made.' He took a slurp of tea. 'Marzipan should be gritty, Verity, it shows it's real. And wine should be French, at least five years old and it should have a cork in it, even if the cork sometimes goes off and ruins the wine. You know what I learned in the filtration and stoppering module? Can you guess?'

I shook my head.

'I learned that the cheapest, most reliable, most efficient way to seal a bottle of wine is with a plastic screw top. They showed us the figures and it's true. Also it means you never need a corkscrew and you know how many picnics and barbies and midnight feasts go up the creek because someone forgot the corkscrew. What do you think?'

'I think,' I said slowly, trying to decide between winding him up and talking sense to him, and then I stopped and realised that actually I didn't want to wind him up. Actually, I cared. 'I think it's an abomination,' I said. 'I really do. Wine ... What do you call people who make wine?'

'*Les vignerons*,' said Phil, firmly.

'OK, *vignerons* sound worse than florists, if you ask me.'

He drove me back to the hotel, after making arrangements to meet up the following day and after extracting my agreement that Sweet Caroline's was the finest that southern California had to offer in cups of tea. Phil was always that way. Not exactly boastful, never claiming glory for himself, but guilelessly enthusiastic about his finds and determined to have you agree. It did make you feel lucky, in the end, to think that somehow you had got the best table, chosen the best off the menu, were hearing the best band in London from the best seats in the house.

'Can you drop me on the corner?' I said as we turned back on to Wilshire Boulevard. 'Instead of taking me up to the door. I need a little time to gather my thoughts before I rejoin my party.' What I meant was, I need to make damn sure that if my party – the new friends of The Widow – are still there, they don't meet you, the old friend of the live and kicking husband.

'Your party?' said Phil. 'Rather mysterious, Vert. You never did say what you were doing here.'

'You wouldn't believe it if I told you,' I said, and then thinking that he might find the thought of a movie producer so diverting that he'd try to meet them, I went on: 'Just boring old business. So if you could drop me?' He crossed two lanes of traffic and drove up on to the shoulder again almost exactly where he had found me that morning. As I was getting out, shaking a Chinese food carton off the heel of my shoe I heard a screech of brakes and a long blast of a horn. Even before I looked I knew what it was.

Up ahead just at the Plaza entrance, Jasmine's convertible had pulled over and she and Patrice were hanging out of the driver's window, shouting unheard in the traffic din. I could see their mouths opening and shutting and the glint of Jasmine's rings as she ran through an extensive repertoire of Italian gestures at me. Still shouting as the door opened, they both tumbled out of the same side of the car and hurried towards Phil and me.

'Oh God,' I said. 'Phil, do me a favour, will you? Don't mention Kim. Don't mention the divorce. Don't even mention the fact that I've ever been married. Can you do that for me?'

'Why?' said Phil, without meeting my gaze. He was watching Jasmine and Patrice striding along the verge and he began to smooth his hair and tug his collar straight in preparation. Before he could get out of his seat, I sprinted up to intercept them.

'Hi!' I said, wildly.

'Verity,' said Patrice, with her face all darts and puckers like an Origami rosebud, 'Where have you been? Who is that man? Tell me you didn't get in a strange car.' Jasmine folded me into her arms and pressed me against her white linen breast.

'Come and meet an old friend,' I sang out, loud enough for Phil to hear me, then added under my breath just for the two of them, 'Only for God's sake don't mention my husband. I'll explain later but please just pretend there never was such a person. Do it for me!'

Phil shambled up and all three of them regarded one another in silence. Phil's verdict on the two females was as clear as a blue bum on a big baboon. He took one look at them and raised both his hands to run them through his hair and show how broad his chest was. Not very, in fact, and the main feature on display were the two dark stains in his armpits and a very white belly with a wad of grey fluff in the navel that dropped out as he stretched and fell on to his shoe. Jasmine and Patrice stared back at him with identical masks of disbelief and revulsion and I felt a giggle begin to form in my throat.

I could read Phil, of course. I knew that the floppy hair, threadbare striped shirt, orange cords going bald at the knee and ancient boat shoes over bare feet, the long yellow teeth, half-smoked Camel and thick layer of dirt were all of a piece, but to these two he must have looked like some new and undreamed of species of bar-room trash that could not be worked into their world in any way that made sense.

But as Clovis had pointed out, Americans – sod them – have beautiful manners and so, of course, they invited him in for a drink.

'Sir, sir,' a waiter shrieked, rushing up to Phil who had just shaken another Camel out of the packet and put it between his lips. 'Sir!' Phil waved a hand to try to calm him down.

'I'm not going to light it,' he said. 'I'm just going to chew it and dream of freedom.' The waiter turned away doubtfully and checked over his shoulder once or twice on the way back to the bar.

'So how ...?' was as far as Jasmine got before her diplomacy ran out. She was still gazing at Phil and, since he'd thrown his arm along the back of the sofa behind her, she was wrinkling her nose too. If she had tried to frame the question, it would have come out like when an *Antiques Roadshow* expert tries and fails to find a nicer way of saying: 'This is a beautiful piece. How did it come to be owned by a grubby little oik like you?'

'Phil and I were at school together,' I said, which seemed fair enough to me; after all, I had been at school with lots of boys. But Phil snorted.

'Ah, schooldays,' he said. 'Lusty lads and toothsome lasses all tucked up together in the dorm and splashing around together in the showers after games. If only ...' He drooped one eyelid at me briefly.

'If only what?' said Patrice.

'If only those days were here again,' said Phil.

'And now he's a winemaker,' I said. 'A *vigneron*. He's studying American wine know-how at Fresno. Aren't you, Phil?'

'Fresno's a long way from here,' said Patrice suspiciously.

'You make wine in England?' said Jasmine.

'Exactly!' said Phil.

'Outta grapes?'

'Exactly!' said Phil again. 'Look at that face, Verity. Only a very unnatural practice could put that look on a face.'

'And Jasmine and Patrice are in the movie business,' I went on.

'Exactly!' said Phil yet again. 'Here we are in Beverly Hills and this pair of beauties are film stars. Of course they are.'

'Just ignore him,' I said, squirming. I had forgotten what a oleaginous creep Phil could be around pretty girls. 'Patrice is a producer and Jasmine's an executive.'

Phil nodded, clearly impressed.

'And where do you come in?' he said.

'Hasn't she told you?' said Patrice. 'Verity wrote the book that's going to be the screenplay.'

Phil whistled and held up his hands to the side of his face to give me a sarcastic round of soft applause.

'What's it about?' he said. Darting glances, as fast as pinballs, shot between Jasmine and Patrice. God, they really did think it was the last chapter of Kim's life, didn't they?

'It's early days,' said Jasmine.

'It's under wraps,' said Patrice.

But my heart warmed to see how seriously they took my request. Don't mention my husband I had told them and – bless them – they wouldn't even mention the story I wrote to get him out of my mind.

Another ten minutes and Phil was gone, fishing out his lighter as he crossed the lobby and ignoring the rumble from the desk staff watching to see if he put the flame to the fag before his feet were over the threshold and into the open air. Then, of course, the fun began.

'A skeleton from your closet?' said Jasmine.

'And is he really a winemaker?' said Patrice.

'Even though he looks like he sleeps under a bridge?' said Jasmine.

'And can I ask now?' said Patrice. 'Unless it's too upsetting for you to explain?'

I was ready for this. I had prepared while Phil flirted with them and they took it politely.

'Phil was with Kim when he died,' I said. 'And afterwards he ... well, he went to pieces. A breakdown, it used to be called. Post-traumatic stress disorder, I suppose we'd say now. Then slowly, slowly, he clawed his way back up—' I cut myself off short. This was beginning to sound a bit like the hole in the ice scenario. 'But he's never talked about Kim again. I've hardly seen him at all since it happened and today when I met him by chance I was worried, I can tell you. I thought if his family sent him all the way over here to get away from the pain, and here I was – a walking reminder of it all – it might send him back down into the chasm.' I bit my lip again. 'But he seems fine! Which is lovely. And I just thought that even though a psychiatrist would say you can't have ghosts in your past and you shouldn't have things you don't talk about, I'm not so sure. I think if Phil's holding it together, he can do it any way he chooses and I won't interfere.'

'You are so right,' said Patrice. 'We all have shadows, and we all have just this one life. I think it's fine to leave things alone. I really do.'

'He had a breakdown?' said Jasmine. 'Is that why he doesn't wash?'

'And while I was out walking,' I said. 'I changed my mind. Patrice, I'd love to go on a trip out of town. I'm sure Kim would tell me – if he was here – to live life to the full.' Because the further away I was from Phil and the chance that he would try to see this 'pair of beauties' again, the better it would be.

'Yeay!' said Jasmine. 'Let's hit the road!'

'Seattle?' said Patrice.

'If you wanna fly 700 miles to get a cup of coffee in the rain,' said Jasmine. 'It's your dollar.'

'Let's all go have a wonderful dinner tonight anyway,' said Patrice. 'Verity, I'll send a car and driver for you.'

'Lovely,' I agreed. 'And then in the morning we go?' I would call Phil from the airport once I was safely on my way.

The phone rang three times while I was changing for dinner, substantially undermining the best thing about staying in a hotel, which is that nobody bothers you for once. First up, was Bradley (Honey) on the desk.

'Your London agent called in to IFA,' he said with an accusing tone in his voice. I tried to assemble an apology for God knows what crime. 'And I have to say from what my cousin heard and told me she sounds like one tough lady. But Halford Meer – yes, don't faint! *The* Halford Meer still wants to meet you. He wants to meet you day after tomorrow!'

'Ah,' I said. 'And does Clovis know this?'

'It's just a meeting,' said Brad. 'It's only breakfast. Halford doesn't like to go through a million different middle men.'

'The thing is Brad,' I said. 'I'm not going to be here. I'm going on a little jaunt with Patrice.'

'This is the independent? She's taking you on a trip? Is she scouting locations? What has she heard? How did she hear? Who told her?'

'Scouting *snow disaster* locations?' I said.

'Who knows,' said Brad. 'Only Halford's PA told my cousin who told me that he's thinking of pitching heat instead of cold. Desert instead of snow? Rock slides instead of avalanches? Save a fortune on the second unit if it's right here in California, you know?'

'We're going to Seattle,' I said.

Bradley gave a theatrical gasp. '*Not* locations!' he said hoarsely. 'Money!'

'Sorry?'

'Only reason to go to Seattle. Wait till I tell my cousin to tell the PA to tell Halford you're on a fund-raising trip with the independent. He's going to tell me that the PA told him that Halford freaked!'

Before I could sort any of that into units of sense, almost before my ears had stopped ringing, while I still had my hand on the receiver, the phone chirped again.

'Are they a couple?' said Phil's voice, no lead-in, no greeting.

'Who?' I asked. 'Jasmine and Patrice? I don't think so.'

'Hmm,' said Phil. 'I thought there was a frisson there. Probably just wishful thinking.'

'You're a pig,' I told him.

'Oink,' said Phil. 'In that case, do you happen to know—'

'Although, to tell you the truth, I did wonder about it too,' I said, remembering. 'They're both as free as birds, as far as I know.' *What was I saying?* 'That is … um … I'm surprised that's what you're asking, Phil. I thought you'd want to know why I needed you to keep Kim under your hat.'

'I do. I was just prioritising. Well?'

'Well, the thing is that I didn't tell them I'd been married. I mean, I told them I'd never been married and it would look strange if they found out now that I was. Wouldn't it?'

'Why did you tell them that?' said Phil. 'Was this when you thought they were gay? Were you trying to get in on their thing and make up a threesome? Wait! Don't tell me until I've lit another fag.'

'You are such a pig. What is it with men and lesbians anyway? It makes absolutely no sense.'

'I'll explain it sometime when you're too drunk to slap me,' said Phil. 'Why did you tell them you'd never been married?'

'Because . . .' I began slowly, pretending that I was trying to decide what to do. Another mistake that people make – I've even done it myself sometimes when I've been flustered – is adding too many details, being too ready to tell things they would never breathe a word of if any of it were true. A much better strategy is what I was doing now: no details at all, lots of hints and solemn assurances that you're keeping the horrible truth secret for everyone else's good except your own. 'At our first meeting, they told me something that made me just really not want to have to make either of *them* think about me and my problems, and the easiest way to avoid it seemed to be to remove Kim from my history completely.'

'Go on,' said Phil. 'Tell me what they said. I can take it.'

Either for everyone else's good except your own, or out of honour, because you gave your word.

'I can't Phil,' I said. 'I promised them I wouldn't tell a soul. But – I'm not kidding here – it's something that makes it a bad idea for you to . . . pursue them.' People will always fill in something worse than the truth for themselves if you leave them hanging.

'Either of them?' said Phil. 'Is it the same thing?'

That didn't seem very likely. Somehow, I was making a bit of a mess of this.

'It's a different thing for each. But both things are pretty terrible. Hey, maybe that's the closeness we sensed, eh? I wish I could tell you more, but I gave my word.'

'Hmmm,' said Phil again. 'And they each told you their deep dark secret the very first time you met?'

Shit.

'What can I tell you, Phil?' I said, trying to keep my voice steady and calm. 'We were all women together. We bonded.'

'Three way bondage!' he yelped.

'Pig,' I told him, and hung up the phone.

I was almost ready now, just shoes to go, and I crouched down on the over-stuffed footstool to try and slide my sandals on without smudging my toe polish, two hours old and courtesy of a hotel manicurist with thumbs of iron and zero tolerance stamped on her soul like a cattle brand.

'How could this be?' she had shrieked when I took my socks off and put my feet up on her bench. 'Where have you been?'

'Europe.'

'Don't tell me any more,' she had said in a sepulchral voice and reached for her rasp.

I got my shoes on with the help of two biros and a rolled-up drinks coaster and sat back clicking my heels like Dorothy and admiring myself, but when I stood up my smallest toe squished against the front strap and threatened the unbroken glossy disc of polish, so walking on my heels I went to the bathroom and got a cotton ball to wedge in. While I was in there the phone rang for the third time.

'Hello?' I said.

'Is that The Widow?' said Kenny Daateng's voice. 'Where are you? It sounds like the bottom of a well.'

'I'm in the bathroom,' I said. 'Isn't it kind of disgusting to have a phone in the bathroom? Who would you call?'

'And speaking of the bottom of a well ...' he said and waited.

'What?' I said.

'Or should I say "a chasm"?'

'I'm sorry?'

'I hear you're off on a junket.' How did he know? 'Scouting locations?' His voice dripped with sarcasm. 'Raising some money?'

'Not really,' I said, trying to remember where that idea had come from.

'Because I have to tell you, there's no deal I ever heard of where the producer takes the writer location-scouting or fund-raising before the ink's even dry on the option. There's something very bogus going on with those two. I told you that the first time I spoke to you and every new thing I hear only confirms it.'

'We're not scouting locations,' I said. 'That was just someone else's assumption. And I wouldn't know how to raise money for a movie if I … I can't even finish the sentence. That's how much I don't know. Actually, we're just going on a trip.'

'What for?' said Kenny. 'Press? Pre-publicity? After all, once people know what the hook is everyone's going to want to hear from The Widow.'

'It's not a true sto …' I began.

'Obviously,' he said. 'I've been very clear about that. It's Based On. Very important distinction. So *is* it a press trip?'

'I don't know,' I said slowly, deciding to play it dumb. 'The producer wants to take me and my agent thinks I should go.'

'Your agent thinks it's a good idea to let a producer sweeten you up with treats?' said Kenny.

'No, she thinks it's the scout.'

'Who is this agent? What's his name? This whole deal sounds worse and worse.'

But, I thought to myself, why should *you* care? Even if I didn't know what I know, who would I listen to? Clovis that I know and trust or you that's trying to buy my script and telling me that everyone else *except* you is doing me down? Clovis was right. I needed to leave this side of it to her.

'It's a she,' I said. 'Clovis Parr. From London. Hasn't she called you yet?'

'I've never heard of her,' said Kenny. 'Who else does she represent?'

'She hasn't left any messages today? She hasn't tried to get in touch with you?'

'She must be busy with other things,' said Kenny, drier than the crumbs in the bottom of a toaster. 'It's the first time I've been left hanging with a six figure offer, I can tell you. This is a new experience for me.'

I was almost late for dinner but I had to try.

'Clovis?'

'At last,' said Clovis's voice. 'Why is your mobile off? And have you had your room phone off the hook? I've been trying to ring you all evening. I stayed up specially.'

'Sorry. Listen, I just want to ask about Kenny Daateng.'

'As I suspected,' said Clovis, and her voice grew tender. 'Verity, love, please don't take this too badly, but I spoke to your Mr Daateng's people and, as I thought, he wasn't serious. He was just dipping a toe in the water trying to see what he could see.'

But he had just told me he was still waiting for her call. Why would he string me along like that? Was he trying to cut Clovis out of the deal? Turn me against her? If so, he was wasting his time. I owed Clovis at least all the loyalty she showed me; I was growing an ulcer here, just from knowing that I was hiding things from her.

'Now,' said Clovis. 'The last thing I want is for Jasmine's buyer to get wind of this and be frightened away, so best just put it right out of your mind.'

'Right,' I said. 'And IFA?'

'Nothing doing, I'm afraid,' said Clovis. 'Just a kid in the mail-room with ideas above his station.'

But Bradley had given me an actual name. Halford Meer, he had told me. Was he making it up? Was he some kind of fantasist? Or, it suddenly occurred to me, was Clovis being less than frank here? Impossible.

'Please don't be disheartened,' said Clovis. 'The news is all good. Jasmine has got the offer up to a hundred and forty. What do you think of that?'

'What do I think?' I echoed. 'I think, why?'

'What?'

'Why? If she hasn't got wind of Kenny Daateng and if IFA was just a kid in the mailroom, why has Pat- Jasmine's buyer upped the offer?'

There was a long silence at the other end of the line.

'OK,' said Clovis, 'OK. I'll come clean. In recognition of the work you've – inadvertently – done there, I'm willing to reorganise the split and your share's going to come out at a hundred and forty now.'

Clovis was finally admitting what I'd done.

'I've made a zzub,' I said. 'Haven't I?'

'Sorry?' said Clovis.

'Kenny and the kid in the mailroom. I've created a zzub.'

The silence lasted even longer this time.

'You have,' said Clovis, 'and it's really not the done thing at this stage of the game. We had a gentlemen's agreement with a buyer, you know. This visit was just a courtesy call, really. It's not good manners to work up a zzub when you've got someone at the table ready to go.'

Hah! I thought, I may be dumb but I'm not that dumb. This was the perfect time for a zzub. But if she wanted clueless, clueless was what she could have.

'So,' I said innocently, 'when Kenny said he could break an option contract ...'

There was a noise like an emergency tracheotomy on the other end of the line.

'He said what?' croaked Clovis.

'Didn't you know? His people didn't mention that?'

'I'm serious now,' said Clovis. 'Please will you stop mucking around? Go off with Jasmine. Have some fun, spend some of the money and then get on a plane and come home.'

'Don't you think it would be worth Jasmine meeting Kenny?' I persisted.

'Verity,' said Clovis. 'I'm getting a headache.' And she slammed down the phone.

I smiled at the handset as I replaced it. Clovis was a patronising control freak but, as the saying went, she was *my* patronising control freak and I loved her for every paranoid, Machiavellian, puppeteering move she made for me. I could even bear the thought of her patting me on the head and telling me the final number Patrice came up with for the stellar deal. Clovis would never know that it was me pulling her strings all along.

Now I was really late, and when I got downstairs the driver was waiting for me with the engine idling. He seemed to know where he was going at least, which was more than I did, although the streets did have a familiar look about them: Grecian temples, lumps of adobe with tiny windows and bell towers, Victorian wedding cakes, all flashing by as we bowled along, and surely there couldn't be more than one Swiss chalet in banana yellow with blue and white striped shutters and commedia dell'arte masks worked into the wrought iron of the gates to the driveway? I sat forward, peered out of the front windscreen and right enough there, dead ahead, was Germolene Towers.

I told myself that their staff must be huge, that the chance of Merle and the bitches even being on duty were tiny. Still, my heart was clunking and I felt as if I had a ball-bearing in my throat as I entered the lobby, as I walked back into a place whose people had thrown me out on to the street once already, to try again.

I needn't have worried. Maybe they saw me stepping out of the car and saw that it wasn't a taxi this time, or maybe tonight I looked like someone who had a right to be here, but I was met with a smile by a little nut-brown man in a tailcoat and told that my party had arrived and were waiting for me in the Polo Lounge. I followed him and there they were. There was Jasmine in satin, there was Patrice in cloudy panels of voile, with squares of net giving odd glimpses of flesh, and there in a hessian blazer like a potato sack and a Dixie string tie, with clean hair and shaving wounds dotted around his face, was Phil.

'Surprise!' said Jasmine and Patrice. They were sitting on either side of him, leaning in. I knew Phil's tricks. Whenever he was talking to a beautiful woman he spoke softer and softer and softer so that she had to come in close to hear him and then, because he was completely without bashfulness, he would look her straight in the eyes from inches away and just keep murmuring. It was surprising how often it worked.

'His eyes are his best feature,' Kim would say loyally.

'They just get drunk and fall on him in the end,' I maintained.

'Surprise!' he said to me now, standing up and leaving Patrice and Jasmine gazing at each other from ten inches apart. They looked startled and sat back. 'I'll get more drinks,' he said. 'We're on watermelon daiquiris, Vert. Felt like going all classy.' Jasmine and Patrice simpered and clinked their daiquiri glasses as he left.

'I couldn't not ask him,' said Patrice. 'Not after hearing about the breakdown and everything. I hope you don't mind.'

'Although I have to say, he seems OK to me,' said Jasmine. 'I'm no professional, but I'd say he's over it. Whatever it was.'

Oh yes, I thought. Whatever it was. I was sure Jasmine and Patrice were full of sympathy, but I would have laid good money that that wasn't all.

Of all the guff my granny ever told me – and there was a fair selection of it what with the admonitions about not washing your hair when it was *that* time, or not swallowing gum because it would stick to your heart, peach stones because a tree would grow in your tummy, and toothpaste because you would grow enamel on your intestines and your food would slide straight out without stopping – the biggest crock of all was the one about people being too interested in their own troubles to care about yours.

I wish it *was* true; it would make life much easier if nobody was paying attention and you didn't have to keep your story straight for them, but how could Patrice and Jasmine not be wondering about my husband, his life, his death, his very existence, and why none of this could have a word breathed about it? As for Phil, I was sure he was well up to his usual level of random lust, but I thought I could see a spark of interest in his eye too as to why Kim was so deeply under wraps that his name could not be spoken. That was the question, and I still had no answer to give.

Chapter 6

The Silence of the Gladioli

There are nights in life that stay in your mind for ever with a sheer grade of gauze over the lens and a gel-filtered light on them; nights when ties are formed never to break; nights when just for an instant life makes glorious sense and you can see your past behind you and your future ahead; nights when you can imagine how new religions might be born. The night of the water melon daiquiris was one of those for Jasmine, Patrice and Phil. But not so much for me.

'How many scripts would you say you have to read in a typical week?' asked Phil, out of nowhere, as we were studying our menus. He was back to talking at a normal volume now, since even he couldn't do husky murmurs to three at once, not when one was on the other side of the table and was me.

'Oh, upwards of a hundred on a bad week,' said Patrice. 'But you can tell within a page or two if they're not worth pursuing.'

'It's not the reading that's the headache,' said Jasmine. 'It's the getting rid of the paper without having to pay a contractor to haul it away.'

I felt a surge of ungenerous pleasure to think that mine was one of the few that hadn't caused Jasmine this problem.

'They don't have garbage cans on the streets outside small production companies,' she went on, 'or there's always some poor schmuck with the job of taking the slush pile out and dumping it for free.'

'And there was that scandal with the grifters,' said Patrice. 'Taking the scripts back *out* of the garbage and scamming the poor writers into thinking they had a deal.'

Phil whistled.

'I have enormous respect for the American conman,' he said.

'In polite Hollywood circles,' said Jasmine sternly, 'we don't talk of it.' She glared at Patrice but luckily at that moment a waiter arrived and stood frowning until we gave him our full attention.

'Can I make a suggestion?' said Patrice. 'Jasmine? How much do you care about your make-up tonight?'

'Oh yes!' said Jasmine, instantly sunny again. 'A seafood platter. It's gotta be.'

'*Plateau de fruits de mer*. Yum, yum,' said Phil.

'Verity,' said Jasmine, 'have a Beverly Hills Hotel seafood platter and you can die happy before dessert. Platter for four, honey. Lemon butter and salsa and keep those daiquiris coming.'

'Bad news about the scripts,' Phil went on, unusually persistent, once the waiter had gone. 'I thought slogging through them all would mean you were a fast reader. Only I was going to ask you a favour.' My heart dropped inside me. Surely Phil wasn't going to ask Jasmine to read a script. Phil was disgusting but he never used to be gormless too. I could see Jasmine getting ready to brush him off politely but he swept on before she had a chance. 'I was going to ask you to read a paper I wrote. I can pay, although not exactly handsomely.'

'A paper?' said Jasmine.

'An academic essay,' said Phil.

'I don't know anything about winemaking,' said Jasmine.

'*Le vinification*,' said Phil automatically. 'It's not about *le vinification*. It's about Ernest Hemingway. "Hemingway and the trope of the hunter".'

'I don't know anything about Hemingway either,' said Jasmine.

'I was a real Hemingway fan as a teenager,' said Patrice.

'Phil?' I said. 'Are you kidding? You're doing a literature course on the side?' Kim had told me that the achievement Phil was most proud of in life was getting his English A level without having read a single book, poem or play on the syllabus.

'Not exactly,' said Phil. 'I'm branching out into freelance writing, that's all. And I need someone to read it over for American idiom. I've had a couple of pieces returned because they sound too English.'

'Sure then,' said Jasmine. 'I could look it over and score out all the double-decker buses and Royal Majesties for ya. How long is it?'

'Two thousand words,' said Phil. 'I'll fax it to you with the terms in the morning. Ahhhhh!' Two waiters carrying one end of the tray each had brought our food. Phil took off his tie, tucked his napkin into his collar and dived for a lobster claw. 'I absolutely heart America,' he said. 'I want a T-shirt that says so.'

Patrice picked up a lobster claw of her own and, spurning the pliers, put it down on the wooden board in front of her and smashed it open with the flat of her hand. Then she blushed.

'Two big drinks and a lifetime of karate,' she said.

'I love to see a woman enjoying her grub,' said Phil. 'All you get in London these days are walking xylophones who won't order pudding and then can't take their eyes off yours.' He glanced hurriedly at Jasmine as he said this. Phil, as I say, was a pig but he was a gentleman too and he would never be unintentionally rude. He was safe here, though; at that moment Jasmine was using two hands to get more salsa into an oyster shell without the oyster sliding out. Phil grinned at her and then at me.

'It doesn't bother you that America doesn't heart you back?' I asked him. 'What publication is this that won't accept a bit of British in its papers?' He didn't seem bothered but I was smarting.

'Oh, it's not for publication,' said Phil. 'It's just for submission. It's my little business on the side. To make me some cash – you know how tight my old man is, Vert – and to stop me going insane with boredom on the *baccalauréat du vin tres émétique*. And anyway, who cares? You really need to watch out for this chippy Celt routine you're working up, my dear.'

'What's that?' said Patrice.

'Verity's so well practised at feeling slighted by the English for being a bit tartan round the edges that now she's getting in a huff about being British over here too.'

'Oh no, Vee!' said Jasmine. 'You'll end up worse than the frigging Canadians.'

'You'll end up like those New Zealanders who fly right over Australia for a weekend in PNG,' said Patrice.

'Laugh all you want,' I said. 'None of you know what it's like to be a minority, and I would have thought that here in California of all places I could rely on a bit of political correctness gone mad.'

'Me not know what it means to be a minority?' said Patrice.

Phil and I frowned at her, both puzzled and Jasmine concentrated on peeling a prawn. Patrice's face went completely still after she'd spoken. I was getting used to Patrice's face. It was as though I had reset my expectations on muscle movement and now I could read her expressions with ease; it was the same as giving up salt – in a day or two you can taste all kinds of subtle flavours under the bland.

'I'm Jewish,' she said loudly.

'Really?' I said. 'Patrice? What's your second name?'

'Carmichael,' she said. 'But only since I got married.'

'Come off it, hon,' said Jasmine. 'Jews aren't a minority in New York. At least not in the neighbourhood you come from. *I'm* the minority here.'

Patrice laughed gratefully and relaxed again.

'Because you're Italian?' I said. 'Does that count?'

'Not because I'm Italian,' said Jasmine. 'Because I'm aesthetically prominent and it attracts a lot of prejudice from other professional women.' I threw a scallop shell at her.

'My heart bleeds for you,' I said. 'You've struggled your whole life against being beautiful?'

'I should have a telethon,' said Jasmine. 'How about you, Phil?'

'Oh easy,' he said. 'I've got all the social disadvantage going these days. I was once nearly stabbed in a pub because two Liverpudlians overheard me ordering a drink and decided they didn't like my accent. D'you remember that night, Vert?'

I did. One night in Kilburn, Phil had hailed the landlord and asked for a stoup of his finest ale and it was only Kim telling them it was a line from a movie that made them put the knife away.

'But I think they were Brummies,' I said.

'So,' said Phil, 'all that disapproval for the perceived over-privilege just hanging by a thread waiting to crash down on my head every minute of the day and not a bean to my name – hence my little business plan. And it's actually rather fun, you know.'

'I don't see how you can make money from submitting things that don't get published,' I said.

'Me either,' said Jasmine. 'And I want to hear. I thought I knew every way to squeeze a buck outta this town.'

'Jasmine,' said Patrice mildly. 'You're so uncouth sometimes.'

'Last week,' said Phil, 'I did an advanced "Who is the Other in Seventeenth-century Central America?" and a basic level "Reciprocity as a trading system in the Trobriand Islands". As well as the Hemingway. Ch-ching!' He raised his glass, emptied it and burped.

Patrice and Jasmine said nothing, and I should have said nothing too and let it pass, but I couldn't help it. I had always known that Phil was a pig and philanderer and, as my granny would put it, a clarty toe rag that needed a good clout from a bar of soap, but what with the ancient code of the Coateses' and stiff upper everything that could be stiffened and women and children first, I had always assumed that he was as straight as a line.

'Plagiarism?' I said.

Phil nodded through a mouthful of food.

'For the undergraduates,' he said, 'Yes.'

'Wow,' said Jasmine. 'How does that work? You upload them to the Internet, do you?'

'God, no,' said Phil. 'Bespoke plagiarism, my dear. The faculty are getting far too wily for off-the-peg. No, I offer exclusive, custom-designed humanities essays for the rich but thick students with which LA is so lucratively endowed.' He grinned at us all again. 'Who would have thought there was something I was training for my whole life without knowing it. It's what I was put on earth to do. Only I can't expand it – which is death to any enterprise as I'm sure you'll agree – because I don't know enough about business and management even to fake my way through. So I'm stuck in the liberal arts.'

'I majored in business administration,' said Jasmine.

'I did management and economics,' said Patrice.

'Well, slap my thigh and call me Belinda,' said Phil. 'We need to talk.'

'Can I just—' I began.

'What about science and tech?' said Jasmine. 'You got them covered? I have a cousin back home in Chicago, got the social skills of a drainpipe, but what he doesn't know about computers and stuff . . .' Phil was shaking his head.

'Does no one else think—' I tried again.

'No, it doesn't work with science and tech,' said Phil. 'It's too right and wrong and no space for bullsh- I mean, it's not amenable to my specialised strategy. Besides, a lot of those science boys actually need to know what they're doing. It wouldn't be right. Too many potential repercussions for tonsillectomies and aircraft design.'

'Oh, *that* wouldn't be right,' I said, getting a word in at last. 'What about the repercussions for the rest of it?'

'Hemingway and the Trope of the Hunter?' said Jasmine.

'Patrice, what do you think?' I asked, turning to her.

'I could care less about Trobrianders,' she said. 'But as a woman trying to make movies I think it matters who gets othered, actually.'

'I didn't mean that,' I said.

'I think it matters too, honey,' said Jasmine. 'Of course it does.'

'I meant the business plan as a whole,' I said. 'Don't you think it's a bit . . . fake?'

'It is a bit,' said Patrice. 'But say this: what about some poor little rich kid who's troubled, someone who's brought a ton of baggage from home, can't get his act together in time and sees his future slipping away? Why shouldn't that kid be able to turn to Phil and get the help he needs like the lucky ones in grade school who had parents helping with homework and proofreading scholarship appeals instead of passing out on top of their secretary or under their gardener every night.'

'For instance,' said Jasmine into the silence that followed this.

'Of course,' said Patrice. 'Just for instance. Of course.'

'Well,' said Phil, 'I have got to admit, with my hand on my heart, that most of my clients are not so much troubled as just bone idle, but who's to say? I'm pretty sure that bone idleness is a symptom of something now. ADHD, maybe? Bipolarity? I wouldn't have thought we could sit in judgement these days.'

Jasmine and Patrice both nodded their heads slowly at him. I shook mine, in disbelief. Phil busied himself trying to jemmy open a clam.

'And this is what you were put on earth to do?' said Jasmine. 'What did you mean by that?' Phil laughed and did that comprehensive napkin manoeuvre that's mostly wiping the face but with a bit of nose-blowing thrown in; truly revolting but deemed to be acceptable by men when they're eating anything with chilli. Patrice sipped her drink in dainty disapproval.

'It just sometimes seems that way to me,' said Phil. 'I've found a business that uses my unique combination of talents: the unshakeable confidence that's all you really get from a public school education these days and then three years as a student scamming my way through on a pub to library ratio of at least fifteen to one.'

'And then you've a long history as a forger too,' I reminded him. It was one of my favourite stories about Phil, one of the first that Kim ever told me.

'Not a forger,' said Phil. 'A butter-in, perhaps. But it wasn't forgery.'

'Tell them,' I said. 'Let Patrice and Jasmine decide.'

'Well, it's my father's fault, really,' said Phil. 'After my parents divorced, my first stepmother had five daughters one after the other, like lottery balls, and I suppose my nose must have been out of joint. Anyway, when the fourth one was born, I was just eighteen and so, in a spirit of helpfulness, to save either one of the busy parents having to bother, I went to register her birth. It wasn't forgery. I was a blood relation of legal age. All perfectly proper.'

Patrice and Jasmine were looking at him expectantly.

'They were going to call her Harriet, I think,' said Phil. 'But I registered her as Lettice Lolita Lollobrigida. Dear Lottie, she'll be fourteen this year.'

'But was it legal?' said Jasmine. 'Would it stand up in court?'

'Oh yes,' said Phil. 'There was nothing they could do about it. And you'd think they would have learned. But no – a year and a half later when she popped the next one, they were still trying to decide on middle names to keep the godparents happy when I paid another visit to the registrar.'

'And what did you call her?' said Jasmine, her eyes dancing. Patrice was strangely silent.

'Oma,' said Phil.

Jasmine's shoulders slumped.

'And the middle names, Phil,' I said.

'Darlin Clementine,' said Phil. 'I'm still very proud of it.'

'Oma Darlin Clementine?' said Jasmine, crowing with laughter again. 'That's so mean. Patrice, isn't this guy *mean*?' Patrice was staring at Phil, her face – even for *her* face – blank.

'I don't see how that could be true,' she said. 'How could you go and register your sister's birth? It's a funny story, but …'

'Why not?' said Phil. 'Anyway, it stopped them. No more baby sisters after that. And now they're divorced and he's on to wife number three. At least this one shows no signs of breeding. Probably doesn't want to spoil her figure.' He groaned. 'Only interested in demolishing the family name. That's what you should be worried about it you're so concerned about fakes, Verity. Chauteau Coates – *appellation* not nearly *controllée* enough. Bloody English wine.'

'Well, you don't need to worry about English wine here, Phil,' said Patrice. 'How about some American champagne?' Phil glanced at me and drooped one eyelid just ever so slightly, but as I say, he is a gentleman and so he grinned.

'Splendid idea,' he said. 'Delicious. Make it pink for me.'

The thing about a *plateau de fruits de mer*, the thing I've always found anyway, is that even though there's a heap of food it takes two waiters to carry, it's mostly shells and it needs such a lot of cracking and winkling out that you don't really get that much to eat for your efforts and so, when you add three jugs of watermelon daiquiris, you don't always have the solid base you would hope for to chuck down two bottles of pink champagne. I stayed sober, of course; there was far too much going on for me to risk it, but as for the others …

'The trouble with Vegas,' said Jasmine not so very much later, 'is that there are no men.' She thumped the table with the handle of her oyster knife. 'All there is is gamblers.'

'It was a flower farm,' said Phil. 'Not a *vignoble*. Cornwall should be covered in flower farms. That's how it always was. And they went on the train to Covent Garden market every night.' He folded his arms and stuck out his bottom lip. 'Whisky from Scotland, wine from France, and flowers from Cornwall, via Covent Garden market, by train.'

'There's always a roadblock,' said Patrice. 'It's always this far and no further, so you struggle and get past it and then it's *this* far and no further.'

'They can't all be gamblers, Jasmine,' I said. 'And things change, Philly. Life moves on. Nobody wants to pay for Cornish flowers any more. I should know that. It's cheaper to fly them in. And Patrice ... what the hell are you talking about?'

'Gamblers and losers,' said Jasmine. 'I can't go back to Vegas. I'll die alone there.'

'At least when my mother moved to Kenya she started growing coffee,' said Phil. 'She didn't import a load of geese and start making African foie gras.'

'So you keep trying, smiling sweetly, doing everything you're told to do, on and on and on.'

'Why would you want to go back to Vegas, anyway?' I said. 'I thought you were from Chicago. And coffee's different, Phil. There's nowhere cheaper it can come from. Your dad's just living in the real world. And Patrice ... huh?'

'My branch of the family has always been Vegas based,' said Jasmine. 'Right from when we came over. My great grandfather, Silvio, was in Vegas before the railroad. His cousin in Chicago set him up there.'

'You just get so tired,' said Patrice. 'You just get to the point where you're sick of being nice and hoping they'll like you and you just say ... No! *My* money, *my* call, *my* way. Now!'

'What would you know about the real world anyway, Vert? You're a florist, for God's sake.'

'Maybe you'll meet someone nice in Seattle,' I said.

'Nerds,' said Jasmine. 'Nerds, geeks, and losers. I've been to Seattle. I've seen them.'

'And Patrice,' I said. 'You're getting your movie. There's no need to shout.'

*

As bad as this was, with them all talking, all talking nonsense, and all talking it to me, as much as I felt it was giving me three migraines at once, once they started listening to each other and agreeing it got worse.

'Don't go back to Vegas, darling beautiful gorgeous Jasmine,' said Phil. 'And don't go to Chicago. It's too windy there.'

'And the men are all gangsters and losers,' said Jasmine.

'I don't even care if it's wrong,' said Patrice. 'It's right for me. I need to climb my own mountain now.'

'Come to Cornwall,' said Phil. 'Everybody should come to Cornwall and tell my father they'd spend a lot of money for flowers and honey and tell him they want to get their wine from France.'

'I love flowers,' said Patrice. 'And I have money.'

'You are a flower,' said Phil. 'You're so beautiful. You look like an orchid. No! You look like a lily.'

'I'll never find a man in Cornwall,' said Jasmine. 'They're all … What are the men in Cornwall, Phil? Where is Cornwall, Phil?'

'They're surfers,' said Phil.

'Losers,' said Jasmine.

'Money doesn't make me a bad person,' said Patrice.

'Jasmine, you need to get real,' I said. 'You shouldn't go looking for a man with a shopping list of—'

'What would you know about "real"?' said Phil. 'You're a florist. You make posies for a living.'

'I love posies,' said Patrice.

'Of course you do,' said Phil. 'You're a posy. Both of you are a posy.'

'So are you,' said Jasmine. 'You're a posy too, Phil.'

'What about me?' I said.

'You're so lucky,' said Phil. 'Making posies and never having to live with our problems, Vert. Never having to deal with the real world.'

'What problems?' I said, which started them all off again talking at once.

'English wine.'

'Losers.'

'Knocking on a locked door begging to get in.'

'Let me tell you something about being a florist,' I said. *Let me tell you something about not being a beautiful film executive, or a beautiful movie producer, or a spoiled, smelly, overgrown schoolboy who's never done a day's work in his life.* Except I didn't say that bit. What I did say was: 'Let me tell you about gladioli. Do you know that even when you put gladioli into a vase at an angle, they always turn up their little faces and reach for the sun? So do you know what florists do?' All three of them shook their heads. 'They put wire down the backs of their stems, stapled on, so that they have to stay sticking out to the sides in the arrangements. That means that all the time they're in the vase, they're straining against the wire, struggling to turn up into the light, and they're not strong enough and they never make it before they wilt and die.'

Six brimming eyes, all slightly crossed, gazed over the table at me. Then Phil reached across and squeezed my hand.

'I'm sorry, Vert,' he said. 'I had no idea.' His voice broke and Jasmine and Patrice turned in to comfort him.

And then I took them all home. I mean I literally took them back to my hotel. I didn't have much choice. Patrice all but passed out when the night air hit her, and I couldn't wake her up enough to get her address out of her. Phil was awake and could remember his address but when the taxi driver heard it he answered: 'No deal, pal. Not that neighbourhood, not this time of night, no way.' And Jasmine, also awake and capable of reciting her name and address – although clearly pretty drunk or she would have said her address without her name and would have missed off the zip code – decided that she wanted to come with Phil and Patrice and me because we were a posy.

I had never had to check three drunk guests into a hotel at midnight before but it went better than I might have imagined. Perhaps it was because two of them were so beautiful, or because one of them was Phil at his grandest, or because the Plaza was that kind of place and it would have been a different story at the Beverly Hills, but nobody called security and the three of us got Patrice upstairs and laid her gently on the bed, then stood looking at her.

'How are we going to do this?' said Phil, looking hungrily at Jasmine. 'Where are we all going to go?' She flashed a glittering smile back at him and turned to me.

'Verity?'

The skin on the back of my neck contracted. I didn't want to be the gooseberry here. If Jasmine and Phil were determined to ravish each other I should bed down with Patrice and give them my room, but there was the pillow talk question. I couldn't leave them alone together all night. My widowhood would be in tatters by the morning, and Patrice would be livid and pull out of the deal, and Jasmine would tell Clovis what I had done and Clovis would never trust me again and would stop being my agent and I would be back torturing gladioli full-time.

And Jasmine couldn't seriously be considering Phil. How drunk was she?

'We should have put Patrice in my room,' I said. 'But we three girls can share these two big beds, surely. Phil can have mine.' Phil and Jasmine both smirked at me. Patrice moved slightly on the bed and moaned. 'Phil, you go to my room, anyway. That's for definite. Jasmine and I will get Patrice undressed and then we'll come and join you for a nightcap. OK, Jas?'

Jasmine had stopped smiling, had begun in fact to look rather sick. Perhaps she had just taken one of those quantum lurches into sobriety that can hit you at the end of the night. Or maybe she had caught a fresh whiff of Phil: booze and seafood hadn't helped his signature scent any.

'God, I must be drunker than I realised,' she said, not looking at him. 'I don't know what I was thinking. Verity, you're old friends right, you and Phil? You don't mind sharing? I'm going to get Patrice into bed now. You two just run along now. Sleep well, see you in the morning.' If she'd had a broom she could not have swept us more effectively out of the room.

'Hmph,' said Phil, standing in the corridor, swaying slightly with his hands on his hips, staring at the closed door. 'That all ended with a bit of a bump.' He saw me looking at him with one eyebrow raised and my tongue in my cheek and mustered himself into some flattery. 'Not that I don't see compensations,' he said.

'It's OK,' I said. 'I won't be offended if you turn it off for the night.'

He grinned at me cheerfully and slung an arm around my neck as we made our way to my room.

Lying in the dark, I listened to what I was sure was only the first stage of a night-long repertoire of drunken snores from the other bed. This early stage was no more than a rumble on the way in and a soft pop as his lips opened on each breath out, but it would be drying out his dehydrated throat even more. He really was disgusting, I told myself, in all sorts of ways. Only, after watching Patrice and Jasmine fall for it and watching Phil slavering over them, wasn't there just a tiny bit of me that was hurt because he had waited chivalrously in the bathroom while I got undressed, then crept out in his underwear, kissed me on the forehead and climbed into his own bed without so much as a wink? Suddenly I was aware that the rumble and pop had stopped.

'Are you still awake?' whispered Phil.

'Yeah,' I said. 'What is it?'

'It's not because I'm not tempted.'

I said nothing.

'It's just that ... the whole marriage question gives me the willies. My parents were a disaster. And then my father left the next one, and I think number three is on the way out. And my mother's not with the original bloke she moved to Kenya with, you know.'

'I didn't.'

'Mm. But I thought you and Kim were different. I still think you are. I think you should get back together. That's why I'm lying here like a boy scout. It's not because you're not luscious. It's a considerable struggle, actually. But I want you to get back together, to restore my faith in humanity.'

'OK, then, I will,' I said. 'Since it's you.'

'Good,' said Phil, matching my tone. 'I thought you'd agree.'

'Only it's not me you need to tell,' I reminded him.

He puffed out a huge sigh.

'I still can't believe it,' he said. 'Helen Marlowe? What's he thinking?'

'She's very attractive in her way,' I said. 'Very clean and soft and all that.' I knew that wouldn't endear her to Phil.

'Yeugh,' he said, right enough. 'She sounds like a milk pudding. Anyway, you're clean. All girls are clean. I wonder how girls live long enough to get old without wearing themselves away and vanishing down the plughole.'

He was beginning to slur again now and I knew the rumble and pop would begin again soon. But I had something to say before I lost him; I'd had a brainwave about how to put him off Jasmine.

'Phil?'

'Mm?'

'You know what you were saying about marriage.'

'Mm.'

'I said I wouldn't, but I think I should warn you.'

'Mm?'

'The reason I didn't want to discuss Kim? The reason I pretended I'd never been married?'

'Oh yes?' said Phil, and I heard the sheets rustle as he propped himself up to listen.

'The thing is, she's been married a lot of times.' I wondered how many I could push it up to and still be believed. 'Six times.'

'Six? How old is she?' He sounded suitably shocked.

'So I decided just to stay off the whole topic of marriage completely.'

'I don't blame you. And thanks for warning me. I'll steer clear.'

'I would, if I were you. She's lovely, of course, but not exactly stable.'

'Pity,' said Phil. 'What about Jasmine?'

'What?'

'What's the story there?'

'Jasmine?' I was stumped. 'Who were we . . . ? Isn't it . . . ? Are you interested in Patrice?'

'You know me, Vert,' said Phil. 'I'm just sort of generically interested.'

'But Jasmine's the pretty one.'

'She is, she is, and it's not to be sniffed at. There's something about Patrice though, don't you think? Not just being fit and knowing about economics and karate. Something elusive. I mean, come on! There must be if she's got six men to marry her.'

'Yeah,' I said. 'So ... Jasmine ...' But before I could think of anything to say, before I could even decide whether to say anything at all, the rumble and pop had started up again and this time he was out for the night.

Jasmine and Patrice woke me, coming into my room in their hotel bathrobes the next morning; there was no sign of Phil.

'God above me,' said Jasmine. 'I can't remember the last time I had so much to drink. I feel like a gravedigger's instep.' Perhaps, but she looked as perfect as ever, wet hair slicked back and tied in a knot, smudges under the eyes but the rest of her scrubbed face smooth and glowing, the snowy robe no more snowy than her glittering little white teeth. Patrice, on the other hand, with her hair flat and her coloured contacts out, with her body swaddled in towelling instead of swathed in panels of silk, even though she had slapped on some make-up already, was pitiful.

'I'm so sorry,' she croaked, as she lowered herself gently on to the end of the bed. 'I can't even remember what I'm sorry for.' She groaned as she lifted one leg and then the other leadenly on to the bed and sat back carefully. I threw a pillow down to her.

'You're fine, honey,' said Jasmine, kissing the top of her head and pushing the pillow down behind her. 'You didn't do anything you need to worry about. Did she, Vee?'

'Not that I can think of,' I said, reaching over and squeezing Patrice's ankle, just above her little towelling sockettes. I could feel bristles of hair, which only melted my heart that bit further. Patrice, even if she looked as perfect as Jasmine when she was assembled, was just like me underneath.

'I made a spectacle of myself,' said Patrice. 'I know I did. Stop being kind.'

'One time,' said Jasmine, 'I went to a party in a dress that had to come off to go to the bathroom – you know, with a real tight skirt that won't lift up, so you have to roll it down? Anyways, a long time after midnight, I went to the bathroom, took it off, hung it on the door, peed, and went back to the party. That's a spectacle, sweetie.'

'No, that's a story,' said Patrice. 'Last night I was just a bore.'

'Sh-sh,' said Jasmine. 'You were fine.' And I squeezed Patrice's leg again. Once again, it seemed, and still without knowing why exactly, we were rallied around her like two mother hens with one joint-custody chick.

'I know I was rude to Phil,' Patrice said, still troubled-looking. 'I remember that. When he told us the story about his little sisters' names? I remember that part clearly. And he's right, you know. I googled it all this morning and what he said was true. What must he have thought of me?' She put her hands up to her face and bowed her head down, although she didn't actually touch flesh to flesh. Even without full make-up, the well-learned habit was holding.

'You googled it?' I echoed. It was a funny way to handle a hangover, if you asked me.

'I love all that stuff,' said Patrice. 'You can find out a lot about a place from government websites and I think England sounds divine.'

'*That's* what you were doing?' said Jasmine. 'That's why I got woken up by you typing at seven o'clock in the morning? Jeez, I miss the days when all you could do in a hotel room was empty the mini bar and watch adult TV.'

Patrice was staring morosely towards her feet.

'I bet if you'd googled eBay for shoes, it would have cheered you up more,' I said, but she didn't respond. 'Do you actually want to know what Phil thought of you?' I said, trying again. She looked up at that. 'He thought you were beautiful and interesting and he was impressed that you understood economics and knew karate and he thought that there was an elusive something about you that he couldn't quite put his finger on but that he knew he liked.'

In spite of the hangover, Patrice's eyes brightened a little.

'He was drunk,' she said. 'He was just riffing.'

'No way,' I said. 'Phil doesn't lie. Especially not when he's drunk. He's famous for it. It's -' I remembered that I should have a firm view on this aspect of Phil. 'It's what I like most about him. Always have.'

'Looks like you picked the wrong one then,' said Jasmine.

I blinked at her. For someone who hated being 'aesthetically prominent' she sounded pretty sour to hear that Phil could resist her. She saw me seeing through her, blushed and flounced to her feet.

'Coming, Patrice?' she said.

'I'll stay here for a while,' Patrice murmured. 'If I have some coffee and an Advil I could see myself getting dressed in an hour or two.' Jasmine shrugged as if to show that she didn't care and then spoiled the effect by banging out of the room.

'Where is Phil this morning anyway?' said Patrice, looking around as if expecting him to reappear from somewhere. Too late, I realised that when you're trying to keep people apart in case they compare notes and your web begins to unravel, the last thing you should do is tell them they fancy each other.

'Gone home, I think,' I said, and then I went on slowly, 'Patrice, I have to say that – much as I love him – Phil is not a good bet. I'd hate to see you fall for his stuff and get burned.'

'I was joking,' she said. 'I know he was only flirting last night. Anyway, that's not what I want to talk to you about. I've been thinking more about our trip.'

'Oh, yeah?' I said. 'Not up to flying today?' This was a blow. I had never heard Phil sound so enthusiastic about any woman as he had about Patrice the night before and, looking at her pink cheeks and shining eyes, I could see that there was trouble coming from her end too; more than ever, I needed to get away.

'I'll be fine flying,' said Patrice. 'But Jasmine's right about Seattle. So I was thinking ... One place that's beautiful in the fall is New York City. My home town. How about that, Verity? Have you ever been to New York?'

I stared at her.

'Isn't it thousands of miles to New York from here?' I was quite happy to be thousands of miles from Phil, but what did it get Patrice?

'A plane ride's a plane ride,' she said. 'It was when we were talking last night – well, this morning really, when I was surfing around on the net – I got a new idea for the movie deal. A renegotiation. Only Clovis is going to hate it. So I'm trying to get you on my side.' She reached down to where my hand was still resting on her leg and grasped it, speaking earnestly and looking hard into my eyes. 'You know how much this … movie means to me, don't you?'

'I'm beginning to,' I said. 'But I still don't see why.'

'Because it's real,' said Patrice. 'It's true.'

'It's not.'

'It's close enough for me,' she told me. 'So will you back me up? With Clovis? Will you?'

I didn't know what to say. Clovis was my agent, the girl in my corner, and if she hated some idea it could only be because it was a bad idea for me.

'I know what you're thinking,' said Patrice, 'and I know we got off to a bad start. But I promise you, Verity, I will be one hundred per cent totally straight down the line about everything from here on in. I give you my word of honour.' She was staring at me, as solemn as an owl.

'Let's change the subject,' I said.

'OK,' said Patrice. 'Phil. You said you'd hate to see me fall for his stuff. What stuff? What's wrong with him?'

'Oh he's just a pig, the usual sort. A flirt, a flatterer, a philanderer.'

'That doesn't sound like a pig,' said Patrice. 'That sounds like a guy. You shouldn't be so harsh on them all.'

Now, this was puzzling. I had always thought that American women, at least successful American businesswomen, had such high standards and so many rules that no man on earth could live up to them. Certainly that was Jasmine's problem.

'Which reminds me,' Patrice went on. 'What you said yesterday, about your husband? When you said he was a liar? What exactly did you mean by that?'

'He lied about everything,' I told her. 'All the time.'

'A compulsive liar?' said Patrice. 'Did he say his daddy was an astronaut?'

'No,' I admitted slowly. 'Not things like that. Just little things. If you asked him how much he'd drunk, and it was three pints, he'd say two. If you asked him whether he'd posted the letter he'd promised to post, he'd say he had when what he meant was he would, sometime. If you asked him how much something cost – a camera, or a squash racket – he'd halve the amount and say it was in a sale. Lies after lies after lies all the time. It would have destroyed us in the end.'

Patrice was shaking her head and smiling at me, her lips beginning to curl back and float in front of her head in a real grin.

'As I suspected,' she said. 'Your husband wasn't a liar. All guys say things like that. If he went fishing, would you expect him to tell you he caught a two-pounder when he caught a two-pounder?'

I was speechless, and I felt a surge of rage that I struggled to hide from her.

'Look at it from his side,' she went on. 'He could just as easily call you a nag.'

'Does that mean the same thing over here?' I said. 'A nagging wife?'

'Sure, from what you just said to me. Asking him how many drinks he'd had, checking up on him that he's posted your mail, demanding to be told how much money he was spending. That would sound like nagging to most men. He could say no way he was a liar, but you were a nag.'

The rage was still boiling. For one thing, all guys didn't say things like that. Kim didn't – I had borrowed the examples from the tearful moaning of a girlfriend. And for another, if I had known that Patrice was going to laugh them off in that patronising way I would have picked some better ones that had the power to shock her. And over and above all of that, where did she get off understanding him? Her job was to understand *me.*

'The trick is,' she went on, 'not to get too hung up on labels. Don't go around calling him a liar to everyone. It's harsh; it's damaging. And you know what else? I don't think it's helpful for you to call yourself a widow either. Why call yourself anything? Why pigeonhole everyone all the time? Or if you must have a name for your situation, why don't you just say you're single? It'll help you heal in the end.'

'I'm not hung up,' I said, through gritted teeth. 'I just prefer to make my own labels before other people make them for me.' I could not believe she was saying these things. Even my granny, who was forever telling me that pride came before a fall and reminding me of how the pounds would take care of themselves if I saw to the pennies, had never said that names couldn't hurt me. Well, only once. Remembering made the rage boil faster than ever.

It was after school, I was in my bedroom, crying, trying to scrub a bad word off the cover of my jotter with an ink rubber that was wearing the paper away. I didn't hear my granny come in, didn't know she was there until she spoke.

'Have you been crying?' she asked me.

'No,' I said.

'That's a good girl.' Then she pulled my jotter away from me to look at it. 'Who's done this now?' she said. 'Who's been scribbling on your book and spoiling it? Did you tell the teacher?'

I shook my head. I had stopped sobbing and was only gulping every now and then and taking big wuthering breaths in.

'Janice said if I told the teacher she'd tell everyone that I was that bad word,' I said, pointing to where I had rubbed it out.

'But you're not a bad word,' said Granny. 'Orphan isn't a bad word.'

Orphan wasn't the word Janice had written on my jotter either, but I said nothing.

'So you just tell this Janice one, whoever she thinks she is, that she has got it wrong.'

I nodded, accepting but not believing. Granny had never met Janice; she couldn't know. And although Janice was only seven, same as me, I never forgave her for the day she called me a bad word and wrote it on my jotter in thick black ink. And years later, when *she* did what amounted to the same thing, the same hatred flooded back, as hot and urgent as before, hatred that could only be cooled by a fight in the playground, grinding fat bare knees into the gravel and pulling handfuls of hair out by the roots.

We had been talking, the way we did, about how busy we all were, how stressed, how time-poor, how burned out. All except Phil and Kim, of course.

'Speak for yourselves,' Phil had said, lighting a cigarette and blowing the smoke straight up. He was sitting with his arms spread out along the back of the bench in a pub garden.

'But what about you, Kim?' *she* had said, obviously discounting Phil. 'You must be a busy man now you're a partner.'

'So-so,' said Kim. 'But I don't let it get to me. One day I'll die and it won't matter whether the in tray is empty or full when I do. Why fret?'

'You know your problem, don't you, Hilda,' said Phil.

'Helen,' she said, frowning.

'Helen, I do apologise. Your problem is that you obviously haven't taken enough drugs. You need to wear out a few more irreplaceable brain cells like Kim and me and you'll soon mellow. We're always telling Verity, aren't we, Kimbo? Just fry a few more connections and you'll stop worrying so much about things like work.'

'*You're* worried about work?' she said, turning to me. 'But you're a shop assistant, aren't you?'

'I'm a florist,' I said.

'Yes, but in a shop, right?' said Helen. 'You work behind the counter in a shop.'

'*You* work behind a desk in an office,' said Kim.

'I'm sorry,' she said opening her eyes very wide. 'I didn't mean to offend you. There's nothing *wrong* with being a shop assistant.'

But of course, as far as she was concerned, there was plenty wrong with being a shop assistant. Just like there was plenty wrong with being a divorcee, no matter how much everyone in California stuck their chins in the air and called it something softer on the ear and the ego; just like there was plenty wrong with being what Janice had scribbled on my jotter so that I tore the paper trying to rub it out.

Chapter 7
Pod People

In mid-flight that afternoon, stretched out in the first-class BarcaLoungers, with our complimentary blankets over our legs and our complimentary eye masks being cooled in the galley fridge by an obliging steward, while Patrice slept away the last traces of her hangover, Jasmine and I sipped our complimentary hairs of the dog and I got another crack at the coconut.

'Sorry about this morning,' Jasmine began.

'This morning?'

'I was mean,' she went on. 'About your choice of husband. I snapped at you.'

'Don't give it a thought,' I said.

'I should never drink,' said Jasmine. 'It makes me cranky.'

'Hmm,' I said. I was still sure it was Phil preferring Patrice that was the problem, but I kept quiet.

'I've been thinking about him,' she went on. 'About what Patrice said? How it's harder to get over him because he was a dud? And I don't agree. I mean, you said he was a lying hound, right? But how bad was it, really? Because it seems to me that if he was as bad as all that, then it's not grief you're feeling at all, it's guilt because you're *not* grief-stricken and you should just forgive yourself and start enjoying life again. But if he was only a little bit crappy, then maybe you're obsessing on it to stop you feeling the grief and you should just let it in, because until you do you'll never work it through to the end.'

'Amazing,' I said. 'When I think about people, I rarely get past wondering how they keep their hair so shiny. You wondered all of that?'

'So,' said Jasmine, sticking to her point. 'Tell me about him. Tell me how bad it was. It's going to help you either way.'

I looked over at Patrice to see if she was really asleep. Her head was lolling on her neck pillow and her mouth was hanging open.

'Well,' I said, determined not to hear, once again, that Kim was 'just being a guy'. 'It was like this. Conversations would just suddenly cease to make any sense.'

'How do you mean?'

'He would just tell silly lies, little stories, little massages of the facts, so that I was never quite sure what version of events was real.'

'Yeah, but like what kind of thing?'

'I just told you,' I said.

'When?' said Jasmine.

'Just then,' I said with my eyes wide and my hands spread out to the sides. 'I said he would tell little lies to trip me up like saying someone had rung him as he was leaving the house and that's why he was late meeting me.'

'You didn't just say that.'

'What? I didn't just say what?'

'You didn't tell me the example about somebody calling the house.'

'Of course I did.'

'You *didn't.*'

'Well, how else do you know? I just said that he would say that a phone call had made him late meeting me. How can you tell me I didn't say that?'

'Yeah, OK. You said it, but you didn't say it until after you said you'd said it.' Jasmine was staring at me with her eyebrows drawn together, then all of a sudden her face smoothed and she whistled. 'Oh!' she said. 'Like that?'

'Like that,' I said, nodding.

'Jeez,' said Jasmine. 'That's mental torture.'

'And the worst of it was that I couldn't tell anyone.'

'Why not?'

'Because whenever I tried, you know what they would say?'

'Leave him now and take him for every penny in the divorce?'

'God, no,' I said. 'They'd say that everybody tells little white lies and I should learn to lighten up and not overreact to them.'

'They wouldn't say it twice,' said Jasmine. 'They'd get a smack in the kisser from me.'

'Patrice said it this morning,' I told her. 'She said I shouldn't label him a liar. She said I sounded like a nagging wife.'

'Patrice called you a nagging wife?' said Jasmine rounding on the sleeping form beside her. 'Typical!' she spat. 'Typical Patrice. Always taking the balanced view, always seeing the other side of the coin. Patrice has never learned that us gals need to stick together.' She was talking very loudly and I saw Patrice flinch.

'Jasmine?' she said, opening her eyes. 'What are you saying about me?'

'I'm saying you're a traitor to womankind,' said Jasmine.

'What do you mean?' said Patrice, sitting up abruptly as she pulled on the recliner lever. 'What have you been talking about?'

'Just about how you reckon Vee shouldn't call her husband a devious, lying shitbag even if it helps her get over him.'

'Oh,' said Patrice. 'That.'

'Patrice's problem,' said Jasmine, 'is that she's never been betrayed.'

'Not now,' said Patrice. 'My head still hurts. Wear me out tomorrow if you have to, but not today.'

I frowned. I didn't want to think that only the broken-hearted would agree with me about Kim. Phil was on my side, after all. Only, I had to admit that Phil had come a cropper over marriage too, his parents' marriages anyway. I turned and stared out of the window at the clouds.

'God I'm bored,' said Helen, looking at her watch. 'Tell me a story, Kimmie.' Kim played a rhythm on the steering wheel and thought. He was crawling in second gear towards the back of the car in front, and unless the traffic started to move he was going to have to go down to first, hit the brake and put the clutch down. He let the car drift slower and slower, until the engine began to chug, then reluctantly he stopped. He let out his breath and leaned heavily on the horn.

'Kim!' said Helen. 'That's not going to help.'

'It might,' said Kim. 'Might set someone off on road rage and we could watch. It would pass the time.'

'A story would pass the time,' said Helen, like a spoiled child.

'OK,' said Kim slowly. 'Here's a good one. This is very subtle, but it gives you another angle on the phenomenon under study. About a year before she finally left, Verity became convinced that I was having an affair.' Helen raised her eyebrows at him.

'Which you weren't, I take it?' she said.

'Which I wasn't,' Kim said. 'It all started because one day I decided to come home for lunch. I've no idea why – I just took a notion to come back at lunchtime. Anyway, when I got there, I looked around and I thought, God this place is a mess. You know how you can be rushing in and out never stopping, away from dawn till dusk every weekend and then you suddenly take a good look round on a Tuesday lunchtime in March and realise that you've crossed a line?'

Helen shrugged and Kim looked around the inside of the car. Box of baby wipes in the key tray, lined rubbish pouch hanging from a hook on the back of the driver's seat, an A-Z in the door pocket.

'Anyway,' he went on. 'I thought I would tidy up a bit. Scrape off the top few layers of grime and make a nice surprise. God, if only I'd done the cooker and hoovered the sitting room carpet! What I chose to do in my innocence was change our bed sheets and clean the bathroom. Then I went back to work and thought no more about it. But for a few months after that our household appliances developed a string of unlikely intermittent faults that no repairman could ever find or fix. And even stranger than that, Verity, living in the middle of London with every Thursday off to go shopping, took to buying a lot of mail order and giving the couriers my work address to deliver it to. I was forever coming home on the tube laden with sets of saucepans and Boden cardis.'

'What was it all about?'

'Well, as far as I could tell, she decided that the only reason I would change bed sheets and clean the bathroom was because I'd had somebody in there. So she'd ask a repairman to come between twelve and two to look at the washing machine, or the telly or some other perfectly functional bit of kit. Or she'd scrutinise the date and the signature of the mail-order delivery note to check that I'd been at my desk when it arrived.'

'Why did you put up with it?'

'There wasn't really anything to put up with,' said Kim. 'It wasn't until months later that I realised what had been going on.'

'She just stopped?'

'No, she had a brainwave that she thought would catch me out for sure. She got a cleaner. Gave this woman a key and told her she could suit herself as to hours, come and go as she pleased. After six weeks, when the woman – I forget her name – said that she'd not seen hide nor hair of me, not once, Verity decided that it had been a one lunchtime stand and called off the watch.'

'And you just never mentioned it?'

'Actually, in this case, I did,' said Kim. 'In a roundabout way. It so happened that about that time old Phil ...' He paused to allow Helen the obligatory frown and tut that Phil's name always brought from her whenever it was mentioned. 'Old Phil got a visit from some cousin, a girl, sent over from South America with Phil's name and address like a lamb to the slaughter. And oldest friend or no, I couldn't sit and let this doe-eyed little angel be ravaged and tossed aside in the usual Phil fashion. So I warned her off; I roped Verity in to help me and laid it on the line. I told the girl she'd better get out of London, right away from Big Bad Phil and go down to Cornwall to his father's house, hang out there with the stepmother and all the daughters instead.'

'And that convinced Verity?'

'Partly,' said Kim. 'She knows how much I think of Phil.' Again the quick frown tugged at Helen's smooth brow. 'And seeing me take the side of this sweet girl against him was a hint that she'd misjudged me. Then Phil and I had some very sharp words about the whole affair when the thing had played itself out and Verity overheard me giving it great guns about fidelity and commitment and everything, and she ended up confessing all, more sheepish than I've ever seen her.'

'So you forgave her? For being so suspicious?'

'Oh yes. Well, actually we were rather taken over by events, because this sweet young South American angel I'd been trying to save from the clutches of Phil duly went down to Cornwall to the family homestead, lured Phil's father away from his stepmother and promptly became wife number three. He's old enough to be her grandpa.'

Helen wrinkled her nose. The more she heard about Phil the less she liked him and now it seemed that his entire family was the same.

'But didn't you say she was a relation?' she said.

'Yes, she was – let me get this right. She was the daughter of Phil's mother's sister – that's it. She came from the farm in Argentina where Phil's mother grew up. So she was just an ex-niece by marriage to Phil's father. Easily far enough away not to count as incest, apparently. Still – eeuuww!'

'No wonder you and Phil had sharp words then,' said Helen, highly diverted.

'Indeed. And no wonder Verity's little bit of nonsense didn't register all that high on the sin-o-meter.'

'No, but really, was that the beginning of you and Phil not being such pals any more?'

Kim said nothing. He had been going to dispute this take on matters until it occurred to him that actually it was true. When had he even seen Phil last?

'It's not like that,' he answered eventually. 'There's no rift or anything. It's just that he's away at the moment and we're not big phoners or mailers. He didn't blame me.'

'I would have,' said Helen. 'I wouldn't have let Verity off with such outrageous behaviour either. And I'd have had plenty to say to little Miss Argentina.'

'No doubt,' said Kim, and he added under his breath, 'You're hardly one of life's letters-go.' And then he thought to himself: you'd still have the couriers and cleaning lady checking me out if I'd raised suspicions in you.

'What in God's name are we doing all the way out here, Patrice?' said Jasmine, slumped on a trolley at the carousel. Their luggage had rolled out early on, as if even the baggage handlers knew A-list cases when they saw them; I felt I was letting the side down badly making them wait for mine to appear.

'It's actually not as far into Manhatten from here as it is from JFK,' said Patrice.

'It must be,' said Jasmine. 'It's in Jersey. I can't believe I'm in Jersey. You know how hard I worked to get out of Jersey, all those years ago?'

'I thought you were from Chicago and Las Vegas,' I said. 'How can you be from New Jersey too?'

'I started work here,' said Jasmine. 'In my family business, everyone starts out working in Jersey. I never dreamed I'd ever be back.' She glowered at Patrice, who ignored her.

'Here they are,' I said, catching sight of a Morrisons' suitcase appearing through the flaps.

'Thank God,' said Jasmine. 'Let's get a limo into town.'

I had thought she was joking, but Patrice sashayed straight past the Hertz and Alamo desks, managing to look as though her little case on wheels was an expensive breed of dog she was taking for a walk on the Champs Elysées, and sat down in a grey velvet armchair in front of a polished table.

'Get one with a bar!' Jasmine called over to her. And then to me: 'I know I shouldn't. This is exactly why I don't drink these days. Once I start, it takes me weeks to stop again.'

We didn't have to set foot outside at the airport – the limo pick-up service took us from carpet to car seat in centrally heated warmth, so when we reached the other end the cold made me catch my breath. Jasmine and I were still dressed for California, although Patrice had sprung a pashmina from somewhere during the ride and was swathed in it now as she stepped out and tipped the driver.

'Where are we?' I said, turning around, enchanted in spite of the cold by the statues, the fluttering flags, the horse drawn carriages clopping past.

'What do you mean where are we?' said Jasmine. 'Stop gawping around like that, Vee, you look like a tourist. We're on the corner of Fifth Avenue and Central Park.'

'Really?' I said, gazing across the road at the railings and the trees beyond. 'That's Central Park? Where are we going?'

Patrice put her arm around me and began pointing.

'That's Central Park. Down there is everything you can buy with money. Up there is all the museums full of everything you can't buy with money. Over there with all the teddy bears in the window is FAO Schwarz, and we're going in here. I thought, after that dump last night, you might like to stay at the Plaza.'

And she meant it; it was the actual Plaza Hotel, the real one this time.

'The Plaza?' wailed Jasmine. 'It's not even twenty storeys high. We might as well sleep *in* the traffic.'

'You can have a room at the back,' said Patrice, sweeping up the steps towards the door. 'Verity, come and see.'

Of course, I was overawed by it all – the lobby was like a Venetian cathedral only with more gold paint – but not so much that I didn't think to ask on the way up in the lift: 'Isn't this place really expensive, Patrice?'

'I told you, I'm trying to sweeten you up,' she said.

'What's this?' said Jasmine.

'I've got a new idea to put to Clovis and I want Verity on my side.'

'A new idea?' said Jasmine. 'Any plans to tell me?'

'I'm moving the project,' Patrice said. It was an Announcement, with a capital A and even in the plushy womb of the lift with its deadening velvet walls, it rang out. 'I always knew a Hollywood movie wasn't real enough, and now I know what is.'

'Oh?' said Jasmine.

'It was meeting Phil that did it,' said Patrice. 'He's the realest thing I've ever seen in my life. He's Hollywood anti-matter.'

'I see what you mean,' I said. 'The yellow teeth, the BO, the fag-breath. But what's it got to do with the movie?'

'I'm moving it to Europe,' said Patrice. 'I'm going to make it in England, maybe even in Cornwall. Where Life,' she paused, 'is Real.'

'Well, Cornwall's maybe not the grittiest—' I began, but Jasmine interrupted.

'Cornwall?' she said. She was staring hard at Patrice, thinking furiously, popping her lips to make a little tune. She should have – anyone else would have – looked like a fish, but not Jasmine.

'Why not?' said Patrice.

'In a word?' said Jasmine. 'Clovis.'

Patrice leaned towards her and spoke very slowly.

'I know,' she said. 'Hence the sweetening.'

I was lost but the lift glided to a cushioned stop and the doors swept open before I could ask for directions.

In my room, the sweetening continued but as I stood dropping cold cherries into my mouth from the bowl laid out next to a decanter of Madeira, I reassured myself that Jasmine was wrong. Why would Clovis care where Patrice made her movie? The Madeira and cherries and the view of the floodlit skating rink below were totally guilt-free. I didn't even have any reason for the twinge I felt from thinking of Clovis's name. It was guilt – what else could it be? – but I had no reason to feel it. For one thing, what Clovis didn't know was never going to hurt her and she was never going to know that the three of us were stringing her along. For another, when Jasmine got her dazzling deal through everyone would be a winner. Clovis included. And for one more, Clovis wasn't exactly being candid with *me*. Hadn't she pretended to me that my zzub was a damp squib? When in fact it was as dry as a tinderbox and ready to pop?

At least I hoped so. I hoped it hadn't got damp somehow when I wasn't looking. Wincing at the thought of a coast to coast call on a hotel bill, but telling myself that, as Jasmine said, it was Patrice's dollar and, as Patrice had said, she'd hack off her arm for this deal, I punched Bradley's number into my phone.

'Are you still in Seattle?' he asked me. 'My cousin told me the PA said Halford's gagging with his tongue out. Can you get back down here to meet tomorrow?'

'I'm calling from New York, Brad,' I said. 'Patrice brought me here instead.'

'This is the independent? She's brought you to New York? *Is* she scouting locations? What has she heard? How did she hear? Who told her?'

'Scouting snow disaster locations in New York?' I said. 'What are you talking about?'

'Only Halford's PA told my cousin who told me that he's thinking urban. Shafts, you know. Ventilation, wiring, the subway, even sewers and drainage. Only I don't think sewerage entrapment could ever make a date movie, do you? But whatever, he's kind of like *Die Hard*, but vertical? *Straight Up!* Definitely with an exclamation point. Wait till I tell my cousin to tell the PA to tell him you've gone to the other coast with the independent.'

'He's going to tell you that the PA told him that Halford freaked!' I said. I was learning.

'But dontcha worry, girlfriend,' said Brad. 'IFA has an office in Manhattan. You can take the meeting there.'

Reassured, I began to think about dressing. I unzipped the biggest case and looked inside. I should unpack, I knew, but the padded hangers in the closet were of more sumptuous fabric – mouse-coloured satin and mouse-coloured suede – than the fanciest of my dresses and so the thought was too depressing. If the man who designed the closets in the suites in the Plaza, with their mirror-backed shoe racks and revolving rails, had seen my clothes he would have saved himself the effort and just banged in a lot of nails.

It's a curious thing how the eye becomes so quickly accustomed to what it sees. At home in Edinburgh, at work, or popping out for a sandwich at lunchtime I always felt reasonably well turned out. Even in London if I paid attention I could pass unnoticed in a crowd. But two days of looking at Jasmine and Patrice and I couldn't stop my lip curling as I stirred the heap of clothes in my case and pictured what I would look like wearing any of it. Was there a chance that either of the others was a sharer? I wondered. Was there any chance that I could get into one of Jasmine's dresses and do it up, or work out which bits of one of Patrice's outfits was supposed to go where?

I padded out of my suite and along the corridor. Jasmine's door was ajar, but before I could knock, I heard my name.

'... still shouldn't have started talking about it in front of Verity,' Jasmine was saying. 'That was dumb.'

'No, Jasmine,' said Patrice, 'that was *open*. Verity likes people being open.'

'You have to let me steer this now,' said Jasmine. 'It just got a lot more complicated. We had a deal and a timetable all ready to go.'

'But if Clovis is like everyone else – and I'm sure she is – we can have a different timetable, another deal, as long as we have a new price too.'

'I'm not so sure,' said Jasmine. 'Five years ago, maybe, but Clovis is strictly US only now. This is going to take some careful steering, that's all I'm saying.'

'We'll see,' said Patrice, and I could tell from the warm, lazy sound of her voice that she was doing that thing she does, closing her eyes and opening them, looking like a cat. 'Verity's perfectly happy.'

'Verity doesn't know dog dick,' Jasmine replied.

I kept it out of my head. I kept my head full of anger instead. Pulling on jeans and a jersey back in my room I imagined being repulsed by some snooty doorman at Patrice's favourite midtown haunt and laughing in his face. Spitting in his face even. I took off my earrings and scraped my hair back into a band. Take that, I told them in my imagination. Wheel that around Manhattan in a limo.

'You're psychic,' said Jasmine, hugging me as she opened the door to my knock. She was wearing jeans, sprayed on and embroidered, but jeans, and a Vassar sweatshirt. Behind her, Patrice was arranging a poncho over a collection of Hessian panels that might, just might, have been joined up to make a pair of pants.

'We're going to Carnegie's,' she said. 'Good to see you've dressed down.'

'And nice work with the facelift,' said Jasmine, batting my pony-tail. I *had* pulled it back quite tight, as a matter of fact, fuming away in front of my mirror. 'I sometimes do that after a long flight too.'

I said nothing.

'Verity? What is it?' said Patrice, just the way she had said it once before.

'I want to know dog dick,' I said and waited.

'What?' said Jasmine, as if saying that about me when I wasn't there was so insignificant, so everyday, that she didn't even remember. She went back to brushing her hair in front of the dressing mirror.

'I heard you talking,' I said, and I could feel my throat drying out as I spoke. 'You said I didn't know dog dick, and I'd like to.'

'Oh, Verity!' said Patrice, her eyebrows quivering as if she was trying to draw them up in the middle and look concerned. 'I'm so sorry. What a hurtful thing to overhear.'

'No!' I said. 'No, it's not. Not particularly. Who cares? Not me.'

I swallowed hard. 'It's just having heard you talking – which is neither here nor there – I think you haven't been exactly honest. Again.' I gave Patrice a significant look. 'I don't understand why you want to move the movie. Or why you think Clovis would care. What's going on?'

'Verity, my darling, nothing!' said Patrice. 'I tried to talk to you earlier and you changed the subject, remember? I'm sorry.' She was gazing earnestly into my face with her face at its blankest and most beatific. 'But of course I need to explain, of course I do.'

I waited.

'I just decided it would work better in England,' she said.

'You know there's no snow there?' I said.

'I'm not talking about locations,' said Patrice. 'There's more to this than a pretty backdrop. I'm not even talking about the movie. I'm talking about the making of the movie, the whole experience for everyone involved. The ... totality of the ... ethos.'

'Well, that clears that right up then,' said Jasmine, shaking her head. 'Can we get it in words of one syllable for the foot trade, Patrice?'

'I'm talking about reality. I want it to be real. And in England it can be. In England anyone can do whatever they want to. You must know that, Verity – you live there.'

'I ... um,' I said.

'Have you heard of the Right to Roam?' said Patrice. 'Jasmine, did you know you can walk into an emergency room in England and get an appendectomy without even giving your name? Did you know that you don't even need a driver's licence to drive a car?'

'Yeah, actually, you do,' I said.

'No!' sang Patrice. 'I checked it all out. You don't. If you get pulled over, you get a whole week to produce one. A week! Can you imagine, Jasmine?'

'And we call ourselves the land of the free,' Jasmine said.

'OK,' I said. 'I can see why all that sounds lovely, although I have to tell you, Patrice, you might be disappointed when you get there, and I'll take your word for it about the totality of the ethos – you're the artist here – but, like I say, why should Clovis care?'

'It's complicated,' said Jasmine, looking over at Patrice as she spoke.

'It's all about profile,' said Patrice. 'Clovis wants to do an international deal with a Hollywood producer. It's higher status, better publicity for her agency. And for all the same reasons it's better for Jasmine too. Jasmine is being very sweet, saying she'll help me move it, you know.'

'OK,' I said, nodding. 'But that's always seemed a bit off to me. You care so much about what's real and what's true and yet your whole deal was set up to get Jasmine a corner office and a bigger set of shoulder pads. Doesn't that bother you?'

Jasmine stood smacking her hairbrush into her palm and looking at me speculatively.

'That's pretty insensitive, Vee,' she said.

'Oh come on,' I said. 'I have to be sensitive about *that*? About something so shallow?'

'The truth is,' said Patrice, seeing Jasmine's face turning mulish and watching the hairbrush slapping faster and faster into her palm. 'That's not really ...' She took a deep breath. 'We haven't been one hundred per cent straight with you on that one.'

I could feel my eyes opening wider.

'Don't look at me that way,' she said.

'You said you would never lie to me again.'

'I didn't,' she said. '*I* told you everything. The rest is Jasmine's story.'

'OK,' I said, settling down on the edge of the bed and folding my arms. 'Tell me.'

'Jasmine didn't lie to you either,' said Patrice. 'She does need to put through the stellar deal, but we're all agreed about the shoulder pads. Scouting, tracking, sniffing? Jasmine hates it, don't you, Jazzie?'

'That's right,' said Jasmine nodding furiously. 'I hate it. I didn't want to tell you—'

'In case it offended you,' supplied Patrice.

'— but I want out. And the only way I can *get* out is to impress someone in the family so much that they give me what I need to start up on my own. Enter Patrice.'

'Start up on your own doing what?' I asked Jasmine.

'I have no clue,' she said. 'None. I've even thought of settling down in Connecticut – that's how much of an idea I don't have. But …'

'All men are losers?' I said, guessing.

'Well, yeah, plus the bill for settling down is a lo-hot steeper than the bill for starting up.'

I nodded slowly. I couldn't see why Patrice didn't just give Jasmine some of her endless money, why Jasmine cared so much about looking good in her family business if she was so desperate to leave, but I bit my tongue. After all, it was my book that was getting tossed around between all the middlemen, and gathering money like a snowball rolling down a roof. I wasn't going to show them a simpler way where they could do without it.

'So that's all it is?' I said. 'You both just want to get out of plastic Hollywood and do something real? That's it?'

'We're your dream team, if you think about it that way,' said Jasmine. 'We'll make up for all the bullshit that lying dog laid on you. And if we'd known the way you feel about truth and honesty – yadda-yadda – we could have told you all this from the get-go.'

'We'll never hide anything from you ever again,' said Patrice, 'if you'll only forgive us this time.'

They beamed at me and I managed some kind of grin back to them.

'Noodle soup and cheesecake,' said Jasmine twenty minutes later, without even looking.

'Twice,' said Patrice. 'Only tourists eat the sandwiches, Verity.'

'Lovely,' I said. 'Noodle soup and cheesecake for me.'

'Got it,' said the waiter.

A couple of thin women, squawking at each other on the next table over, paused and looked at us briefly. Jasmine leaned in and whispered to me.

'When the waiters speak to you, all the other locals look around to see if maybe you're a star.' She waved at the walls where signed photos of baseball players and country singers were five deep above the dado rail.

'They don't say "got it" to stars,' said Patrice. 'They say "ma'am" or "sir".'

'Really?' said Jasmine. 'I never heard that.'

'Oh yeah,' said Patrice. 'They used to say "ma'am" to my mother.'

'That's right,' said Jasmine. 'I forgot she used to bring you here.'

'Every Fourth of July,' said Patrice. 'It was always full of tourists but we never had to wait because it was my birthday.'

'And because your mother was a star, right?' I said.

'She wasn't,' said Patrice. 'She was just a New Yorker.'

'Hah!' said Jasmine. 'Just a New Yorker with a room named after her in all the museums, her name engraved on the wall of the Met and her dress size memorised by every assistant in Bergdorf Goodman.'

'Stop it, Jasmine,' said Patrice. 'That's not true.' She paused. 'It was her ring size by every assistant in Tiffany's.'

'Wow,' I said. 'Who is she?'

'I'd rather not say,' said Patrice. 'We don't talk any more, Mother and me.'

Jasmine spat three times to the side. I wasn't sure what that meant; perhaps a curse on Patrice's mother, perhaps an appeal to the gods of fortune to heal the rift. All I did know was that it was a Jewish thing and that Jasmine was Italian, so maybe she didn't know either, maybe she just had a hair in her mouth.

'She didn't approve of my marriage,' Patrice went on. 'And then having disapproved of that she also managed not to approve of my divorce. And now she doesn't approve of what she calls my "lifestyle".'

'Patrice, honey,' said Jasmine. 'Don't think about it. Don't talk about it.'

I nodded sympathetically. I had no idea what Patrice could mean by disapproval of her lifestyle – I couldn't really say, for that matter, what her lifestyle might be – but I could certainly relate to the rest of it.

'It'll end in tears,' Granny said, after the first time she ever met Kim. 'You'd better stick to your own kind, lass. It'll all end in tears.'

'She didn't take to me much, did she?' said Kim when I called him to talk it through. 'A tough nut to crack, your grandmamma.'

'It would help if you didn't call her my grandmamma,' I told him. But it would take more than that. Me, she was proud of. She'd brought me up right and I had a trade behind me, a solid, respectable job with a good wage coming in. Her family was back on track, she used to say. And now here was Kim – and what kind of name was that for a laddie? – flinging kisses around and laughing at her all the time under the surface. Oh, don't think she couldn't see through that nicey-nicey routine, she told me. She wasn't as green as she was cabbage-looking.

In time, of course, she came round. She never got over him taking me to London – all that way, she used to say, what if anything happened? – and on her only visit to us she was puzzled and disappointed by the house on the Wandsworth Bridge Road. A wee bit of a place, in a terraced row. Not even the whole of the house either, but neighbours up the stairs and us all topsy-turvy with our kitchen over our heads and downstairs to the bedrooms. We kept finding her turning around and around in the hallway, lost – even in that wee bit of a place – unable to make a map for herself, unable to accept it, the front door upstairs and the bedrooms down. It just wasn't right.

'What about your father?' I asked Patrice. 'Do you still see him?'

'Long gone,' Patrice told me. 'Wore himself out making all the money for my mother to give away.'

'Typical New Yorker,' said Jasmine. 'Typical American. We do things different in Catania.'

'Catania?' I said. 'In Sicily? I've been there.'

'It's where I come from,' said Jasmine. 'Everybody keeps tight hold of their money and lives for ever.'

'You come from New Jersey, Las Vegas and Chicago,' I said. 'What's with Sicily all of a sudden?'

'Oh, Jazzie always gets very Italian when she hits New York,' said Patrice. 'And who can blame her? I was married to an Italian and now my ex-in-laws are the nearest things to family I have left.'

'I can imagine,' I said. 'The Italians I met – they bought TV rights in *Straight Up* as a matter of fact – had practically adopted me after three days.'

'Small world,' said Jasmine, and her voice sounded rather wooden somehow.

'Hardly,' said Patrice. 'My ex-in-laws are a bunch of bankers from Milan.'

'Anyways,' said Jasmine, 'after this, how about a club?'

'We are not going on to a club,' said Patrice.

'Oh come on!' said Jasmine. 'We gotta show Vee the New York club scene!'

'Yeah, come on, Patrice,' I said. 'Jasmine could land a hot date with the love of her life. You can't deny her that.' But Jasmine's smile had disappeared as though someone had flipped a switch and killed it.

'A hot date?' she said. 'In New York? I have one word for you, Vee, and please excuse my language. Lawyers.'

'And losers?' I guessed. Jasmine nodded, her eyes closed in pain.

'Anyway, wouldn't you rather have a moonlight boat ride round the harbour, or a carriage ride through the park?' said Patrice.

'Oh sure,' said Jasmine. 'Don't order Carnegie's pastrami but by all means go round the park in a buggy. That's not going to make you look like a tourist – no way.'

In the end we did both and even Jasmine, although she complained about the cold, the smell of the horse, the choppy water and the hokiness of it all, was shiny-eyed and giggling when we got back to the Plaza long after midnight and went our separate ways.

Back in my room my phone light was blinking at me, telling me that I had a message waiting. Three messages, it turned out.

'Hello darling,' said Clovis's voice. 'And who's a lucky girl, then? Jasmine is rapidly becoming your biggest fan. But I think at a round two hundred you really should just sign the contract, don't you? Call me back when it's in the bag and I'll organise flowers for her. Easier for me to get them from Interflora than for you to get bilked for a bunch of marigolds at midtown prices. Sleep tight and speak in the morning.'

Message received and understood, Clovis, I thought. I wasn't to call until I'd signed on the line and yet she would hear from me in the morning. And the little dig at florists hadn't gone unnoticed either. Except maybe I was being unfair. Clovis always thought she could get everything, from a hire car to a headstone, at a knock-down price and usually, let's face it, she could.

The second message was from Kenny Daateng.

'What happened to Seattle? I'm just calling to tell you about another sniff of interest from a studio. They're very keen – I spoke to one of their junior development executives who I happen to know – love the title, love the concept, not so keen on the snow and no way they're going to go for high desert plains and canyons. But submarines: now you're talking. Still vertical but with the dwindling oxygen supply thrown in to crank up the tension? Now, I know what you're thinking: how could one man be on a submarine on his own? But she was talking sole survivor, independent diver in a wreck, treasure seeker. Or make it a whole crew of them. More dialogue. Easier script in the long run. I can see the title sequence: like *Panic Room* but floating on the surface of the sea.'

'Hardly vertical, though,' I said to the machine. 'That's about as horizontal as it gets.'

And, of course, Brad.

'There she is, riding the subway, talking the street talk,' he sang. 'Nine-thirty tomorrow morning. IFA building, Lexington Avenue. That's fiftieth and Lex, Verity. As in around the block from the Waldorf? Have *you* arrived or have you arrived? Huh? You're meeting with the PA to the assistant to Mr Bojangles himself. Ben Jankel. I've faxed over the script already and my cousin? In the mailroom? Here in LA? He said that Mr Meer's PA said to him to say to me to say to you that you should probably keep a lid on the whole London agent side of things just for now. And I agree, I have to say, I do agree. But you should plug the independent and Mr Daateng. I'd plug them deeper than Elton's implants, if I were you – and I have to say I wish I was. So anyway, call me after the meeting and let me know how it goes. And just be yourself. They love it. I told them all about you. The Widow. And about you being a mortician. You don't mind me saying you were a mortician, do you? I mean, you practically are, what with flowers and funerals and whatnot. Right? So they're thinking definitely not snow. Something darker. But they love it like their mama made it. Speak tomorrow. Mwah!'

One good thing about a message from Bradley Honey, I thought, is that he could make the midtown night traffic in NYC sound quiet in comparison. The silence positively tingled as I put down the phone.

The next morning, Jasmine and Patrice waved me off like proud parents at the school gate.

'Don't take the subway,' said Patrice. 'Keep a twenty in your pocket to pay cabfare. Don't open your purse. Don't look at a street map outside – step into a lobby. Don't talk to any—'

'Patrice,' I said. 'I have lived in London for seven years. I won't let anyone sell me a bridge.'

'Don't sign any petitions,' said Jasmine. 'If a cop talks to you don't tell jokes. If anyone mentions bombs, don't be ironic.'

'I'll see you later,' I said. 'Lunatic.'

'Are you going to be warm enough?' said Patrice.

'I'll see you later,' I said again. 'Mom.' She grinned, one of the big grins that turned her lips outwards.

And then they practically shooed me out of the door. Jasmine wiggled her eyebrows, spiky lashes flashing.

'We've got a surprise for you,' she said. 'At lunch.'

I walked down Fifth Avenue, turned at St Patrick's cathedral and strolled along East 50th, heading for the Waldorf. Why would I look at a street map? It was all so easy. No wonder New Yorkers in London stood around in huddles, turning their A-Zs and trying to find themselves in the heap of street spaghetti. This was a breeze. I rounded the Waldorf and entered the foyer of the IFA building.

They were charming. There were three of them – two women and a man – all beaming, solicitous, enthusiastic, altogether like a little slice of LA and not the wise-cracking, coked-up, hard-bitten New Yorkers I had been expecting. And they spoke about 'Mr Jankel' in the kind of voices I had only ever heard speaking about 'Mr Mandela' before.

'Mr Jankel said he'd try to stop by, Verity,' said Erin, one of the women. 'He sent an email around to all of us this morning saying he really might be stopping by.'

'Wow?' I hazarded.

'Wow,' Melanie confirmed. 'So what are we going to tell him about this fabulous project when he gets here?'

'*Straight Up*,' said Beau, the man. 'I'll talk you through our brainstorming, show you where we got to. Funeral homes . . .'

I blinked.

'Have basements,' went on Beau. 'But they're not nearly deep enough. Crypts, of course, are a possibility but then the bodies would be embalmed and inedible. And how deep, really, could a crypt ever be?'

'Sorry?' I said, trying to catch up.

'So,' Melanie went on, 'we're thinking of other worlds. More vertically-based communities in other worlds where body storage is a problem and we could have chasms of corpses. Kind of *Cliffhanger* meets *The Matrix*.'

'Zombie Zion,' said Erin.

'I'm sorry?'

'But don't worry,' said Beau. 'We're keeping the central character human, from old earth. An adventurer, maybe. On an expedition, just like in the book.'

'Did you say inedible corpses?'

'That's the part we think everyone will be able to relate to,' said Beau.

'*What?*'

'Oh absolutely,' said Melanie. 'That's going to be the hook. You gotta keep body and soul together somehow for the climb. So what you gonna do? That's what they'll all be talking about on the way home from the theaters, I can tell you.'

'And you didn't really develop it in the book,' said Erin. 'I mean, I loved the book, don't get me wrong. I bought and read it even before we got involved. I have it on my bookshelf in my apartment.'

'You do?' I said, cringing for her. I've claimed to have read a few unread books in my time, but not an unpublished one, I hope.

'We all do,' said Beau. 'It's a huge cult hit, as you know.'

'But you could have done so much more with the question of what did this guy eat? What did he eat? What did he eat all that time, clawing his way up through the pods?'

'The snow,' I reminded her.

'Sure, the snow,' said Beau. 'You see? That's the big question. *What did he eat?*'

'Kendal Mint Cake,' I said.

They all smiled at me.

'Intergalactic Mint Cake?' said Erin, holding out one hand to the side as if weighing up a bar of it. 'Or,' she turned to her other hand. 'Cold-stored corpses?' She see-sawed her hands up and down like a Siamese dancer. 'What's going to get them all talking on the way home?'

I was speechless, which went down rather well.

Mr Jankel, Mr Bojangles himself, never did stop by, but as Erin, Melanie and Beau were quick to assure me, an email to all three of them saying that he really might was quite an achievement for me at this stage. I left the building again and set off, zigzagging up the avenues and along the cross streets. What would my granny say about that? She always liked a good film, often went to a matinee with her knitting and a box of wine gums, but a simple tale of corpse ingestion in a galaxy far, far away? I didn't think so.

I swerved into Trump Tower to jolt myself back to reality, thinking even as I did so that when you start looking to Donald Trump to make the world seem normal, you're in trouble for sure.

Back at the Plaza at noon, my eyes refreshed by the pink marble waterfalls and my available credit shaved down to a sliver by a gifted shop assistant who had told me I was just 'Doo-awling' in the raw silk 'paaant suit' that could go anywhere, anytime and was 'Goo-awgous' with my colouring, I hurried to the elevator to hide the bag up in my room. I had been flattered – I'd never thought of myself as having 'colouring' before – but looked at soberly that was no reason to buy a grey trouser suit that made me look like a check-out supervisor. Patrice and Jasmine must never see it. Patrice had been right: I shouldn't have spoken to anyone or opened my purse. In fact, the trouser suit wasn't the only way I was getting walked over here. Even forgetting about the corpses, cannibalism, and zombie Zion, I couldn't really be said to be steering this deal. I was just going wherever Patrice, Jasmine, Clovis, Bradley, Kenny, Halford Meer, and Mr Jankel cared to roll me. The only thing I *had* managed to achieve for myself was to get the supporters of The Widow away from the Husband's Best Friend.

Downstairs again, in the palm court, I rounded a pillar and found them.

'Surprise!' sang three happy voices. Jasmine, Patrice and, of course, Phil were well into what I hoped was their first bottle of wine.

No, I thought. Not that much of a surprise really. Pretty much par for the course, if you asked me.

Chapter 8

The Night of the Baby Turtles

'I just couldn't stay away from you,' said Phil, and then after a pause added, 'all.' The smiles on Jasmine's and Patrice's faces faltered then redoubled and the sickly grin I had managed to hoist to my lips disappeared completely. Multiple Flirty Phil, my least favourite Phil of the entire set.

'Seriously,' I said. 'What are you doing here?'

'Patrice invited me,' he said, blowing a kiss to her and making her twinkle. 'And besides, there's an enormous wine-growing area in upstate New York.'

'Uh-huh,' I said. 'How far from Manhattan exactly?'

He grinned.

'A six-hour drive,' he said. 'So, yes, I admit, there's also Columbia, Princeton, Harvard and Yale in the vicinity. An untapped market as lush as a maple tree bursting with syrup in spring.'

'Phil, no!' I wailed. 'Those are Ivy League colleges. There's no way there would be a market for your … I don't even know what to call it … there.'

'That's a good point, Phil,' said Jasmine solemnly, nodding. 'We're talking about the kids who will become the lawyers, bankers and brokers of all our tomorrows. None of them would ever dream of buying a little advantage.'

'A wasted trip,' said Patrice, with her mouth twitching. 'Oh, sit down and have a glass of wine, Verity. It's Chablis and it's delicious.'

'French Chablis?' I asked and had the satisfaction of seeing Phil wince.

'Come off it, Vert,' he said. 'Before, when I thought you were a sweet unworldly posy-maker that was one thing, but since you came clean about those gladioli and admitted you're in the same dog-eat-dog world as the rest of us I don't really see where you get off.'

'But I hate it,' I told him, sitting down and slumping a little. 'I keep trying to get my boss to sell these beautiful old roses: Gloire de Dijon, Albertine, Rosa Mundi. Gorgeous, blowsy, billowy things with a scent that would knock your head off. And do you know what she says? She says: no vase life. You might as well have plastic and be done with it, I say. And do you know what she says to *that*? She says we do a good trade in fakes – or "faux" as she insists on calling them – and so people have high expectations if they're going to shell out for fresh instead. It makes me sick, the whole thing.'

'Actually,' said Phil, 'you're wrong about essays, but as far as roses go, you might have a point.'

'It's not about things being fake,' said Patrice.

'Of course it is,' I said. 'People don't want to have to dead-head, refill the water, salvage the long-lasters, move them to a smaller vase when half the original bunch is wilted. They just want the look. They want a dozen identical stems they can plonk with a sachet of powder in the water and forget about them for a fortnight.'

'It's nothing to do with fakes,' Patrice insisted. 'Dead-heading and refilling and changing the water is creating an illusion too, just like using plastic flowers is, really. It's all about taste.'

'True,' said Jasmine. 'Take tits.' Phil perked up like a dog who'd heard his lead being unhooked from the back of a door. 'There are real tits. Beautiful ones and all the other kinds. The empty purse, the banana, the tote bag.'

'Bad boobs have names?' I said.

'Whatever. Then there are fake tits, beautiful ones – indistinguishable from real – and all the others. Grapefruits, beach balls, life vests, porn stars.' Phil was sitting with a spear of asparagus halfway to his mouth, dripping egg yolk on to his lap, spellbound. 'Patrice is on the money,' said Jasmine. 'It's nothing to do with fakeness, everything to do with taste.'

'You could be right,' said Phil, coming back to life again and staring very hard at Jasmine's face, willing himself not to look down a bit and wonder. I was doing the same. 'If only someone would do a really good smear campaign on the forecourt carnation, we could have a flower farm in Cornwall again. And the world would be the place it was and should be.' He finally ate the asparagus, biting off its head with a snap.

'Hmm,' I said to him. 'Has it escaped you that you're sitting eating asparagus in October? If the world was the place it used to be, you'd be dipping turnips into that boiled egg.'

'I'm doing my bit for the third world,' said Phil. 'Some of my mother's neighbours in Kenya depend on the Plaza lunch menu to send their kids to school.'

'That's right,' said Jasmine, leaning in. 'You said your mother has a farm there.'

'She does,' said Phil. 'Lovely spot. Well worth a visit sometime.'

Jasmine lit up like a set of fairy lights, while Patrice's smile faded and she attempted to look coldly unperturbed. Her face was perfect for looking unperturbed, but she wasn't well placed to do the coldness. Her mouth and her eyes were permanently turned up at the corners, living testament to the flick of the surgeon's wrist, so that when her mood was doleful she looked, behind her perky face, kind of hijacked sometimes.

Phil, of course, was preening himself like an oiled duck, loving it.

But they couldn't be serious, I told myself, when I was alone again. Neither of them could. I was standing at my window, after lunch, looking down at the ice rink, watching an ambulance crew with a stretcher slithering across to pick up yet another casualty and cart them off to the emergency room. All around on the footpaths, business people were striding along with phones clamped to their heads. Homeless people were shambling up and down with bottles clamped to their lips and upper east side mummies were sauntering at toddler speed with minds, I imagined, clamped to their coming divorces. I took a swig from my water bottle. I was still one city behind; I had spent a week in LA dehydrated, now I was in New

York guzzling Evian and next week back home I would probably be mainlining espresso and walking twice as fast as everyone else.

I told myself that Patrice was only cultivating Phil because she had fallen in love with the idea of England and he was the only bit of it around and Jasmine, *surely*, was only acting on instinct, on reflex even, not used to seeing a man flirting who wasn't flirting with her. She couldn't really be considering him. *Could* she? Could someone like Jasmine really look at someone like Phil – not a gambler, nor a nerd, nor an actor, nor a gangster – and think he wasn't a loser either, one of the very few?

A knock came at my door, making me clunk my head against the windowpane.

'Ow,' I said.

'Vee?' said Jasmine's voice. 'Can I come in?'

'Nothing's happened,' I said when she'd sat down. 'Nobody's called me all day. I'm beginning to think Clovis is right, you know, I scared them all off somehow.'

'Nah,' said Jasmine. 'It's still cooking. Believe me. I might hate my business, but I know my business. I'm the fourth generation of my family in this business.'

'You're the fourth generation of your family to be a script sniffer?' I said. 'A talent scout? Did they even have movies four generations ago?'

'Hey,' said Jasmine. 'What can I tell you? We're Italians, we marry young. Which brings me to my point.' She subjected me to a long quizzical stare and I could feel my cheeks flushing. What had she heard about my marriage? Who from? What was I going to say?

'It's Phil,' she said. I nodded, glumly. Of course. He had told her. 'I don't know how to read you guys, so I thought I better ask if I can go for it.'

'Go for *Phil*?'

'Woah! OK, forget it,' said Jasmine. 'But I should warn you that you're not sending out the right signals. You need to mark your territory a lot stronger if you want everyone else to back off.'

I stared at her. Her hair gleamed like treacle, her eyes sparkled like chips of jet, her teeth glittered as she flashed me a grin. I thought back to Phil at lunchtime, hair in greasy hanks, eyes bloodshot, egg yolk on his chin. What was she thinking?

'Seriously?' I said. 'You would walk into a party, where people know you, with Phil on your arm?'

'No way,' said Jasmine. 'The guy is a walking "before" picture from every makeover show there ever was. But it's like real estate, Vee. You invest in potential and do the work yourself. A hairstylist, an orthodontist, two days in a spa and a trip to Barney's and Phil could look great.'

'You *can't* be—'

'I am,' said Jasmine. 'I told you I want out. How much further out could I get than Phil?'

'All the same,' I said. 'I wouldn't if I were you.' Jasmine raised her eyebrows and waited. I thought furiously. 'I know things about Phil that I don't want to tell you,' I told her, 'but if you knew them too, you wouldn't either. Trust me, you really would not.'

'I know a lot about Phil,' said Jasmine. 'The guy's not exactly inscrutable, is he? His family is broke and dysfunctional; he plays tricks and cheats for money; he's the worst flirt I ever met in my life. That's what I like: all the bad stuff is right there in your face from the get-go. What else could there be?'

'I wish I could tell you,' I said. 'But I really can't. Trust me.' I could tell from her face that it wasn't going in. 'It's tied up with Kim,' I said at last, putting a break in my voice. She looked unimpressed to hear it. 'And anyway,' I said, 'it's Patrice he's got his eye on.'

'That won't happen,' said Jasmine.

'How can you be so sure?'

'Believe me,' she drawled. 'You might know Philly but I know Patrice and that will *not* happen, OK,' she said, standing and flipping her hair the way they only ever do on shampoo adverts. 'To work. I'm gonna ask him to come ride the merry-go-round in the park.'

'Promise me one thing,' I blurted, scurrying after her as she strode to the door. 'Don't mention—'

'Kim, I know, I know,' said Jasmine. 'Give me some credit, Vee.'

I cursed her as she disappeared out of the door. Her and her perky, can-do, not-a-problem, Oprahfied self-belief. I would never get her to stay away from Phil. But, I thought to myself, walking back into my room, I could probably persuade Phil to stay away from her and concentrate on Patrice instead, and I could certainly persuade Patrice to ignore his efforts – how much longer could this trip last anyway? Phil would have to go back to California soon and if Patrice got her way she would be leaving for England. I could hold them all steady until then. After all, I was the common link among them; they shared nothing except through me.

There was no answer from Patrice's room when I stopped by before dinner to begin the anti-Phil campaigning; no one there at Jasmine's either. I stood in the hallway with my hands on my hips, wondering, then with a groan, the puzzle was solved. Phil hadn't mentioned where he was staying and it would have been the YMCA if he was footing the bill, but Patrice had said it herself – she was sick of holding back and getting nowhere and money didn't make her a bad person. I buzzed down to reception.

'Mr Coates is in Room 1721,' said the desk clerk. 'Would you like me to put you through?'

Room 1721 was on a higher floor, with thicker carpet, older paintings and bigger lilies – stamens snipped out – than you got down on my ordinary, everyday, nicest-hotel-I'd-ever-imagined floor. I knocked at the door and it was opened by a buzzer. I trudged through the entrance hall past the antique hat stand and jardinières of ferns, crossed the drawing room, skirted the dining room and eventually arrived in a bedroom where, on a bed bigger than my flat, which nevertheless looked rather lost in the expanse of floor, Patrice, Jasmine and Phil were sprawled. I could see at once that they were all fully dressed and they were miles apart – they would have had to stretch even to touch one another with a finger – so whatever they were doing, I knew what it wasn't, but it took me a while to process the details and work out what it *was*. Phil was skimming through a pile of thick books, bristling with Post-it markers, Jasmine was looking at a stapled-together sheaf of paper with a red pen held in her teeth, and Patrice had a laptop propped on her knees and was busily typing.

'No!' I wailed. 'What are you doing? Oh, please tell me you're not!'

'Proofing *Hemingway and the Trope of the Hunter*,' said Jasmine, after spitting out her pen. 'And I must say Phil, it's pretty good. I'm changing the "whilst"s to "although"s and I've killed the bit where you say "you drive a coach and horses through the theory", but otherwise, it's pretty good. I could buy a kid from Boston writing this.'

'Oh Phil,' I said, sinking down on to a vacant patch of bed. 'How could you?'

'They wanted to help,' said Phil. 'And I'm busy. This essay's due on Friday and I'm really behind.'

'No, you're not,' I said to him. 'You don't have an essay due on Friday because you're not a student at . . .' I twitched the essay rubric away from him and read the logo. 'Columbia. Patrice, I'm surprised at you.' Patrice, who had kept frenziedly typing, now looked up and flashed me a smile.

'I'm comparing two methods of market modelling,' she said. 'And I'm amazed at how it's all coming back to me. I had completely forgotten I knew how to do this!'

'OK, I'm done here,' said Jasmine. 'She wrote the essay and the essay was finished,' said Jasmine. 'She gave the finished essay back to Phil. It felt good. The essay was good and finished and back with Phil. How did we ever fall for that guy?'

'I loved Hemingway when I was a child,' said Patrice. 'Nick and the fish and the two-hearted river? Loved it.'

'Hated it,' said Jasmine, 'and I'm right. Now I need a big drink and a bloody steak.'

'You go down and I'll follow,' said Phil. 'I need to call the old man and sound like someone who's in LA on a wine course.'

'Devious pig,' I said.

When he joined us later, he was frowning and troubled.

'Everything OK?' I asked him as he sat down. He must have been fiddling with his hair while on the phone; it was sticking up in twists and I could see that both Jasmine and Patrice were longing to reach over and smooth it down.

'Strangely, no answer,' he said. 'Which is most unlike them at this time of day. Nobody in the house, the *cave*, all mobiles off. Nothing from the coven. Has anyone seen a newspaper today? Has a freak wave carried off the Cornish coast?'

'The coven?' said Jasmine.

'The land of sisters,' said Phil. 'My first stepmother's house. My father is often to be found there, since the ex can cook and the current can't. But not today.' He frowned and clicked a little tune with his tongue against his teeth.

'You're not seriously worried, are you Phil?' I asked him. 'They're out, so what?'

'It's the *vendange*,' said Phil, then seeing our blank looks, he relented. 'The tail end of the picking season. He's busy with the *pressage*, getting it all *en chais* – the one moment of the year where he has a chance for something to go right – and he never stirs from the place till it's done. That's half the reason I was so sure he would ring me up in California and start hassling me and why I thought I'd better call him first. Bored and spoiling for a fight, you know? And it's half-term. The sisters never go out. Not all at once and not without their mobiles.'

'Well,' said Jasmine. 'Maybe the third wife has run off with a gardener and your dad is face-down drunk in his own wine cellar and the ex and her daughters are out in the yard, quietly unloading a van full of their stuff to move back in and they didn't hear the phone.'

'You've met them!' cried Phil, his frown smoothing. 'Ignore me – I'm being a bore.' But although he tried, he never managed to get the worry out of his eyes and he left right after pudding, without even ordering a brandy and moaning about not being allowed a cigar.

'What a sweet, caring man,' Jasmine said, gazing after him.

'You can tell a lot about a person from how they are with their family,' Patrice murmured, which wasn't very diplomatic since we were busy trying to put together a deal that would let Jasmine shake off her family for ever.

Jasmine didn't miss the dig; she frowned at Patrice, really knitting her brows, probably because she knew Patrice couldn't do it back. I said goodnight and left them to it.

My phone was ringing when I got back to my room.

'Still no one around,' said Phil, when I lifted the receiver. 'Should I be worried, Vert?'

'Of course not,' I told him.

'Then why am I so worried?'

'Guilty conscience? At last?'

'Oh, gimme a break,' he said doing quite a creditable Jasmine impersonation and hung up. The phone rang again before my hand was even off it.

'What now?' I said.

'It's Clovis. And I'll tell you "what now". Sign the contract is what now.'

'Well,' I began, 'before you speak too soon, let me fill you in on what happened this morning. I had a meeting with three executives and every one of them told me that they had bought my book long before the film rights were even an issue and they had all read it and they all loved it. One of them even described how she'd kept the copy and could put her hand on it right this minute on the bookshelf in her apartment.'

'Bought a book that doesn't exist?' said Clovis. 'Who were these people?'

I didn't want to say they were agents, so I said in a haughty voice:

'Junior development executives. You know what the movie business is like, all first names and no details? But my point is this: if all three of them were sucking up hard enough to lie about it, that means I've set off a hell of a zzub. And before you say it wasn't fair on our buyer, just let me remind you that our buyer has upped her offer fairly substantially since the zzub started to tickle and I don't think it's topped out yet. Nothing like.'

There was a long silence at the other end.

'Have you spoken to Jasmine about this?' said Clovis, at last.

I had no idea how to answer *that* one.

'About what?' I settled for at last.

'Suffice to say, Verity, love,' said Clovis in her patient voice, 'that the buyer hasn't so much upped her offer as thrown the whole deal up in the air and started again. Which wouldn't have happened if you had signed the damn thing when you landed like I told you. This may well all go belly up now, I hope you realise that.'

'So we go with another buyer,' I said, trying to sound breezy. 'Where's the harm?'

At the other end of the phone I heard a sound like a tiger eating a toaster, the unmistakable snarling crunch of Clovis biting the mouthpiece of her hands-free phone. I said a gentle goodbye and hung up softly. What I needed, I decided, was some good old fashioned manic optimism, and the voice of someone who was pleased to hear mine.

'Hi,' I said as Bradley answered.

'Hey, hey, hey,' said Bradley. 'Live from Manhattan we give you! So, tell me all about it.'

'You're kidding,' I said. 'You mean you don't know?'

'Oh all right, all right, all right, if you insist. I'll tell you. You were punctual to a fault, dressed in blue with matt black accessories.'

'They're not matt,' I said. 'I just hadn't polished them.'

'And you were very British, very deadpan, very professional. You listened with respectful attention to all their suggestions.'

'I listened with my jaw on the floor,' I corrected. 'Have you *heard* their suggestions?'

'Uh-huh. Kind of out there, but when you think about it, gross-out comedies, horror, and tear-jerkers are big coconuts. If you can knock off all three at once with a gross-out horror-jerker you got a licence to print your own money.'

'Hold on,' I said. 'Where does the tear-jerker come in?'

'What do you mean? It's right there in the original. It's a tragedy, a doomed and lonely quest. It's *Cyrano de Bergerac* meets *March of the Penguins*.'

'Don't remind me of that film!' I squeaked.

'C de B?' said Bradley. 'You have nose issues? I always said that nose should have had a higher rating than the rest of the movie. Talk about separate billing – it was obscene.'

'Not that one, look it doesn't matter.'

'*March of the Penguins*?'

'Shut *up*!' I pleaded. 'I don't want to talk about it. And anyway, it's not a tear-jerker.'

'It's hardly a comedy, hon,' said Bradley. 'If only it was. I mean a gross-out horror romcom-jerker is a whole extra coconut.'

'It was supposed to be a thriller,' I said. 'An action thriller.'

'Really?' said Bradley his voice an octave lower than I had ever heard it before. 'Slowly crawling up a hole in the ice? A thriller? OK.'

'Hey, it's no worse than slowly crawling through air vents in a dirty vest,' I said. I always made out I hated being flattered, but I had got used to everyone saying how much they loved my book, even when I knew they were lying, and it turns out I preferred it to this. 'Or slowly getting everyone into lifeboats before a ship goes down.'

'Please,' said Bradley. 'Don't diss *Titanic* in front of me. Anyway, my cousin says that Mr Meer is telling everyone in the LA office that Melanie said to Mr Jankel that she would be happy to have you on the development team. They're very art house highbrow in the New York office and they think it looks better to have the original writer on the script all the way to the door.'

'Ah, that's what it was,' I said. 'They threw me a little with the corpses, but now that I know it's a highbrow art house thing ...'

Bradley assured me not to worry, told me that the staff in the New York office were used to dealing with all kinds of people and they wouldn't judge me. How, I asked myself, could one and the same person completely get Monty Python and yet not see through me?

I wasn't aware of choosing to dial again. It was almost as though the process began with Clovis and Brad and natural forces wouldn't let me stop without completing the set. Or maybe it was nothing more than not wanting to be alone with my thoughts.

'Mr Daateng?' I said.

'Kenny,' he answered. 'So tell me what you thought of those suits over at IFA. Tell me you didn't buy their shtick.'

'Do you know what their shtick is? Not snow, not desert plains, not subway shafts. Interplanetary mausoleums.'

'Yeah,' said Kenny. 'I heard. The thing to remember is they are not a studio and they are not a production company. They're an agency. Don't be fooled by the size of their development team; all the effort goes into getting you to square one, where a studio starts to look at you. Well, I've got you past there already. I've got a studio who's had a good look and is very interested in talking.'

'And before I met you I had a producer who had looked and talked and was very interested in signing,' I said. 'I'm going backwards here.'

'Only every third step,' said Kenny. 'That's good progress, believe me.'

After that, there was no one else I could think of to phone and with a shudder I realised I had been so distracted I hadn't got undressed when I came in. My palms began to sweat and I could feel my heart knocking in my chest like a pipe with an airlock. I tried to think about something else – anything else – but what Brad had said just wouldn't go away and I could feel it all joining up, getting soft, starting to fill me. I tried to think about Patrice, but all I could remember was Patrice saying she didn't see her family any more. I tried to think about Jasmine, but all I could hear was Jasmine saying she had to get away from her family too and Phil couldn't find his family, not even on the phone. I wouldn't think about it. I would not. I refused to. I couldn't help it. Here it came.

It was Sunday night, bath night, clean sheets night, and we should have spent it tucked up together in Granny's big chair, me in my pyjamas and her in her curlers, drinking Horlicks and watching nature red in tooth and claw. Granny, like all adults I knew, approved of David Attenborough for children. None of them seemed to suspect what might happen to the minds of a generation subjected to the gang wars of the macaques and the ripping apart of the springboks every Sunday night for years. To be fair, though, in my pyjamas, on Granny's knee, high on Horlicks and setting lotion, I could cope. Only, tonight was different. Granny had been out in the hall, whispering on the phone since *Songs of Praise*, and I hadn't had my bath, and now David Attenborough was talking about the coming of spring and the first of the baby turtles was hatching up in the dunes and beginning to plod down the beach to the sea.

The fire was dying down. Granny was making noises, gulping as if she was trying to drink hot tea too fast and hurting her throat. The turtles were heaving themselves towards the breakers and endless, relentless battalions of gulls, huge and screeching, were swooping in and carrying them away. I couldn't tell which whispering voice was David Attenborough talking about the turtles and which was Granny talking about me, and all the time the gulls were swooping, pulling back their heads and then crack! crack! crack! drilling the points of their beaks into the shells and the baby turtles kept plodding and Granny was gulping and David Attenborough was whispering and something I heard or something I saw – I'll never remember – made me, at long last, scream.

The next thing I knew the telly was off, the phone was back in its cradle and I was sitting on Granny's knee on the shut toilet lid in the bathroom, while she rubbed me clean and dry.

'I'm sorry, I'm sorry,' I said, shaking with shame.

'It doesn't matter,' said my granny. 'Look: all better now.' She folded the towel so that the bit she had used to wipe me was in the middle and she dropped it into the laundry basket beside her.

'It's late,' she said. 'Too late for a bath now. I'll just pop you straight into bed and bring you a nice hot drink.' She was smiling at me and her voice was soft but her face looked like drunk men's faces in the streets sometimes, grey except where it was red and, all over, kind of puffy.

'I'll not get you clean jammies tonight, though,' she said. 'Since you've not had your bath.' And she stretched over to the basket, where she had just put the wet towel, picked out my pyjamas from last week and shook them. In bed, in my dirty pyjamas and clean sheets, waiting for my Horlicks, listening to Granny sniffing in the kitchen below, I wondered about that last baby turtle on its way down the beach, but it was too late; the programme was finished, and even if I asked Granny what had happened, there was no way for her to find out.

I knocked at Patrice's door and she called out, asking who it was.

'Verity,' I said. 'Can I come in, please?'

There was a long pause and then an awkward laugh.

'OK, but don't look at me.' She was hiding behind the door as she opened it and she went straight into the bathroom, telling me to sit down and get myself a drink. I had taken two gulps of whisky and was shuddering when she appeared at the bathroom doorway, looking very white and blanker than ever.

'Are you OK?' she said.

'Not really,' I answered. 'Are you? You look kind of …' But I saw as she advanced towards me that it was only that she had no eyebrows, lashes, cheeks or lips.

'You've caught me with just my foundation,' she said. 'I look like the creature from beyond the grave.'

'You do a bit.' She had one of my wrists in her hand and was taking my pulse. 'How do you manage to remove your make-up item by item? How do you get your blusher off without your foundation coming away too?'

'I wasn't taking off,' she said. 'I was putting back on. Nobody sees me bare faced, Verity. But nobody.' This was vanity on a scale I couldn't dream of, but I said nothing. 'Now, tell me what happened. I'll get you some Advil.'

Could I tell her? Could I tell her about the gap between your skin where the outside starts and the bit inside that you have to watch out for, how you need to shrink it down so none of it touches and there's a gap all round? Could I tell her that for me this shrivelled little thing was a peach pit, as small and hard as that, as easy to hide? Would she understand? Would anyone, who hadn't been brought up by my granny, with her digestion horror stories, understand? I know it was Granny because the other way I think about it is as a tiny blob of very cold gum chewed hard and stuck somewhere. And sometimes I feel angry for the litter she left lying around my brain, but mostly I'm just glad it's a peach pit or a blob of cold gum and not, say, an inner child.

When she came back, it had stopped trembling and was safely tucked away. I managed to smile at her.

'I had a bad dream, that's all,' I said, trying to sound calm. Actually, I realised, I wasn't just trying to sound calm, I was beginning to feel calm too. If my granny was a mug of Horlicks in front of a fire, sometimes with skin on top and embers jumping out and one side always colder than the other, Patrice was more like … drifting in a punt on a very still lake, sipping rainwater and listening to a harp being played on the far shore. Even without doing anything, even when she was in the bathroom and you couldn't see her, she just exuded a bottomless, endless calm. Maybe it came from Pilates; I wouldn't know. 'But I wanted to talk to you anyway,' I said.

'Fire away,' she invited. She had brought her make-up case with her and opened it on the table at her side. It fanned up and out in three tiers of trays like a stage-set by Busby Berkeley. Patrice unclipped a lip brush from inside the lid and opened a lipstick tube. I had never seen anyone, outside of a professional beautician, actually putting on lipstick with a fine brush, like they tell you to.

'It's about Phil,' I said. 'You said he was a sweet, kind caring man and he said he thought you were one in a million and I think we need to talk.'

'We don't,' said Patrice, and she sighed hugely. 'It'll never happen.'

'Yeah, that's what Jasmine said.'

'About her and Phil?' said Patrice, her eyes narrowing the only way they could which was to bunch her collagen-padded cheeks upwards. She looked a bit like Jack Lemmon and not to be crossed.

'About you and Phil,' I said.

Patrice released the Jack Lemmon squeeze on her cheeks and blinked slowly.

'Well,' she said. 'Jasmine's right.'

'Why?' I said, relieved but puzzled.

Patrice regarded me solemnly before she spoke. Her face was perfect, dewy and fresh looking.

'I'll never marry out again,' she said at last.

'Marry out?' I said. 'What does that mean?'

'Did you forget that I'm Jewish?'

'I did,' I admitted. 'It's your name that does it.'

'It doesn't exactly reek of the shtetl,' said Patrice, with a laugh.

'Were you christened Patrice?'

'No,' she said slowly. 'I'm from a strange little Jewish sect that's not so much with the christening, don't you know.'

I slapped a hand to my head and groaned, but she was laughing.

'God,' I said. 'I feel like my granny. It took me the last decade to get her to refer to a particular chocolate shade as "N-word brown". So were you … I have no idea what Jewish people do to baby girls. I mean, is that the name on your birth certificate? Patrice? Only it sounds so Irish. Especially with Carmichael.'

'Carmichael's my married name,' said Patrice.

'Oh, yeah,' I said. I was watching her painting a line above her lashes now, with an even finer brush. Then I remembered something. 'Didn't you say your husband was from Milan?'

She was breathing heavily and trying to hide it; I could hear her nostrils whistling.

'They changed it at Ellis Island,' she said. 'Carmichael was the nearest sounding thing.'

'Ah,' I said. 'That explains it. And Patrice?'

She lowered the lid of her make-up case and looked at me over the top of it.

'Wouldn't this be easier if you shone a bright light in my eyes?' she asked. 'Or at least dripped some water?'

'I'm sorry,' I said, and she stretched out one of her bare feet and poked me with a toe to show me she was only joking. She had, I noticed, very ugly feet, exactly the kind of feet my granny always warned me that you got from wearing beautiful shoes.

'My name was chosen for St Patrick,' she said.

'Why? When you were born on the fourth of July?' I said. Patrice laughed and fluttered a hand near her throat.

'It was more about New York than about Ireland.' She had finished the construction and she shut her make-up case and rested her hands on it. 'So, you see, even if my name is Irish and should really be Italian, I'm as Jewish as Jackie Mason and there's no need for you to talk to me about Phil,' he said. 'He's all yours.'

'I don't want him!' I said. 'Why does everyone keep saying that? I wouldn't touch him with a ten-foot pole,' I took a deep breath and shuddered, 'knowing what I know.' Patrice was definitely going to rise to it, definitely going to ask me what I knew but before she could there was a knock at the door and she swished across the carpet to open it, her robe rippling out behind her. I heard Phil's voice.

'Sorry to disturb you,' he said. 'Is Verity there?'

Patrice turned and led him into the room, smirking at me, her eyes twinkling.

'Phil,' she said. 'For you.'

As soon as I saw him I knew something was wrong.

'Philly?' I said.

'I finally got through,' he told me, coming forward and dropping into the chair where Patrice had been sitting.

'And? Where were they all?'

'At the hospital,' said Phil. 'With their mobiles switched off. He's had a stroke, Vert. The sodding stupid old bastard has gone and had a stroke. They were trying to get me in California all day to tell me.'

'Are you going home?' I asked him. He nodded. 'Do you want me to come?' He nodded again.

'That's what I was trying to find you to ask,' he said. 'I don't think I can do all the tickets and packing. I feel as if I've been hit on the head with a shovel.'

I made that useless, caring face people make – eyebrows up, mouth turned down – but Patrice swung into action.

'Pour Phil a brandy,' she said to me, as she picked up her phone. She was on to JFK in under a minute and had a car booked in about as much time again. Then she phoned downstairs and spoke very firmly. 'Boil the water, until it's coming up the sides of the pot and then pour it in *on top* of the teabags. And use at least four. Put the lid on and wrap it up to keep it warm. I don't know – use napkins or something. There's a fifty dollar tip in this if you get it right. Now move it.'

'I do love the way you Americans get exactly what you want,' said Phil.

'It's an emergency,' said Patrice. 'A Brit in shock needs tea. I've watched enough BBC to know that much. Now, Verity,' she turned to me. 'You better pack. The car's going to be here in forty minutes. If I'm finished packing before you I'll do Phil's. If not you take care of it.'

'If you're finished packing what?'

'Everything,' said Patrice grimly. 'I'm not coming back.'

'You're coming to England with us? Right now?'

'No time like it,' said Patrice.

'Has Clovis agreed about the move?' I asked her. Patrice glanced at Phil and then looked back at me, a far-off expression on her face, like Clint Eastwood on a horse, on a rocky bluff, looking for outlaws or trying to keep cheroot smoke out of his eyes.

'She will,' she said.

'And you're sure it's the right thing? I mean, I know you've looked at a lot of websites and there's your ethos totality angle, but ...'

'For tonight,' said Patrice, 'let's just worry about Phil.'

Chapter 9
Napoleon at Waterloo

I raced downstairs to tell Jasmine. She could stop this.

'Jeez,' she said. 'Bummer. How old is this guy?'

'Late fifties,' I said. 'Sixty maybe.'

'Jeez.'

'And Phil asked me to go with him.'

'Of course.'

'And Patrice is coming too. To England. With Phil and me.'

It worked. It worked like an electric shock would have worked, from where I was standing. Jasmine's eyes flashed, her fists bunched, her jaw contracted so tight, so fast, that I heard her teeth snap.

'Oh she is, is she?' she said, when she managed to unclench her jaw again. 'Well, let's just see.' And she stepped out into the corridor, slammed the door shut behind her and stalked away towards the lifts.

'Jas?' I said, scurrying after her. 'Have you got your room key? Haven't you just locked yourself out?' I caught up with her just in time to see her poke the lift button so hard that the scarlet tip of her fingernail pinged off and landed on the floor. She didn't seem to notice it; she waited, drumming a foot and breathing like a bull, for a second or two and then wrenched open the door to the stairway and began pounding upwards to Patrice's floor. Now she had lost me. She was California fit and angry enough to lift a car. Panting, I went back, caught the lift and pitched out at Patrice's landing, neck and neck with her. Patrice answered her door smiling beatifically and, glancing over her shoulder with an expression of concern before pulling the door to, she joined Jasmine and me in the hallway.

'Yes?' she said mildly and, before Jasmine had time to catch her breath and start in on her, she laid a hand on her arm and said, 'But can you keep it down, Jazzie? I don't want Phil disturbed.'

'Don't call me that,' said Jasmine. 'And get your mitts off me too.' Patrice put her hands behind her back and waited for more. 'Were you just going to sneak away?' she hissed. 'Weren't you even going to tell me?'

'I would have called,' said Patrice.

'Yeah, sure, right, from the plane,' said Jasmine. 'Listen, Pat—'

'Don't call me that.'

'Listen, *Pat*,' said Jasmine again, 'you're not leaving with this hanging in the air. I took the relocation plan to Clovis. She said no. I agreed to keep trying, but ... you can't just steamroller your way into a completely new deal. It takes time and finesse, and negotiation. You can't just up stakes and go.'

'I'm taking Phil home,' said Patrice. 'Don't be so—'

'And that's another thing,' said Jasmine. 'You're buying an option on a book. Where do you get the idea that you own rights in Phil? Huh?'

Patrice ignored her and turned to me, smiling sweetly. 'Would you go in and see that he's OK? I don't want him to get upset again, what with a long flight ahead and everything.'

'You're not his mother,' said Jasmine. 'It's not up to you to see that he's OK.' She turned to me. 'Vee, go check on Phil for me, will you?'

I didn't want to go – I didn't want to miss any of this, but I hardly had a choice with both of them on me.

Inside, Phil was still in the same chair with an empty teacup in his hands and a tray on the footstool before him. I looked at the lump of napkins, the swaddled teapot, and marvelled at what an air of authority and a fifty-dollar tip could do. If I'd had even a fraction of Patrice's chutzpah, I could have blagged my way into the Beverly Hills Hotel, where Patrice would have come to have lunch with Jasmine and me, so I would never have met Kenny Daateng, Bradley (Honey) or Phil, who would therefore have been in LA when his stepmother called him and would not now be dying of guilt and worry and wondering if he was ever going to see his father again. However, I told myself, he would also be flying home cattle class and all alone instead of taking me even if, as the fight I could hear hissing and whistling away in the corridor suggested, he was going to have to do without Patrice after all.

'He'll be OK,' I said. 'He's a young man and a stroke's just more or less a wake-up call, isn't it?'

'He's sixty,' said Phil. 'He smokes like a train, drinks like a fish and uses a sit-on lawnmower to get from the house to the car.'

'What about the nubile South American?' I said. 'She must have been keeping him in shape with the odd workout?'

Phil laughed, but the laugh turned into a sigh before it was over and his chin settled back down on to his chest. Outside in the hallway the hissing and spitting had stopped to be replaced by a low grumble and presently Jasmine and Patrice came back in. Patrice went back to the phone and Jasmine sat down on the footstool in front of Phil and gathered him into her arms.

'I'm coming with you,' she murmured into his hair.

'That's very kind of you,' he said, sounding muffled, making no effort to move his face away from where it was clasped to her bosom. I didn't think I could stomach this, so I left.

I wouldn't go so far as to say Patrice and Jasmine had made up by the time we were in the air. Phil, knocked out by shock, brandy and a pill produced by Jasmine at check-in, slept through the night, splayed out like a dead bear on a roof rack in his first-class seat, his head lolling, mouth wide open and occasionally dribbling, feet hanging over the end of the footrest and waving gently at each rattling snore. Every time the stewardess went past, a quick frown tugged at her face to see Phil's big toes and long yellow toenails poking through the holes in his socks and more than once she dropped a blanket over them, but he soon kicked it off with a grunt and went back to the drooling, waving and snoring again. On either side of him Jasmine and Patrice flicked through thick magazines and watched for any sign of him waking up, ready to jump in with an extra pillow should he need it.

I shot a surreptitious look at each of them and another at Phil and tried to figure it out. Jasmine couldn't want Phil, not really. She was just annoyed that he preferred Patrice. And Patrice didn't want

Phil; she had practically told me so. And anyway, would it matter if one of them, or even both, got close enough to him to start talking about me? Would it really matter if they found out I wasn't a widow after all? Would it matter if Bradley Honey and IFA found out that The Widow was actually The Dumped? If Kenny Daateng found out that the Story was anything but True? If these two women who had taken me to their hearts like no one in my life ever before, discovered that I was too ashamed to admit I was just like them? If they found out they had been grovelling for forgiveness for being less than open to someone who had topped their whoppers by a mile? Would it matter if Clovis found out that all this trouble that was mucking up her careful deal had not, in fact, come out of nowhere like a plummeting boulder of sheer dumb luck but had been heaved on to its trajectory by them and that I knew all along?

Yes, I decided, it would.

So ... could I rely on Jasmine and Patrice each exerting her own gravitational pull on Phil to make sure he stayed suspended between them and didn't actually touch down on one or the other? Clearly not. I remember Kim telling me about him before we had ever met.

'He should be the most hated man I know,' Kim said. 'He two-times, three-times, forgets their names, stands them up and yet everywhere we go old girlfriends fall on his neck and call him Pippin.' He gave a laugh that bounced my head off his chest – we were having this conversation in bed one Sunday morning. 'You've got to love him,' he said fondly. 'I mean, he's excellent entertainment value and he never keeps any of it to himself.'

'Hmmm,' I said. 'I don't know. *I've* got to love him, clearly. I've got to love him because he's your oldest friend, but I'm not sure you shouldn't cast him out now that you're with me. He's a very bad influence. He must be.'

Kim growled into my neck, nipping me with his teeth and making me giggle.

'Thank God you're joking,' he said. 'There are plenty of girls who would say that and mean it, you know.'

*

Of course, *she* hadn't let Kim keep his oldest friend, who might be a bad influence on him. And actually, although it pained me to put her in a good light, she had a point. After all, when I was joking about it with Kim, I really was joking – I was so complacent back then – but *she* knew for a fact that Kim was a cheat since it was her he had cheated with and so of course she wouldn't want to see him hanging around with the world's most notorious unrepentant hopeless philanderer. Second-generation hopeless philanderer at that. What *she* didn't know, of course, was that while Phil had no morals of his own, for himself, he had believed in Kim and me and if he ever got the chance to get Kim away from *her* it wouldn't be to lead him astray; it would be to lead him back to the straight and narrow.

Which was a comfort in a way; it's always nice to have a champion for your cause, but who wants to be the straight and narrow when you get right down to it, really? Who wants her husband to be resolutely sticking to the path and just about managing to ignore the winding lanes leading to the tempting grotto of *her*? Let's face it, all any woman ever wants is to be married to Paul Newman. Not literally, although few would put up a struggle, but in the steak and hamburger sense. I didn't want Kim spending his life telling himself that a big, fat, juicy steak, cooked to perfection by a master chef was over-rated and he had perfectly good burgers in the freezer at home.

Helen was talking to the owner of the shop, or rather he was talking and she was listening, nodding slowly and with a great show of concentration. Kim sucked a cube of cheese off a cocktail stick then flipped the cocktail stick into the little dish provided and sighed.

'Well, I think we'll take one, won't we Kimmie?' she said at last.

'Absolutely,' said Kim. 'Sounds delicious.' Both Helen and the shop owner frowned.

'It's an antibacterial breadboard,' she said.

'Mmm,' said Kim. 'I love bread with no bacteria. Yum, yum.'

Helen sighed ostentatiously and unzipped a compartment in her bag to get her chequebook out.

'We take all cards,' said the shop owner and Kim tuned out as Helen

launched into the explanation of why she preferred to write a cheque. It was an explanation Kim knew well, but if he had ever been called upon to share it with a third party he could have boiled it down to: because a cheque is the only method of payment which, if you rolled really tightly into a tube, would fit up her airtight arse. He was looking along the shelves of wine behind the counter to distract himself and suddenly he pointed.

'Hey!'

'What?' said Helen.

'Trepolgas Ruby Red,' said Kim. 'We'll take a bottle of that.'

'Kimmie,' said Helen, waving the cheque in his face. 'I've already written it out.'

'It's Phil's dad's wine!' said Kim. 'I've never seen it in a proper shop before.'

'Friend of yours?' said the owner.

'Not really,' said Helen. 'Someone my fiancé used to know.'

'Well, between you and me, if you want a bottle you'd better take one now. I won't be reordering. And you'd better decant it and watch out for the sediment. And don't lay it down, because it won't keep.'

'I'm surprised you bought it at all,' said Kim coldly, attempting to stare the man down. Waste of time, obviously. The man had a goatee and it was well known that a man with a goatee was not open to nuances of facial expression and tone of voice, otherwise he wouldn't want his chin to look like a woman's waxed bikini line and he wouldn't be able to ignore everyone he met giving out the subliminal message that he was a prat.

'What's got into you?' said Helen when they were walking back home, with the antibacterial breadboard but without the wine. 'You were almost rude.'

'Almost?' said Kim, stopping and turning around. 'Hang on while I go back and finish the job.' Helen didn't laugh. 'I just hate London food shops, especially on a Saturday afternoon. I work right next door to a twenty-four hour Tesco, for God's sake. And the rugby's on.'

'I know you don't mean that,' said Helen. 'There's no comparison.'

'No,' said Kim. 'In Tesco the bread isn't crawling with bacteria for one thing.'

'It's not like you to be so grumpy,' said Helen.

'I just think we could have bought a bottle of Phil's dad's wine,' Kim said. 'If I started a business I'd expect everyone who knew me to wear it, or visit it, or choke it down. That's what friends are for.'

'He's not a friend though, is he?' said Helen. 'I've never met the man. He's not even on the invitation list for our wedding.'

'Neither's Phil,' said Kim, half under his breath.

'Well then,' said Helen. 'Now stop being such a grumpy-pumps. How can I cheer you up?'

'He was my best man last time.'

'Exactly,' said Helen. 'We agreed. It wouldn't be right.'

'Did I ever tell you the story about my stag night?' Kim said, smiling again at last. 'It's a Verity story in a way. At least, Verity by proxy.'

'What happened?' said Helen.

'We went to Edinburgh to see the rugby. England against Scotland, the week before the wedding. Phil arranged it all. Up on the overnight train, rugby match, pub crawl, posh hotel, plane home. A real 24-carat stag night.'

'You won't be doing anything like that this time,' said Helen, and Kim wished there was a way he could have heard it as a question.

'As you might expect,' he went on, 'I had a drink or two. There's this one street in the middle of Edinburgh – I forget what it's called – with more pubs on it than … well, I forget the statistic but you get the gist. Now, the thing about Scotland is this. Wonderful whisky, absolutely hellish undrinkable beer. But it was my stag party, and I couldn't believe I wasn't going to wash the night away with gallons of beer. So we'd go into one place, I'd have a disgusting pint and then try, say, a gin. Then we'd move on. Try another pint – unspeakable – remember that the gin hadn't seemed to hit the stag-night spot and try a brandy. Then on we'd go. Surely this third place had beer worth putting in the barrels? No? Whisky and Drambuie to take the taste away. And after that it's a bit hazy so everything else I'm going to tell you I heard later from Phil. No point going into all the details; suffice it to say, shortly after midnight Phil and I were to be found standing in our shirtsleeves on a street corner, having been chucked out of the posh hotel.'

'What for?'

'Don't ask. And we couldn't even get the fascist on the desk to let us phone up anyone else from the stag night for help. They wouldn't put us

through. At this point, I apparently mumbled to Phil to phone Verity, which is what he did. He told her more or less the truth: that we were on the street, I had lost my wallet, he had precisely seven pounds left to his name and that I was pretty much too drunk to stand.

'"Where are you?" Verity said.

'Phil looked around, spied a street sign and told her we were at the bottom of Cockburn Street.

'"Hm," said Verity. "Cockburn Street. OK, here's what to do." Just like that. No thinking time, no false starts, just a perfect ingenious, devious, classic Verity scam fully formed in an instant. "There's a restaurant," she said. "Viva Mexico! just up the street and down a lane to the left. Leave Kim outside, go in and either bribe or charm a waitress into either selling or giving you a couple of the paper sombreros they dish out for parties and a couple of empty beer bottles. Then go up the street, turn right, then left, then take the right fork and you'll see the hospital. Ask for directions if you get lost. When you get to the hospital, phone my granny – here's the number – and tell her this: You took Kim for a Mexican meal – wear your sombreros, mind – and he ate kidney beans and had to go to hospital and get his stomach pumped. Use the word haemagglutin; it'll knock her dead." – Verity's granny knew how allergic I am; she was always heavily into ailments and allergies, you know. Rather a hobby of hers – "Tell her," Verity said, "that the sedatives they gave Kim have made him terribly woozy and the hotel won't believe he's not drunk."'

'Did it work?' said Helen.

'Did it! Phil thought she would tell us to jump in a cab and say that she would pay it when we got to her house out in the suburbs, but dear me no! There was her soon-to-be grandson-in-law who'd always seemed so hoity-toity, laid very satisfyingly low with a nice dramatic complaint and turning to her for succour. Also, remember, it was Phil doing the talking. Phil who could charm the birds off the trees. Or in this case, charm an old lady in Portobello into waking up one of her neighbours and demanding that he get dressed and drive into the city centre in the small hours – she doesn't drive – to pick up two stag-night casualties he'd never met in his life. So half an hour later Mr Sangster from next door rolls up, also Granny Drummond with blankets and a flask and Mrs Sangster who presumably hadn't had so much excitement

since Coronation Day. There we were, still in our sombreros still with a couple of Mexican beer bottles in our pockets, Phil looking rather worn out after all the worry and me looking exactly like someone whose throat had almost closed over from a bean allergy and who had then had his stomach pumped.'

'But what a dismal end to your stag night,' Helen said.

'Not at all,' said Kim. 'Not a bit of it. We slept in Granny Drummond's spare room and were greeted the next morning with a port and brandy each to settle us down.'

'First thing in the morning?'

'Land of the gleaming river, land of the purple liver,' sang Kim. 'And then a fry-up that I still dream about sometimes. She even made chips.'

'For breakfast?'

'Land of the deep fried Mars Bar,' sang Phil. 'Scot-land the Brave!'

'Kimmie,' said Helen. 'You're not there now. You can't sing in the street in the daytime in Fulham.'

Kim said nothing.

'And how did you explain why you'd eaten kidney beans in the first place?' Helen asked.

'Oh that was easy,' said Kim. 'I didn't have to explain. She said she sympathised entirely. Said what a terrible dilemma for me – to have to turn their hospitality back in their faces that way saying I was allergic when they'd gone to all the trouble to book me a lovely meal with the special hats and everything. It was exactly what she would have done herself. Granny Drummond's code of honour. I never did work out all the ins and outs of it. All the shades and gradations of mortification and affront. I miss her sometimes.'

'The grandmother?' said Helen.

'Yes,' said Kim. 'The grandmother, of course.'

Patrice got a car and driver to take us to Gatwick to connect with the Plymouth flight.

'Women are amazing,' said Phil, making Patrice twinkle and Jasmine glint. 'When did you organise all this?'

'All what?' Jasmine grumbled, looking at the plane. 'Do we stick our arms out the window and flap them?'

Even Patrice was nonplussed later on, however, to find that there was no limo service at Plymouth airport.

'None?' she said. 'It doesn't have to be a stretch. We don't need a bar. Just a regular limousine with a driver for a day or two.'

'We can hire a car,' I said. 'I'll drive.' I looked at the luggage: three trolleys stuffed with Patrice's pigskin cases, Jasmine's mock-croc, my Morrison's £39.99 set and Phil's rucksack with the cricket tie holding it shut. 'Better make it a van.'

Phil called his second stepmother again once we were under way and from the conversation we could hear at our end it seemed she was telling him not to worry. He didn't take it lying down.

'Yes, but is that a doctor telling you he's going to be fine?' he said into the phone. 'Or just you telling me?' A pause. 'Oh yes you do sodding well understand, don't give me that English proficiency that blinks on and off like a neon light whenever it suits you. Look, is he attached to any machines? How many? Does one have a screen and a wavy line?' He hung up. 'Vert,' he said. 'Put your foot down, will you?'

'Where are we going?' said Jasmine.

'I thought I might pop in at the hospital,' said Phil. 'But if you had plans ...' I caught his eye in the rear-view mirror. For Phil to be as sour-sounding as that, I knew he must be beside himself.

'I didn't mean that,' said Jasmine. 'Of course you're going to the hospital, Philly, of course you are. I meant Patrice and me. Where are we going to go?'

'Stay with us,' said Phil. 'There's tons of room.'

'Oh no,' I put in, hastily. 'We'd hate to impose at a time like this. We'll go to a hotel.'

'You'll never get in anywhere,' said Phil. 'It's half-term. Now, shut up and let me concentrate on directions.'

We had reached the Bodmin bypass and in the light midday traffic we soon threaded our way around the outskirts of the town to the hospital. Phil leaped out and galloped towards the door as I drew up, but before he got there he stopped and turned.

'Come with me?' he said. It wasn't clear which one of us he was talking to and so, leaving the van in the maternity night-admissions space, I jumped down and, followed closely by Jasmine and Patrice, took his arm and led him through the revolving door.

'God, hospitals stink,' Phil muttered as we scurried along an endless corridor to where the receptionist had told us his father was to be found. 'Whose idea was it to do away with Dettol?'

At the door of the ward, a flustered staff nurse asked if we were all family.

'Yes,' said Phil.

'All of you?' She looked suspiciously at Jasmine and Patrice. I guessed that after just one night in the Plaza and only a single pedicure I didn't look too glamorous to be one of the Coateses.

'Yes.'

'There's only supposed to be two to a bed,' she told him. 'And visiting's not until after lunch really. I keep telling them. Different when he was in the HDU.'

'You're very kind,' said Phil, and squeezed her arm. 'Thank you so much.' And she pointed the way.

It was an old hospital and the ward was one of the traditional kind, like a Victorian school gym hall, all clanking radiators and rattling curtain rings. In beds down either side old men, yellow and papery or red and bloated, lay suspended between their drip bags and their catheters staring up at the pipes on the ceiling or asleep – I hoped although I wouldn't have bet on it. The ward was silent except for the whirr and beep of a few rather ancient machines sitting on trolleys at some of the bedsides. Right at the end a curtain separated off one bed from the rest and as we drew level and rounded it, we saw a haggard looking middle-aged blonde woman and a young black-haired girl, grey in the face and with dark smudges under her eyes, sitting on either side of a bed as close as they could get in spite of the machines. In the bed between them lay a grey-haired, white-faced ... Phil.

The real Phil breathed in sharply and the other (ghost) Phil opened his eyes. They stared at each other for what seemed like half an hour.

'Jesus Christ, Pa, you look like shit on toast,' said Phil.

'Thank you!' bellowed the old man in the bed, paddling his legs in their yellow compression boots. He slurred it slightly so that it came out like 'rank oo' and his mouth hung open at one side after he had spoken. 'That's what I said, after they let me look in a mirror, at long last. But to listen to this pair wittering on, like Florence Nightingale's bridesmaids, you'd think I could beat,' he gasped for breath, 'George Clooney in the swimsuit round.' The two women started to protest, but he kept talking over the top of them. 'Now, young Phillip, where the sodding hell,' another gasp, 'have you been?'

Phil sat down on the bed and, by way of a caress, flicked one of the tubes leading into or out of his father. 'I would give you a California man-hug, Pa, and blame you for sending me there to pick up the habit, but I don't want to get stuck with a needle and catch a hospital superbug off you.'

'Where were you?' said the old man again.

'Aren't you supposed to lose the power of speech after a stroke?' said Phil.

'They've downgraded it,' said the blonde woman. 'It wasn't a stroke after all.'

'Cerebral vascular accident,' said the girl in a very glamorous accent. 'CVA with no lasting aphasia.'

'Still, it didn't look too cheery for a bit back there, I can tell you,' the old man said. 'See all these machines?'

'Pulse, temp and meds,' said the girl. 'That is all.' The old man ignored her.

'Not too cheery at all. And I thought, Oh, super! Oh, bloody marvellous! Here I am, on my sodding deathbed,' he gasped, 'ten years before it says on the contract, with two bloody wives, yammering in my dying ears, and no bloody effing son.' This speech seemed to have tired him and he sank back a little deeper into his pillows at the end of it.

'I was in New York,' said Phil. 'On a spree.' He waved vaguely behind him as though the three of us would serve as an explanation. 'No harm done. And, dear father, you shouldn't disparage your many daughters that way. After my incarceration in California I find it offensive.'

'Hear, hear,' said the blonde woman. Phil leaned over and kissed her and then kissed his father on the top of his head. 'You're hot,' he said.

'Of course I'm bloody hot,' said his father, rousing himself again. 'They won't so much as crack a window in this place. The radiators are belching out steam,' – gasp – 'every minute of the day and night, I'm wearing pyjamas, for the first time in my life – Araminta had to go and *buy* them – and they're pumping enough blood through me to keep at least,' another gasp, 'three young farmers on the go.'

'Why are they giving you blood if you've had a stroke?' said Patrice.

'God knows,' said Phil's father. 'Probably because it's blood they've got, and they've run out of whatever it is I need. Who are you?'

'Don't listen, Phil,' said the young girl. 'He's got the blood because he fell and hit his head open and the medicine they give for the CVA is make him keep bleed too much.'

'True, true,' said Phil's father. 'I've got a scar down the back, like a badly repaired teddy bear. I haven't seen it, but I've felt the sodding stitches, catching on the pillow case, so I know it's there. And I know it's a beauty, because when the nurse came to take the dressing off it, she brought a little student nursey, on her first day, who promptly fainted. But never mind all that, I say again: who are you?'

'Yes, sorry,' said Phil. 'Don't know what I've been thinking. Father, this is Patrice Carmichael of New York. And Jasmine ...?'

'Cammeggio,' said Jasmine.

'Of Catania, Chicago, Las Vegas, New Jersey and latterly Los Angeles,' went on Phil. 'And Verity Drummond from Edinburgh, you know.'

'I do?' said Phil's father.

'She's K—' began Phil.

'Kind of an old friend,' I broke in. 'But actually Philly, I've never met your family.'

'Ladies,' said Phil. 'This is what's left of my father, Pollie Coates.'

'Pollie?' said Patrice.

'Short for Napoleon,' said Phil's father. 'It's a very long story. And these are my ex-wives, Josephine and Araminta.'

'Finnie,' said the blonde woman, smiling.

'I am not your *ex*-wife,' said the girl.

'Oops,' said Phil's father, but he didn't look at all perturbed. 'Well, it looks like you've got me beat, Philly boy. Three against two.'

There was a commotion at the end of the ward and the sound of squeaking wheels.

'Ah, lunch!' said Pollie Coates. 'The jewel in the crown of the NHS. What will it be today?'

'You chose roast beef and gravy on the menu card this morning,' said Finnie.

'Shoe soles in mud,' said Pollie. 'A nice glass of chlorinated tap water, in a Tupperware cup with teeth marks, and a warm pink yoghurt afterwards as a treat. Finnie, please go home, and cook me something. Anything. Please.'

'I will,' said Finnie, looking uncomfortable. 'I will very soon. Just as soon as I can.'

'Hah!' said Araminta and she tossed her black hair.

'I tell you what,' said Pollie. 'Now that Phil's here, why don't you both go. Araminta can take our guests home, and get them settled into the house. I take it you're all staying at Trepolgas, aren't you? Good, jolly good. And, Finn, you go home and cook me something? Hmm? Doesn't have to be a cake. Could be a nice joint of cold roast pork. Bit of apple sauce, a new loaf. I could live off that for days, with a grape or two.'

'I'll go if Araminta's coming too,' said Finnie.

'I'll go home, but I'm come back when you're bring the food,' said Araminta.

'Excellent,' said Pollie. 'And in the meantime ... Phil, you can help me, with this little problem I have.' Phil looked doubtful, but said nothing. Which is,' went on Pollie, 'just in case all of this, this neck-and-neck wifery, that's going on here, hadn't told you ... I am staring down the barrel of mortality, close enough to read the maker's name on the sodding gun, and I quite simply cannot bloody well afford to sodding die. Now, short of robbing a bank or winning the lottery, what the hell am I going to do?'

*

We followed Finnie and Araminta back to the farm, rattling down the A roads to St Austell just over the speed limit. I was tired, and glad when the indicator flashed and we swung off into the deep Cornish lanes. I relaxed, glanced at the speedo, looked up again, and the Corsa was gone.

I hadn't seen who was driving it but now, judging from the way I had to lean on the accelerator to keep up as it bounced along, whisking out of sight, careening around blind bends in the middle of the road with brake lights winking, I guessed it wasn't the placid, blonde mother of five.

'Jee-zuss,' said Jasmine, clutching the dashboard beside me, her knuckles as white as mine. Patrice, in the back, was crunched up into a ball, looking with wide eyes at the hedges whipping past inches from either side of the van.

'Is this a one-way system?' she asked, in a wavering voice.

In answer, the Corsa, which had just disappeared around a corner, came hurtling back round with its reverse lights on. Patrice screamed. I stamped on the brakes, threw the van into reverse too and started whizzing backwards. Eventually, at a place in the lane about six inches wider than the rest, the back of the Corsa shot up the bank and it hung there, at what looked like ninety degrees to the road. I could hear an advancing rumble and I hastily edged the side of the van up into the hedge roots as well. A second later, a milk tanker came thundering into view. This time all of us screamed and I hitched the van higher up into the hedge. Jasmine slid towards me, and I could hear the luggage thumping about in the back. I closed my eyes and kept them closed until I heard the whack against my side mirror as the lorry passed. The driver, holding the wheel with one hand while he propped his phone to his ear with the other shoulder, waved a casual thanks out of his open window and was gone.

I looked up at where Jasmine hung, suspended by her seat belt above me, and then I glanced in the mirror at Patrice.

'Quick,' she said. 'We're losing them.'

Out of the windscreen I could just see the dust as the Corsa shot away out of sight again and I took my foot off the brake, but nothing happened; at some point we had stalled. With numb fingers,

I checked the gearstick, handbrake, and mirrors and started again. Driving along at twenty-five miles an hour, with my headlights on and my hands at ten-to-two, I had no chance of catching up again, but there was nothing I could do about it. I couldn't have gone into fourth gear if someone had paid me. We trundled along in silence, each of us slowly starting to breathe again and gradually letting our shoulders drop down. At last, Jasmine spoke.

'Trepolgas,' she said, raising an arm and pointing out of the window at an enormous sign, painted with what looked like piles of rabbit droppings but must have been bunches of grapes. I turned in and negotiated a cattle grid just in time to find the Corsa barrelling towards us again, face forward this time, obviously coming back to see where we had gone. Araminta, at the wheel, swerved off the track on to the edge of the field, made a wide U-turn at our backs and overtook us on the other side, snapping back the other wing mirror, before disappearing like a rocket back up the drive.

'Welcome to England,' said Patrice, once the dust had settled. 'I can't believe British tourists are scared to drive on the freeway.'

'Every guidebook I ever read,' Jasmine said, 'tells you to praise where you can and keep quiet about everything else. So . . .'

We looked around at the pale dry earth, the straggling vines, stripped of fruit and beginning to lose their leaves, and the rutted track ahead with tufts of yellow grass growing up the middle and potholes half-heartedly filled with pink gravel here and there. Speechless, we went on our way.

Actually, though, away from the road and into the rolling fields, the sky above dappled with high mackerel-skin clouds and far ahead the unmistakable clear brightness of sunlight coming off the sea, Trepolgas, and Cornwall, started to show us their charms and when we crested a final rise and saw the house both Jasmine and Patrice were forced into grudging praise.

'Quite a pile,' said Jasmine.

'This is a farm?' said Patrice.

It was a long white I-shaped house, stuck with chimneys like a birthday cake with candles and approached by rounding what was either an enormous pond or a tiny lake where a pair of black swans and a handful of scruffy adolescent cygnets were gliding. I drove around the side into a yard and parked beside the Corsa, which was ticking as the engine began to cool.

'Come in, come in, have tea, find rooms, take a bath,' said Araminta, coming towards us tying on an apron. I wondered about that until Finnie followed her out in one of her own. Finnie in an apron looked, as most of us do, like a sack of potatoes tied in the middle and I was sure that Araminta, who made hers look like a new take on a wrap dress, was out to needle her.

We trudged after them into the kitchen. It was the typical kitchen of a big, posh house where big, posh people had lived for hundreds of years, a kitchen I had seen in my life with Kim, many times, but I could tell that Jasmine and Patrice were puzzled. (The expressions on their faces were the same as when they'd first seen Phil, in his bald cords and sockless boat shoes with the turned up toes.) Thirty feet long and floored in stone it had an Aga the size of a skip, which you could only get to by stepping in the four dog baskets that lay in front. There was a pair of stained porcelain sinks with a tap dripping into one of them and a black oak dresser, ten feet square, laden with much-glued antique tureens and mugs from Ikea.

'Sit down, sit down,' said Araminta. 'I make coffee. Or wine, maybe?'

'Don't sit on that one,' said Finnie pointing to one of the chairs, as she came back into the kitchen from a pantry swinging a freezer bag like a club. 'It's riddled with worms. One day, Araminta,' she said.

'I know, I know,' said Araminta, filling a dented kettle from the hot tap. 'One day somebody is going to break the back and sue the arse off. I know.'

'I always kept a pot plant on it, as a warning,' said Finnie. 'When I lived here.' She ripped open the freezer bag and rolled the frozen meat into a tray. Then she sloshed in some wine – Trepolgas Ruby Red – from an open bottle, poured corn oil on to it and unhooked the door of the oven with her foot.

'Pork?' I asked her.

'His favourite,' she said. 'Couple of hours and it'll be just how he likes it.'

'So you don't live here any more?' said Patrice, obviously trying to straighten things out in her mind.

'No, the *family*,' said Finnie with emphasis, 'lives over at the dower house. But I keep a few staples here, just in case. Pollie can't *always* be running over to me for his meals, especially in the picking season when he's so busy.'

Araminta held out a long leg in front of her letting her shoe dangle from her foot and inspecting her gleaming brown ankle, as if to say to all of us that there was more to marriage than cooking. Despite myself, I glanced at Finnie's legs. They were mottled pink and rather stubbly, rising straight from the tops of her shoes to the hem of her skirt like two sausages.

'Why do you keep the chair, if you can't sit in it?' said Jasmine.

'Oh, it's fine for children,' said Finnie, 'so long as they don't squirm. And we can't throw it out. Pollie's father was conceived in that chair.'

We all looked at it, particularly at the old and rather stained cushion cover on the seat pad. Patrice rose a few inches in the air, as though she had tensed her thighs to reduce any contact between her bottom and whatever piece of Coates family furnishing history it was resting on.

Araminta was digging in a jar of coffee with a teaspoon, waiting for the kettle to boil.

'Any milk?' she said. 'Any sugar?' She tossed the teaspoon into a sugar bag and put it on the table, then picked up a bottle of milk and sniffed it. 'Gone bad,' she announced and held the bottle upside down over the sink to let it plop out in three big glugs before she rinsed it away.

'Araminta!' said Finnie, sounding scandalised. 'When will you learn? That could have been the start of some yoghurt there. Not much of a housekeeper,' she explained, smiling fondly but not very convincingly at Araminta's back as she went off to the pantry and, I hoped, the fridge. I couldn't help glancing at the oven and I only just managed to nod.

'So, black coffee,' said Araminta, coming back and hopping through the dog baskets to get the kettle from the stove.

'Where are all the pets from those baskets?' asked Jasmine.

'Ah,' said Finnie. 'Yes, Araminta's not too keen, so the dogs live with the girls and me.' There was a glint of triumph in her eyes and I had to agree. Araminta might be right about the balance of sex and cooking, but she had missed a trick if she had let the dogs go.

We were still at the kitchen table, watching Finnie mashing together the fixings for some scones and trying – at least I was – to forget that she hadn't so much as wiped her hands on her apron since doing the pork, when we heard the sound of a diesel engine coming into the yard. Araminta hopped up to look out of the window.

'Is Phil,' she said. 'In a taxi.'

'Philly?' said Finnie as he came in. 'Is everything all right? Is Pollie …'

'He's fine,' said Phil. 'I'll go back tonight for visiting.' He went to throw himself down, looked behind and moved on to the next chair along before he let go. 'I'm knackered for one thing. And the nurses are starting to get seriously hacked off.'

'But they can't complain about this!' said Araminta. 'One bedside guest, his most beloved son. They are not kind, these nurses. They are not kind people at all.'

'It wasn't just me,' said Phil, and he kicked me softly under the table to get my attention before he went on. 'Mum's there.'

There was a silence during which all we could hear was the sound of the poison pork starting to sizzle in its corn oil.

'Your mother?' said Finnie at last.

'Straight off the plane from Nairobi and come to bury the hatchet, mop the brow –' he paused while Finnie and Araminta both leaped to their feet, tore off their aprons and grabbed their bags, '– and check the will for codicils,' he finished quietly.

'Araminta, you drive,' said Finnie. 'Verity, can you chuck those scones together for me? Raisins in the pantry. Phil, you'll have to show the girls to their rooms.' She disappeared out of the back door as the sound of the Corsa engine roared into life. 'And someone keep an eye on that pork!'

Chapter 10
Six Symbolic Husbands

Phil made no murmur as I tipped the scone mix into the bin.

'The freezer's full of them, anyway,' he said. 'Finnie thinks there's a critical mass of baking and, when it's reached, some law of physics will make my father just slide out of Araminta's bed and back into hers.'

But he wouldn't let me touch the pork.

'It'll be fine,' he said. 'I was brought up on Finnie's cooking after my mother ran away. Chicken portions straight from the freezer to the grill, every boiled egg a boost to the immune system. All Finn's family recipes start: first scrape off all mould and rinse away any maggots. Now,' he said, 'Let's see about getting you installed, shall we? And then I'm going to crash for an hour or two.'

Jasmine gave a low whistle as Phil led us out of the kitchen wing and into the main room of the house. It had to be fifty feet long at least, with five high windows running down each side and two encampments of sofas drawn up around each of two fireplaces. In its lines – the bones of the fireplace pillars and the ogee curve on the tops of the windows, echoed on the sofa backs – it was pure Georgian elegance, but overlying all of that were layers of tie-dyed rugs, striped blankets and clashing patterned cushions littering the surfaces. Ornamented poles and sticks, as well as various long and unmelodious-looking horns, were lashed to the walls and, in lieu of occasional tables, moth-eaten djembe drums were arranged here and there.

'What's with all the stuff?' said Jasmine. 'Shouldn't it be French antiques in here?'

'They're my mother's,' Phil explained. 'She started going on trips to Kenya when I was a kid, and brought it back by the lorry load. Longer and longer trips, shorter and shorter breaks at home in between. We should have seen it coming really. Then one time she cleared out her clothes and that was that.'

'That's terrible,' said Patrice.

'I know,' said Phil. 'She could at least have taken some of it with her.'

Through the hall, at the other end of the house, a staircase rose up grandly around three sides of a square tower, topped, high above our heads, with a dome of coloured glass. Here too a flavour of Kenya remained; tribal masks ranged up the walls above the panelling, glowering down at us as we mounted the stairs.

'There used to be a great big tree just off to the south-west there,' said Phil, pointing. 'It hung right over the house and when the wind blew, the shadows of the leaves would move across the bits of coloured glass up in the skylight and make it look as if the ju-ju masks were winking and sticking their tongues out at you.'

'Jesus,' said Jasmine. 'That's what these things are? That's what all those tourists are bringing home all the time?'

'Not all the time,' said Phil. 'Sometimes they're just plain old death's heads. Ancestors' spirits, you know. I'm not sure how you tell the difference, if I'm honest.' He was looking up in an interested way at a nearby face, and Jasmine, Patrice and I drew a little closer together behind him on the stairs.

The bedrooms, thankfully free of African crafts, were easily as big as the rooms in the Plaza, but any resemblance stopped there. Phil flung open a door at the top of the stairs. 'Adam Room,' he said, waving vaguely around at the bed and the view, then he opened a door into a second, even larger one and started to cross it. 'This is the Gallery Room. All the pictures my mother took out of the hall to make space for her treasures ended up here.'

We followed him, murmuring politely at the flaking portraits of stern Coates ancestors and studies of unfeasibly fat farm animals on miniscule little legs.

'Next, the Fleshpot,' said Phil as we passed through a connecting door.

'Fleshpot?' said Patrice, standing in the middle of the floor, looking around at the candlewick bedspread and the mild watercolours on the walls. Phil pointed to the ceiling and we all looked up.

'Jesus,' said Jasmine again.

'Yeah,' said Phil. 'We've never quite worked this one out. It was either some horny old git who saw the like on his grand tour and didn't have the nerve to put it in one of the public rooms, or perhaps this was the honeymoon suite for some poor unsuspecting bride and it was supposed to be a turn-on.'

'Was this here when you were growing up?' asked Patrice. 'Didn't they cover it?'

'God, no,' said Phil. 'It saved no end of awkwardness. First time I asked where babies came from, my mother sent me up here to lie on my back for half an hour and I learned all I'd ever need to know.' Patrice nodded slowly, looking at him with a hint of compassion. 'And finally,' Phil went on, disappearing again, 'the back landing. Bathroom's in there,' he pointed, 'family rooms are round that corner and that little door over there leads to a staircase that takes you to the kitchen passage, only watch out because there's no light and no banister and Araminta tends to fling the Hoover in at the bottom and leave it there.'

Jasmine and Patrice had looked around the bathroom door and were now waiting, smiling politely at Phil with just a hint of desperation. I knew what was wrong, of course.

'We missed the other bathrooms?' said Patrice.

'There's one downstairs,' said Phil, 'but I can't really recommend it. This is your best bet.'

Jasmine and Patrice continued to stare at him, bewildered.

'So,' he said. 'All you need to do is work out who's the lightest sleeper and who's got the titchiest bladder and decide on rooms. Although there's always the trek down past the death's heads, across the hall and up the Hoover stairs instead. Also, I should say, there's never more than one bathful of water in the morning, so you need to work out who if anyone is washing her hair so she can go first, and don't worry about me: I'll get in after everyone else and just slosh about in all the leftovers.'

Jasmine and Patrice had let their jaws drop open.

'Honestly,' said Phil, misreading their expressions. 'I got used to it when the five sisters started to hit puberty. I didn't have to touch a bar of soap for years and I smelled lovely.'

'Do we have to factor in Araminta?' I said, trying not to giggle.

'Hmph,' said Phil. 'No, you don't. She's put an en suite loo and shower in my father's bedroom. 'Cost a fortune, ruined the cornice, and keeps leaking into the pantry.'

Jasmine and Patrice both gazed wistfully at where he was pointing, and I knew that they would storm Araminta's stronghold and get into that shower if it killed them.

'Now,' said Phil bounding down a few steps and up again on the other side of the landing to wrench open the staircase door. 'I'll start ferrying your things.'

I had a quick look around the bathroom door – a cavernous bath with a green stain under each tap, a wooden-seated lavatory with a green stain running down the back and a washbasin big enough to bath a five-year-old, with two green stains and a line of black mould where it joined the wall. There was a pile of rather thin and dingy towels stacked on a deckchair and a Homer Simpson bathmat on the floor. I had seen worse and it was country dirt, not London dirt – clean dirt as my granny would say – but I was worried about Jasmine and Patrice. I hurried back to the bedrooms to find them.

Fortunately, they were laughing, lying side by side on the bed in the Fleshpot looking upwards, pointing out highlights. I joined them.

'You better have this one, Patrice,' said Jasmine. 'You sleep on your front anyway.'

'OK,' said Patrice. 'But only if I get first bath.' They broke into streams of helpless laughter again.

'I could do my hair yoga again,' said Jasmine and Patrice yelped.

'What about me?' I said. 'And what's hair yoga?'

Patrice propped herself up on her elbows and kicked off her shoes.

'Years ago, Jazzie read this article by some guy who lived in a tree in India.'

'He lived in a condo in Florida,' said Jasmine. 'He *was* a master of Hatha yoga, though. He ran classes.'

'And this guy reckoned that once every five years you had to stop washing your hair long enough to let the oil get right to the ends.'

'It lets the life of the body flow into your hair,' said Jasmine. 'Because it's bad for your chi to carry around dead lifeless hair on top of your head all the time.'

'Chi's not yoga,' I said. 'Did it work?'

'Well, it certainly brought life to her hair,' said Patrice. 'Every time you went outside, Jazzie, remember? You had a whole zoo flying around up there.' Jasmine scratched her head busily with both hands.

'Don't talk about it,' she said. 'I'll never forget the smell. Anyways, forget hair yoga. I have a better idea.' I was right. 'Every morning two of us grab Araminta, tie her up, lock her in the dark stairway then we all have a nice long shower before we let her go again.'

'Every morning?' I echoed. 'How long are you planning on staying?'

Phil never did get his couple of hours crashing out time. Patrice, standing up and going to gaze out of her bedroom window, said:

'Did you know that all the swans in England belong to the Queen?'

'Now, how on earth do you know that?' said Phil, putting down a load of bags in the doorway and knuckling his back.

'Government homepage,' said Patrice, predictably. She really did have the worst taste in websites of anyone I knew.

'So they're just passing through on their way to Buckingham Palace?' said Jasmine.

'They've been here four years,' said Phil. 'The mating pair arrived and this is the fifth lot of cygnets they've hatched here. God knows where they came from, but it doesn't look like they're leaving.'

'I can believe that,' said Patrice stretching her arms out euphorically and taking a deep, joyful breath. 'It's heavenly, isn't it? I don't suppose anyone who comes here ever wants to go away again.' She turned and blinked slowly, just once, at Phil.

'The Queen doesn't mind?' said Jasmine. She came to stand

beside Patrice and gave an even more luxurious stretch, looking like a ballerina as her arms unfurled and her hands waved delicately against the light. Her dress strained, less delicately, against her body. Phil stared at both of them, gulping.

'Yes,' I added. 'Quite a view.'

'What happened to all the other ones that were born down there?' said Jasmine. 'It's pretty sad if they keep trying to start a family and then losing them.' Phil looked taken aback.

'Not at all,' he said. 'They're all still with us. They bring them up and then they drive them out of the nest to make homes for themselves.'

'Kinda shitty parents, aren't they?' said Jasmine.

I couldn't help but think that Patrice's gazing and sleepy cat-blinks were bound to be more successful in the end than Jasmine's approach of a quick gaze, a quick stretch and then a string of gratuitous insults.

'It's natural,' said Phil, unperturbed. 'They're quite happy. They all live down at the bottom lake, where it runs into the sea. Sometimes, when it's calm, they bob right out into the bay. Causes a bit of a stir with the sunbathing tourists, I can tell you.'

'I'd love to see that,' said Patrice. 'How far is it to this bottom lake? Could we walk there?'

'If you like,' said Phil. 'It's only a mile or two.'

'Excellent,' said Jasmine, through gritted teeth. I would take a bet that the only time she had ever walked a mile was on a supervised cross-trainer in a nice warm gym.

'Oh yes, let's!' said Patrice, clasping her hands together girlishly under her chin.

'Really?' said Phil.

'Absolutely,' said Jasmine. 'Patrice is such a big fan of nature. Aren't you, sweetie? Anything *natural*, Patrice can't get enough of it. Well, you only have to look at her to see that.' Every word was a barb and even Phil, not the most attuned to undercurrents, was picking up a whiff of it.

'I'll look out some gumboots for you,' he said deciding to ignore it after all. 'What size? And how about you, Verity?' I hesitated. 'Only if you wouldn't mind too much, could you bear to stay in case someone phones from Bodmin? I'll take my mobile, and if the hospital calls, you call me?'

I took a minute to think it through. It seemed to me that with the two of them scrabbling for advantage with Phil, and his mind on his father, there was no way they would get through a walk in the woods and fields without at least touching on the fleetingness of life, the inevitability of death, and the cruel game of dice that throws love, loss, and sorrow in our way. And there was no way they would get through all of *that* without someone forgetting the perfectly simple facts I had laid out for them and mentioning either my tragic loss or the rupture into ulcerous divorce. On the other hand, I could hardly say no, I couldn't care less about swans of any colour, and I doubted my ability to stomach the floor show Jasmine and Patrice would put on for Phil.

'Of course,' I said. 'Actually, I wanted to make a call anyway. Where's the nearest phone, Phil?'

Phil explained to me, while Jasmine and Patrice were trying on wellies in the far regions behind the kitchen, that there was only one phone these days.

'Araminta's doing,' he said. 'I suppose no third wife wants to live in a house with a lot of extensions. And since Pa has never learned to use email and thinks you get ear cancer from mobiles, she reckons she's safe.' He sighed. 'I suppose she really is safe now,' he said. 'I can't see the poor old bugger getting up from his bed after this and running off with number four, can you?'

'Remember not to say too much about divorce in front of Patrice,' I whispered. 'Mine, your father's, divorce in general ... She's looking for number seven after all. And I have to say, if I was Araminta,' I said, putting my arm through his to comfort him, 'I'd be more worried about number two.'

'And if I were number two,' said Phil. 'I'd watch out for number one. My mother might have had the will in mind when she left Nairobi, but there was anything but a hard glint of finance in her eyes when she saw old Pollie. She went quite misty for a minute there.'

'No offence to your father, Philly,' I said, 'But I can't quite see ...'

'Me neither,' said Phil, twinkling. 'A gormless pillock like him with three lovely ladies swarming around like flies at a jam pot. He must have something, eh?'

Just as he said this, Jasmine and Patrice re-entered the kitchen and each gave him a dazzling smile which fluttered as they saw his arm around my waist. I sighed. They could take it from me that no matter what Pollie's total was up to, there were only two lovely ladies inexplicably panting for Phil.

I drew them aside when he went to get his coat on.

'See if you can cheer him up a bit,' I said. 'Try not to let him dwell on his father too much.'

'I thought the old guy looked in pretty good shape,' said Jasmine.

'Exactly,' I said. 'And yet Phil's been acting as if he's a definite goner. I think this is bringing it all back to him, you know.'

'All what?' said Jasmine.

'Jas,' said Patrice, nudging her. 'Kim, remember?'

'Sorry,' said Jasmine. 'I forgot. Oh Jeez, Vee, I *forgot*. Say, are you OK?'

'I'm fine,' I told her.

'What with the hospital an all?'

'Kim didn't die in a hospital,' I said. 'But please just keep off the whole subject of death. Kim's, Pollie's, anyone's.'

'Pollie's anyone's what?' said Phil, coming back. 'What are you saying about my beloved parent, Vert?'

'That he's anyone's for a smile and a free drink,' I said. 'That he's where you get it from. I'm telling them to watch out for you once you get them in the woods.'

Phil beamed.

'They don't look too worried to me.'

As soon as they had gone, I settled down in a fairly sturdy-seeming chair, and pulled the phone on to my lap.

'Gemma?' I said, trying to sound casual. 'Is Clovis—'

'Is that you, Verity?' said Clovis's assistant.

'Is that Verity?' I heard Clovis's voice bellow from the background.

'I'll put you straight thr—' Before she could finish, Clovis had wrenched the phone from her hand.

'Verity?' she said. 'I tried the Plaza, and I tried Beverly Hills, Jasmine's office and cell phone and pager service. Where the hell are you now?'

'Co—' My nerve failed me. 'Colorado?'

'What?'

My nerve failed me again.

'Cornwall,' I said. There was a long silence.

'There's one way for what you've just told me not to mean that you're in the worst trouble you've ever been in in your life and any past lives you may have clocked up as well,' said Clovis. 'And that's if you tell me that you signed the contract and left the buyer in New York and now she and Jasmine have gone off on a little celebratory jaunt, without leaving US soil.'

'Not exactly,' I said. 'Look, Clovis, I know all about the profile and the status and why a Hollywood deal is so much better than a domestic one, but if I'm happy why aren't you?'

'Who have you been talking to?' said Clovis.

'Um,' I said, but luckily she was too annoyed to wait for me to answer.

'I don't know where you're getting all that nonsense from,' she said, 'but just leave the business decisions to me. Now why, if you don't mind telling me, are you in bloody Cornwall?'

'A friend of mine who was with us in New York—'

'A friend?' roared Clovis. 'A new friend? One you met in New York or one who followed you from LA? And was this new friend an agent, or a producer? Or have you moved on to directors now?'

'No,' I said. 'Not a new friend. An old friend. A school friend. He had to come home unexpectedly because his father is ill and he didn't want to come on his own.'

'Oh,' said Clovis. 'In that case, I apologise. But have you any idea where Jasmine's got to?'

I considered this. Technically, I didn't. I didn't know where the bottom lake was, only that it was near the sea. I hesitated.

'And the contract?' said Clovis, sounding friendly enough now. I hesitated again, and then squeezed my eyes shut and let it all come out in a rush.

'I haven't signed it I'm still in talks with other people Jasmine's in Cornwall too.' I smacked down the phone and stared at it. She didn't know the number, but I was sure the Coateses wouldn't have the ID blocked and she would be ringing back any minute, unless ... I picked it up again and dialled the international code.

'Bradley, honey!' I cried.

'Verity?' said Brad. 'Where *are* you, girlfriend? I've got half the housekeeping staff of the Plaza hotel checking under dust ruffles for me. Where did you go?'

'Cornwall,' I said. 'We're all in Cornwall now.'

'Corn-wall?' echoed Brad. 'That doesn't sound like a place. That sounds like a medical procedure.'

'How are you?' I asked. 'What's happening? What have you heard?'

'What have I *not*?' said Brad. 'You know my cousin? Who works in the mailroom?'

'Yes, you've mentioned him.'

'Well,' said Bradley. 'He copied me a puff piece from IFA's in-house, all about you, all about your circumstances, the tragedy, the book, the happy ending. I mean, except for your husband may he rest in peace and angels watch over him it's happy, right?'

'Why are they writing about me?' I asked him. 'I haven't even signed with IFA. Yet.'

'It was a motivational piece,' said Bradley. 'Give me your fax number there in – Corn-wall, was it? – and I'll copy it to you. It's inspirational, you know. If life hands you lemons ... squeeze out a script.'

'Inspirational,' I said.

'For the agents, honey,' said Bradley. 'I didn't mean for you. That would be insensitive of me.'

'God forbid,' I said. 'So ... you think the biographical stuff really matters? You think it would be different if it was all just made up? Really?'

'What do you mean? If The Widow wasn't a widow? I'll say it would matter. If The Widow was just some hack, sitting in his undershirt out in the valley, shuffling his story cards and seeing what he came up with? I'll say. The script is great, don't get me wrong. It's even better than the book was and who can forget how great the book was.' Not you too, I thought. 'But *you're* the hook, hon.'

'As far as the agents are concerned,' I said.

'Darn tootin',' said Bradley.

So I decided to check someone who wasn't an agent.

'Kenny?' I said.

'Well, look who it is,' said Kenny Daateng. 'I thought you'd left us for ever. Where are you?'

'Can I ask you a question?' I said. '*Straight up*? How much would it matter if it wasn't a true story after all?'

'It's not a True Story,' said Kenny. 'Nobody would touch it with a pole if it was a True Story. There would be lawyers crawling over lawyers to sue. If someone else is telling you they want to go with a True Story, they're lying. They're either lying or they're in television. There's no money in television. Nobody ever sues them so they can say what they like.'

'So it doesn't matter at all?' I said. 'OK, but we've been at pretty comprehensively crossed purposes then, all this time.'

'What?' said Kenny. 'No, the thing is, the beauty of the Based On, which is what we have here, is that you get all the good of True and none of the lawyers.'

'So it would matter if it wasn't Based On?' I said.

'Honey, we wouldn't be talking to each other if it wasn't Based On,' said Kenny Daateng. 'And I certainly wouldn't be talking to who else I'm talking to. My phone's ringing off the hook on this one.'

'Oh,' I said. 'I see.'

'And I'm hearing some wonderful things. Picture this: closing credits, silent, no music. Black screen and then a clip: *Straight Up* is Based on a True Story. Then the next clip: In memory of ... what was your husband's name?'

'No!' I said. Oh my God, no!'

'No?'

'No. I mean, could we not just have ... something else?' I recovered. 'Something like: This film is dedicated to all those who climbed the mountain—' Kenny cut me off.

'If they go mountain,' he said. 'If they go snow. But I take your general point. So how about: Dedicated to all those who came home from the journey and in memory of those who rest there,' he said. 'Beautiful. Now, see the thing about Based On is it's true enough for that dedication but we have leeway for ... are you ready? The Kid.'

I waited.

'The Kid. A father and son. Last shot of the movie, the father's holding out the kid to the mountain rescue stroke diving team stroke fire fighters.'

'So they survive?' I said.

'Nah, the dad bites it, the kid survives. The father hands the kid over and lets go. Scream splash the end. Good, huh? See, this way we get the tragedy and happy ending all rolled into one and also we get some dialogue under the ice stroke ocean stroke debris instead of just in scenes with the mountain rescue stroke diving team stroke firemen.'

'Do I have to write this?' I said.

'We're a long way from anyone having to write anything yet,' said Kenny. 'Everybody knows the story, everyone remembers the book.'

'They certainly seem to,' I said.

'So we're good with a pitch and coverage for now.'

I stared at the phone in my lap. There was no one else I could think of to call, but if I didn't call someone, Clovis was sure to call me. She would probably have Gemma checking the line right now. But I shouldn't tie up the phone too much longer. What if the hospital needed Phil? I looked along the flex to where the phone jack was plugged into the wall. I could pull it out, but again, what about the hospital? I agreed with Jasmine; I thought Pollie was going to be fine, but still I had promised. I shrieked as the phone in my lap started ringing, a loud old-fashioned, piercing ring. With my hand on the receiver and my mind racing I stared at it. It was Clovis; it had to be. I could let it ring until it stopped and then check to see who it had been and then call back and ... Oh what could she do to me after all? I lifted it.

'Hello?'

'Cornwall! You think I don't know what you're doing in Cornwall? You think I think you're just going shopping and having buttered scones for tea over there? You think I came over from the old country on a toasted bagel? You think you can fool me?'

In other words, it was Brad.

'Who else, girlfriend? Cornwall, huh? Are you going to say it or am I?'

'It had better be you.'

'Cornwall or in other words: pot holes. Right? Underground caves? Tin mines? Cavers? Potholers? Underwater caverns? Divers? And who knows – how cold does it get in Cornwall? – there could even be snow. Is this still the independent?'

'It is,' I said. 'But honestly Bradley she's not even thinking about locations.'

'How else could she do it? She's building a set? Where's she getting the money? Or … no! CGI potholes? Is she going totally animation? Is she using an animatronic cast? Wait a minute! Are you over there talking to Nick Park?'

I pressed my finger down on the cradle and, still holding the receiver to my ear, listened to the silence hum. As soon as I put the receiver down, though, it rang again.

'Brad,' I said. 'I don't know what CGI is, but she's not using Wallace and Grommit and she isn't raising money. That's not why we're in Cornwall.' I stopped talking. Bradley had never been this silent for this long on a phone.

'Who's Brad?' said Clovis. 'And what are you talking about? CGI? Verity, is that what all of this is about? You actually think someone's going to make this thing? You won't sign the contract because the buyer might not make the movie? Let me explain a few things to you, love. Options are not like that. A producer buying an option is like a human being buying life insurance. It's just in case. It's like an airbag. It's there in case everything else fails and there's no *other* option. Verity, hear me. No one is ever going to make this story into a film. Now, please take the quarter of a million pounds – it's pounds now, not dollars any more – that Jasmine is practically shoving down your bra for you, and move on.'

'You're wrong,' I told her. 'The producer told me this project means more to her than her right arm. It's the start of a new life for her.'

'That was very unprofessional of her.' Clovis's voice was quiet and hard. 'Does Jasmine know the buyer said that to you?'

'I'm not sure,' I said, buying time.

'Because a buyer has no right to tug your heart strings,' Clovis said. 'And you shouldn't even have met her. This is a business deal, pure and simple.'

'Not to Patrice it's not.'

When I put the phone down this time, as well as the humming silence I could hear a faint fizzing inside my head. I shook it, but the fizzing wouldn't stop. Only, when I thought about it it wasn't really fizzing and it wasn't inside. I had the inside bit sorted, tiny, hard and tight, tucked right down where no one could find it. This fizzing was different, more as though there were insects circling me, but faster than insects, going whoooooosh! when they passed my ears and each leaving a trail, until I felt as Saturn must feel, all tangled up in those rings trying to see out at what was beyond them. What were they, these insects in orbit? Were they words? Were they stories? I closed my eyes but I could still see them pinging past. They had faces, I could tell that much. They weren't stories at all. They were Clovis and Kenny and Bradley and Erin and Beau and Melanie. They were Phil and Patrice and Jasmine and Pollie and Finnie and Araminta. They were the dad and the kid and the mountain rescue stroke firemen stroke lifeboat crew. And they were Kim and *her*, and Granny was there too shuffling round me. But who were the others? Who were the ones whose faces I couldn't see? I pressed the heels of my hands into my eyes. Who were they? Mr Jankel, maybe. And Bradley's cousin in the mailroom in IFA. Jasmine's publicists and PR people, Clovis's endless contacts at home and abroad. Maybe they were all Phil's sisters, maybe they were Patrice's six husbands. Or wait: was it Jasmine who had the six husbands? I tipped forward and put my head down between my knees.

Which is how Jasmine, Patrice and Phil found me when they came back from the swans.

'Vee?' said Jasmine, who was the first into the room. 'You sick?'

'Verity, your poor darling,' said Patrice. 'You're as white as a ghost. What's wrong?'

'Oh shit, Vert,' said Phil. 'Did the hospital phone?'

'No,' I said. 'It's nothing like that. In fact, it's nothing.'

'It must be something,' said Jasmine and all three of them stared at me, waiting.

'I'm just tired,' I said and I let them bundle me off upstairs to lie down.

The bed was lumpy, made of a substance I had never experienced in a bed before, and high above me, strands of spider silk thick with country dirt billowed in swags across the ceiling, but the light was soft and the only sounds that came in the open window were birdsong and the distant shushing of the sea. Seaside, seaside, seaside, I said to myself. A dance at dusk on the hard sand below the high tide line. Driftwood sticks to mark a path from the dunes. Ropes of seaweed, hung between the sticks and heads of *Crambe maritima* twined into them. Pink thrift blossom posies as rosettes where the swags join the driftwood. At the end of the path a circle of split bamboo candle holders pushed into the sand and vanilla-scented candles – no! Unscented candles, with crushed cinnamon sprinkled on top to release scent as the wax melted. The guests would dance in bare feet on the cool damp sand, and on the tables set up under the shelter of the dunes, more candles and ... what? What would live up to the sunset? Euphorbia Fireglow like a little sunset in every vase. Thundercloud lupins, sooty black, but I would have to weave them into the Fireglow with cotton thread to hold them steady. And ... one more. *Rosa glauca*, pink flowers to clash, like all good sunsets do, and blue-red leaves like little bruises, like little dusty grapes. I would have to snap the thorns, or if I had time I could file them blunt. Slowly, the Saturn rings began to fade and I propped myself on my pillows to think things through.

All was well, I told myself, all was well. Jasmine was still trying to get Clovis to change her mind, except ... if Patrice didn't stop flirting with Phil then maybe Jasmine would get annoyed enough to *stop* trying. I wouldn't worry about that now. Clovis wasn't capable of turning down that much money, except ... since my zzub was working so well, she had other deals she could turn to, hadn't she?

Well, I wouldn't worry about that either. After all, Patrice was far too desperate for my script to give up, except ... she might stop flirting with Phil to make Jasmine try harder with Clovis, and then Jasmine would have Phil with one snap of her teeth and he'd tell her about Kim and she'd tell Patrice and she'd drop my script like a live grenade because she'd think it was fake and ... I wouldn't worry about any of it right now. I just had to hold it steady a little while longer then I could just walk away from them with my suitcase full of money and I'd have no worries at all. I'd be a woman of private means working on her next book, possibly for ever like Margaret Mitchell and Harper Lee but even that was better than being an unemployed florist's assistant after all.

So, when Phil knocked softly on my door a while later and crept in with a mug of tea and a packet of Jaffa Cakes, I asked him to stay and told him I had something I needed to share with him.

'They're both after you, you know,' I said. His expression told me that he knew. 'And if I know you ...' His grin broadened even further. 'So, which one were you thinking you would go for, first?'

'Oh decisions, decisions,' said Phil stretching out on my bed and putting a whole Jaffa Cake in his mouth. 'There's something about Patrice, isn't there? I'm pretty sure I know what it is too. And it gives her that vulnerable air, makes you want to say: it's OK, you're safe, I'll take care of you, no one's going to hurt you.'

'I know what you mean,' I said.

'And yet at the same time, she's so: it's OK, Phil. I'll take care of you, nothing's going to go wrong. I'll never forget how she got a hot cup of tea out of New York room service for me. There's just ... something about her.'

This was much worse than I thought. I had expected to see no more than a glint of lust but, talking about Patrice his eyes had softened and the grin had gone leaving a small smile – not a leer – playing on his face.

'Yeah,' I said. 'What about Jasmine?'

'Perfection in female form,' said Phil. '*Perfezione*. It would be an insult to the race of men not to at least try. Only, I wanted to ask you something too, you know. That night in New York when we had all been drinking. You said one of them had six husbands and I can't remember who.'

Me neither, I thought, but what I said was:

'Patrice.' And I said it very decisively. I would get her out of the way first and deal with Jasmine later. 'And you know what, Phil? She didn't divorce them.'

'What are you saying?' said Phil. 'She's a Mormon?'

'No,' I said. 'They died. She told me. They all died.'

Phil slowly put another Jaffa Cake into his mouth and sat there, waiting for it to melt, looking like a guppy.

'What of?' he said, indistinctly, at last.

'Car crash, heart attack, boat accident, heart attack, renal failure – he was the old one she got all her money from – and another heart attack.'

'She's finished off three men with heart attacks?' said Phil, rubbing his chest. 'Boy, she must know some moves.'

'Oh God,' I said. 'Only you could think that was a plus, Phil. You're a pig.'

'Oink,' said Phil, thoughtfully. 'You know what? I don't believe you. That just doesn't sound true.' I stared at him. I could feel the colour rising in my cheeks.

'What exactly are you saying?' I said. 'Spit it out, why don't you.'

'I'm saying,' said Phil, 'that I don't think she was being straight with you when she told you all that. I think the six dead husbands are probably more symbolic than real.'

'Symbolic of what?' I said. Phil shrugged. 'Well, even if they are she must be fairly nuts to make it all up. Either way, she's best left alone, don't you think?' He shrugged again.

'We've all got our dark places,' he said, which was maddening. How could he sit there and say that anyone who would come out with all of that wasn't seriously screwed up? If Patrice actually marched up to him and told him straight that she'd made up a story like that one he would turn on his heel and she'd never see him again. If I told him even half of what I could, he wouldn't be lolling about eating Jaffa Cakes with me. Oh, people are all very understanding and forgiving so long as it's not for real.

Chapter 11

A Feast in the Freezer

The consultant, on his evening round, told Phil, his mother, Araminta and Finnie, who were clustered at the bedside, that Pollie had passed some vague but significant milestone on the road to recovery, that what he really needed was a good night's sleep, and that they should all go home and calmly work out a visiting rota to provide Pollie with company while sparing him any stress. He hoped, he said, staring at them sternly over his glasses, that there would be no more far-flung family members flying in the next day.

Slightly with their tails between their legs then, Phil and the mothers came bucketing back to Trepolgas in Araminta's Corsa, picking up the five sisters and Finnie's space wagon on the way, for what promised to be a family reunion with several bells on.

Actually, it could have been worse. For one thing, Jasmine, Patrice and I had pulled out as many stops as you can really pull in someone else's house. We cleared the kitchen tabletop, scraping bills, wine catalogues, newspapers and library books into black bin bags, and then dragged the table out into the yard to a spot in a corner where the wall was hidden right up to the upstairs windows under a sprawling Spanish jasmine. It was heavy with blooms and in the twilight the fragrance was just beginning to unroll.

'It's kinda cold though, isn't it?' said New Jersey Jasmine, standing shivering in the crook of the whitewashed wall where the Indian summer had beaten down all day.

'Put a vest on,' I said, hearing my granny's voice under my own. But by the time I had made the trip back to the kitchen to search for a cloth and some napkins and had realised that we would have to make do with a sheet and some squares of kitchen roll, Patrice and she had gone digging around the sheds and barns and had found a pair of chimeneas.

'Verity,' shouted Jasmine. 'Help us drag these mothers. They weigh a ton.'

'There probably won't be anything to burn in them,' I grumbled, bent uncomfortably and staggering as I tried to lift one of the iron legs clear of the cobbles to stop it scraping them.

'It's OK,' said Patrice. 'There are bags and bags of some kind of pellet fuel back there.'

'Pellet fuel?' I said, and groaned. 'You mean peat bricks, don't you? Yeah, why not – let's burn peat to heat the garden. Who needs a planet, anyway?'

'What?' said Jasmine. 'Vee, stop babbling and lift your end up, will you?'

We went together into the pantry to look for food; none of us could have entered that place alone. There was a hare hanging by its back feet from a hook on the door, cloudy-eyed and just beginning to rustle with oxidation under the skin, and we almost lost Patrice to a hotel for a moment, but I threw Finnie's apron over it and she dug deep and went on.

'We're not using anything perishable unless it's unopened and it shows a date,' said Jasmine. 'Nothing from the freezer unless it's in grocery store packaging OK?' I had unearthed a pie and, poking in the air hole in the top, I thought I could identify gooseberries under there.

'A gooseberry pie,' I said, wheedlingly. 'What harm could come from a gooseberry pie?'

'She might have run out of butter and made the pastry with goat's grease,' said Patrice. I threw the pie back into the freezer and slammed the door. In the end, we emerged with a packet of bacon, three tins of chickpeas and a box of noodles, but out of the pantry window over the yard wall I spotted crests of wigwams and the waving tips of what I was sure were bean plants, and when we found the door in the wall and Patrice shouldered it open, we were in luck.

'So, who grows all this stuff, do you reckon?' said Jasmine, twisting a lettuce from its roots and flicking off centipedes with a sharp red fingernail.

'Finnie, without a doubt,' I said. 'What you got, Patrice?'

'Tomatoes, zucchini, and herbs,' said Patrice, coming up. She was holding her harvest in her skirt like a child and smiling dreamily.

'And I've got enough runner beans to reach around the moon,' I said. 'That should do it.'

'Don't you love this place?' said Patrice. 'Can you believe how near the sea is when the air is this soft? And look at that sky! Huh? Jazzie? This reminds me of my great-aunt Tatty's house. Oh, I wish there was something I needed to dig up with a fork.'

'Tatty had four gardeners,' said Jasmine. 'Tatty didn't even carry her own flower basket.'

'Speaking of which,' I said. 'I'm going to have a scout round and see what I can see.'

So Jasmine and Patrice cooked, Patrice in Araminta's apron, running the show, and Jasmine moaning but attacking the slugs, earwigs and greenfly that had come in on the vegetables as if she was a contract killer paid by the hit. Meanwhile, I searched around the walls of the kitchen garden and in the long grass at the edge of the little lake and came back with white dahlias to match the jasmine, furry sweet-pea pods and blue grass heads that clattered together like maracas when the breeze moved them.

'And,' I said, coming into the kitchen, 'I found a pear tree. Rock hard but is there time to cook them?'

There was. They had just gone in when we heard the screech and spray of Araminta returning and Finnie's following rumble.

'How is he?' said Patrice offering a cheek to Phil, who kissed it and looked with interest into the frying pan.

'Honey! I'm home!' said Jasmine under her breath, and they did have that look about them. It was probably only the apron, but still.

'He's really coming along,' said Phil. 'He's perked up no end. In fact, if it wasn't for the fact that his face has done that melting thing, I'd say he was just throwing a sickie to get us all buzzing round him.'

'Hear, hear,' said a loud but smoky voice from behind him. Phil turned, beaming.

'Girls,' he said, 'This is my mother, Ruth. Ma, these are Jasmine, Patrice and Verity.' His mother nodded with a quick tight smile for each of us, but spoke again to Phil. 'Bloody waste of money sending you to that school if you can't make a simple social introduction. Everyone's on a game show.' Phil took a deep breath and started again.

'Verity Drummond, my old friend from London days, Mother. Her business associate, Patrice Carmichael, my new friend who very kindly paid for my last-minute flight home when I heard about Pa. And *her* old friend and business partner Jasmine Cammeggio.'

'That's better,' said Ruth Coates and turned to Jasmine. 'What business are you in?'

Jesus, I thought, seeing Jasmine think it too. I glanced at Patrice who was shooting a look at Ruth which, even without the benefit of narrowed eyes, could have pierced armour. We agreed then, the three of us.

'The movie business,' said Jasmine. 'Patrice is developing a project of Verity's and I'm ... managing the deal.'

'Of course,' said Ruth. 'California.' She gave the quick nod again and then dismissed us as unmistakably as if she had clapped her hands and summoned guards to take us away. 'Where am I sleeping?' she said and strode out of the room with Phil following her.

'What a prize—' Jasmine began, but she was interrupted by sounds of whispering at the back door and what looked like at least a dozen girls poured into the room, to stand goggling at Jasmine and Patrice although not, I was unsurprised to notice, at me. The biggest ones were whip-thin and dressed like hookers with a lot of midriff on display, but they ranged down to a chubby one of about twelve, unpierced and unhighlighted and still wearing a ribbon in her long, straggly hair.

'Are you the movie stars?' said the smallest one at last.

'Movie *executives*, doofus,' said one of her sisters.

'We are,' said Patrice, smiling and inclining her head in a small bow.

The girls, even the oldest ones, opened their eyes wide, enchanted by the treacly vowels of this real live American movie mogul standing in their kitchen.

'You must be Oma,' Patrice went on, putting out her hand. 'And Lottie.' She moved on to the next tallest. 'And . . . ?' Solemnly she shook hands with a Sophie, a Celia and a Poppy, murmuring what pretty names they had and by the time she was done they were in her thrall for ever.

'So girls,' said Jasmine, and five pairs of eyes swivelled to take in this even more fabulous creature. 'Dinner's nearly ready. Why don't we raid your dad's wine cellars and see what we can find?'

'No point,' said Celia, the oldest girl. 'It's all home-made muck down there – Trepolgas Ruby Red and Trepolgas Sparkling White.'

'Trepolgas Rough as Rats and Trepolgas Spit it Back Out, we call them,' said Sophie.

'But,' said Poppy, trying to sound languid but betraying a hint of hopefulness, 'there's usually some gin around somewhere if you know where you look.'

'Behave, girls,' said Finnie, coming in behind them with Araminta. 'Daddy's wine is delicious and if your palates aren't sophisticated enough you must just stick to orange squash until you all get jobs and can afford to buy your own. The table looks lovely, you three. Jolly well done. Now, give me an hour and I'll knock up some supper for us all.'

'No need,' said Patrice. 'It's done. Hummus and flatbread. Garden salad with bacon and croutons, Idaho baked potatoes and Pears Beau Napoleon, which is really just Pears Belle Hélène except they're picked from Pollie's garden, and poached in Pollie's wine. And the chocolate sauce is melted Snickers because they were all we could find.'

'You're an angel,' said Finnie, blowing Patrice a kiss. 'You found some ice cream then? God knows what's in that freezer if you dig deep enough.'

'Don't look at me,' said Araminta. 'Is you fill it all the time. I don't eat frozen food.'

'Yeah,' said Jasmine. 'We found some. But I must say if we'd known who was coming it could have been home-made, huh?' We all looked at her, puzzled. 'I mean Patrice could have knocked up some custard and got Ruth to look at it.'

There was a moment's stunned silence after this and then Finnie, Araminta and the older girls broke into whoops of laughter. Even Oma and Lottie, who didn't understand, joined in.

'Oh, that's the first time I've laughed in days,' said Finnie, blotting her eyes with the backs of her hands. 'Jasmine, my love, you've hit the nail on the head. Only for gawd's sake,' she lowered her voice, 'don't let Philly hear you.'

It's a funny thing, but despite all the cross currents running amongst us, despite the worries we shared and those that some of us harboured secretly, that first supper in the garden at Trepolgas with the Spanish jasmine and peat smoke heavy in the air was magic. And even Ruth couldn't spoil it; not now the rest of us were in league against her and were waiting, hoping, for her to do something we could flash our eyes and nudge one another about. She was rather sour about the sleeping arrangements.

'It seems that all the good rooms are taken then,' she said, coming back downstairs with Phil and joining us outside.

'What do you expect?' said Araminta. 'We did not know you were going coming. What do we? Keeping a room all ready all times in case you arrive?'

Ruth's only answer was to shake a cigarette out of a packet she took from her breast pocket and light it in a candle flame. Jasmine coughed ostentatiously like a true Californian and Patrice, just at that moment arriving at the table with her dish of hummus, shot another skewer of a look at the cloud of smoke in front of Ruth's face.

But other than that … the girls were raucous, flirty, slightly showing off to Jasmine and Patrice and disarming both of them and me. Phil was almost as relieved to be home again as he was to have good news about his father, I thought, and Finnie and Araminta were warmer to each other than I had seen them up until that moment. The food was delicious – and safe to eat – and the wine, even the white sparkling, was masked by all the lemon and garlic in the hummus and Pollie wasn't there to be offended if we put ice cubes in it to see if the cold would mask it some more.

'Why aren't you a movie star?' said Oma, halfway through the meal, after staring fixedly at Jasmine for a while. 'It's a shame when you look like that, isn't it, Mummy?'

'Everyone in California looks like that,' said Phil. 'No offence Jazzie, but it does get dull.'

'But how can they?' said Oma, who was at the age when doggedness is the main conversational style.

'Because they spend all of their days have plastic surgery,' said Araminta, a little irked to have been shouldered so completely out of the role of resident beauty. 'Peeling, waxing and dyeing.'

'And what do you do all day long that's so—' said Celia, but her mother wagged a finger at her and she shut up.

'Anyone can look beautiful, girls,' said Jasmine. 'You want me to tell you how?' Six heads nodded eagerly. The five girls' and mine. 'Well,' she began, 'the best way to *look* beautiful is to *be* beautiful. And the first step to being beautiful is ... Can you guess?' Five heads shook. I had recovered some of my poise and arranged a fond look on my face like the rest of the grown-ups – except Ruth who was staring into the distance, smoking hard. 'Beautiful skin,' said Jasmine.

Sophie put her face down, but Jasmine took hold of her chin and raised it again. 'Honey,' she said. 'Puh-lease. If you had seen the zits I had when I was a kid. They go away. They're nothing. Now, here's how you get beautiful skin. You drink water until you're peeing clear.' Oma and Lottie giggled but Jasmine ignored them. 'You sleep at least eight hours a night with a window open. You don't run around with bad boys who make you cry, cos crying is not good for your complexion. You only go out with nice boys and, even then, you make them cry if anyone's gonna. What else? You don't drink too much booze.' She lowered her voice. 'You don't smoke, cos if you do you end up looking like a rhino's kneecap. Unless you're very lucky and you got that gorgeous Latin skin that forgives all.' She winked at Araminta and glanced at Ruth, who wasn't listening. 'And finally, you slap on any old beauty cream you find lying around. It's all the same. Save your money. Cos you know what?' They shook their heads. 'If any of those damn things worked, why would rich people ever look old?'

'I always suspected that,' said Finnie. 'Thank you. I'm going back to Tesco's own brand until I die.'

'Is that what you do too, Patrice?' said Sophie. Patrice laughed.

'All that and more,' she said. 'Jasmine isn't telling you the whole story, girls.' But Finnie had her hands clasped in a prayer, beseeching Patrice not to spoil it for them, and Patrice relented. 'No,' she said. 'Jasmine forgot the most important thing of all. If you want to be beautiful, you have to feel beautiful, you have to believe it. You have to walk into every room full of strangers believing it, because if you believe it . . . they will too. Now . . . do you believe?' The girls looked around at each other in the candlelight and slowly one by one they began to nod.

'I thought you were a New Yorker?' said Phil. 'That's the biggest load of California I ever heard.'

'All women are from California inside,' said Patrice softly, making him blink in surprise.

'See, girls?' said Jasmine. 'That's exactly what I was telling you about good boys and bad boys. Was that a kind thing Phil just said, or was that a mean, nasty thing that could make a girl cry?'

'Mean and nasty!' came the chorus.

'Right,' said Jasmine. 'And he has no girlfriend. Do you see? All the girls in the world are too smart to let Phil turn them ugly. So you take a good look, sweethearts. Here's what you *do not* settle for, when the time comes.'

'Oink,' said Phil.

By the time Patrice was hacking into a Costco tub of supposedly soft-scoop vanilla, we'd all had enough of Pollie's wine to admit how filthy it was. Almost all of us, anyway.

'Araminta, he's not here,' said Finnie. 'You don't need to be loyal, he can't hear you.'

'But I believe what he say to me,' Araminta said stoutly. 'If we let it out when we are all alone we can't make it true to fool the buyers who need to buy to make a business. Is like method acting. Have to believe.'

'OK, I dare you,' said Phil. 'Have a mouthful of ice cream and then a slug of Spit it Out. I bet you a fiver you can't do it.'

'Is not a dessert wine,' said Araminta.

'Tenner,' said Phil.

'I've tasted worse,' said Ruth.

'You haven't tasted anything since you were twelve, Mother,' said Phil. 'The last thing you tasted was a packet of jujubes that you bought at the same time as your first twenty fags.'

Ruth brayed with laughter, sending out a puff of smoke with each note.

'I'm the best taster on the whole plantation,' she said.

'Oh well then,' said Phil, spreading his arms. 'I rest my case. You have the palate for munching newly roasted coffee beans – and I've tasted your blends, remember.' He turned to me. 'My mother goes in for several cheeky little coffee beans for their home roast to catch the safari trade. They range from Breakfast in the Crackhouse to one they call the Destructor.'

Ruth laughed again, still with an edge of something that could have been menace, but might just have been nicotine.

'That explains a lot,' said Finnie quietly. There was a silence, while everyone waited to see if everyone else was going to let it pass.

'What did you mean by that, Mummy?' said Oma at last. 'Ow,' she added, and glared across the table at Celia.

'Yes, do tell,' said Ruth, aiming for a purr in her voice but ending up with a growl.

'Oh nothing,' said Finnie. 'More ice cream, anyone? Say now or it'll have to go away to stop it melting.'

'Well, why did you say it?' said Oma. '*Ow*!'

'Very well then,' Finnie said. 'I was just thinking that perhaps someone with the taste buds of a woolly mammoth wasn't the best person to make the decisions in a coffee bean enterprise if you want it to be a success.'

'Is a good point,' said Araminta.

'What would you know about making a success of anything?' said Ruth, turning on her. 'Your bloody father's run the finca into the ground and this place is a joke.'

'We're just starting,' said Araminta. 'This place was a joke when I got here.' And she glared at Finnie. I couldn't help but notice that, contrary to the usual pattern, Araminta's English got better when she was annoyed.

'Well, don't look at me,' Finnie said. '*I* never pretended to be a farmer.' She stuck her tongue out at Ruth. 'And if your so-called coffee plantation is doing so well, my love, why have you scuttled over here to see what you might be able to lay your hands on if Pollie's for it?'

'Is Daddy going to die?' said Oma and she shot back from the table, getting out of the way of any sisterly kicks.

'Of course not,' said Patrice. 'He's much better now. Finnie, I really think the girls should go see him tomorrow, don't you? Just for a minute. They need to see their poppa and he needs to see them. It'll help with his healing.'

Phil and Finnie were looking at Patrice wondering whether to disturb the picture of family bliss she had painted or leave it be, when Jasmine stuck her oar in.

'So the whole family are farmers, huh?' she said. It sounded as though, ignoring her own beauty advice, she was slightly drunk. 'That's nice. A family isn't a family without a family business, you ask me. What does the place in Argentina grow?'

'A plantation's hardly—' said Ruth.

'Is not to talk about,' said Araminta. 'Ruth is right.'

I agreed. How could it help the course of the evening to remind any of them that they all came from the same big happy incestuous family.

'I'm interested,' insisted Jasmine, ignoring my flashing eyes. 'My family is always interested in other people's business. You keep your ear to the ground wherever you go, you learn a lot.'

'We have a big farm in Argentina where I come from,' said Araminta. 'Beef cattle and horses.'

'Once upon a time,' said Ruth. 'It's more rusty fences and prairie grass these days.'

'My father,' went on Araminta, 'big shot, big ideas, you know – he spent all his money buy farmland in the north, in Colombia and Ecuador and … things don't go so well.'

'So what do you grow in Colombia then? Heh heh heh,' said Jasmine.

'Is no joke,' said Araminta. 'We can't grow anything – not corn, not coffee, not even grapes for …' She put her head down on the table and groaned again 'For wine so disgusting it make me sick inside my stomach.' At that Finnie cheered and Phil shouted that Araminta owed him a tenner.

'Hence,' said Ruth, 'sending the prettiest of the daughters over here to see what she could make of my leavings?'

'Pollie wasn't your leavings when Araminta came,' said Finnie. 'He was my husband.'

'I came to London to learn English,' said Araminta.

'Why can't you grow anything?' said Patrice, hastily, judging that farming was perhaps the safest topic on offer right now after all. 'I thought South America was ...'

'Is the drugs,' said Araminta. 'The co-co boys. My stupid father never ask why the land is so cheap, good rich land so very cheap like a desert. But we can't use it. Those sodding co-co boys have a ... I don't know what to call ... a stop the road, stop the supply come.'

'A blockade?' said Jasmine.

'My benighted brother-in-law doesn't have the sense he was born with,' said Ruth, taking up the tale. 'He never stopped to wonder how it was that he could buy however many thousand acres of freshly cleared forest at a snip and why no one else was doing it. Now, he can't even afford to run the Argentinean place and he can't sell up in Colombia because he was the last person in the world stupid enough to buy there.'

'Why doesn't he sell it to the co-co boys?' said Jasmine.

'Jazzie!' said Patrice 'How can you even say such a thing? You must excuse Jasmine, Araminta. She's drunk.'

Araminta shrugged.

'He would if he could,' she said. 'But who you think sold it to him? They sold him the land and then they use anyway. Who is go stop them?'

Jasmine was frowning with her lips pushed forward in a pout.

'That's just rude,' she said. 'That's disrespectful and rude. You should never let people push you around that way. People get the idea they can treat you that way, what they gonna do next time?'

Araminta shrugged again. 'Nothing we can do,' she said. 'What we do?' And the doleful sound of defeat in her voice infected everyone.

Ruth glowered at the tablecloth.

'The effing Colombians have got the coffee market stitched up too,' she said. 'Finnie's right. We're going under.'

'Well, it was the effing Kenyans that pinched the flower trade from Cornwall,' said Phil. 'So it serves you right. Them and the effing Dutch.'

'But Cornwall could steal the wine market from under the effing French,' said Finnie and raised her glass of Trepolgas Ruby Red. 'Only not with this stuff it can't,' she admitted and put her glass back down.

'Is effing the same as fucking?' said Oma. 'Ow! Mummy, that was *you*.'

Even so, it was hard to stop my spirits lifting when I woke the next morning in the Adam Room. The sky outside my window was a pale pinkish blue promising another glorious day and I had thought of a way to keep Jasmine and Patrice away from Phil. An absolute dead cert of a way. *Schadenfreude* lifted my spirits even further when my bedroom door opened and Jasmine came in, eyes shut, hands out, tottering a little on her pony-skin mules.

'They should change the name of that stuff,' she said, lowering herself gently on to a slipper chair by my bed, 'to Trepolgas Once is Enough. It's poison.' She was dressed in a short silk nightie with spaghetti straps and I could see goose pimples on the backs of her arms.

'You cold?' I said.

'Nauseous,' she replied. 'Shivering with revulsion at the memory. It'll pass.' We heard Patrice's bedroom door open, far in the distance.

'Jas?' she called.

'Through here,' I shouted back and we listened to the sound of her footsteps advancing slowly through the Gallery Room. She was wearing a sleep mask pushed up on her head and was still in a pair of complicated-looking Japanese pyjamas but she had already put on a film of foundation and some lipstick.

'Never again,' she said, dropping on to the foot of my bed.

'Good one,' said Jasmine. 'Trepolgas Once is Enough and

Trepolgas Never Again. You're a very bad influence, Vee. We hear about you Brits and your boozing and, my God, it's true.'

'I feel fine,' I said, getting more cheerful by the minute.

'Wait till you move your legs,' said Patrice.

'Still,' said Jasmine. 'It was a fun night. Great kids, aren't they?'

'Finnie's a lucky woman,' said Patrice.

'Except for being shoved out of her house and her marriage by the Argentinean bombshell,' I reminded her. 'Although she doesn't seem to have been shoved out that far, does she?'

'And if you ask me,' said Jasmine, 'Araminta would be back in the Andes like a rocket if she could see a way to get there. You should have heard her last night when we were doing the dishes, her and me. She was looking around that God-awful kitchen down there as if she wanted to torch the place. Homesick as hell.'

'Do you think she married Pollie just to get a roof over her head?' I asked.

'Oh please,' said Jasmine. 'Look at him, look at her. What do *you* think? God, people like that drive me crazy. Letting some two-bit hoods keep them off their own farm. And Ruth! Can't run a coffee farm in Kenya – that must be like taking candy from a baby. Even Phil, sitting on this beautiful, lush, parcel of land, complaining. These people are too dumb to live.'

'Actually,' I said. 'I need to talk to you about Phil.'

'Ahhh,' said Jasmine, sliding down in the chair so that her short nightie wrinkled up even higher. She wriggled her toes in the bedside rug, making the long tendons in her legs ripple under the olive skin. 'Yes, let's talk about Phil.' There was a glint under her lashes as she peeped up at Patrice, checking the effect. Patrice looked up and down Jasmine's body, then down at her own, and her face made one of the infinitesimal shifts of alignment that did her instead of a frown.

'I can't ignore the fact,' I went on, 'that you're ... both ... I can't see it myself, but that's another story.'

'It's because you're still grieving,' said Jasmine. 'Another six months and you won't be able to believe you let him slip by. He's a honey. Potentially, anyways. A unique opportunity for honey development.'

'I would just hate to see either of you get mixed up with him unless you knew the whole story,' I said. 'Because honey potential or no, when the chips are down, when it comes to the crunch ... well, I'll just tell you and you make up your own minds from there.'

They waited, expectant, Jasmine with her eyebrows slightly raised.

'You know I said they were together when Kim died?'

'He killed him!' said Jasmine. 'I knew it.'

'Shut up, Jas,' said Patrice.

'No, he didn't kill him,' I went on. 'Kim died ... in the ice. It *was* a true story. Or based on one. Clovis doesn't know. That's why I didn't want you to tell her about Kim dying. In case she put two and two together and thought I was callous to write it. And that's why I didn't want you to tell Phil anything about the script. Because Kim died and Phil survived, you see?'

'You mean Phil just abandoned him?' said Patrice.

'No, he tried to save him. He failed, but he did try. Then ... he ... survived. For four weeks, in a hole in the ice, waiting for help to come.'

'Wow,' said Jasmine. 'Four weeks? How did he keep going?'

She was waiting for me to answer, eyes wide and cheeks still rosy. Patrice however, had gone waxy under her foundation cream.

'Oh God,' she said.

'What?' said Jasmine. 'He *did* kill him, didn't he?'

'No,' I told her. 'He ate him.'

And then I watched as the blood drained out of Jasmine's face until she was white from her hair to her lace-edged nightie trim.

'He ate your husband?' she said, weakly. I nodded. 'And you're still friends with the guy? Vee, what is *wrong* with you?' She rose up and stood towering over me, then shook her head slowly once or twice, turned and marched back into her bedroom, slamming the door.

'What does she mean "What's wrong with *me*"?' I said, staring after her.

'The thing you have to remember about Jasmine,' said Patrice, 'is that while she's very ... earthy, she has a strict sense of honour. Especially family honour.'

'What, like, I've been disloyal to *family* so shoot me but Phil's OK because the guy he ate was just a friend?'

Patrice put her hands up in front of her face to block the words as if they were birds pecking at her.

'And she's upset anyway,' she went on, 'because she thinks I'm screwing up her deal.'

'Well, I have some very good news for you on that score,' I said. 'I spoke to Clovis yesterday.'

'Go on.'

'And she doesn't care about Hollywood.'

Patrice sat up sharply, too sharply for her hangover, but her eyes were shining.

'Sorry! No!' I said. 'She cares – cares very much – about it being a US deal, don't get me wrong, but she's not interested in PR value. In fact, Patrice, she doesn't even think you're going to make the film.'

'She said that to you?'

'She did, but I don't think she meant to be insulting, she was just trying to stop me getting my hopes up. She told me that producers buy options like other people breathe oxygen and it might come to nothing in the end. And don't you see? This is good news. Great news.' I waited, but she stared back at me blankly. 'If she doesn't care about the *movie*, then she must care about the *money*. See? Because what else is there? And if it's money she wants, then you're home free. Because isn't money what you've got to spare?'

Patrice only stared some more.

'It's a bit more complicated than that,' she said at last.

'How can it be?'

Another long stare.

'Well, because we haven't exactly been one hundred per cent open with you,' she said at last.

'You ... You ... You promised me,' I said. 'And then you promised me *again*.'

'I know, I know,' said Patrice. 'And I was completely straight with you, Verity. Truly I was. The rest of it is Clovis's story. You see, if Clovis needs this ... transaction to be international, and it goes through domestic, then it's going to attract attention.'

'Who from?'

'Officials.'

'Official what?'

'I don't know what you would call them,' said Patrice.

'You mean like taxmen and all that?'

'Exactly,' she said, clapping her hands. 'Taxmen, auditors, accountants. All of that. And if the deal goes through domestic for no good reason that anyone can see, say because the other party – that's me – is from somewhere else, then it's going to attract even more attention. And in that case, more money is worse. More money is just more conspicuous.'

'This all sounds very ...' I said.

'It's just business,' said Patrice.

'No wonder Jasmine wants out of it.'

'But what Clovis doesn't see,' Patrice went on, 'and Jasmine doesn't see either, and what I'm only just beginning to see, is that if I *do* have a good reason to be here, if I move here, if I live here, then there's nothing ...'

'Bent?' I said, 'Crooked? Dodgy?'

'... *concerning* about me doing business here.' She beamed at me. 'So I just need to figure it out.' She stared at me as if hoping that I would say something useful. I stared back. 'If Jazzie would only get behind me,' she went on. 'Or maybe Phil could help.'

As she said Phil's name, she remembered what she had just found out about him and shivered once more.

'How *do* you sleep at night?' she said. 'How do you get up in the morning and go to sleep every night with those thoughts in your head? How have you not gone crazy and how – I don't want to sound like Jasmine – but how *can* you still be friends with him? You must be the most forgiving person ever born.'

She was making me feel bad now. Perhaps I had underestimated how other people would take this. What could I tell her? I decided to fall back on the truth.

'I think about flowers,' I said. 'I plan things, with flowers.' Patrice looked puzzled. 'For instance ... do you ever imagine getting married again?' She nodded hesitantly. 'Spring, summer?' Patrice shook her head.

'I'd love to get married in winter,' she said. 'In a fur-trimmed gown. I don't like to show a lot of bare flesh.'

'OK, a winter wedding,' I said. 'A tough call, but here goes. We're going to have to import some of them, obviously. I need to make that clear from the outset. And the most important thing is to make it seasonal without it being at all Christmassy. It's not Christmas. That comes round every year. It's your wedding day!'

'Plus I'm Jewish,' said Patrice.

'Of course, there's that too. So, green, white, lilac and blue-red for a colour scheme. We'll get red roses – I don't care if they're a cliché. Weddings are a cliché. And you so rarely get to use them in summer because the light's too strong and they can look vulgar. But fragrant red roses in winter sunlight coming off snow? Beautiful. I'm making it snow on your wedding day, I hope that's OK. Rosa Guinée for your bouquet, dark red, smelling like heaven – they're a climber and you can't even get them with reliably long stems here in England, never mind imported, but I'm talking about my dream world here. So Guinée in your bouquet with dark philodendron leaves – heart leaf, they're called. No holly and ivy here. And Lachenalia – you know what that is? I didn't think so. It's sprays of little white waxy flowers just blushed with lilac, they're like tiny little ballerinas all strung together, fragrant, adorable. God knows where I'd get them but they'd be perfect. For the big arrangements at the ceremony, more red roses but this time Roseraie de l'Hay. Same colour as the Guinée but they're huge, must be six inches across, so they're the right scale and they'd fill the whole place with perfume. And your flower girls – if you're having flower girls? I thought so – could carry little boxes of dried red rose petals to sprinkle on the aisle for you to walk on. Not baskets, baskets are too summery. Little dark green velvet boxes, or perhaps cones. No, suede. Nicer. Green suede the shape of hatboxes hanging from ribbons over their arms. And they wouldn't be those freeze-dried petals. We'd order them air dried from somewhere and when you stepped on them they would smell sublime. And then afterwards, on the tables at the reception, I think we should have more of the green suede hatboxes – you could bet your life every woman in the room would be wishing she was a flower girl when she saw the first ones. And in these boxes, set into moss, we'd have living snowdrops and red cyclamen. Wintry still, but with just a hint of "new beginnings".'

I sighed happily and Patrice did too. 'That's what I think about, when things get too much,' I said.

Patrice nodded then came slowly and reluctantly back to the autumn morning, back to her hangover and her pyjamas instead of her fur-trimmed white dress.

'Oh, Verity,' she said. She pulled her sleep mask back down over her eyes and shuffled down until she was almost horizontal on my bed. 'Tell me again.'

Chapter 12
Cold Cloths and Aspirin

I arrived downstairs after a dip in Jasmine's bathwater to find Finnie, Ruth and Araminta trying to thrash out a timeshare for Pollie's bedside. Patrice was presiding and Phil was providing useless sarcastic commentary. I made myself some toast and left to find a perch in the garden.

'But I'm his wife,' said Araminta for the fifth time in my hearing.

'Three years,' said Finnie. 'I put in eighteen long winters in this house and bore him five children.'

'I'm the mother of his son,' said Ruth. 'I'm the wife that continued the Coates line.'

'You sodded off to Africa, Ma,' said Phil. 'I think you've lost a bit of leverage there. And it's me he wants to talk to anyway. We hardly scratched the surface yesterday.'

Outside, I crossed the kitchen garden and went out through the far gate into what should have been a meadow but was now a dusty field of stripped and tortured vines, twisted around stretched wires, the posts dug in at angles to pull the wires even tighter. At the far side of the field the land disappeared and a flat rock promised a view of the sea, so I made my way towards it. Of course, when I got there I saw only another two rolling vine fields – the sea, like the brow of a hill, is never as close as you think – but I sat down on the rock anyway and gazed out to where I thought it must be.

How could Finnie bear to be here, in what should be her home, where she had spent eighteen of the best years of her life? How could she sit there with the woman who had thrown it away and the woman who had stolen it from her? I couldn't have sat at a table with *her*. I couldn't have gone and hung around my kitchen on Wandsworth Bridge Road, making tea and bickering with *her*. If Kim ever ended up lying ill in a hospital bed, I wouldn't even get to know.

Helen was lying down in her underwear on top of the bed, flipping through paint catalogues, sticking little page markers against the colours she liked enough to discuss.

'There's no point in looking at paint,' said Kim, coming through from the bathroom, dripping, with a towel around his waist. Helen frowned.

'How many times?' she said. 'Why can't you get dried in the bathroom, Kimmie?'

'Because it's too hot,' said Kim. 'Because you won't let me open the door, because it steams up the bedroom. So take your pick: drips or steam? And don't try to change the subject. We're not decorating a house we're only going to move out of and sell.'

'I don't want to talk about it,' said Helen.

'We're going to have to talk about it sometime,' said Kim.

'I can't see why,' Helen insisted, flicking over a page.

'You don't have to see why,' Kim told her. 'It's the law.'

'I'm sure you could contest it,' Helen said putting the catalogues down with a smack and closing her eyes. 'Your ex-wife brought no property into the marriage, produced no children during the marriage; why should she take a half of a London house out of it?'

'Since when is she my "ex-wife"?' said Kim. 'What's happened to her name?'

'Now who's changing the subject?'

'I don't want to contest it,' Kim said. 'You know that. I've told you before. Verity leaves the marriage with a good slice of a London house because I stood up in front of a lot of our friends and promised – no, vowed – that I would share everything I had with her. If you would like a different arrangement for our wedding vows, just let me know.'

Helen scowled, without opening her eyes.

'And anyway, she does have some property of her own, as a matter of fact.'

At that Helen's eyes snapped open.

'And are you splitting it with her?'

'No,' said Kim. 'It's her granny's house. Verity was born there. And it's only an ex-council flat anyway.'

'It must be worth something,' said Helen. What sort of area is it in?'

'It's offset against this place,' said Kim. 'Do you know, I think your eyes actually lit up just then. Pink. Not really your colour, pink.'

'But you're still going to have to sell even with this council flat in the frame? We still can't afford to stay?'

'Helen, why on earth would you want to stay? This was the house that Verity and I lived in together. Why don't you want a home of our own?'

'It's a good postcode,' said Helen. 'And it's very handy for the Heathrow tube. Anyway, I'm the one who wants to decorate away all traces of your ex-wife. What's that if it's not wanting to make a home of my own?'

Kim laughed suddenly and once again Helen opened her eyes.

'What?' she said.

'Nothing,' said Kim. 'You just reminded me of something.'

'A Verity story?'

'A little Verity sidebar,' said Kim. 'I said exactly the same to her, you know. When we came here. I said we couldn't afford to decorate it and we would just have to live with it as it was for a while. So you know what she did? She accidentally left the kitchen window open one day when we went out to work.'

'All day?'

'And when I got home, vandals had come in and spray painted over the walls.'

'Did they steal much? Did they break everything?'

'Nothing. Not a sausage. Well, one lamp that Verity wasn't too keen on. And actually, they didn't even spray everywhere. Not the bathroom. Not on the plain white tiles that no one could object to.'

Helen was giggling too now.

'She didn't!'

'Oh, she did. The insurance covered everything, including carpets. It was hard to be angry really.'

'And how did you know?'

'Because she wrote "shite". With an "e" on the end. The local coppers said they'd keep an eye out for a vandal with very neat writing and a northern accent, but they never found him.'

I had only just finished my coffee when I heard Patrice calling for me.

'Over here,' I shouted, standing up on the rock and waving my arms as she put her head around the door in the kitchen-garden wall. She loped over to join me, stumbling now and then in a pair of borrowed wellies, but setting a good pace.

'You're a very efficient runner,' I called as she drew near. 'You don't hug your chest and shilly from side to side like I do. I saw myself once on a video and I looked like I was doing the Charleston.'

'It's all in the bra,' said Patrice climbing on to the rock beside me. She fanned her face with her hands. 'I can't believe it's October – everyone always said England was cold and grey.'

'You seem very happy all of a sudden,' I said.

'I am,' Patrice twinkled back at me. 'I've got a plan. Only, I don't know what you'll think of it, or of me for even suggesting it.' She took a huge breath. 'Because I'm going to have to do Phil quite a big favour to get it to pan out.'

'Why would I …?' I said. And then I remembered. 'Oh. That. Kim.'

'You're such a lovely person,' said Patrice. 'Even after what you told me, you don't mind if I help Phil prosper?' She was smiling at me so kindly that, not for the first time, I wanted to put my head on her shoulder and tell her all about it, about how the putty that held my marriage in place dried up so that my life fell out of its frame and crashed on to the pavement with a resounding *Divorce!*

I didn't go that far, obviously, but I went further than I would have believed, further than I ever had before. Without planning to, I suddenly found myself saying:

'Can I tell you something? Can *I* trust *you*?'

Patrice nodded and took my hands.

'It wasn't true,' I went on. 'What I told you this morning, about Phil and Kim, it wasn't true.' I didn't black out exactly, but the bright day went dim around me and my hands felt cold as I waited for Patrice to say something.

'Thank God for that,' was what came out at last.

'I was just trying to make sure that you didn't – you and Jasmine, I mean – that you stayed away from Phil. I was trying to put you off him.'

'Why?' said Patrice.

'I just really need you not to talk to Phil about my husband,' I said. 'And I can see you getting closer and once you're closer to him than he is to me or you are to me ...'

'You poor little thing,' said Patrice. 'Poor baby, what is it that's wrong?'

'I can't tell you any more,' I said. 'You would hate me and I couldn't stand that.'

'OK, OK,' said Patrice and she smoothed my cheek with one of her long cool hands. 'That's OK. But you know what? As gruesome as this is going to sound, I don't think it worked on Jasmine, sweetie.'

'I'll take care of it,' I said. 'Somehow. If that didn't put Jasmine off Phil I don't know what could, but I'll put Phil off her instead. Just leave it to me.'

'What are you going to tell him?' said Patrice. 'The mind boggles after what you tried this morning, but I'd love to know.'

I ran my mind over the possibilities. At least, I ran my mind over the place where the possibilities should have been, but there was nothing there. What was happening to me?

'I'll think of something,' I said.

'I'm just so glad it's not true,' Patrice said, almost laughing.

'You're being very kind about it,' I said. 'Considering I basically told you a ... well, a great big ...'

'A necessary misdirection,' said Patrice. 'And I'm sure you have your reasons.'

'You're not angry?'

She shook her head.

'I know you have this thing about being totally straight up all the time,' she said. 'I haven't forgotten what you said about your husband. You took a tough line with him. But most of us can see that … yes, honesty is great but life is complicated. We all have to do things we wouldn't tell our mommas sometimes. And when we do it's best to keep the details to ourselves.'

I tried to follow, but nothing made sense to me any more. Sitting on that rock, in the sunshine, nothing that came out of my mouth or out of Patrice's mouth seemed to make any sense at all. She was saying she had a secret plan and yet I still trusted her. I had just come clean to her about a major whopper and yet she was telling me she trusted me. She was smiling at me. What would happen, I asked myself, if here in this place, I chipped away a bit of that tight little clenched thing and let her see it? I had no way of knowing. I couldn't tell how anything would work, here. I felt as if I'd left my home planet and was sitting on a little flat rock sticking out of the moon.

The house was heaving when we got back. Finnie was slicing the roast pork from the day before, which I had to say looked lovely, the girls were racing around the kitchen scrabbling in the glued tureens and dresser drawers looking for a charity pen that was still working to write cards for their father; I noticed that Poppy and Celia were glistening with cheap face cream and had bottles of spring water on the go. Jasmine was making herself an egg white omelette at the stove, standing in two dog baskets in her mules, and Araminta and Ruth were crouched at the table over cups of coffee and cigarettes and trying to ignore the room around them.

'Where's Phil?' I asked.

'Gone to get the dogs,' said Finnie, with a note of triumph. 'Much too complicated without having to keep rushing over to the dower house to feed them and let them out. They're coming home.' She turned back to her slicing and Araminta blew a thin jet of smoke towards her back.

'Elephant's kneecap,' said Oma, giggling.

'Rhino, doofus,' said Sophie.

'Patrice, my love,' said Finnie. 'Explain again how this is going to work.'

'It's not complicated,' said Patrice. She turned to me. 'I worked out a rota. The girls get ten minutes each first thing, while Daddy's feeling fresh. No one has to sit in the dismal lunchroom all alone, no one has to take a taxi and all the immediate family gets an hour each. Only, you need to come with us now, Verity, as the coffee-break companion and you won't be back until the afternoon. I hope that's OK?'

'Us?' said Jasmine. 'Who exactly is "us" these days, Patrice?'

'Phil and me,' said Patrice.

'And where do I come in?' Jasmine asked, sliding on to a chair.

'You can stay here with Ruth and Araminta until later,' Patrice told her.

Jasmine scowled, jabbed up a square of omelette with her fork and flicked it into her mouth, closing her teeth on it with a snap.

I drove Patrice and Phil in the hire car. We were following Finnie and the girls in the van but they soon shook us off. It wasn't just Araminta clearly, and it wasn't the Latin blood that did it. Sturdy, solid Finnie who had only taken her apron off as she turned the key in the ignition and who was ferrying a precious cargo of offspring as well as a brimming bowl of apple sauce to go with the pork, roared off across the cattle grid at the end of the drive and disappeared around the bend in the lane with daylight visible under two of her wheels.

'How is he this morning?' said Patrice. 'Did you hear any news when you called in?' She was hunched forward, her face between the two front seats. Phil turned his head, smiled at her and reached over to ruffle her hair.

'He's bloody annoying, I gather,' he said. 'That's not what the staff nurse said in so many words but that was the message just the same.'

'But that's wonderful,' said Patrice. 'If he's goosing the nurses and complaining, he's going to be fine.'

'I only wish *he* would believe that,' said Phil. 'He's convinced he's going to die and he's in such a temper about not being able to afford it that he's going to give himself a proper stroke and make it come true.'

Patrice caught my eye in the mirror and then shuffled in her seat until she was looking at Phil.

'I need to talk to you about that,' she said. Phil looked puzzled.

'Do you think if your father could afford to die – you're talking about the taxes, right?'

'Death tax, the overdraft, the business loan, the ex-wives, the hordes of daughters clamouring for braces and MP3s,' said Phil. 'God, no wonder the poor old bugger had a stroke, eh?'

'But if he knew he was free and clear, he'd live for ever, don't you think?'

Phil nodded again, and I hoped Patrice was going somewhere with all of this. If not, it was cruel just to dangle it in front of him.

'Well, I have something to put to you.' Patrice went on. 'I need somewhere to stay. A permanent address. And a reason to be at it. So, what I'm asking is, can I come and work for you? Can I help you at Trepolgas? Because if you give me a job you can convince Immigration that only I can do – and remember I did major in management and I have lived in two of the biggest wine-producing states – then basically I get residency and bingo! I'm in.'

'I don't quite ...' said Phil. 'I'd be glad to have you, obviously, but why would buying Verity's book mean that you had to ...?'

'The film business is a very complicated thing,' said Patrice. 'Like the bespoke essay business. And the wine business.'

'Oh God,' said Phil. 'The wine.'

'Yes, but what I'm proposing is that you employ me – as a manager – at Trepolgas wine and I'll see if I can simplify it for you, a little bit.'

Phil let out his breath in a long hissing whistle.

'Patrice, you're very kind,' he said. 'And you're a fiend with a spreadsheet, but we can't afford to employ someone to wash out the bottles, never mind someone to explain why.'

'Well, that doesn't matter so much,' said Patrice, 'because as well as being your employee, I'd invest. Heavily. On excellent terms.'

'I have to advise you against it,' said Phil. 'There is no way a single glass of drinkable wine is ever going to come off that land. And not even to light my dear old father's dying hours can I pretend that it will.'

'I'll take that chance,' Patrice told him.

'Why, for God's sake?' said Phil. 'You've tasted it.'

'To repay you for what *else* you're doing. Fingers crossed. If you agree.'

I looked round sharply at her. This plan had sounded odd from the start but, as Kenny Daateng would say, it got worse the more I heard about it.

'What else *am* I doing?' said Phil. 'You can uncross your fingers, because of course I agree. But what is it?'

'Backdating my arrival,' said Patrice. 'Greasing – no, that sounds tacky – expediting my residency by saying I've been here a while.'

'Sure thing,' said Phil.

I managed not to tut, but my eyes rolled and I couldn't stop them.

'But you're going to lose your money, you know.'

'I could care!' cried Patrice. 'I've got more money than I'll ever need if I live to be a hundred. I want something money can't buy. I want to live here. I just want to be allowed to stay.'

'Why not just buy a place and stay then?' I said, ignoring Phil blowing a raspberry at me. 'No offence, Philly, but there must be an easier way than putting your shirt on Trepolgas wine.'

'Easier but not quicker,' Patrice told me. 'I need to have something secure, all set up, for the deal.'

'Why is it so important?' said Phil.

'Verity, I wish you would tell him about your flowers,' said Patrice. 'You can explain it so much better than me. Phil, I came from a place where nothing was natural, and even when you make it look real, you can't ever escape. But here is different, here it could *be* real. Everything's so easy here. Nobody cares whether things are perfect, everybody just trusts each other and lets it all happen, and if I was here I could be the same. Do you see?'

Phil and I had exchanged a glance while she was talking.

'Not really,' I said, but to my surprise Phil said:

'Kind of, yes. I think so.'

'Of course you do.' And she squeezed between the two front seats and kissed him, actually touching lipstick to skin, leaving a print on his cheek.

'Let's go and tell the old man,' said Phil, swivelling round in his seat, hoping for mouth to mouth contact. Patrice sat back and Phil shrugged. 'I can't wait to see his face.'

Pollie was lying in bed looking, I had to agree with Phil, rather anxious. All his awareness seemed to be turned to the inside as though, his body having let him down once, he was determined to pay attention and catch the next catastrophe before it happened.

'Finnie's got the girls downstairs,' said Phil, stooping and kissing his father's head. 'She's tanking them up on Coke and chocolate before she lets them in to bounce on you.'

Pollie tried to smile.

'Five sodding daughters,' he said. 'At least, I thought, with me as their father and old Finnie as their mother they had a chance of turning out as plain as puddings. I mean, Finnie's a wonderful girl but she's no oil painting. But look at them. All as pretty as angels, and you know what that means. Five sodding, bloody weddings to pay for. I'm almost glad I won't be here to see them.'

'That's what I need to talk to you about,' said Phil. 'Pa, Patrice here – remember from yesterday? – has a proposition to put to you.'

Ten minutes later, Pollie was sitting straight up in bed, nodding briskly, his eyes darting from side to side.

'Inward investment,' he was saying. 'See, Phil, my boy? And you told me going to California was a waste of money.' Patrice was doing her best not to hear, studying the lunch menu and frowning. 'And in the nick of time!' Pollie went on, 'because between you and me,' and at least he lowered his voice, 'between you and me, this year's vintage isn't looking too hopeful, not quite going to be up to my usual standard, and we needed something to get us over the sticky patch. Did we ever!'

Patrice cleared her throat and I could hear a slight whinny as she did so, a laugh that she was far too kind to let out. Pollie fixed her with a hard stare, one eyebrow up and one pulled down making him look like a hawk.

'I take it you're serious about this. In it for the long haul? You won't get tired of it in six months' time and float away back to Tinseltown to dabble in something else instead?' he asked her.

'This is for real,' said Patrice. 'I won't be floating away anywhere ever again. I'm going to be rooted to the ground right here.' She sounded, after less than twenty-four hours, as if she had only been waiting to see Bodmin to know what her life was for.

At that moment, Finnie put her head around the curtain.

'Come on, you lot. Ten minutes, we said. The girls are dying to see their daddy.'

'And the good news,' boomed Pollie, the loudness of his voice making Finnie blink and bringing the sound of nurses' hurrying feet, 'is that their daddy is only dying to see them! And you Finnie, my old armful of alimony. That's all the dying I'm doing today.'

We couldn't talk much in the hospital cafeteria while the daughters were trooping up and down in shifts, but when Patrice took them away in the van at noon, and Finnie was at the bedside for her allotted hour, Phil and I sat at the table and faced each other across its crumb-strewn surface, with a fresh cup of grey coffee and a four pack of custard creams.

'Bit of a turn-up for the books this, then,' he said. 'Do you think Patrice really wants to come and live in darkest Cornwall?'

I shrugged. Not just Patrice, I thought. Try stopping Jasmine too.

'I can't say I get it, do you?'

'Phil,' I told him, 'what I don't get about the movie business gets bigger every day.'

'So are you going back to your vases and ribbons, or off to Hollywood to wait for the Oscars?' I shrugged again. 'Or,' he went on, 'back to London, to Kim?'

'Philly, he's probably sitting planning his next wedding right now, this very minute, as we speak.'

'They're definitely getting married?' asked Phil.

'Why not? Why shouldn't they?'

'Because she's a slimy little chilblain and you and Kim are ...'

'Were,' I said. 'We were, and actually as it turned out, we weren't. We might have looked right on paper, but it wasn't to be.'

'It's not too late. You had a commitment.'

'You've caught California off Patrice,' I said. 'It's not too *late*? Just because we're divorced and he's engaged to someone else?'

'Take a chance,' said Phil. 'Call him. Have some courage for once.'

'Look who's giving advice,' I said. 'Where's *your* courage? Where's *your* commitment? Why don't *you* take a chance ever?'

'I might do,' said Phil.

'Only not right now,' I added, hastily. 'I don't want to interfere, but I have to warn you, I really do.'

Phil clapped his hands to his face and groaned.

'No!' he wailed. 'Don't warn me! Don't you get it, Vert? I don't care. I don't care what Patrice is up to. You saw the old man. This good news is going to save him and that's good enough for me.'

'It's not Patrice I'm talking about,' I said. 'It's Jasmine. I think she's coming in for the kill. She's after you. And – believe me – you really don't want to know.'

'Why not?' said Phil. 'Six symbolic husbands again?'

I reached for another biscuit, playing for time. What could I tell him about Jasmine? She was, quite simply, perfect. Beautiful enough to make people walk into lamp-posts, independent but chummy, funny but full of heart, laid-back but feisty, sassy, sexy, successful. What could I possibly say that would put Phil off the perfect woman? Nothing, obviously. So I would need to move one step beyond.

'The thing about Jasmine,' I said, and I took a deep breath, 'is that she hasn't always been female.' Phil inhaled a crumb and then coughed it out into his hand. 'In fact,' I went on. 'She's not actually all the way there yet.'

'Jasmine?' said Phil, still coughing. 'Jasmine's a tranny? *Jasmine*?'

I nodded, but put my finger to my lips to try to shush him. Jasmine might be laid-back and chummy and all the rest of it but if Finnie rolled up, overheard us and passed on what I'd just said, I wouldn't be surprised if Jasmine forgot California and led with New Jersey, at least for long enough to lay me out.

'I can't believe it,' said Phil.

I shook my head to show him that I could hardly believe it either, but I knew it was true.

'Jasmine,' he said again.

'Jasmine,' I agreed.

'Stone me,' said Phil. 'I thought it was Patrice.'

I was very glad I didn't have a mouthful of custard cream on the go. I gaped at him, waiting for the punchline, but he only nodded, unsmiling, perfectly serious.

'That's what I always thought was the thing that was the thing about Patrice,' he said.

I continued to stare at him, speechless.

'You know, the thing?' he went on. 'We've talked about it.' I nodded slowly. 'And her clothes, all the make-up, the crazy Joan Collins hairdo. Does she seem like a girl who's always been a girl to you?'

I thought back to my very first impression of Patrice. The carefulness, the watchfulness, the sense I had that she was holding herself, placing herself, as if she had only just moved in to her own skin.

'Philly,' I said, 'I think you might be right.'

'It makes sense of a lot of stuff.'

'Like what?'

'Well,' said Phil slowly, 'it explains some of the cobblers about feeling at home and wanting to be where nobody cares if you're perfect. And it explains why Jasmine's always so … protective, doesn't it?'

'Of course!' I said. 'Jasmine knows. Ooh, and you know something else it explains: how her name got chosen on St Patrick's day when her birthday is in July. And why she thinks she's a minority.'

'And knows so much about computers and karate.'

'And loved Ernest Hemingway when she was a little …'

'… boy.'

We spent another short while nodding at each other, becoming more and more sure that this was right.

'Poor old thing,' said Phil at last. 'God, what a palaver, eh?'

'Changing your sex?' I said. 'Just a bit of a one, yes.'

'And quite a significant "ouch",' Phil said, and I could tell that under the table he was crossing his legs.

'I don't really want to think about that,' I said. 'It doesn't seem right to be so interested in it when she's a friend … Oh!'

'What?'

'You said you suspected this?'

'Yeah?'

'But yet you were still …' I said. 'I mean, you said you quite fancied the idea of Patrice. Did you mean if she's not … What *did* you mean?'

Phil laughed.

'You should see your face, Vert,' he said. I flushed 'Talk about Granny Drummond, the next gen.'

'What do you know about Granny Drummond?' I said.

'Kim always talked a lot about her,' said Phil. 'She made a big impression on him, you know.'

'You should have seen the one he made on her,' I said. 'She'd never seen anything like him.'

'And don't forget I met her once, on the famous stag night.' He gave a laugh that turned into a sigh.

We both sat in silence for a while, wondering, remembering. The more I thought about this, the more I was sure it was right. It explained why Patrice was so peculiar about anything to do with fakes, why Jasmine wound her up about being natural, even why she put on foundation to answer her door in her nightclothes. It all made a lot of sense.

'Still can't believe it,' said Phil at last.

'Neither can I,' I said. 'Even though I'm sure it's true. Why doesn't she have an Adam's apple, for one thing?'

'I don't mean Patrice,' said Phil. 'I mean Kim. I can't believe he would do that. Not just that he would go for Helen Thingy, but that he would walk away from you. You and Granny Drummond were all Kim had. That was the point, wasn't it? That was what you had in common when everyone – don't take offence, Vert – but when everyone in Kim's crowd was wondering where the hell he had dug you up. Actually, I'm being really offensive so take all the offence you like, but it's true.'

'It wasn't *just* that,' I said. But of course, he was right. I remembered the day we met, Kim hugging me at the wedding and saying it sucked and me saying I was dreading my own wedding, dreading all the holes where the people should be.

But when it came around, our wedding, Kim's and mine, was

lovely. I did the flowers and my granny was bewildered when she saw the baskets and the limp cotton ribbons and heard about the falling petals, as well as black affronted that it wasn't going to be in a church, or even in a hall, and there wouldn't be a proper dance or a proper dinner, just a lot of standing around and wee bits of nothing to eat. She wiped her eyes and said she had tried her best and it broke her heart to see me getting wed in a second-hand dress; she even whispered that I should think carefully about what I was doing, because Kim had a bob or two, she could tell, but if he was keeping me short already, before the wedding day, she could only imagine what he would be like once the ring was on that finger and the door was shut behind me. I told her it wasn't second hand, it was vintage, and I showed her the receipt. Then she told me that I could have booked the Willowbrae Lodge, with a band and a sit-down meal for eighty guests and had change.

I took Finnie home soon after, leaving Phil with his father and passing Ruth and Araminta on their way in to cover the afternoon shifts. The inside of the little Corsa was fugged with cigarette smoke and we could just make out their two heads of straight hair, one black, one grey, hunched forward as if ready to challenge the rest of the traffic to a duel. I was dying to talk about Patrice but they were the next best thing.

'So, her mother is Ruth's sister,' I said, looking in the mirror at the Corsa's exhaust fumes. 'What does *she* make of it all?'

'Gawd knows,' said Finnie. 'Nothing, I shouldn't imagine. She's one of those women who's got such a spectacularly bad marriage that she spends her life in a state of disappointed dismay and doesn't notice anything else very much.' She gave a sharp laugh. 'Rather like me when I was married to Pollie.'

'That's a bit harsh, isn't it?' I said. 'You look to me like the least divorced divorcee in the world.'

'Oh, I'd go back in a flash,' said Finnie. 'He's an old goat but he makes me laugh and the girls adore him. Besides, it would be so much easier all round not carting the kids and the dogs back and forward.'

I stole a glance at her out of the corner of my eye.

'If you could forgive him,' I said.

'Nothing to forgive,' said Finnie. 'I brought it all on myself. Araminta landed down here from London, Pollie flirted as Pollie does, I threw an enormous strop and huffed off to the dower house expecting him to run after me and beg me to come back. What I *wasn't* expecting was for Araminta to move quite as fast or quite as determinedly as she did. Pollie, led by the trousers as ever, was powerless to resist.'

I couldn't think of a thing to say, dumbstruck by this. She could hardly have hidden the fact that she was divorced but she needn't have come out with all that mea culpa stuff to a practical stranger. Unless, of course, it was easier to pretend it was her fault than to admit that she'd been traded in and it was killing her.

'And how do you rate your chances?' I said, deciding to take her at face value and talk about this as though it was a simple bit of household organisation and not the crushing betrayal that it must really be.

'Not bad, not bad,' said Finnie. 'Araminta's bored out of her skull at Trepolgas, of course, and she's already been seen eyeing up the beach talent. Then, in the last couple of days, I've thought I could detect a fair measure of frantic despair about her – she certainly wouldn't want to be lumbered with an invalid – so I did wonder whether perhaps if the doctors forbade Pollie his favourite hobby, she'd really have no purpose left in his life and he might as well come back to me, for the cooking.' She looked across at me and laughed. 'I know how it sounds,' she said. 'But you did ask and that's the truthful answer. Now, however …' She heaved a mighty sigh. 'If Patrice is serious about this massive cash injection and if Araminta gets wind of it, you won't be able to prise her out with a crowbar. On the other hand, Pollie's so cock-a-hoop about the idea, and it is good to see the old sod happy. I do love him in my way. So, I don't know what to think. I'm …'

'Conflicted,' I said. 'That's what they call it in California anyway.'

'Precisely,' said Finnie. 'I'm conflicted.'

Me too, I thought. Because listening to Phil telling me he could handle what Patrice was hiding and listening to Finnie just blabbing out what any normal person would rather die than have to tell someone, it was almost as though all my … all my … almost as though none of it would have mattered after all.

Back at Trepolgas, what little stores of conflict Finnie and I brought home were, as my granny would say, a drip in a pail. The five girls were sitting in the kitchen, their eyes out on organ stops and their mouths hanging open.

'Mummy,' said Lottie. 'You should hear what Jasmine and Patrice are saying to each other. You should just *hear* it.'

'They've been screeching at each other in the main hall ever since Ruth and Araminta left,' said Celia. 'Language like you wouldn't believe.'

'And I didn't think there *was* language we'd never heard in this house before,' Poppy said. 'Not considering the way Daddy goes on.'

'Wait here,' said Finnie, and she and I hurried towards the passageway leading to the front of the house. We could hear them as soon as we opened the door.

'… can have your motherfucking dream-come-true *anywhere*.'

And then a muffled murmur as Patrice answered.

'Fucking selfish bastard that you are,' screamed Jasmine. 'After everything we've been through, you'd think you could do this one fucking thing for me!'

Another stream from Patrice, out of which I understood only one word: 'Clovis'.

'What in the name of Jesus Fucking Christ are you *talking* about? How have I not helped you with Clovis? It's all good to go. Clovis has done exactly what she said she would do, like I have, like everyone has. And you … you spoiled … you spoiled selfish *freak*! It's still not good enough for you.'

Finnie and I burst in through the double doors. Patrice was huddled on one of the velvet sofas, with her arms around her knees, weeping piteously, deep channels running down through her made-up cheeks, while Jasmine stood over her, her fists bunched and her chest heaving. On the floor, on its side, lay a set of djembe drums with one of Jasmine's mules stuck in the torn skin where she had kicked it.

'Oh well,' said Finnie, nodding at the drum. 'Not all bad then.'

'Jasmine!' I said, going over to Patrice and sitting down beside her. 'Stop shouting and back off. You have no right to speak to her like that.'

'Hah!' said Jasmine, so loud it must have hurt. '*I've* no right? *I've* no right? What makes you think she's the one . . . ?' But she was too angry to finish it. She wheeled around and booted another drum, making it skitter across the floor and crunch against a window frame.

'Hurrah!' said Finnie. 'Only five more to go.'

'Patrice, you poor darling,' I said, trying to wipe her face with my sleeve. 'What's happened? What's going on?' Patrice could only moan and try to pull away from me.

'Oh sure,' said Jasmine, throwing herself down on the opposite sofa. 'Patrice is a poor darling. What about me?'

'You're behaving like a nasty little bully who should be smacked on the legs and sent to bed with no supper,' said Finnie. Jasmine blinked. 'I'm sorry, but I've seen it too often over the years to mistake it for anything else and I speak as I find.' She turned to Patrice. 'And as for you?' She sat down on the sofa on the other side of Patrice who was now honking and gulping as you do when you've cried your heart out until there are no more tears left but still plenty of whatever made you start in the first place. Finnie patted her knees with her hands. 'Come on,' she said.

Patrice looked at her, puzzled, out of sodden, puffy eyes.

'I don't care how old you are or how tall you are,' said Finnie. 'I mean it. Hop on.'

So Patrice shuffled over and lifted herself on to Finnie's lap, while Jasmine and I boggled at each other.

'Now,' said Finnie, pulling Patrice's head on to her shoulder and beginning to sway back and forward, ignoring the snot bubbles that grew on every breath and popped against her neck. 'Shush now, my love, shush now. You don't want to make yourself sick.'

'I have now seen fucking everything,' said Jasmine.

'You're not fooling anyone, miss,' said Finnie, fixing her with a glare. 'So just stop showing off and start acting like a person who has a right to stay in the room.'

Jasmine shaped her mouth to answer – it looked as though the first word started with an 'f', but taking another look at Finnie, at last she subsided.

After a minute or two, silent except for Finnie shushing and the creak of the sofa springs as she rocked back and forth, Patrice sat up and slid down to one side of her. Finnie fished in a cardigan pocket and produced a cotton handkerchief.

'Blow,' she said, handing it to Patrice. 'And now I'm going to get you a cold facecloth.' She stood up and faced Jasmine. 'And the same for you, although you don't deserve it. Your head must be splitting after that tantrum. Now, while I'm gone I want you both to say sorry and make up like good girls. Verity, you tell me if they don't, my love.' And she swept out of the room.

I don't know which one of them started giggling first.

'I'll say sorry first if you help me with my spelling homework,' said Patrice.

'Give me a stick of your gum and we'll call it quits,' said Jasmine.

They both sighed and sat back weakly against the cushions.

'So,' I said. 'What was it all about? What happened? If you can tell me without starting again.'

Patrice blew her nose one more time and dabbed her eyes with the hem of her jacket, leaving black smudges of mascara behind.

'Clovis said no,' she told me. 'She won't do the deal here. She doesn't care about me being resident instead of just visiting. She said it would be "flying a flag of convenience".'

'Well, she's got a point,' I reminded her.

'I know she would change her mind if Jasmine backed me up . . .' said Patrice.

Jasmine started talking over her. Well, shouting. Ranting, actually.

'You don't know *anything*,' she screeched. 'It's not *about* nagging her till she changes her mind. You have to do business the way people do business! That's why you should have left it to *me*. Like I told you. Over and over and *over*. The deal's gone sour for Clovis now. You've dicked her around and acted like a big shot and she's sick of the sound of your voice and if she could see ya she'd be sick of the sight of ya and if she could smell ya she'd be even sicker and . . .'

'. . . but Jasmine won't back me up,' said Patrice.

'Yes,' I said. 'I'm getting that.'

'I've backed you every step of the way for years,' said Jasmine. 'Now, for the first time, I'm thinking of myself. Verity, just listen to my side, will you?' But she broke off as Finnie came back with two washcloths wrung out into twists and handed one to each of them.

'We had a deal,' said Jasmine, scrubbing her neck with the cloth. Patrice laid hers over her head and leaned back. 'All set up, all smooth, no worries, set up by two people – Clovis and me – who know what they're doing. And I was going to shine. Until Patrice – who doesn't have a fucking clue about *anything* – decided she could just wade in and throw the whole thing over her selfish, fucking shoulder and now Clovis is walking away – like I said she would – and I'm going to look like the biggest schmuck that ever lived. Forget a corner office, forget leaving with blessings, I'll be making the coffee and xeroxing for the rest of my life after this is through.'

'So strike out on your own,' said Patrice, as if she had said it ten times before, which she probably had, while Jasmine was shouting.

'Doing what?' Jasmine spat back at her. 'You think it's easy? Look at Ruth going under, and Araminta's family going under. Why do you think I'm ready to give up and get married again, for Chrissake? Huh?'

'So let me help you,' said Patrice, in the same exhausted tone.

'No. Fucking. Way,' said Jasmine. 'A deal is one thing, but if I walk away from my business with nothing and then all of a sudden I'm riding high, you think no one's gonna wonder where it all came from? You think no one's gonna find out this deal was a set-up from day one? What do you think my family's gonna say? Huh? What's Clovis gonna think? Huh?' Her voice was rising again and Finnie nudged another drum forward with her toe. 'And just as if that wasn't enough,' Jasmine said, wheeling round to face me and making me step backwards away from her flashing eyes and glittering teeth. 'As if that wasn't enough, just to insult me, she snaps her fingers and she's got Phil dancing too.' She took a huge breath and turned back to Patrice. 'Well,' she said, 'as far as Phil goes, we'll just see.' She shook her hair back. 'We'll see whether Phil would rather have you in his wine cellar or me in his bed, huh? Honey?'

'Hang on, hang on,' said Finnie. 'What are you saying? If you stay, Patrice goes?'

'This vineyard ain't big enough for the both of us,' said Jasmine.

'But if Patrice goes, Araminta will go too,' said Finnie, chewing her lip and looking between them. 'But if Patrice stays Pollie will stop worrying and get better.' She looked over at me. 'Conflicted,' she said. 'Aspirin all round, I say.' And she left to get it.

There was silence once she had gone. Patrice was too shattered to speak, Jasmine too angry. And me? Something was happening inside me that had never happened before. I could see what to do, a plan, a way to make it work. But it wasn't my usual kind of plan at all. It was all tangled up in reality, clogged with facts, making – from every angle, even straight on – sense. What was happening? I had never had an idea like this before. Obviously it would never work for me; I wasn't going that far, but bizarre as it seemed, I really did think that the truth might be just what was needed for the rest of them.

'Jasmine,' I said, 'you really think Clovis is just digging her heels in because Patrice pissed her off?'

Jasmine nodded.

'Well, don't you think someone with your experience in negotiation and facilitation and someone with your skills in delicate diplomacy,' I tried not to glance at the shoe sticking out of the drum skin, 'could smooth things over again?'

Jasmine nodded, looking interested to hear more.

'So, I went on, 'if there was something you could do for your future, you know, and Patrice could help get it started – strictly business, you understand, not charity – would you go back to Clovis and get the deal through?'

'I might,' said Jasmine.

'And what if it meant that Ruth wouldn't go under and Araminta could go home and Finnie and the girls could come back here? Wouldn't that be great?'

Finnie arrived in the doorway just in time to hear this and it stopped her in her tracks.

'Sure,' said Jasmine.

'Here girls,' said Finnie. 'Swallow your aspirin.' In her distraction, she gave me some, and in my own I took them.

'But what is it?' said Jasmine. 'Because I am sick to death of my business and I can't do it any more.'

'It's not your business,' I told her. 'It's mine.'

There was a silence and then Patrice clapped her hands.

'I see!' she cried.

'I'm happy for ya,' said Jasmine. 'You wanna tell me?'

'No,' I said. 'You'll think it's a better idea if you believe you worked it out for yourself. But just to give you a hint, I'm going to get Patrice to describe her dream wedding for you. Just listen and tell me what you think.'

Chapter 13

The Family Business

By the time Phil came home with Araminta and Ruth, Jasmine did indeed believe that it had been her idea all along. She was sitting on the floor in the hall with two phones, a calculator, a laptop and a notepad that was already half full of big excited scrawls and long sums.

'Flowers, Phil,' she said. 'Flowers. Wilting, stinking, crappy flowers with thorns and bugs. Aw, don't look like that, Patrice, I'm not gonna write the ads.'

'Bulbs in moss,' said Patrice. 'Air-dried rose petals that smell like heaven when you walk on them.'

'There's no money in flowers,' said Phil.

'How many times?' said Patrice. 'Why does no one ever believe me?'

'But actually,' I put in, trying to help, 'if we're talking about bridal bouquets full of things no one has ever even heard of ...'

'Like that whatchacallit I want in mine,' said Patrice.

'Lachenalia,' I reminded her.

'What about it?' said Phil.

'I just think,' I said, 'that if you've got the nerve to grow them and charge what they're worth I think it could work. I always have, only I could never get anyone to listen to me.'

'I agree,' said Finnie. 'Things have changed since we were in flowers the last time. The bridal market – as I should know with five daughters of my own – is a licence to print fivers.'

'OK,' said Phil. 'I can see that. But where does Jasmine come in?'

'I'll run it,' she said. 'From Beverly Hills. We don't need a farm in California, cos the season is basically the same as the season down in Argentina and the wages are higher, but we do need that California wedding market. We need those Beverly Hills princesses and their daddies' checkbooks. So I see the California farm being a kind of showplace. Like this place down here is gonna be for those Kensington babes. They'll come along and see rose-cheeked peasants with wicker baskets and it'll all be part of the dream, but the real grunt work's going to be in the other places with Ruthie and Araminta where the costs are cheaper and nobody's looking to see how pretty it ain't.'

Patrice was shaking her head, slowly.

'No,' she said. 'No way. Not one cent of mine goes anywhere near this unless it's all above board. I want fair trade. I want Amnesty taking lessons from us. I want to make Oxfam look like Enron. I want happy people with good jobs and their kids in school and I want anybody to walk into any one of our places in the world and see what we're glad for them to see. That's my deal. Take it or leave it.'

'You'll never make any money,' said Jasmine.

'Yes we will,' said Patrice. 'My father and his father and his father were wrong – screwing everybody who worked for them into the ground to make the money to give to their wives to give away to good causes so they could sleep at night. I ask you: how dumb is that?'

'And what does Verity do?' said Phil. 'Is she jetting around, overseeing the welfare of the gladioli in all four corners of the world?'

'She can do whatever she wants,' said Patrice. 'Verity, honey, do you want to be a suit or a posy-picker?'

I couldn't answer. They were all so excited, so full of their dreams. And I knew that I couldn't be part of it with them, I was the only one here who was hiding grubby little secrets while everyone else pitched in together, and sooner or later they would all find out. I was just going to have to keep a smile on my face while the dust settled and then slink away and forget I had ever known them.

Well, I could do that. It wouldn't be the first time and it wouldn't kill me. I concentrated on shrinking it down, shrivelling it up even more, harder than gum, harder than a peach stone, smaller than ever before, and when I was sure that nothing would show, I smiled at them.

'First things first,' I said. 'Shouldn't one of you call Clovis and get her on board?' I swear to God, I think Jasmine and Patrice had forgotten all about her. Their faces fell.

'Who's Clovis?' said Ruth.

'She's my agent.'

'And what does she have to do with any of this?' asked Finnie.

Jasmine and Patrice stared at each other for a bit until Jasmine finally piped up.

'It's complicated,' she said. 'Movies are a very complicated business, up at the financial end.'

'I don't understand,' said Araminta. 'If we have the land and Patrice has the money, where do movies come in?'

'It's really very complicated,' said Jasmine again. 'Don't worry about it.'

Patrice and Jasmine both stood up.

'I'll go,' Patrice said. 'You don't need to do this for me. I'm going to offer more money and keep offering more money until she says yes. If she gets pissed with anyone it should be me.' She smoothed her clothes and hair as if she was about to walk out and wrestle lions in front of Caesar. I found myself looking closely at her hands, her feet, the front of her throat, until Phil caught me looking. He mouthed 'Granny Drummond' at me making me flush. Patrice moved towards the kitchen and the phone with a slow steady tread. She was back in less than a minute.

'She's on another call,' she said. 'Gemma's going to get her to ring me back.' All six of us exhaled in a rush together. 'But can someone else come and wait with me?' Patrice went on. 'My knees are trembling. The girls have gone out with the dogs and I can't go through there all alone again.'

'Oh, for Gawd's sake,' said Finnie, scrambling to her feet with a scowl at Araminta. 'One bloody phone in this mausoleum? It's ridiculous.' She marched away to the kitchen calling over her shoulder. 'You think he couldn't run a mistress with no access to a phone?' Her footsteps died away and then immediately grew louder again as she reappeared carrying the big black telephone from the kitchen. 'Crawl under the table there and plug this in, Philly, my love,' she said. 'Let's wait it out together.'

Clovis must have already been calling back because as soon as Phil pushed in the line, the bell sprang to life making us all jump. Finnie slapped the phone down on the tabletop and we all stared at it.

'Why don't I talk to her?' I said. 'Tell her I'm ready to sign? That'll put her in a good mood to start with.' There were nods all round and so, trembling slightly, I lifted the receiver.

'Hello?' I said.

'Hello!' came the squawk from the other end of the line. 'I'm honoured that you'll still talk to me, Princess Big Time. It's touching that you still have space in your life for the little people. Have you heard? You must have heard? Have you heard? You haven't heard, have you? You will not believe, you will not be able to comprehend, who is talking about discussing looking at a proposal for a meeting to think about your script. I can't even say the name. Are you sitting down? Are you kneeling? Face the flag and place your right hand over your heart, girlfriend.'

'Bradley,' I said, 'this isn't a good time.'

'Oh!' squawked Brad, right in my ear. 'You *don't* have time for me, huh? The little people are yesterday for you, huh? Well, fan me flat with a wafer-thin mint – why am I not surprised?'

'It's not that,' I said. 'It's just that I'm waiting for a call.'

'Oh my *God*! Ohmigod! *The* call? You're waiting for *the* call, right now? OhmygodIcan'tbelieveI'mtyingupthe line. Call me.' And he slammed down the phone.

'Sorry,' I said.

Patrice shushed me. 'So,' she said, 'now we just wait.'

Jasmine was wandering around the room, looking at the wall hangings and throws.

'Is it racist of me to say this?' she asked. 'I just don't *get* African textiles. They're ugly, right?'

'Jasmine!' said Patrice. 'Yes it is racist of you to say that. It certainly is.'

'And rather rude,' said Ruth. 'Since they're my things, in my house.'

'My house,' said Araminta.

'I am so looking forward to the end of this nonsense, if nothing else,' said Finnie. 'Can't we just agree, starting right now, if you two are hightailing it back to the colonies, that it is my house?'

'Actually,' said Phil. 'Not to put my foot down or anything but taking the long view, it's my house.'

'I'm sure African people love them,' said Patrice, judging that the ugly cushion covers were the best bet after all.

'Yeah, like the Chinese love Chinese opera,' said Jasmine.

'Exactly,' said Patrice. 'It's a question of cultural expectations.'

Jasmine held up a cushion. On a background of cream and orange squiggles floated black and green striped lozenges and hexagonal spirals of pink.

'Tell me the truth about this, Patrice,' she said. 'Would you have this in your house?'

Patrice tussled with herself.

'I would,' she said. 'I would have it to honour the African aesthetic and to pay tribute to the artisans who made it, in recognition of their skill, and out of respect for their difficult lives from the comfort of my own.'

'But you'd keep it in a cupboard, right?' said Jasmine. 'You'd honour it from there?' She tossed the cushion down.

'No one like an American for rudeness,' said Ruth, glaring at Jasmine.

'True,' said Finnie. 'Some of them are nearly as rude as you.'

And then the phone chirped and Patrice snatched it up before it even started ringing.

'Clovis?' she said, then she closed her eyes, swallowed hard, and held the receiver out to me.

'Listen, kid,' said Kenny Daateng. 'I'm bowing out here. I love the book. I love the whole father-son sacrifice thing, I always did right from the beginning. But I can't compete with a guy like that. I only called to congratulate you and to say don't forget who gave you your start.'

'Who did give me my start?' I said.

'Oh come on,' said Kenny. 'You know as well as I do what the hook is. It was me who pushed the Based on a True Story. Remember?'

'Yes,' I said, glancing around the room at all the people who knew how loosely based it was, 'but I don't want to talk about it right now.'

'OK, I understand,' he said. 'You don't need me. But be careful. There's only one way to go from the top, and the people you meet up there ain't coming back down with you.'

'I'll bear that in mind,' I said, but I really didn't need any lessons to teach me that I was all alone.

'Give me that thing,' said Jasmine, when I had hung up again. 'Clovis was never on a call this long in her life.' She dialled and waited. 'Clovis Parr, please,' she said into the phone and, sticking her thumb up, she passed the receiver to Patrice. Ruth, Araminta and Phil all lit up and smoked furiously.

'Clovis,' said Patrice. 'It's Patrice Carmichael here. Yes, the buyer. I want to make a new offer … Still in Cornwall … No listen, listen to me. I'm living here. I'm going to stay. I'm going to be a resident, so it's completely diff … Uh-huh. OK.' And then she went quite silent. We could hear the faint chirrup of Clovis talking, but Patrice didn't utter a sound, and she put her head down so we couldn't read the look in her eyes. 'Jasmine agrees with you, that's why I'm doing my own nego—' she said at one point but she didn't get a chance to finish, just went back to listening, looking down at the floor. 'I see,' she said at last. 'I didn't know that.' And very carefully, so that there wasn't even a click, she put down the phone.

She took a mustering breath, and shook her head slowly so that the tears, just beginning to fall, slid out to the sides and ran into the curly side locks of her hair.

'I have to go back,' she said. 'I'm sorry. I'm sorry about everything, but I've got to go … home. I've got to do the project there.'

There was a long silence in the room. In the distance we could hear squeals and barks and splashes. The girls must have taken the dogs to play at the pond.

'I'll still help out here,' said Patrice. 'I still want to invest in the flower farm, obviously, but I have to go home, go back, before the time runs out on the deal.'

'Why?' said Phil.

'Because Clovis wants it that way,' said Patrice.

Jasmine walked around the back of the sofa and leaned over to squeeze Patrice's shoulders. This only made the tears fall faster.

'Wait a minute, though,' I said. 'God, I can't believe I never thought of this until now!'

'What is it, Vee?' said Jasmine.

'It's *my* book,' I said. 'We're all sitting here saying Clovis says this and Clovis says that, but it's my book.'

Jasmine was shaking her head.

'You never read your agency contract, did you?' she said. Of course, I hadn't. Reading your agency contract before you signed it would be like checking the small print on a Valentine's card.

'It was a stupid idea,' Patrice said. 'I can see that now.'

'But what's the problem?' said Phil. 'How can it possibly matter? Can't you just do the deal in America anyway? Is it the exchange rate? Only you keep saying money's not a factor with you.'

'Phil,' I said, thinking it was my turn. 'It's just that it's—'

'Don't tell me it's complicated,' Phil said. 'Not again.'

'Hear, hear,' said Ruth.

'It's more than complicated,' Patrice said quietly. 'It's personal.'

Finnie got to her feet.

'Ruth, Araminta, Verity?' she said. 'Can I have a word with you in the kitchen?'

Patrice smiled at her.

'Verity can stay,' she said, and she turned to me. 'I don't want to keep any secrets from you.'

I tried to smile, feeling sick. If only she knew me, if only she knew.

'It was you that started it, Phil,' she began, when the others had left. 'Telling us about the British attitude. I just thought life could be different here. I thought I could make it all real. So that the outside, the official version, matched the inside, matched the feelings.' She gave a little laugh and put out a hand to Phil and to me. 'This won't be making much sense,' she said.

'Actually, I understand,' said Phil. 'Verity and I worked it out, you know.'

Then Patrice gave me that look again, the one I saw on the very first day, the look that was waiting for a kick and made me want to hug her.

'I lived in San Francisco for seven long years,' said Patrice. 'Hated every minute, but it meant that I got my California birth certificate, a real one, one that matched the inside. My birth certificate says "Patrice Jasmine Rachel Carmichael". Rachel is my mother's name. But my passport doesn't come from California, and my medical records, and my driver's licence and social security number … it's all still in there. *He's* still in there in all of them and he always will be. Only, I got this idea that if I came here, stayed here, all I would need would be my beautiful precious birth certificate, "Patrice Jasmine Rachel Carmichael", and I could start again here. Start my new life. Start this … project. Start again.'

'Well, why not?' said Phil.

'It takes time,' Patrice told him. 'Until I get that British passport I'm still a US citizen and as long as I am, *he*'s going to be there. I can't get to be one of you lucky people,' she said looking at Phil and me. 'The only way to get to be one of you lucky people in a hurry is to be born here. Or … Well, in my case, to be born here. Otherwise it takes years. And I've only got weeks.'

'Until you lose the chance to buy the option?' I said.

Patrice nodded, biting her lip.

'If I go back and start the … project there, my history's going to be all over it. He's going to be all over it. It won't be the same.'

'Patrice, sweetie,' said Jasmine, 'you could always wait and then go ahead with a different project.'

Patrice turned brimming eyes towards her.

'You mean a different … story?' she said. 'Just abandon this one?'

'Sorry,' said Jasmine. 'Forget I spoke.'

Patrice stood up.

'Now if you'll excuse me,' she said, 'I'm going to go and sit on that flat rock in the field and cry my guts out. I don't want company, because it's the one thing I just can't do. I never did learn to cry pretty.'

And she walked over to one of the long windows, unlatched it, stepped out and moved away.

'Classy lady,' said Jasmine. 'Always was. No way Patrice is gonna kick the hell out of a drum kit just because she's in trouble.'

Then she too rose and disappeared out of the window to the garden.

'Jasmine,' I called. 'She wanted to be alone.'

'Nobody wants to be alone, sweetie,' said Jasmine. 'And anyway, I've seen Patrice cry plenty – usually it was me making her – and it could be worse.'

Phil and I remained, slumped on the sofa.

'She's still going to help you out,' I reminded him. 'She said that, remember.'

'I do,' said Phil. 'She's going to honour the commitment. Classy lady, like Jasmine said.'

'She is,' I agreed. 'God, I wish there was something I could do. It's hurting me, physically, hurting, in my chest.'

'The Patrice-related ache,' said Phil. 'I know it well.'

'It's been that way since the first day I met her.'

'Me too.'

'Like ... you would do anything for her?' I said.

Phil nodded.

'What I don't see,' he said, 'and don't be offended, Vert, but why exactly does she care so much about this book?'

'I honestly don't know,' I said.

'What's it about, anyway?'

'It's about a struggle. A person – Actually, yes, I *can* see it now – a person who's trapped and then escapes in the end. And I suppose I did put a lot of ... suffering in it. I suppose Patrice might think it was very real and think she had to make it somewhere that was very real too.'

'And she'd be willing to underwrite Trepolgas wine to swing it?' Phil was half laughing in a weary way.

'That's nothing,' I told him. 'You've no idea what Jasmine was willing to do to get what *she* wanted.'

'What?'

'To escape from Hollywood, and in the absence of better options, she was seriously considering making her next career ... you.'

Phil sat stock still and silent for a moment and then, as if he had been jolted with a thousand volts, leaped to his feet, hurdled over a coffee table, and crashed out of the window.

'Phil?' I shouted, scuttling along behind him. 'Phil?'

'She was wrong,' he yelled over his shoulder. 'Being born here isn't the only way at all.'

'What? Phil? What do you mean?'

But he didn't stop. He wheeled around the corner of the house and disappeared. Oma and Lottie, standing in wellies at the reedy edge of the pond, looked after him.

'Where is everyone going?' Oma shouted.

'The flat rock across the field from the kitchen garden,' I called back, which slowed them down for a minute or two.

'Why?' called Lottie at last. 'What's going on there?'

I mimed a huge shrug and they went back to poking in the reeds with what looked like ski poles.

I never got there. I met Phil, Patrice and Jasmine halfway across the vine field on their way back. All three were beaming from ear to ear, although Patrice's face was still wet with tears.

'Well?' I said.

'We're getting married,' said Phil.

I stared back.

'All three of you?' I said, and Jasmine snorted.

'We're not in San Francisco, Verity,' said Phil. 'We're getting married *here*. Which is rather the point, after all.' Then he turned to Patrice and caught her hands in his. 'I didn't mean that the way it sounded,' he said. 'I mean, yes of course, it's for the passport and everything that we decided it today and that's it's all got to be so quick. But I would have got there in the end.'

'I know,' said Patrice. 'I don't believe it yet, but I know.'

I was determined, for once, not to be like Granny Drummond and so instead of letting my mouth drop open in wonder, I rushed forward and threw my arms around Patrice's neck. And whether she had cried off so much make-up that there was nothing left to save or was no longer frightened that I would feel how very firm and strong she was under those floating panels of silk, or whether she had just crossed some line that separates LA and New York from the dusty fields of Cornwall, I don't know, but she didn't freeze or clamp her hands around my arms and move me backwards. She just hugged me too.

'Congratulations,' I said. 'I think you're mad, but if looking at Pollie and seeing what Phil's going to turn into doesn't put you off, then good luck and can I do the flowers, please?'

'Of course,' said Patrice.

'I take it it's going to be a winter wedding?' I went on. 'Roseraie de l'Hay and Lachenalia?'

'Who?' said Phil. 'What are you wittering on about? It's going to be an autumn wedding, in three weeks' time, with hardly a minute to spare.'

'But you still have to do the flowers,' said Patrice. 'And Pollie has to be better and out of hospital in time.'

'I'm sure he will be,' said Phil. 'Mind you, we might have to wheel him in a bath chair. In fact, I could see him insisting on the bath chair whether he needs it or not. He'd hate not to be the centre of attention, Patrice, just because it's your wedding day.'

'Is he going to give you away?' I said. 'Don't you think any of your family is going to be here? Don't you think they would come if you called and asked them?'

Patrice shook her head, but she was smiling.

'I don't care about them any more,' she said. 'I've got a new family now.'

'Hey,' said Jasmine. 'I'm standing right here listening to this, you know, and if anybody's going to give you away, it's gonna be me.'

'Oh God,' said Phil. 'I knew it. A heartfelt American wedding, all throbbing emotion and no decorum. Jasmine, my dear, it's supposed to be a man who gives the bride away.' Patrice giggled and Jasmine gave him a look.

'Phil, my *dear*,' she said. 'At this wedding, with this bride? I really don't think that matters, do you?'

Back at the house, in the kitchen, Finnie was prising apart frozen sausages with a bread knife and dropping them into a frying pan for the children's supper while Araminta and Ruth sat at the table, smoking.

'There now, my love,' Finnie said, when she saw Patrice. 'You're looking brighter.'

'Is the phone still in the hall?' said Phil.

'Wait here, Verity,' said Jasmine. 'This is where you get off.'

'What are they up to now?' said Ruth sourly to their departing backs. 'Those two girls are running rings round my poor boy. Out for what they can get and not even trying to hide it.' But I had had enough of Ruth by this time. I glanced at the pad she had been scribbling on.

'If they're out for what they can get,' I said, 'why are you doodling dollar signs?'

'And if you're only here because you're so concerned about my poor Pollie,' said Finnie, 'why did you just call and book a flight home?'

'*My* poor Pollie,' said Araminta automatically, but then she spoiled it by adding, 'You going home, Ruth? Do you think I need to go home too, to begin set up everything? I will tear me away if I'm have to.'

Finnie, speechless, shook her head a couple of times and turned back to the stove.

At that moment, very faintly, from the hall, we heard the sound of three voices raised in a cheer.

'Hang on to your hats,' I murmured, and went to meet them.

'She said yes!' said Patrice, her eyes gleaming in the dim light of the passageway. 'Clovis said yes.'

'Of course she did,' said Phil. 'She had no reason not to. The day the deal goes through you will be a loyal subject of Her Britannic Majesty, just like me.'

'So, Vee,' said Jasmine, 'wait there, will ya?' She hared off up the Hoover stairs and reappeared a minute later with a rather dog-eared set of papers in her hand. 'You need to initial the bottom of each page and sign the last one. So easy, huh?'

I took the contract from her. It had a ring from the bottom of a daiquiri glass on the top page and a smudge of cheesecake stuck in the staple.

'There's one more thing,' said Jasmine when I had finished signing. She was looking rather uncomfortable. 'As a condition of the new deal. Clovis wants *you* to deliver the manuscript.'

'To Patrice?' I said, looking from the contract in my hands to

Patrice, two feet away.

'No,' said Jasmine. 'To a third party.'

I turned and stared questioningly at Patrice. She was looking uncomfortable too.

'A third party? Your precious book? Your precious project? What's going on?'

'Jazzie,' said Patrice, 'we have to tell her. We're a long way past normal protocol now. Wait in the kitchen, Phil. Verity, honey, let's talk in the other room.'

Our footfalls as we processed along the empty passageway to the hall sounded like the steps of three prisoners walking to the gibbet. Maybe only because all of us were slowing down, each more reluctant than the others to get there.

We sat in a row on the same sofa, facing the fire.

'We haven't been entirely candid with you,' Jasmine said.

I gave a laugh that sounded hollow even to me.

'Forgive me if I don't faint from the shock,' I said.

'I'm not making the movie,' said Patrice.

'Why not?' I asked her.

'I'm not a producer.'

'So why is Jasmine selling you the option?'

'I'm not a scout,' said Jasmine.

'So why is Clovis working with you?'

'Clovis isn't an agent.'

'What?' I said, wheeling round. Jasmine was staring straight ahead, refusing to meet my eye. 'Of course Clovis is an agent. She's *my* agent.'

'Verity, honey, sweetie,' said Jasmine, and she might as well have said Verity comma love. 'You're a florist.'

'So what *is* going on?' I asked them. 'Is nothing anyone's ever said to me *true*?'

'I'm so sorry,' said Patrice. 'I've been hating myself for lying to you. But what could I do?'

I was thinking it all over, trying to make some sense of it somehow.

'You're *not* really trying to get out of your family business? Patrice *isn't* really trying to help you? It's *not* really a big secret?'

'No, no,' said Jasmine. 'That's true. I'm getting out, Patrice is helping, nobody knows that her and me have history, everyone thinks I put this deal together for real.'

'So you see,' said Patrice, 'a lot of what we said was gospel.'

'Only my family business ain't movies.'

'So why do you buy books?' I said.

'To help move the money around,' Jasmine said.

'What does that mean?' I was completely lost now. 'And if your family business isn't movies, what is it? Why are you so desperate to get out of it? Why can't you just leave?'

'Because my family business,' said Jasmine, 'is a business you have to leave with their blessing, because the only way to leave without it is not a way you'd want to go.'

I thought about it for a moment.

'And it's some kind of publishing?' I said.

'Oh, for the love of Jesus Christ!' Jasmine said. 'Wake up, Vee! Do I have to spell it out to ya? OK, the Corleones import olive oil. The Sopranos haul away garbage. The Cammeggios buy unpublished books.'

With a dull thud, everything dropped into place.

'You're the ...' I swallowed hard and whispered the next words. 'You're the Mafia?' She didn't slap me, so I spoke a little louder. 'You're the *mob*?'

'No!' said Patrice, but then she spoiled it. 'Not really.'

'Does – Does Clovis know?' I asked, my brain still reeling.

'Clovis is my second cousin,' said Jasmine.

'And so the deal,' I said, speaking quicker now, catching up at long, long last, 'had to be done in the States because that was where the money had to go? That was the problem with moving it over here?'

'Kind of,' said Patrice, looking uncomfortable. 'Pretty much, yes. In a way.'

'Oh God,' I said. 'How dumb am I? *Sicilian* television? I signed a contract in with a family, in Sicily and they gave me money to bring back to London. I signed a contract in Prague and they ... How dumb *am* I? Where will I be going this time? Where's this third party?'

'Minsk,' said Patrice, and with so much make-up gone I could tell she was blushing.

'Minsk,' I repeated. 'Oh God, just exactly how dumb am I?'

'You're not dumb at all,' said Patrice. 'You're just a little too trusting sometimes.'

'Yeah,' I said, almost laughing. 'I trusted Clovis when she said she loved my book for one thing.' I was having trouble giving up on the idea that I'd written a story that everyone loved and facing the fact that the only good thing about my writing was Patrice's money. It was like Bradley had said: nothing gets people interested like someone else getting interested first. It was all just a great big bubble of nothing. A big, deafening, empty zzub.

'Don't look so forlorn,' said Patrice. 'You feel bad now but it's good to be trusting. We wouldn't have you any other way. Stick to the flowers and let Jasmine deal with the big bad world out there.'

'But you're telling me it's Jasmine who *makes* it a big, bad world out there,' I said, almost shouting. 'Jasmine and people like her. I can't believe I didn't see through it. How many businesses are there where Italians work Vegas, Chicago, New Jersey, and LA?' I sank back against the cushions, exhausted. Then sat up again.

'Tell me this,' I said. 'Does Clovis get the manuscript from the bins outside real agencies?'

'I'm so sorry,' said Patrice.

'Do you do that too, Jasmine?' I demanded. 'Do you actually rake through the fag ends and banana skin with your own bare hands?'

'Hey,' said Jasmine. 'Two things I need to say, Vee. One: I'm getting out. And two: it's not as bad as you think. The Cammeggios' family business—'

'No, Jasmine,' said Patrice. 'Please. Verity, trust me. It's not drugs, it's not guns and it's not girls. It really could be a lot worse.'

'Trust you?' I said, glaring at her. At least she had the courage to look back at me, out of her streaky eyes. Jasmine was still staring at the fire. 'Trust *you*? You're buying off Jasmine's family. You used my book as a front so you could move the money. You lied to me about everything, every day.'

'I have my reasons,' said Patrice, and I remembered that when she caught me lying to her that was what she had said to me.

'Sorry,' I told her, gruffly. 'I'm sure you do.'

'It's one last deal,' said Patrice. 'Jasmine gets out. You get rich.'

'And you get Phil,' I said. Patrice, in spite of the remorse – which I could tell was for real – couldn't help smiling.

'Yeah,' said Jasmine. 'Let's concentrate on that and forget the other stuff, huh?' Let's go tell 'em the good news.'

At the kitchen doorway, we met Oma and Lottie tramping in, still in their wellingtons.

'Why were you cheering before?' said Oma. 'Why is everyone running about?'

'Let me see,' said Patrice, sitting down and pulling Oma on to her lap. 'It might be because ... I'm getting married. Can you guess who to?'

'Oh Lord,' said Lottie. 'Not Daddy!'

Patrice's answer, if any, was lost in the tumult. It even brought the three older sisters out, blinking, from the television room to see what was going on.

'In three weeks?' said Finnie. 'It doesn't give us much time. But we can have it here. I'll do the food.'

Patrice was so happy that she agreed.

'My flight's non-refundable,' said Ruth.

Patrice was so happy she pretended she cared.

'Will there be lots of your family people comes from America?' said Araminta.

Patrice shook her head and I don't think it was only because she was so happy that it didn't seem to bother her a bit.

'There won't be anyone here from my side at all,' she said. 'Except Jasmine, of course.'

'Exactly what relation are you to Patrice, anyway?' I asked Jasmine.

Jasmine looked around to see if anyone was listening.

'I was her wife,' she said, and cackled with laughter to see the look on my face. 'So, it really has to be me who gives her away.'

'Why are you wearing your Granny Drummond face, Vert?' said Phil, coming up to us.

'Will you be an American now, Phil?' said Lottie, before I could answer.

'Of course not, doofus,' Celia told her.

'But if you have babies,' said Oma. 'Will they be American babies?'

I froze. I didn't want anything to spoil Patrice's day and how could this fail to? But Phil took it in his stride.

'They won't,' he said. 'We're going to live here, so any babies that might come along would be little Cornish pasties just like you. Only with a rich American mummy who could take them to Disneyworld on their birthdays.'

Patrice looked quite happy with this as an answer and Finnie looked on, misty-eyed and convinced that all was well, which I supposed was the point. Phil didn't want any throat-clearing and shiftiness to make anyone start asking questions. Fleetingly though, I wondered what Pollie would think of his only son marrying someone who couldn't provide Trepolgas with an heir.

I slipped away then, leaving them discussing the biggest problem of all.

'It will break my father's heart,' Phil was saying. 'We've got to serve it one last time. At least for the toasts.'

'We can't, Philly,' said Patrice. 'Toasts are supposed to be for luck. They're supposed to represent good fortune. Tell him it's tradition for the bride to provide the wines. Tell him it's a Jewish thing.'

'Possibly,' said Phil, 'but I was going to lead up rather gently to telling him about the Jewish thing too. He has just had a stroke after all.'

I went back to the flat rock, picking my way over the stones in the field, stumbling in the near dark. Jasmine had told me she was a script sniffer when really she was a ... whatever it was she was, and I was trying very hard to believe Patrice that it had nothing to do with girls, guns or drugs, although that didn't seem to leave much. And as for Patrice ... I hardly knew where to begin. What if I could tell them the truth about me and they would just shrug and say that life was complicated and they forgave me? What if I let the little thing unshrivel and it wasn't a tree that would grow up my throat and choke me or a piece of gum that would wind itself round my heart and kill me. What if – embarrassing as this would be – that wizened little lump really was my inner child after all and, if I let it, would just grow up, leave home and only come back to bring its washing? Then I could stay here making posies. There was nothing for me anywhere else after all. I tried not to think about Kim. I tried to think about the wedding that was coming at Trepolgas and not about the other one, soon to come in London.

'I don't want a big family wedding,' Kim said. 'I'll give you three guesses why.'

'Oh Kimmie,' said Helen. 'I know, my poor darling, and I'm sorry. I wish you had a family but the fact is you don't. And I do and I don't see why I shouldn't have the wedding of my dreams.'

'Seriously?' said Kim. 'You don't see why having a mother, father, brother, sister-in-law and two nephews, not to mention, what is it?, eighteen aunts, uncles, and cousins should mean that you have to show a bit of understanding to someone who's got one ex-wife and a cat?'

Helen's lip began to tremble. She clicked her propelling pencil until the lead was safely inside and began to roll up the piece of graph paper she called, utterly without irony, her wedding master plan.

'I think it's very unkind of you to mention your ex-wife when we're planning our wedding.'

'We're not,' said Kim. 'You are. Please tell me you're not thinking of having a groom's side and a bride's side of the aisle.'

'Why not?'

'Because I don't think they allow cats,' said Kim. 'And unless you want me to invite Verity, my side's going to need a bit of ballast.'

'There you go again. Verity, Verity, Verity.'

'You love Verity stories,' said Kim. 'Don't you?'

'For a laugh,' said Helen. 'But I don't want you just dropping her into conversations, as though she's your aunt or something.'

'I wish I had an aunt,' said Kim.

'You have friends, don't you? You'll be inviting friends. They can sit down your side.'

'Yes, I suppose so,' said Kim. 'That should even things up. So I can invite any friends I want, then?'

'Of course. Within reason.'

'The trouble is,' said Kim, 'that some of the friends you don't think are within reason are the very ones that might just turn up anyway and make a scene.'

Helen's face froze for a moment and then she laughed.

'Why am I so gullible?' she said. 'You get me, every time, Kimmie. People don't turn up to weddings uninvited. Everybody knows that.'

'They do in Albert Square,' said Kim. 'And on Coronation Street.*'*

'But not in real life.'

'True,' said Kim. 'I was at a funeral once, though, where a long lost relative turned up out of the blue. It's a Verity story of a sort. Only not one of the funniest ones.'

'If it's a proper story,' said Helen, 'go ahead.'

'No, I don't think I shall,' said Kim. 'Now that I think about it, it's not really funny at all.'

It was pitch black now. Over my shoulder I could see a dim glow from St Austell and Bodmin, but looking out to sea all there was was a perfect inky blackness punctured with stars, the moon a sliver, like a clipped fingernail snagged on the sky.

I wouldn't be completely alone. I could use some of my Patrice money to phone Bradley, honey, every now and then. I was sure *he* would be pleased to hear from me even if Kenny Daateng had decided I was more trouble than I was— All of a sudden the night seemed to get thicker around me somehow, as though someone had let some of the air out of the sky and it had settled down a little heavier against my skin.

Bradley I could just about dismiss, but somewhere amongst all the feints and sleights of hand and stories and nonsense, wasn't there a straight thread that went like this: Clovis wasn't even in the movie industry and yet Kenny Daateng was someone who Clovis had heard of. And Kenny Daateng was walking away from me because he had heard that someone too big for him to tackle was interested in my book. I thought hard about it, but it wouldn't go away. This *wasn't* just zzub. No bits of it disappeared because Jasmine wasn't really a scout. It didn't unravel because the Italian telly people – Cammeggios all, I now saw – were having me on. I tugged on the thread and it gave a sturdy-sounding twang.

'Where is everyone?' I said, sprinting into the kitchen, where Finnie was scraping plates.

'Philly and Ruth have gone to the hospital,' said Finnie, 'and the girls are showing Patrice and Jasmine over the house.' She sniffed and wiped the edge of the sink with her apron hem. 'Apparently, Phil and she are moving in here and Pollie's to come to the dower house to me.'

'If I'm leave him,' said Araminta absentmindedly from the table where she was busily texting someone.

'Yes, yes, yes,' said Finnie. '*If* you leave him.' She rolled her eyes at me.

'Seems a bit daft, when you've got all the kids still at home,' I said.

'No choice,' said Finnie. 'Pollie's signing the whole lot over to Phil. Then he just has to stay alive for seven years. This is the reality of trying to dodge death tax, my love. And it's no joke. The nasty old Inland Revenue are well known for sending little spies round to check that the wrinklies have actually been turfed out, you know.'

I wondered briefly if anyone had told Finnie or Pollie or even Phil just exactly how rich Patrice was and how small a dent forty per cent of Trepolgas would make in her portfolio, then I realised it was none of my business and left.

They were in what I assumed was the master bedroom, right above the kitchen judging from the lingering smell of sausages.

'And I was born right here in this bed,' Sophie was saying. 'All the others were born in the cottage hospital in St Austell, but I was three weeks early and Mummy thought I was wind.'

'You are,' said Lottie and made a farting noise at her.

'And now you're going to sleep here with Phil,' said Oma, giggling.

Patrice looked down at the sagging bed with the dark stains on the brocade headboard where the hair oil of past Coateses had seeped in, never to be removed.

'We'll see,' she said, which I thought was diplomatic of her.

'Patrice,' I said, unable to wait any longer. 'Are you nearly finished with the grand tour? Could I have a word?'

I took her halfway down the Hoover stairs; it would be easier to say this in the darkness.

'I know this is going to be hard to believe,' I began. 'But those two phone calls this evening? While we were waiting for Clovis? It went out of my mind in all the upset and excitement, but I think . . . I really do think that there might be someone interested in buying my book.'

'*Straight Up*?' said Patrice. 'Who?' I could just make out the gleam of her eyes in the darkness.

'I don't know. But if you were to call IFA – I've got the LA and the New York numbers – and ask them . . . I mean, if you didn't feel too silly doing it. It has to be you really, since technically you own it now, don't you?'

Patrice said nothing.

'I know you must think I'm making all of this up,' I said.

'Why on earth would I think that?' said Patrice. 'Apart from the little thing about Phil – and that was so ridiculous it's almost funny – you've never been anything except totally straight and open with Jasmine and me since the day we met you.' She laughed. 'So of course I believe you, honey. Why would I not? You have got to stop thinking that everyone in this world is like that dead husband of yours. Now, who will I call?'

I sat on the arm of a sofa and listened in while she placed the call to the New York number. She was passed from extension to extension, holding the phone out to me so I could hear the muzak every time she got put on hold. Then when she finally got to talk to someone all she said was 'uh-huh, uh-huh, uh-huh' over and over again and then: 'Do you have a number for him? Oh – he'll call me?' And then she had to read the number off the round dial in the middle of the big black phone turning it this way and that to make it out in the lamplight. When at last she hung up I thought she was never going to speak again.

'Did you know there was a piece about you in a magazine?' she said at last.

'Only an in-house one,' I said. 'Who is it? Have you heard of him?'

She nodded.

'Name some of your favourite films,' she said.

'Ahhh,' I thought hard. '*Cinema Paradiso, Women on the Verge, Jean de Florette.*'

'English language films, Verity,' said Patrice.

'Oh! Of course, sorry. *The Crying Game, Secrets and Lies, Four Weddings and a Funeral* ...'

Patrice sighed.

'Hollywood films.'

'Sorry! *Vertigo, Gone With the Wind, It's A Wonderf—*'

'By living directors.'

'OK. *Moonstruck*,' I said.

Patrice shook her head.

'*Mullholland Drive*?' Nothing. '*Brokeback Mountain*?'

'What were your favourite films when you were growing up?' asked Patrice.

'*Bedknobs and Broomsticks*?'

'Newer.'

'*Wayne's World*?'

'Older.'

'*Terms of Endearment*? *Crocodile Dundee*?' I was struggling now. '*ET: The Extra—*'

'Bingo,' said Patrice.

'You are kidding,' I said and I slid down the arm of the sofa on to the seat so that my knees were under my chin.

'I'm not,' said Patrice, hauling me back up again. 'And can I just say: you have very eclectic taste in film.'

Chapter 14
The Scalat Bootstrap

It was long after midnight before anyone got to bed. The girls and dogs lay about in heaps and the rest of us sat looking into the fire, listening to the distant thumps of Araminta and Ruth packing.

'He really was looking better?' asked Finnie, not for the first time. 'Sure he wasn't too overwhelmed by the news?'

'Calmed by it, if anything,' said Phil. 'One wife, six kids, one daughter-in-law and a flower farm. Much less to stretch his dottled old brain around then the recent set-up, really.'

'I'll go to see him tomorrow,' said Finnie. 'How's the roast pork holding out, Phil?'

'You go too, Patrice,' said Phil. 'I'm sorry to say he hasn't really got it clear, and I quote "which one of them" it is I'm marrying.'

Patrice laughed.

'He'll be disappointed it's not Jasmine,' she said.

'There was never any chance of that,' Jasmine said. 'No offence, Phil, but I only gave you the come-on to bug Patrice.'

'Well,' said Phil, giving a mighty yawn as if trying to suck in the contents of the room like a whale with plankton. 'I don't know about anyone else, but I'm all in.' He stood up, scratching his stomach and pushing his feet back into his shoes. There was a long, empty silence, broken in the end by Lottie and Oma giggling. Patrice, her face at its blankest and most mask-like, rose, kissed Finnie, Jasmine and me and walked to the end of the hall towards the staircase. Phil, less serene but managing to ignore the giggling, followed her.

'You horrible little children,' said Finnie. 'Patrice won't want you for bridesmaids now.'

This sobered them and slowly, grumbling and whining, they began to gather themselves for the trip home. Jasmine and I were left, sunk into the cold feather seats of the long sofas, gazing at the logs in the grate, which were just turning pink and grey at the edges as the flames died. I was dying to ask Jasmine for some details. She had to know.

'I can't imagine how nervous Patrice must be,' I said, which I thought would sound caring.

'Forget it, Vee,' said Jasmine. 'I ain't telling.'

Even Finnie was interested enough to be over from the dower house bright and early the next morning, though. She was already scraping the burnt bits from a slice of toast when I got downstairs before eight. Araminta, huddled in Pollie's dressing gown, was nursing a cigarette and a cup of coffee, leaning against the stove for warmth. I think she had already started to let herself anticipate the glorious swamping heat of her equatorial paradise and she stared out of the window at Cornwall with no look of love. The door opened and the three of us turned as though our chins were tied to the handle.

'It's me,' said Jasmine, shuffling in. 'God, you people!'

'Cook you an egg, my love?' said Finnie. 'They're too old to poach, but they'll boil beautifully.'

Jasmine shook her head, coughed ostentatiously in the direction of Araminta's cigarette and went to open the garden door. We were all watching her stretching in the doorway, revelling in the morning sunshine like an otter turning in a warm river, and we missed the entrance of Phil.

'I can see right through your nightie, Jas,' he said. 'Very Pirelli, I must say.'

'Phil!' said Finnie. 'You're up early.' Jasmine came back inside and leaned against the doorframe.

'Just down to get Patrice a cup of tea,' he said.

'Tea?' said Jasmine.

'It's part of the deal,' Phil told her. 'Patrice is going to learn to drink tea and I'm going to stop smoking. I've just flushed my last packet of fags.'

'In the upstairs lavvy?' said Finnie. 'I'd better call the plumber.'

'So, this morning,' said Phil, 'Patrice takes a couple of sips of Darjeeling and I take a quick drag of this.' He plucked the cigarette from Araminta's lips and raised it towards his own, but he stopped before it got there. Jasmine was staring at him.

'You're gonna marry Patrice and you have my blessing,' she said. 'You wanna hear my blessing?' Phil nodded. 'Make her happy or I'll kill you with my shoe.' Phil gave the cigarette back to Araminta and unhooked a mug from the back of the dresser.

'Hear, hear,' said Finnie. 'As the mother of five girls I say, hear, hear to that.'

Poor Phil. His father's recovery was swift and uneventful, but Pollie still had to be protected from all upset and strain, and so it was Phil alone who bore the brunt of eleven females planning a wedding and the much weightier brunt of ten of them all feeling the – now more explicable – impulse to look after Patrice. Well, eight, really. Ruth and Araminta were gone as soon as BA could mail back the confirmations to them and, besides, neither one of them really did looking after, as a rule.

My flights were booked for the triumphant return trip to California to take the courtesy meeting with the director whose name I still couldn't say out loud in case I made it dissolve into the fantasy that it must, surely, be. In fact, it was Clovis who organised this for me; it was to be her last task as my 'agent'. Jasmine urged it, telling me it was only good manners to let Clovis see it through to the end. Of course, Clovis being Clovis, it wasn't straightforward. I had my ticket out, my statement of second trimester health and my ticket back, via Minsk.

'I'm still delivering the book?' I asked Clovis on the phone. 'Why?'

She was silent.

'Why am I still delivering the book when the option's sold on already?'

'That deal needs to be tied up.'

'Oh, I see – the paper trail, right?'

'Umm ... yes, that's it,' Clovis said. 'But actually, I've sent the book through the post already.'

'So *why* am I going to Minsk?'

'Well, the flights were booked anyway and it would be tricky to change them now. Besides, you can do me a favour while you're there. Hook up with a chum of Patrice's who's coming to London. Look after him on the flight, steer him through Heathrow.'

'A friend of Patrice?' I said. 'Don't you mean Jasmine?'

'No, Patrice,' Clovis told me airily. 'Varjan's his name. Nice bloke. You'll like him. Now, hang on, Verity, love, I've got another call.'

I didn't wait for her to get back to me. The less I understood the better. I kept repeating to myself what Patrice had assured me: it wasn't guns, girls, or drugs. And besides, Jasmine was getting out of it after this. I was the last deal she would ever put through for the Cammeggio family business.

The Coates family business was another matter entirely. Patrice didn't have a lot of attention to spare with the wedding and all, but there were contractors ploughing up the fields and new rotation plans in the making – five years of sweet peas, scabious, snapdragons, pinks and sweet tobacco, mapping out Phil and Patrice's fragrant future. I was in charge of sourcing the roses, busy calling up struggling old nurserymen the length and breadth of the country, making their dreams come true. Jasmine, no finer feelings to be troubled by the pathos of it, was winding down Trepolgas Wines and dumping the bodies.

'I can't just pour it out, Vee,' she said. 'There's too much of it. It'll pollute the water table and we'll never get the EPA off our backs. And what about the stuff that's half made? Plus the bottles. It's gonna be the mother of all trips to the recycling centre.'

'You could compost it,' I said. 'Couple of years under some black polythene and it'll be harmless again.'

'We're gonna have some very happy worms,' Jasmine said.

And all the time I tried not to think about afterwards, after the wedding, after the meeting, after the last trip to Minsk to leave Clovis with her paper trail, when I would be leaving these people, before they found out what I was and what I had done, when I would be dumping them before they could dump me. The thing – gum, stone or kid as it might be – was smaller than ever, as tight as I could make it, and I knew that I couldn't let go for one instant, because it wouldn't just soften, or slowly put up shoots like a new young tree, or go off to college; it would blow up like an airbag and obliterate me from the inside out.

Half of me kept expecting every morning for either Patrice or Phil to come and find me, ask me what I had meant by it all. I could imagine Phil's face asking me why I had said that Kim, his beloved Kim, was dead (and maybe that Phil had eaten him). I could imagine Patrice's face puckered with another attempt at a frown, asking me why I had said that my husband was a liar and a dead one at that.

But they were too busy or perhaps just too happy to waste time gossiping about me and day after day I got to stay in the magic circle, planning a future I wouldn't be part of and making sure nobody knew.

The wedding day was the first day for weeks that it rained, the Indian summer over at long, long last. Jasmine marched into my bedroom with her hands on her hips, swearing, shook her fist at the clouds in a very Italian way and then dragged me with her to go and see Patrice. She was looking out at the weather too, standing at one of the long windows in the Fleshpot bedroom – she'd slept on her own the night before her wedding, of course – drinking her cup of Darjeeling and looking out at the pouring rain.

'Honey,' said Jasmine. 'It's gonna be fine.'

'Of course it is,' said Patrice turning. She was wearing a mud mask, almost set, but being Patrice, with Patrice's face, it made no difference. Her face was as immobile as any mud mask could make it anyway. 'It's going to be lovely. I'm sending Celia and Poppy into town for some golf umbrellas. The contractors can't work in this weather anyway so I'll pay them to valet park the cars. And we'll be inside. Don't you think the hall will look even better with rain lashing against the windows? All the candles, and the fires roaring? Don't you think it'll be like being on a ship in a stormy sea? Like an oasis, like a little pocket of happiness in a dark and treacherous world? It's going to be perfect. You'll see.'

'And actually,' I said, 'we could put the flowers outside for ten minutes and get some rain drops on them. It'll look like diamonds on velvet.'

'Perfect,' said Patrice. 'It'll pick up the chandeliers against the tenting.' Because of course, as soon as Ruth had left in an airport taxi, Jasmine, Patrice and I, with Finnie helping and cheering, had opened the long windows and thrown all the African textiles out on to the terrace. Phil wanted to keep the masks on the stairway because, as he said, a house needed its history, but the hall was stripped bare, only the long cold sofas remaining. For the wedding, we had stapled plum-coloured velvet to the ceiling and down the walls and added a banquet table, but there was still room for dancing.

'Reminds me of when I was a nipper,' said Pollie, skating over the bare boards in his electric wheelchair. 'Everything got stored for the war and afterwards it took my mother a few years to be bothered to put it back again.' He drew up near where Patrice and I were laying roses along the top of a mantelpiece. 'We had some fun in here in those days. Bicycle races, tennis, lacrosse with my sisters, brought our ponies in once to have a game of polo. My arse is still tingling from the whacking that got me.'

Patrice laughed and stooped to kiss him.

'Won't be long before those days are here again, eh?' said Pollie. 'Finnie's girls never really lived up to the place, you know. Always fussing with their bloody Barbies and doing their nails. And Phil was just the one. See if you and he can't get me a good crop of grandsons, my darling. Haven't had a game of indoor tennis to put the windows out and get someone a slippering for fifty years.'

Patrice only twinkled at him and went back to her flowers, so he spun round in his chair and hummed off to find Finnie in the kitchen. I wondered whether to say anything, but when I looked at Patrice I could see she was struggling with it herself. The great bell of happiness that was clanging inside her head quietened for a moment. I could hear each breath juddering on its way in and out and the rose stem she was poking into place was shivering as she touched it.

'Think about the wedding,' I said to her. 'Just concentrate on that.'

She nodded, closing her eyes and trying to slow her breathing.

'He loves you already,' I said. 'Pollie, I mean. And look what you're doing for this place. There's more than one way to secure Trepolgas for the future, you know. And—'

'Verity,' said Patrice, turning to me. 'I can't talk about this just now.' And although Patrice couldn't look flushed or pale or anything except perfectly made up I could tell that I wasn't helping and should just leave things be.

This morning, though, looking out at the rain drumming on the terrace and dimpling the surface of the pond, she was all serenity. She put down her teacup and turned towards the dress hanging on the back of the wardrobe door. It was white – like a wedding dress as far as that went – but otherwise it was pure Patrice, ordered from her personal New York couturier, with a touch of karate suit, a touch of origami, a few even more extraneous pieces of fabric than usual as though the designer had, at the last minute, decided to add some placemats.

We went in procession to the bathroom where Phil had tacked a notice announcing that no one was to use any hot water (not a drop) until Patrice was dressed and gave them the all-clear.

'You gotta love him,' Jasmine said.

Three hours later, while thunder rolled and lightning flashed outside, Phil and Patrice stood in the registry office in St Austell and repeated the words of the short service. 'The dog licence version' as Pollie called it in everyone's, even the registrar's, hearing.

'But of course, a church was out of the question. Jewish *and* divorced, don't you know?'

Phil turned round in the middle of his vows:

'Pa, shut up.'

'What?' said Pollie, all innocence. 'I'm not passing judgement. I'm just filling people in. And *I* can hardly talk about divorce, now can I? As for the other thing, I couldn't give a flying—'

'Father, will you please shut up?' said Phil. 'We're in the middle of the ceremony.'

'Hmph,' said Pollie. 'That was my point. If there *was* any ceremony I could hardly have missed it, could I?'

He was right about that. No one gave Patrice away in the end, and Phil had no best man. He had given me a look and said there was only one best man he could think of but he didn't deserve to be at a wedding. So it was a minimalist affair, in a way, just a lot of Coates relations and some neighbours, as well as Jasmine and me, but it was plumped out and made sumptuous by Patrice's happiness and by Phil's air of stunned disbelief in what he had done and his visibly growing realisation that he had been right to do it. No one's umbrella spike got struck by lightning on the way from the cars to the house, there was plenty of food – enough people knew enough about Finnie's cooking not to dig in too deep, I suppose – and the flowers, of course, were beautiful, gleaming and plush, spicing the hall in the warmth from the fires.

Jasmine was having fun. She had picked up the local doctor, a youngster just passing through the village on his way to better things, and was flirting shamelessly.

'So it was you who called the ambulance?' she said. 'And saved old Pollie's life? Well, I'm sure Patrice will want to give you a big thank-you kiss for that. Or if you can't find her, kiss me and I'll pass it along.'

The doctor was blinking, dazzled by Jasmine, but working up to asking her out for a drink some other day.

'It's a lonely life in a single-handed practice,' he said. 'No workmates and all my patients are sick whenever I see them.'

'Jeez, I guess so,' said Jasmine. 'It must destroy some of the magic when you meet a person haemorrhoids first.'

Through it all, Patrice floated around like a sculpted iceberg, kissing a lot of new in-laws, who seemed to find the totality of her so awe-inspiring that they dared not pick fault with any of the details. I overheard a couple of middle-aged ladies in chiffon frocks and matching frilly topcoats saying that they didn't take *Vogue* any more these days – it was all advertisements – so of course Patrice's dress looked peculiar to them.

'Such a pretty face, though,' one said to the other.

'Absolutely,' the other replied. 'A terribly modern face – chemical peels perhaps, like they have at eight-thirty on Channel Four – but terribly, terribly pretty.'

'We met in California when I was doing a course there,' I heard Phil saying to someone behind me. 'Then we spent some time together in New York where Patrice comes from. But when she came over to meet the family we decided to settle here.' And when he put it that way, I thought, why not?

And it wasn't even as if he was lying. He just missed out a lot of the details so that what was left sounded perfectly plausible even though it was true. If there had been any chance of telling my story, the real one, that way, making it sound as plausible and as blameless as that, I could have kept the little thing cold and hard and shrivelled up for ever, never risking being left in tatters if it suddenly went whump! like it felt it was going to.

I thought about it all the way over to LA a few days after the wedding, sitting in my upgraded seat, trying to look five months pregnant while the cabin crew fussed around me and told me not to eat too many of the salty peanuts in case my ankles swelled. I didn't come up with anything, though; at best, I would need three different versions – one each to tell to Jasmine, Patrice and Phil. There was just no way.

I checked into the Beverly Hills Hotel, courtesy of Patrice, and Merle the security man tipped his hat and failed to recognise me, blinded by Jasmine's mock-croc luggage, which I was beginning to think wasn't actually mock at all. The desk clerk gave me one long wondering stare, and I could hear her mental rolodex clicking over, but this time the booking was smooth and soon I was in my room tipping the bellhop and kicking off my shoes.

I changed into my nightdress right away, thinking that Bradley wouldn't mind dinner from room service, not here. That way, at bedtime I would be able to slide inside the crackling cotton sheets all the way to the middle of the bed and lie sleeplessly worrying about the next day without any old ghosts to haunt me. I was right; far from Bradley minding, he insisted on changing into a towelling robe and slippers to match me and he made the room-service waiter spread our supper out on the bed and bring more pillows. And actually, this was a bit of a breakthrough: when bedtime came, everything was creased and crumby and I could have got inside in any nightclothes at all.

I lay thinking. Just one day, one meeting, one annoying, complicated, Clovis-induced flight home via Minsk and I would be free of them for ever, safe from being detonated inside by the sudden explosion of the thing. I was never going to have to look at any of their faces, cold hard and sneering – I was sure Patrice could do something approaching a sneer if she really had to – and have to hold my chin up and keep the tears behind my eyes.

'Don't you cry now,' my granny always told me. 'I've not cried a tear since my sixteenth birthday, you know. Buried my husband and lost my only child and never a tear, whether ourside for folk to see me or in here by my own fire with my door closed. Never a tear.'

But I remember you crying, sitting on the toilet lid, wiping me dry, I wanted to tell her.

'What happened on your sixteenth birthday?' I asked instead.

'My mother gave me a length of cloth and a needle case to make myself a dress,' said Granny.

'What did you want?' I said. 'What had you asked for?'

'I don't remember,' said Granny, turning away from me and beginning to rub a scraped carrot up and down the grater. I watched her shoulders and hips rock faster and faster as the grater wore the carrot away, and said nothing.

Kim swore as he stubbed his toe against the bed in the dark and Helen opened her eyes. Behind the single candle her face looked eerie, owlish with sleep and as pale as the pillow behind her.

'Happy birthday to you,' sang Kim. 'Got a present or two. You can change them if you hate them. Happy birthday to you.'

Helen sat up in bed and blew out the candle then clicked on the light.

'What time is it?' she said.

'Quarter to five,' said Kim.

'I need to leave at six,' said Helen. 'My flight's at seven forty-five.'

'Just time to eat your special birthday bagel.'

'What a lovely idea,' said Helen. 'What's in it?'

'Smoked salmon and cream cheese,' said Kim. 'What else?'

Helen said nothing.

'It's the poshest bagel filling there is,' said Kim, valiantly. 'What else could I have brought you on your birthday morning?'

'Oh, I don't know,' said Helen. 'How about a Danish pastry, my favourite breakfast?'

Now it was Kim who said nothing.

'My God!' said Helen stripping back the bedcovers and springing to her feet. 'I thought you were being inventive. I thought you had brought me a bagel because it seemed too early for anyone to eat sweet things. But that's not what it was, was it?'

'Of course it was,' said Kim, hollowly. 'What else could it be?'

'Hmm, let me see,' said Helen. 'Could it be that you brought me your ex-wife's favourite breakfast treat on my birthday? Could it possibly be that? No, it couldn't. Because what would make you do something so thoughtless, so clueless, so mean and shitty?'

'Wishful thinking?' said Kim, very quietly.

'What did you just say?'

'Nothing.'

Helen stood breathing heavily for a moment and then she turned on her heel and walked into the bathroom.

'Sorry,' shouted Kim through the closed door. 'Sorry I spoiled your birthday. I'll pick you up at the airport on Thursday night.'

They sent a limo to take me up to Glendale. The girl who met me at the front door was very friendly, but she only delivered me to reception so we didn't get time to bond. The man on reception, however, was even friendlier and the girl he paged to come and take me upstairs seemed ready to die happy now she had found me. The woman behind the desk on the tenth floor knew my name and where I was staying and was ready to go back to the hotel and gun them down unless I told her that I'd had a comfortable night. The girl *she* paged hugged me, overheard the receptionist asking about the hotel and urged me three times to let them call and move me to the Château Marmont. This girl took me to a room with a view across Hollywood to the pink smog over downtown LA, where two young men dressed like models from the Land's End catalogue – or I suppose it would be L L Bean – were waiting to meet me. They seemed very friendly.

'We're glad you could come,' one of them told me. 'It's a long way, but Steven likes to meet people.'

'And I'm delighted to be here,' I said. 'It's an honour to be meeting Mr Sp—'

'Steven,' said the other. 'Call him Steven.'

In the end when he breezed in with a brown folder and another three young men, I called him nothing at all.

'We're very excited here,' he said leaning forward, elbows on his knees and hands hanging down. 'The story is going to need a lot of work, a lot of opening out. The minor characters need some serious development.' They would, I thought. 'But we're all very excited.' He leaned back and circled one of his hands. 'It's the central human relationship after all: mother and child. Built on sacrifice. But what we're doing when we move it out of the female, and not even into the male, but out of the human realm completely and into a dimension that's just as much about time as it is about space ...' His words ran out but his hands kept circling.

'Uh-huh,' I said. Then, remembering who I was talking to, I added. 'That sounds like a much better idea than mine.'

'The struggle remains the struggle it always was,' he went on at last. 'The focal image – a powerful image – remains. The idea of a father dying as he holds his son up, pushing him into the sunlight. But we see a different and a much grander sweep. The galaxy – the Scalat Region – from where these ambassadors to Earth have travelled is such a distance away, you see, that the father always knows he will die before they reach the destination. He's not going to make it. He knows that from the start. The child doesn't know that *his* destiny is to be Earth's only Scalat ambassador, living his life in a host galaxy so far from home that he can never return, linked only by the satellites they have built along the way, bootstrapping themselves into communication with that other shadowy planet. He doesn't know that his father will die as he pushes the craft into the earth's atmosphere and ushers his son into the light.'

For a while I said nothing. Then I checked.

'This is *Straight Up*?'

'So far,' he told me. 'It's still deep in development, like I said.'

'Did ... umm,' I began. 'Did anyone here ever read the original story?'

'Oh sure, sure, sure,' said the young men. 'Sure, sure.'

'I took it on my junior year abroad with me,' one of them added. 'I loved it.' The hand waving had begun again.

'The treatment that came from IFA captured the essence. And we've moved it on some. But don't worry: I assure you that our vision is the same as yours.'

'Unbelievable,' I said. Was it not going to occur to anyone here that they really could have gone ahead and made their space odyssey about the bootstrapping Scalat ambassadors without paying Patrice almost as much as she had paid me? Or was it peanuts to this lot? Or were they just so happy to have got the sketch of a germ of an idea for a treatment to explore developing that they had to pay someone? I decided, since they seemed to have got what they wanted, to accept that somehow, as result, I had got a little something too.

And so I was fairly content with my lot as I boarded the flight from LAX to Minsk, via Moscow. I settled back into my considerably less swanky seat – there was no statement of second trimester health for this leg of the journey for some reason – and flopped a pile of glossies on to my lap. Minsk to London was going to be small talk with Varjan, the 'nice bloke', and so I was treating myself to make up for it in advance.

We hadn't, I realised as I stood outside a coffee shop in Minsk airport an uncomfortable sweaty lifetime later, made any arrangements about how I was to recognise this Varjan character, no folded newspaper and red carnations to look for, and there was no one I could see who looked at all likely, not many people at all in this dead time of day, mid-week, far from whatever tourist season Minsk might boast.

There were a few airport security men, looking far too young for their guns, a few grubby students asleep against their backpacks, the inevitable panhandler with shawl and baby, but no one who looked like a pal of Patrice, whatever look that might be. I kept searching around and eventually caught someone's eye, but it was only the fat woman in the shawl. She smiled at me and I smiled back – I never learn – and began patting my pockets for change as she approached. Minsk beggars would take dollars, I was sure. There really was no sign of a man travelling alone who looked like someone who'd need help at Heathrow. The fat panhandler planted herself squarely in front of me and I unzipped my bag, glancing around for security staff in case she grabbed it.

'I go to bathroom,' she said and walked away.

OK, so not a beggar after all. Just a nutter and quite a harmless one. Except that, of course, since she had mentioned it, I had to go too now and the one place that this Varjan bloke definitely wouldn't be waiting was in the ladies' loos. I hurried across the hall and into the door with the skirt symbol. The woman in the shawl was coming out of a cubicle and I flitted past her.

'Verity?' she said. I blinked twice, very fast, and turned back.

'Hello?' I said.

'Hello,' she answered.

'I'm waiting for Varjan,' I said. She nodded very fast, smiling.

I looked more closely at her. She was definitely a woman, and I would say she always had been. Besides, she had a baby and no luggage and just didn't look like someone who was about to get on a plane.

'Here he is,' she said and I looked around expectantly, surprised. What was he doing in the ladies? How much of a bloke, in Patrice's terms, was he? When I looked back she was holding the baby out towards me.

'Um?' I said.

'Here is Varjan,' she said, and she pushed the baby right up against me so that I had to grab him in case she let go. As soon as she had her hands free, she began to empty her pockets and shrug out of a shoulder bag she was wearing across her back. 'Here is diapers for him. Here is clothes. Here is bottle of milk for him. Here is – very important – here is passport for him.' She stuffed the bottle in my bag, but the passport she put right into my hand. 'You read,' she said, nodding at the passport, and then she turned and, faster than I could have believed, barrelling along on her little feet, she disappeared.

'Wait a minute,' I said, rushing along the line of cubicles and banging out of the door behind her. 'Wait.'

She was gone. All around, travellers and baggage handlers strode on their purposeful invisible pathways over the wide stretch of floor.

The baby was beginning to squirm, clearly not thinking much of giving up the embrace of the fat smiling woman for the inexpert grip of me. I walked over and sat down in one of a row of plastic chairs all joined together and bolted to the floor.

'Varjan?' I said, looking down at him, as though I actually expected him to wake up and answer me. I had no idea how old he was, how young. What did I know about babies? He was about the size of a cat, I suppose, a small cat. And the bottle of milk suggested that he wasn't old enough to eat. But how old did that make him? Too young to talk, for sure. Too young to answer questions and far too young to help me. I looked into his sleeping face a little longer hoping for clues, then my glance fell on the passport still clutched in my hand. It was a UK passport. Red and gold. I opened it. Born 8 October. He wasn't even six weeks old. If he had been a kitten he wouldn't have been old enough to leave the litter. I couldn't take a baby not even six weeks old on a plane. He might melt. On the first page of his passport, though, there was a stamp, and a little booking stub stapled to the page. He had flown before? I looked at it more closely. It showed that he had left London two days ago on the same flight as me. I looked at the name under the photograph. 'Varjan Drummond,' it said. Drummond? *Drummond*? And at that moment over the tannoy the nasal voice of the announcer called my flight.

What was I going to do? I couldn't take this baby to London with me. What was going on? I was supposed to be meeting some bloke and looking after him for Patrice. I swear, at that moment, as I thought her name, as the word 'Patrice' leaped into my head, he opened his eyes and laughed at me. Or burped, or clucked, or something, but he definitely opened his eyes and looked into mine. And at last, it made sense. At last, with a clunk like the padlock that locks the chain that chains you to the ship that's sinking, it all fell into place.

This was what Patrice got out of this deal. This was the business that wasn't drugs, or guns or girls. This was what Clovis had all set up for the USA and no way to move it to London. And was what Patrice could do with just her birth certificate and none of her medical records in England that she couldn't do at home in New York. Deep in my bag, far under the baby, my mobile started to ring.

'Have you got him?' said Clovis.

'A bloke,' I said to her. 'You told me he was a bloke. A friend of Patrice's.'

'He is a bloke,' said Clovis. 'Check his nappy.'

'She just shoved him at me and vanished.'

'Good,' said Clovis. 'The nippier the handover the better.'

'You seriously think I'm getting on the plane with him?'

'Jasmine assured me you would.'

I said nothing.

'You're a British citizen, Verity, travelling into Britain with her own baby after a short trip to the USA and a rather awkward journey home. It was the only way to do it. I couldn't bring him in, I told Jasmine that. In my business, it's very important that no officials ever get to know my face. Jasmine couldn't bring him in because she can't do the accent to match a UK passport. None of the Belarusians would dare to try. So you were the only option. And since Jasmine tells me that you know far too much to stay on the outside … you're in.'

'But in what? And why is his name Drummond?'

'Oh catch up,' said Clovis. 'You're in with the rest of us who've got something to lose if anyone squeals, that's all. And his name's only Drummond until you get him through passport control at Heathrow. UK passports I can do by the dozen. As the buyer – sod her – seems to know only too well. The buyer knows so much about so much that I sometimes think she's got more contacts than me.'

'Clovis, stop talking,' I said. 'You're insane. I can't traffic a baby!'

'It's not trafficking,' Clovis said. 'It was the bloody traffickers that ruined my European business in the first place. Five years ago, before all the bloody traffickers, I would have let him come to England without a murmur.'

'Whatever you call it,' I said, breaking in again. 'I can't do it. If you only knew …' I could sense it inside me, rising up, choking me, filling me up, making me feel as if my eyes were bulging. 'Call her and tell her to come back,' I said. 'I can't do this to her.'

'You're not,' said Clovis. 'He's not her baby. She works for me. Varjan came from a nursery in a government-run children's home.'

'I don't believe you.'

'They all do.'

'I don't believe you,' I said again. 'Nobody would leave him in a nursery. He's just a baby.'

'Verity, why are you getting so upset?' said Clovis.

'Why am I …? Clovis, why can't you hear me? Why don't you understand? I cannot take a baby away from his mother.' I said it as slowly and firmly as I could even though my voice was cracking.

'You're not,' said Clovis, even slower and much firmer.

I looked down at him. He had stopped squirming and was just looking back at me, waiting.

'He really came from a home?'

'Six storeys high, two dormitories on every floor, ten cots in each room, one nurse between twenty. They tape their dummies to their mouths, Verity. They only change their nappies twice a day.'

'He's an orphan?'

'Well, abandoned.'

'Because if someone's looking for him and you've taken him away …'

'I haven't,' said Clovis. 'I wouldn't.'

'That would make it kidnapping.'

'Of course it's not kidnapping. Verity, love, do you know the jail tariff for kidnap? I'm too much of a coward to face that, believe me. This is just a nice, ordinary, everyday, illegal, international adoption. Trust me.'

She couldn't fool me with that old 'say something bad about yourself so no one thinks you're lying' routine, but I believed her about the nursery. He smelled of tallow soap and he had a little helmet of scurfy skin under his black hair, little lines of crust in the folds of his ears. I thought about Phil and picnics on the beach with the black swans bobbing, about Pollie and Finnie and the polished hall floor for riding bikes and ponies.

'I'm really not taking him away from his mother?' I said again.

'You're taking him *to* her, Verity, love. Jasmine's bringing her to meet you at Heathrow, and it's going to be you who holds him out and puts him in her arms.'

Finally, I thought about Patrice and the feeling of floating on a lake listening to music every time I was near her.

'Clovis,' I said. 'They're calling our flight. I've got to go.'

I say one thing for him, he passed the time. I fed him on the way from Minsk to Moscow. The cabin crew warmed the bottle and tested it for me so I just had to plug it in and watch him suck. I didn't even have to wind him – a woman across the aisle who said all her grandchildren lived in Canada begged to be allowed to do it. She spread a cloth over her shoulder and banged him on the back until he vomited back up more milk than I remember him drinking. This was the result she had been aiming for, I think, and she handed him back to me with a dewy smile. Then I changed his nappy on the plane from Moscow to home, locked in the toilet, holding him down in the sink with one elbow and trying to read the instructions on the packet of nappies, which weren't in English or anything like it.

'Are you all right in there?' someone asked, rattling at the door.

'We're fine!' I sang out.

'Two of you?' said the voice. 'Madam, it is strictly against the rules to—'

I unlatched the door and smiled at the stewardess as I tried gently to bend his skinny, waving little legs and get them back into the feet of his babygro.

'It's OK,' I said. 'Not what you think.'

'Oh, pretty baby,' said the stewardess. 'Let me hold him while you finish up.'

I felt quite proud of myself as I followed her back to my seat, winking at Varjan who was staring backwards over her shoulder from in front, sucking her shirt. I looked around to see if anyone else felt like cooing or clucking or generally giving me a round of applause for being with him. And that's when I saw her. *Her*. There she was, sitting with her laptop open and her hair pulled back in that loose, shiny coil, with her plain, well-cut suit and her smart navy shoes with the filled-in toes. It was *her*. She must have felt me staring because she raised her head and a vague twitch of recognition crossed her face. She couldn't place me, but she knew that she knew me from somewhere. I unfroze myself and hurried to catch up with the stewardess, taking Varjan out of her arms and huddling down into my seat with him, hiding.

'Of course,' I said to him. 'Moscow, Thursday night. Of course. You know, Varjan, it was one of the first things she ever told me about herself the very first time I met her to speak to. She said that she did a lot of work in Moscow and some weeks she was there from Monday morning to Thursday night.'

'Moscow?' I had echoed. 'That must be interesting.'

'They're a fascinating people, the Muscovites,' she had said, waving away a plate of canapés as it was offered.

'That must be where she got all her razzamatazz,' Phil had whispered in my ear from behind me. 'She probably learned to party in the viewing queue for Lenin's tomb.'

Of course, she was off the plane long before me, since I had carry-on luggage that had to be persuaded to let me put its hat and mittens back on and I got stopped at passport control, while the official looked at Varjan's papers and blew kisses into his face, and got stopped at security while they rubbed his nappy with their scanner and tickled him under the chin, so I thought she would be long gone by the time I had reclaimed Jasmine's luggage and was pushing my trolley, with Varjan wedged into the handbag tray, along the corridor into Arrivals.

But there she was, ten paces ahead of me. What had she been doing all this time? Staring at her back, I realised that she wasn't wearing her suit any more; she had changed into a well-cut, plain silk dress and her hair was twisted into a loose, shiny chignon. I slowed down to let her get away from me again. If she had changed in the loos at the baggage carousel, she must be meeting someone right here in the airport, but it was a big airport, I told myself, and kept walking.

It might well be. Nevertheless as the Moscow passengers squeezed through into the arrivals lounge and started to fan out, straight ahead of me I saw Jasmine, Patrice and Phil waiting, clutching one another, as white-faced as though all three of them were wearing Patrice's foundation. And standing two feet along from them, arms folded and head back, looking the way he always looked when he was getting tired of waiting for something, was Kim.

I watched Helen striding towards him, swish-swishing the hem of her dress and clip-clipping the high heels of her black patent shoes with the filled-in toes. She was making right for him and I felt the vision at the sides of my eyes beginning to blur and close in, as though everything I could see was being squeezed down an egg timer. What was going on here? What was happening inside my head and what was real?

Helen drew up level with Kim and I saw his eyes open wide in surprise. I saw Helen nod at him and then turn with an Ah! as she remembered who that woman on the plane was at last. Kim lifted one hand towards her in a mild wave and smiled. Then she swished past him and clipped away across the airport. I had stopped and the rivers of people flowing past me on both sides made me feel as if I was falling backwards away from them, so in the end I had to start walking again just to stay on my feet at all, but I trained my eyes on Patrice, concentrating very hard on her alone, trying not to see Kim, hoping if I ignored him he would just dissolve and go away.

Patrice stared back at me, her always immobile face a stone mask in pale grey. She leaned towards me, boring into me with her eyes and then, suddenly, she let her held breath go with a ragged gasp and rushed forwards to pluck Varjan out of the tray, pressing him against her chest, sobbing.

'Jesus, Vee,' said Jasmine. 'We couldn't *see* him in there. We thought you didn't *have* him. Jee-zuss!'

Phil, cupping the back of Varjan's head in his hand, was gently prising him away from Patrice's body, trying to get a look at him, but she wasn't having it so he gave up and just wrapped his arms round both of them and rocked them, blinking very fast, determined not to cry in an airport like a Californian. Jasmine was gazing at them and I couldn't catch her eye. I looked at the luggage trolley, at my watch, at the ceiling and then eventually at Kim.

'Surprise!' he said. 'Phil – finally – called me.'

Now Jasmine had all the attention in the world to spare for me; of course she did.

'Yeah, how about that, Vee?' she said. 'A miraculous recovery, huh? For someone who died and got eaten, I think he's looking pretty good.'

'Never mind that,' said Kim. 'Death I can handle and Phil's my best buddy – he can eat me any day he wants. What's bugging me is the shacked up with another woman angle. Where in God's name did that come from?'

'Phil asked why you left me,' I said, staring at my feet. 'I had to say something.'

'And who was it supposed to be?' said Kim. 'Phil wouldn't tell me.'

'No one,' I said. 'Nobody we know.'

'Well, I've got to hand—' Kim began. And stopped. 'Wait a minute! Phil asked why I left you and you had to say something? Phil asked why *I* left *you*? Verity, *you* left *me*.'

'I'm sorry,' I told him.

'To be fair,' said Jasmine. 'Vee always said to us that if you hadn't died and gotten eaten she was going to dump you anyway.'

'Oh really?' said Kim. 'Did she mention why?'

'Jasmine, please,' I begged her.

'She did,' said Jasmine. 'She said you were a compulsive liar. Said you told so many stories she didn't know what to believe sometimes. Said she just couldn't take it any more.'

'She said she couldn't take it any more?' said Kim softly and he stepped towards me. 'Well, that much at least I think was true.'

Chapter 15

Scream Splash the End

'Jesus, kid,' said Jasmine as a stream of milk ran out of the side of Varjan's mouth and spilled on to the cold velvet of the sofa cushion.

'Jazzie, please don't swear at him,' said Patrice.

Pollie and Phil rolled their eyes, then Pollie threw his electric wheelchair into reverse, spun a half circle and shot across the floor towards the kitchen.

'I'll get a cloth,' he shouted over his shoulder.

'And *walk* back, Pa,' shouted Phil. He groaned. 'I'm wasting my time. The old bugger's obviously never going to walk again.'

'I'll get a hold of it and take the battery out,' said Finnie. 'But you know, Philly, when the physio says walk around the house for gentle exercise, they're not thinking about a mausoleum like this. Different when I get him to the dower house. Right, Jasmine, my turn.'

Jasmine picked Varjan up under his arms and held him out across the coffee table, his little jumper bunching up and his skinny body stretching long above the top of his nappy.

'That thing would fall straight off if he uncrossed his legs,' said Kim. 'Jasmine, you're hopeless at changing.'

'And it's a skill I'm not aiming to improve,' said Jasmine, wiping her hands on her jeans. Finnie had tucked Varjan into the crook of her arm, rubbing his back and bouncing him up and down.

'Oh, this feels good,' she said. 'It's lovely to have a baby in the house again. Even if it does make me a gr- gr- gr- … Let's go and look at the swans, my little love. Patrice, do you think he'll be warm enough if we put his blanket on?'

It took five minutes of fussing to get him ready to leave the house and cross twenty feet of terrace to the edge of the pond, and even then Patrice watched from one of the windows.

'Pollie couldn't care less, could he?' she said, looking at the old man waving his arms around, describing the grounds to Varjan, telling about his home. 'About the adoption, I mean. About Varjan not having Coates blood in his veins?'

'Oh, my dear,' said Phil. 'If you only *knew* how little it matters. If he was officially, technically adopted it might be different. But he's going to be in the Parish Book like all the rest of us and I daresay he's not the first that's smooth and seamless on the surface and God knows what shenanigans underneath.'

'That's why our beloved royal family won't ever have anything to do with genetic testing,' said Kim. 'No way they'd all come out related to each other. It would blow the lid off them for good.'

'Are you going to call him Varjan?' I asked Patrice. She giggled.

'I'm going to see what Phil comes up with when he goes to the registrar,' she said. 'I don't care what we call him.'

'That was what gave you the idea, wasn't it?' I said.

Patrice turned to Kim, to explain it to him since he had missed the beginning.

'Philly told me about Lettice Lolita and Oma Darlin,' she said. 'And I thought, my God, with my new California birth certificate and Clovis's way with medical documents, if only I was in England I could be his real mother. Really, really – not just adopted – and then nobody would ever be able to take him away.'

'Nobody ever *would* have taken him away,' said Jasmine. 'I told you that over and over. Him or any other baby. No wonder Clovis was ready to strangle you.'

'You didn't go through it,' said Patrice. 'It's the Fundamentalists, Verity. Those crazy pro-lifers. They've got the US adoption system sewn up airtight, even in California. I waltzed in there, to the first agency, all starry-eyed and innocent to tell them my story and I thought they were going to lynch me.' She turned back to Jasmine. 'You weren't there.'

'But Clovis has forgiven you enough to do you a doctor's note?' I said, trying not to show what I thought of that. They were supposed to be done with Clovis now, done with the whole baby business for ever and it seemed a bad idea to start off owing her a favour again.

'She woulda,' said Jasmine. 'But there's no need. We found a midwife ready to go to the wire for a pay-off.'

Kim and Phil put back their heads and roared with laughter.

'What?' said Jasmine.

'It's nothing,' I assured her. 'It's just that you have such a talent to for making everything sound so ... bent.'

'Perry calls it refreshing,' said Jasmine.

'Perry?' I said.

'The GP,' said Jasmine. I raised my eyebrows at her. 'Oh yes,' she said. 'He's transformed my love life. I didn't even think of doctors, but as soon as I get back to LA I'm going straight to the hospital to check them out. Only I can't decide which kind. A plastic surgeon would be very useful for later, but kinda tacky. A shrink would be way too scary. A gynaecologist – yuck! But that still leaves a lot.'

'So, getting back to the subject in hand,' I said, trying not to laugh at Kim's expression as he gazed at Jasmine. 'What you mean is, you found a radical independent midwife.'

'Who's not going to penalise me for wanting to give birth all alone in a tepee,' said Patrice.

'Yeah,' said Jasmine. 'Cornwall's lousy with them.'

'She's a darling,' said Patrice, 'but she's very annoyed with me because I won't breastfeed.'

'Does she suspect?' I asked.

'No,' Patrice said. 'She saw the wedding pictures. She's having no trouble believing I was eight and a half months pregnant that day.'

'And thanks to our native desire to look the other way and keep family honour intact no matter what,' said Phil, 'I am deemed to be Varjan's legal father because Patrice and I were married on the day he was born, even if the ink wasn't quite dry on the certificate. Smooth on top, shenanigans underneath, like I told you. Makes you proud to be an Englishman, Kim, doesn't it?'

Kim was looking hard at me.

'You see, Verity?' he said. 'Families. All shapes and sizes. All flavours of mess and chaos. Nobody cares.' There was a long silence.

I could feel them all smiling at me. They really *didn't* care. Nobody cared except me.

'You wanna be alone, you two?' said Jasmine at last. I shook my head. 'Well, then you wanna tell us what's been going on before we bust our brains trying to work it out?' she said.

I cleared my throat. Inside me the shrivelled thing was unshrivelling, but it wasn't going to burst out of me like some alien lifeboat and leave entrails hanging from the lampshades, and it wasn't turning into death gum and heading for my heart, or even rooting into my guts and twining its branches through my ribcage. It just slowly unfolded and filled me up, right to the skin and no further, like something that fitted as if it was made for me. I took a deep breath. It was't even interfering with my breathing.

'You know how I said I was a widow and I wasn't?' I began.

Phil and Kim snorted.

'Peckish?' Kim asked.

'So-so,' said Phil. 'I could manage a finger or two if you've got them to spare.' I knew already that they would never stop. There was no point in even asking.

'Well, I'm not an orphan either,' I went on.

'You never told us you were an orphan,' Patrice said.

'Really?' I said.

'You told *me* you were an orphan,' said Phil.

'Yes, and I told Kim. I told everyone. That's what my granny always told me.'

'Ooh, that's harsh,' said Jasmine. 'Your parents are alive and your grandmother told you they were dead?'

'She meant well,' I said. 'She didn't want me to know the truth. Which was ...'

'You don't have to, honey,' said Patrice. 'Remember what I told you? Life is complicated and sometimes you need some cover.'

'No, I need to say it.'

Kim made as though to come and sit beside me, but Jasmine stopped him.

'Back off, boy,' she said. 'This is a job for girlfriends. Only, Patrice, can you sit where the puke is? You're pretty much coated in it anyway.'

Jasmine and Patrice came and sat very close on either side of me, like secret service but with more squeezing.

'My father was someone who drank in the pub where my mother worked,' I said. 'But nobody knows who exactly. And my mother left me with my granny when I was two days old and never came back.'

'Verity,' said Patrice. 'If I had known that, I would never have let you go and bring me Varjan. I'm sorry.'

'No,' I exclaimed. 'That was good, that was fine. Bringing a baby to someone who wanted him so much?' I winced, remembering. 'God, I'm sorry I put him in the tray. Anyway, I never saw her. She used to phone sometimes and ask about me, but it always ended in an argument and eventually my granny told her not to call again. I think I overheard it, but it's kind of hazy.'

'So how do you get from there to walking out on Kim?' said Jasmine.

'My granny died,' I said.

'No!' said Phil. 'I didn't know that. Granny Drummond's gone?'

'And my mother came to the funeral,' I said. 'I met her. Kim met her. He found out the truth about me.' I stopped and waited.

'And?' said Jasmine. 'What happened? Why d'you leave?'

I raised my head and looked slowly around their four faces, three solemn and one creased up into a smile.

'That's it,' said Kim, his smile widening even further. 'That's the whole explanation, folks. That's all you're going to get because that's all there is. Look at their faces, Verity. They're puzzled. *You're* puzzled, aren't you?' He was looking at Patrice, who nodded back.

'I think I might have missed something somewhere,' she said.

'No,' said Kim. 'All you missed was the spaceship to Planet Drummond. On Planet Drummond, you see, I hate Verity for not being able to cope with knowing that her mother didn't want her. I also despise her for not being able to soak up all her granny's stories and not get into the habit of telling a few stories of her own. Finally, on Planet Drummond, anyone who finds out the truth will decide that if her mother didn't want her, there's something wrong with her and they don't want her either.'

'Including us?' said Patrice. 'Jasmine and Phil and me?'

'And Finnie and Pollie and the girls,' said Kim. 'And probably Varjan too.'

'Vee, that's completely nuts,' said Jasmine. 'One hour with a good analyst and that garbage could be popped out like a zit. I'll give you my analyst's number, he can do ya over the phone.'

'As I have long maintained,' said Phil. 'All women are from California underneath.'

'Actually, Philly,' Patrice reminded him, 'it was me who said that.'

'Hah,' said Finnie, opening the door and hearing her. 'Welcome to married life, my love. He'll steal every good idea and serve it up as his own for evermore.' Pollie rolled in through the open window with Varjan crying his peculiar creaky little cry and making his blanket bulge as he struggled to get out of it.

'Mummy!' said Pollie, holding him out towards Patrice. She scooped him up and put the knuckle of her pinkie finger into his mouth for him to suck while she took him through to the kitchen to wait for a bottle to warm. They all drifted after her one by one, leaving Kim and me.

I was remembering. Ganny's coffin was already resting on the rollers at the front of the crematorium when we went in. Her friends, Pearl, Vera, all of them, nodded respectfully as we passed on our way to the front pew. Kim was gripping my hand, rubbing the pad of my thumb with his and I could feel the scrape of a dry hangnail against my skin.

'I don't know,' he said, looking round as we slid into the seat. 'I suppose it's all right. Those so-called velvet curtains are velour, though, and don't try to tell me they're not.' He was doing his Granny Drummond impersonation, to make me smile, pronouncing it 'v'loor' the way she did. 'Still, who can blame them? V'loor comes up lovely and takes a lot less of a heavy ironing.' I could hear her voice; his Granny Drummond was a triumph, always had been, but I turned to check who it was coming to sit beside us in case they might be offended, in case he should stop.

She was about fifty, I suppose. Nice hair, reddish, straightened with tongs, and a black leather jacket over pinstripe trousers. High-heeled black boots. I nodded at her and she smiled at me, thumping me in the heart with that smile, my granny's smile. The music started and I turned to face the front as the minister climbed up into the little pulpit thing.

'Who's that?' whispered Kim. But I just shook my head and said nothing.

Afterwards, at the reception, she stood uncertainly in the doorway, wondering if she was welcome. Then she looked at me, pouring thirty years of love and regret into her eyes, those eyes that I recognised from the framed photograph of my grandfather that sat on the sideboard. I nodded gently and she came forward and took my hands.

'Verity,' she said. 'My darling girl. I've waited so long to tell you how much I—

'No,' said Kim, and he slid down in the velvet sofa until he could reach over to nudge me with his toe.

'What?' I asked him. 'No, what?'

'No more of that,' he told me. 'That's enough. It's time to stop now.'